ALL MURDER IS LOCAL
a Francis and Alicia mystery

by

GEOFFREY HILD

All Murder Is Local

ISBN 978-0-9972671-0-5

Cover design: SelfPubBookCovers.com/Ravenborn

PB10

A special thanks to Angela Bayes for her assistance with the final edit.

And a thank you also to Martha for introducing us to the high culture to be found in the City of Chihuahua.

All Murder Is Local

d

Chapter 1

September 2010

Unlike my fellow travelers, I had neither the name of a hotel nor a street address to give to the harried clerk behind the taxi service counter. I was told to wait outside for the next taxi returning from the city, as the vans and cabs in line out at the curb were reserved for normal people with predetermined travel plans. So, I waited, bag-in-hand, outside the airport terminal, looking off toward the afternoon haze that hung above the City of Chihuahua in the color of fated rust.

This should have been just a simple rescue mission. Perhaps a little more involved than bailing out a friend after a particularly eventful night-on-the-town, but basically, you pay the money and take the friend home. Granted, in this case the town was in Mexico, and the home was in Chicago. I hoped that the six hundred dollars, my life savings withdrawn from my bedroom gun safe, would be enough to pull it off. Beyond that, there was only pocket money for food and beer, backed up by an abused credit card.

But I was sure Alicia would be released following a little questioning and the payment of a hefty fee. I didn't for a minute think she would actually murder someone. In the past, Alicia had never given the slightest hint she'd be so inclined, even when we were married.

When a returning taxi, at last, arrived, I threw my bag onto the back seat, and climbed in after it. I'd ramped back up into my Spanish, during the Q & A with Customs and with the business of converting some drab dollars to colorful peso notes at the Currency Exchange window. So, I'd already regained some comfort with the language when I asked the driver to take me to the police station.

"We are blessed with four police stations, sir," the taxi driver said in languid Spanish. "Which one do you prefer?"

"I know only that my friend was taken to jail this morning."

"Ah, we have just one jail. A nice, big, new one."

"Take me there."

The rest of our conversation had to do mostly with the novelty of taking a tourist from the airport directly to the city jail. Thankfully, once the taxi driver had wrung all the amusement he could from the subject, we lapsed into silence.

I leaned back in my seat, as a wave of fatigue swept through my body. I'd spent four long days wiring in updated controls on a pair of honing machines in North Carolina and had finally flown home to Chicago late Monday night. I was brushing my teeth the next morning when Alicia had called. Her anxious words, spoken above a heavy drone of background noise, now flooded back to me. "Francis, I'm in jail in Chihuahua. It's a city in Mexico. You know where it is? I mean I know you know where Mexico is, but...Yes, jail. It's a freaking nightmare. Dr. Salazar is dead. Murdered. And the police arrested *me*...I tried, but they don't even *listen* to English. What am I supposed to do, suddenly learn Spanish?...Yes, why else would I call?...Francis, don't be difficult. You have to come down here. Come now."

Initially, the taxi's route from the airport to the city had been a four lane, tree-lined highway that cut through open farmland, its broad fields dotted with distant clusters of cement-block buildings – the small villages that surround Mexican cities like poor relations hovering near the keg at a garden party. Next came the typical outer-district mix of light industry, struggling businesses, and low-rent housing that tourists are swiftly whisked through en route to the good stuff.

At a sprawling intersection, where too many streets came together, the taxi turned off the highway, and we cruised at a good clip along a boulevard, skirting around the city center's montage of towering buildings. A few turnings later, the taxi pulled up in front of a vast, imposing building, featureless save for the bars on the windows and the tall chain-link fencing, topped with concertina wire.

"Our new jail, sir," the driver announced with pride.

I arranged for the taxi to wait, while I went in, hopefully, to retrieve Alicia.

The jail's lobby was filled with people, most of them sitting, but many having to stand in the aisles and around the periphery. They waited, I supposed, for a visit with an incarcerated relative or friend, or perhaps, to petition for a loved one's release. I worked my way through to a long, high counter and asked in my rejuvenated Spanish about Alicia Elton.

"Oh yes," the uniformed officer behind the counter said. "There is no need for me to look through my lists. The fiery Gringo woman. Sergeant Gameros will not soon forget her." He chuckled to himself briefly. "She is no longer here. She is your relative?"

"Yes," I answered, even though technically that was no longer true. "Where is she?"

"Your Consulate demanded that she be taken immediately to the Prosecuting Attorney's office at the Palacio de Justicia. She is perhaps a very important person?"

"Yes, very important." I was fairly sure that this also wasn't true, although I hadn't seen Alicia for a while, so maybe. "Is she there now? At the Palacio de Justicia?"

"She is there, she is released, or she is sent to prison to await her trial. There are only the three possibilities."

***

As I climbed back into the taxi, I instructed the driver to take me to the Palacio de Justicia.

Once underway, the driver asked, "Your friend, he is a very important person?"

"My friend is a woman." But now I was curious. "Why do you ask?"

"You told me that your friend was arrested only this morning, but now she is already at the Palacio de Justicia. It is normal for the journey through our justice system to proceed very slowly. There is much discussion, but little progress. It is like a taxi operated by many drivers. And therefore, I ask if she is a very important person."

"She has a way of attracting attention," I said.

The taxi's tires rolled ever more slowly, as the traffic density increased with our approach to the city center. Eventually, we were at a bumper-to-bumper crawl within the afternoon shadows of downtown

4

Chihuahua. A few, massive, government buildings from the eighteenth and nineteenth centuries still proudly stood among the more modern steel-and-glass government and banking structures. The buildings that housed street-level shops, however, made no such attempts at grandeur. Judging by the display windows, their main focus was to get as much merchandise in front of potential customers as possible.

The Palacio de Justicia was a modern and impressive courthouse. A statue of Blind Justice, holding her scales and sword, stood at the street corner on a tall base, which featured a clock whose hands indicated twenty minutes past two. I knew from a previous glance at my cell phone screen, that it was actually nearing five o'clock. Wide marble steps led up to tall pillars and heavy Palladian glass doors. The golden words "Supremo Tribunal de Justicia" triumphantly spread across the façade above the entrance.

The taxi driver left me and my lone piece of luggage on the sidewalk and sped off. Another plane was due in at the airport, he'd explained, and he had to return to meet it.

I mounted the steps and entered through the glass doors. Inside the courthouse, people moved purposefully about their business, traversing the vast polished marble floor beneath a two-story-high expanse of ceiling. In the center, a wide, marble staircase rose regally up to a broad landing, then split to each side and doubled back on itself in its reach to the next level.

I decided against asking for directions from the small knot of uniformed security officers, gathered far off to the left at a tall desk. Security types tend to automatically switch into gatekeeper mode when you ask for the office of a high-level official, and I wanted to minimize the number of times I'd be asked to state my business. And anyway, I knew the offices of the Prosecuting Attorney wouldn't be on the first floor. In government buildings, nothing of great consequence takes place on the first floor. I headed for the massive staircase and prepared myself for an upward plunge into its heavy counter-flows of preoccupied people, ascending and descending, some with paperwork in hand and most with a cell phone held to an ear.

As I put a foot on the bottom step and looked up, I was immediately stunned by the sight of Alicia, aristocratically descending through the bustling throng, each high-heeled foot placement landing on the next lower tread with confidence. For a moment, the rest of Mexico didn't exist.

Although Alicia appeared brave and proud, it was easy to see she'd had a rough day. Her hair, longer and darker than I remembered, was tangled; her smooth, pretty face bruised on one side of her mouth. But her skirt danced with each descending step, and as I now belatedly became aware, her balance was aided by a grip on the arm of a handsome, well-dressed man. The handsome man, tall and slender in his tailored suit, was definitely Anglo, although his full head of hair was combed back in the classic Mexican style. Despite a twinge of envy, I had to admit they made a lovely couple.

When Alicia first spotted me, her only reaction was to comb her fingers through her hair with her free hand.

By then, she was near enough for me to see dots of red spatter on her white blouse, yet she waited until she arrived down at my level, before greeting me.

"Francis, how wonderful of you to have come all this way." Alicia placed a hand on my chest, leaned in, and gave me a peck on the cheek.

Her perfume held no memories for me. But that's not saying the new scent was ineffective. "I'd assumed that the situation was a little more desperate," I said.

"On the contrary," the handsome man's words were crisp, "our dealings here have been decidedly unpleasant. However, I find it most encouraging that Miss Elton's champion has, at last, arrived."

"It really was sweet of you," Alicia added.

I felt like Plan B watching Plan A unfurl the Mission Accomplished banner.

"I'm Francis Elton." I reached out for the handshake. "Ex-husband and rescuer of damsels in distress, if I hurry."

"U.S. Consular Agent Richard Woodstead." His hand was as soft as a priest's. "Given the circumstances of Dr. Salazar's death, we were rather expecting Miss Elton's call at the old outpost. I hope you don't mind my intruding on your endeavor."

What's this guy read in bed at night, I wondered, the Oxford Book of Verse?

"Well," I said. "I'm sure you accomplished in a few hours what would have taken me days."

"Months, more likely, if at all." Consular Agent Woodstead finally disengaged from the handshake and looked at his watch. "My car will be outside by now."

***

7

A sleek, dark blue, Lincoln Town Car, wrapped with smoked windows, was at the curb. The driver – a stocky middle-aged Hispanic in a dark suit – stood on the sidewalk with his hand on the opened rear door.

"I can drop you at your hotel, Miss Elton," Woodstead said, "but then I must be off. A small, evening soirée at the Mayor's residence. Duty calls, and I am partial to fine wine."

"If it wouldn't be too much trouble, I'd appreciate it." Alicia was being gracious too.

"Are you sure I can't slay you a dragon, or something, before I go back?" I asked.

"Just pal along for the moment, will you, Francis?" Alicia said. "You'll feel better with a beer and the story, and you can't get a plane out till morning, anyway."

The driver ushered Alicia and Consular Agent Woodstead into the rear seat. My suitcase was tossed into the trunk, and I sat up front. It didn't feel like the seat of honor.

Woodstead's driver accelerated past the statue of Blind Justice, where it was always twenty minutes past two, paused briefly at the busy cross street, and aggressively swung out into the relentless flow of sedans, pickups, and buses.

The city was still crowded, the traffic thick and the sidewalks bustling. Although it was now well after five, the stores remained open, and there was no place to park. It was as though the city was just getting its second wind. Despite being on a four-lane street, we advanced only in brief rushes from traffic light to traffic light.

"Damn," Woodstead said in muted exasperation, as we were again stopped on red.

I turned in my seat to see the Consular Agent looking at his watch. Woodstead then spoke to his driver in a blur of rapid Spanish that ended with "pronto." The driver, without hesitation, swung out into the oncoming traffic lane, paused at the red light to gauge his moment of opportunity in the stream of cross traffic, and turned right in front of the two lanes of cars lawfully waiting for the light to change.

I looked over at the driver. His face held no expression, but I now noticed the leather driving gloves and felt the smooth, assured accelerations, as the big car weaved through the traffic. This guy was having the time of his life.

Seemingly oblivious to the driver's aggressive maneuvers, Alicia said, "Richard, I can't thank you enough for getting me out of that black hole. But I must look so awful that—"

"Please," Woodstead stopped her. "I won't have you talking about yourself that way. Even in your time of despair, your beauty cannot be denied."

"I could eat you with a spoon."

The driver's smile at this showed a healthy set of teeth. I doubted he'd ever heard the expression before, and I wondered what inner visual his literal translation had produced.

We crossed a bridge over a concrete-lined riverbed with only a shallow flow of water in the center. A street sign indicated that we were on "Ave. de Universidad", and I idly waited for a university to appear, not realizing at the time that we were actually moving away from the cultural center of the city.

"I apologize for the abruptness of this subject," Consular Agent Woodstead said, "but I'm afraid I'm quite constricted for time. The money for the amenities at the City Jail must be restored to our special fund."

"This is where you come in, Francis," Alicia said.

"What?" I turned to the back seat again.

"The money," Alicia said. "You brought it, didn't you?" And then, as though to a child, "Francis, sweetheart, I told you I was in *jail*."

"How awkward," Woodstead said. "You have no money at all?"

"I didn't say that. I have...five hundred dollars."

"Better, but still rather disappointing." Woodstead then spoke a phrase that may have been Mexican slang, or merely beyond my depth of Spanish.

In any case, the Lincoln Town Car noticeably decelerated. I turned back around to look through the windshield. There was no traffic-related reason for the driver to have slowed – unless he was preparing to turn the big, luxury car around.

"Francis, go ahead and give him the money for my return plane ticket, too." Alicia had apparently also picked up on the situation.

"I was going to use my credit card for your ticket." Woodstead said nothing.

"Francis!" Alicia snapped at me.

I pulled my life savings out of my front pants pocket.

"Okay, including the money I was holding onto for food, there's a hair over six hundred. Then I'm tapped out." I had the equivalent of almost a hundred dollars in pesos in my wallet that I wasn't about to throw in. I'd learned the hard way never to be broke when you're more than walking distance from home.

Richard Woodstead sighed. "We'll certainly be covering the cost of resetting the Desk Sergeant's broken nose, and perhaps, some dental work, in addition to the usual gratuities."

I wondered a little about the damage to the jailer's nose, while I waited for Woodstead to suggest that we drive my credit card over to an ATM.

But instead, Woodstead re-consulted his watch, and said, "All right, we'll simply have to make the best we can of it. Let us say the six hundred then, and the Embassy will graciously stand the Director of the Jail and his wife to a lovely dinner."

I reached the bills over the seat back toward the impeccably dressed Consular Agent.

"Please, my man will take it."

I gave the money to the driver. He tucked it into his inside jacket pocket without counting it.

Now that the deal was done, no one had anything further to say. But the silence lasted for only a few more city blocks, before the Town Car turned onto the paving-bricks leading to the entrance of the Motel Vista Suites.

The car swung around the fountain and stopped. While the driver retrieved my bag from the trunk, I climbed out and opened Alicia's door.

Alicia remained seated for the goodbye.

"Richard, you're such a darling. I know you spent some serious political capital on me." Alicia's fingertips

11

touched the far side of the Consular Agent's chin and turned his face to hers. "I'll have to make it up to you somehow."

"All part of the daily slog." Woodstead reached up and gently lowered Alicia's hand. "Now Miss Elton, you must understand your current status. You are not out on bail. Rather, you have been conditionally released. I have no standing as a lawyer here, so it was only my personal influence that allowed me to assert that the police had insufficient evidence to give them grounds for your arrest. Fortunately, the Prosecuting Attorney agreed with me. However, he then directed the Commandant of the State Ministerial Police to pursue a more thorough investigation. I assured the Prosecuting Attorney and the Commandant that you would remain in the City of Chihuahua during the extended investigation and be available for questioning. I'm afraid this was a necessary concession."

"Anything that keeps me out of that hellhole."

"Excellent." Woodstead drew a slip of notepad paper from his jacket pocket. "Meanwhile, here is a list of local attorneys with whom we've successfully worked in the past. Engage one without delay."

Alicia took the list from Woodstead and scanned it briefly, before folding the paper and holding it in her hand. It was then that I noticed that she didn't have a purse with her.

"And one more thing," Woodstead said. "While the police gather further evidence against you, be assured that they will be watching for any little misstep on your part. Thus, for the immediate future, I suggest that you lead the blameless life of a saint." Woodstead let that sink in for a few seconds, before dismissing Alicia with, "But now, if you'll excuse me, I'm really quite pressed for time."

Alicia accepted my hand to assist her up and out of the back seat. I shut the door, and the Town Car sped off, leaving us to fend for ourselves.

Chapter 2

As Alicia and I neared the glass double doors of the Motel Vista Suites, a pair of smiling employees swung both doors open simultaneously and greeted our entry. A third attendant stepped forward to relieve me of the weight of my suitcase. We crossed the tastefully appointed lobby and halted in front of an L-shaped counter, behind which a small assemblage of clerks and computers were stabled.

"Good afternoon," Alicia said in English to a young clerk who came to his feet. "I lost my room key. Alicia Elton, room one ten."

The young clerk immediately deferred to a thin man in a black suit, sitting at the computer with the largest screen. After a few departing clicks, the thin man stood. A tight-pedaled, lapel flower was on display above a plastic tag that proclaimed him as the manager.

"Yes, Miss Elton," the manager spoke in smooth, accented English. "We were informed of your situation. We were told that you would not be returning."

"Well, they were wrong, weren't they," Alicia said. "Now, please, let me have my key. Room one ten."

"Your room is no longer available," the manager said. "I am sorry."

"Now wait just a damn minute." Alicia's hands were on her hips. "I held that room with an American Express card. You don't screw around with those people. I have to pay full freight every month. What kind of funky-assed place is this? Do you understand what business you're in?"

"I am sorry. You were checked out this morning."

The manager laid several papers listing room charges on the counter. A credit card receipt, apparently signed by Alicia when she first registered, was stapled to the top paper. He neatly folded the papers, stuffed them into an envelope, and slid the envelope toward us. The Manager then rested his hands on the counter, fingertips laced, waiting.

"Well, damn it, just check me into another room," Alicia demanded.

"I am sorry. We are full. There are no other rooms available."

"All right, I get it. A little misunderstanding with the police, and suddenly, my persona is non freaking grata around here, is that the drill? Well, this dump isn't all that wonderful anyway. What did you do with my things?"

"The police packed your personal belongings and took them away," the Manager said, with unconcealed satisfaction on his face.

"Francis, let's get out of here." Alicia snatched the envelope off the counter. "We'll go to a real hotel. One where the management treats their guests like ladies and gentlemen. Unlike *this* pompous little popinjay."

Carrying my suitcase, myself now, I ushered Alicia past the superfluous employees, none of whom hazarded leaping ahead of the seething Alicia to open a glass door for her.

***

Out on the paving bricks in front of the Vista Suites, a man, leaning against an old Chevy Cavalier and reading an issue of El Diario, lowered his newspaper and asked in Spanish, "Taxi, sir? The airport, sir?"

I told him in Spanish to take us back to the city center. The driver opened his trunk, and I tossed my bag in.

"Francis, where are we going? I need a shower and some clean clothes. I can't go anyplace looking like this."

"I told him to take us downtown," I said, getting her seated in the back of the taxi. "They sell clothes there, and they must have hotels where they don't know you're accused of murder."

The taxi wheeled around the motel plaza fountain and exited the compound, boldly intruding itself into the rush of early evening traffic. The feel of the ride from the rear seat was a loose, almost floating sensation. I supposed the old auto's carriage was without benefit of functioning shock absorbers and was now supported on springs alone. But the radio still played, and the driver danced with his shoulders to the Latin rhythms and blaring trumpets of Mexican rock and roll.

Alicia sank into the worn fabric of the seat cushions and stared out at the passing storefronts and office buildings. It was a random mix of the ramshackle and the architecturally correct, as though in willful defiance of the very concept of zoning laws.

Temporarily sheltered from the line of life's fire, Alicia appeared drained of energy. Her face in profile looked as lifeless as a relief portrait on a coin. I knew that she just wanted the taxi ride to end, but at the same time, wasn't yet ready to face the task of checking into another hotel.

"I guess it was fairly rough when the police took you in," I broached the subject.

"Yes, it was." Alicia swung her green eyes to me. "And how did I get into this mess? Okay, here goes." Her gaze returned to looking at nothing, as she began. "Dr. Salazar is a Fine Arts professor and my boss for this project down here. We're restoring these huge murals at the State Capitol Building – the Palacio de Gobierno it's called. He's the Director of the Restoration Project, and I'm the Assistant Director. Well, Dr. Salazar gets shot dead, while I'm trying to take a photograph of him sitting in an old car at Pancho Villa's Museum. It was the most traumatic thing I've ever experienced in my life. And I see it through a viewfinder, as though it wouldn't be unreal enough otherwise. It sounded like a cannon went off, and then there's Dr. Salazar slumped over the steering wheel."

Alicia paused, her hand unconsciously drawn to her mouth. After a few moments, she went on, "We were alone and locked in at the time – you know, just Dr. Salazar and me – so naturally the police decided I did it. That's pretty much it."

The taxi stopped, boxed in by a traffic jam. The music and the driver's dancing shoulders carried on.

"But you didn't do it," I said.

"No, I didn't."

"But the police arrested you."

"Not right away. Not till the next morning," Alicia said. "The rest of the restoration group and I were all assembled at the Palacio de Gobierno, but nobody felt much like working on the murals. I'm in this skirt and heels, because I have to go talk to the State Historical

17

people about how we're going to proceed without Dr. Salazar. But I'm delayed, because I'm busy being a grief counselor. Then a couple of policemen, not in uniforms, but in blue jeans and starched dress shirts, plus another one who's in charge and wearing a suit, they show up. And I figure we're in for more questioning. But instead, they arrest me and drag me away right in front of the people that I work with and all these tourists."

"How did you know they were policemen?"

"Teresa told me. She's one of our artists. She warned me not to fight them."

I looked at the bruise on the side of her mouth, but said nothing.

"The one in the suit snatches up my purse, like it's a prize at a carnival. So when we get to the jail, all I had was this fifty-dollar bill stashed in my bra. It's a lot of money for a phone call, but I didn't have a lot of options. So I bribed the booking officer to use his cell phone, and he gives me the number to the US Consulate. And after I explain my situation to *them*, I sneak out the call to *you*, and I was dialing my sister, when he caught on and took his phone back."

"Still," I said, "fifty dollars well spent."

"I didn't know that just yet. So I wile away the next couple of eons sharing a cell with several other women. Sometimes they talked to each other in Spanish, but mostly we just sat there, like lumps. Then a female officer comes and takes me to a windowless room with an examining table, like in a doctor's office. She says I have to give her my clothes, so their lab can process them for evidence."

"That's stupid. Salazar was killed yesterday. And you're dressed in different clothes for your meeting today."

"That's what I tell her. Plus, she can kiss my ass, if she thinks I'm giving up my clothes. But I don't think her English is all that good, and she calls in this big, ugly Sergeant – he's got the three chevrons." Alicia brushed her hand on her upper arm. "They confer in Spanish a bit, and then the big, ugly Sergeant walks right up and backhands me as hard as he can." Alicia touched the bruise on the side of her mouth.

"Damn."

"I'm knocked off my high heels, and I hit the floor like a sack of potatoes. The policewoman flees from the room, and now I'm alone with Big Ugly. I take off my heels, so I have some stability, and I scrabble back up on my feet. I got the message that my clothes are coming off, whether I'm conscious, or not. But I don't like my chances, rushing him and using the spike heels on his head. He looked like minor injuries wouldn't mean a thing to him. So I know I have to take him down hard. And for that, I need him to come into range. I unbutton my blouse and pull it off. He smiles. He thinks it's going to be easy. But I don't want him to think. I want him to react. I reach back and unhook my bra. I hold it in place with one forearm after the other, getting free of the straps. He's breathing heavier now, and I fumble with the bra, like I'm nervous, and he gets a little flash of the goods. And now, he's coming forward, arms bent at the elbow, hands open, head lowered, eyes focused on the bra. I slide my left foot back and bend my knees a little, timing his rush. And just as he commits to a grab for my bra, I twist out of it and thrust the heel of my hand hard up under his nose. Bam!" Alicia's eyes blazed. "He drops the bra and stumbles back, hands cupped over his face. He drops to his knees and blood's streaming out of his nose. He's moaning and bellowing. A bunch of uniforms burst into the room. And while I'm corralling the girls back into my bra, they're laughing and hooting at their Sergeant, along with whistling and making kissing sounds at me. It takes three of them to lift the fat Sergeant up. And he spots me, and I can see the rage on his ugly, bloody face. Thankfully, they're still holding him, which gives me time to get my blouse buttoned. Because that's when he starts yelling again, spraying out all kinds of blood at me. And I shielded my face with my hands and kept my mouth and eyes closed tight. But the freaking animal ruined my blouse."

"But how did you—"

"This is when Richard Woodstead strides in, but I don't know right then who he is. He barks a few words in Spanish, and suddenly they're all stalwart officers of the law again. And he introduces himself to me, and when I hear 'US Consulate,' I just want to melt into his arms. But the next thing I know, I'm being stuffed into the back of a patrol car and whisked off to the Court House. From the basement garage, I'm loaded into an elevator and taken up to the second floor. Then I'm plopped down on an upholstered, but really uncomfortable, chair in a small waiting room, where the walls are crowded with all kinds of original oil paintings. There are some other, nicely dressed people, sitting and waiting, but I'm the only one with a police escort and a bloody blouse. So naturally, I get a lot more look-sees than the paintings."

"That was the Prosecuting Attorney's office?"

"I guess," Alicia said. "Pretty soon, Richard Woodstead breezes in, cucumber cool, and tells me to just sit tight. He goes into an inner office, and I hear raised voices from behind the door, all of it in Spanish. That goes on for fifteen-or-so minutes. Then Woodstead comes out, takes charge of me, and leads me down that grandiose staircase." Alicia's green eyes swung back to me. "And there you are at the bottom of the stairs with that wondrous look on your face."

That Consular Agent Richard Woodstead had saved the day without breaking a sweat was becoming a well-polished stone in my shoe. "Alicia, I wish I could've arrived sooner. Maybe—"

"It happened the way it happened," she said. "And don't you get all jealous, because I was fawning on Richard Woodstead, which is—"

"I wasn't jealous."

"—which is just how you always get, even though that should be long done with."

"I'm fully capable of appreciating what Woodstead did for you without getting my blood up."

Green eyes momentarily fixed on mine, serving notice of the double Pinocchio I'd scored with that gem.

Alicia turned away and slumped back in her seat. "Look," she said. "I just want to put this whole day behind me. And I want to get out of these filthy clothes and into a hot shower."

I leaned forward and asked the taxi driver, in Spanish, to take us to a clean, inexpensive hotel. The driver bobbed his head. "El Hotel Miramar."

***

Halfway down a sloping city block, the taxi pulled into a loading zone in front of a gray, time worn building. While the driver retrieved my bag from the trunk, I helped Alicia out and onto the sidewalk.

Standing within an unbroken line of similarly weathered buildings whose days of consequence had long since passed, the Hotel Miramar did not noticeably stand out. Even its name, cast in ornamental iron and mounted proud of the facade, had faded and was now visually lost against the background of aged gray stone.

After squaring up with the driver, we entered the hotel and were carried along through successive waves of politeness, emanating from jacketed hotel employees, and deposited at the front desk. I registered us as Mr. and Mrs. Francis Elton and secured a room on the third floor. I didn't try for separate rooms, in part because Alicia didn't have a passport to show, but mostly because my wealth now consisted mainly of increasingly unsustainable credit. I was completely at a loss, however, when asked how long we intended to stay.

I took my best guess – "A few nights, maybe more" – and soon found myself signing a blank credit card imprint, so we couldn't skip out on the bill.

I didn't know what the hotel people thought about there being only one small suitcase between us for luggage. They didn't ask, and I didn't offer to explain. But I felt sure we'd be the topic of speculation among the hotel employees for quite some time, after we'd gone upstairs.

***

A high ceiling supported the vintage fan that hovered above the double bed and mirrored, upright dresser. A mismatched nightstand supported a modern touch-tone telephone, and a deep-bodied TV from the cathode-ray-tube era took up half the surface area of a single-drawer desk. There wasn't any dust on the furnishings, but the room smelled like dust anyway.

Alicia sat on the edge of the bed long enough to remove her high heels and then headed straight into the bathroom and closed the door. Soon, faucets squeaked, pipes hammered, and a shower coughed into action.

I surveyed the tarred rooftops of adjacent buildings through the double-hung window for a few minutes, stood at the TV and thumbed the arrow key on the remote through the limited offerings for a few more, and finally kicked off my shoes and flopped down on the bed. The sound of Alicia's shower should have lulled me to sleep, exhausted as I was. Instead, I lay awake, thinking.

I had assumed that springing Alicia from jail would be the hard part. But instead, given the conditions that Woodstead had accepted in negotiating Alicia's temporary release, the hard part had now become getting Alicia back home to Chicago. This meant spiriting her away, while we still had the chance – which would, of necessity, begin with eluding the local police, followed by a knuckle-biter border crossing at the Rio Grande, and then keeping a low profile, as we, rapidly as possible, made our way north to Chicago. True, we'd have a lot of explaining to do, once we got there. But we'd have a US lawyer doing the explaining and a US judge doing the listening in a courtroom reassuringly far away from Mexico.

I mulled over several escape scenarios, a couple of which actually seemed feasible. But it had been a long day, and the bed was soft, and I finally drifted off to sleep, while Alicia's shower droned on.

***

When I woke the next morning, the sun was up, and I was still lying, fully clothed, on top of half the bedspread. The other half was bunched up next to me, and Alicia slept under the sheet with her back to me. Only her hair and a pale mound of bare shoulder were visible.

I rolled out of bed, extracted a travel-worn toiletry kit from my suitcase, and carried it into the bathroom. Draped on a towel bar next to the sink were a bra and panties. The rest of Alicia's clothes lay in a pile on the tile floor. Evidently, she was done with them. I kicked the pile aside and set about my morning routine.

A half hour later, I emerged from the bathroom, carrying my kit and Alicia's pile of clothes. I set her clothes, now roughly folded, on the bed next to a rumpled bath towel that hadn't been there before.

Alicia stood barelegged at the dresser mirror. She was wearing one of my shirts and attempting to unsnarl her long hair with her fingers. "Have you got a comb, Francis? I've got unholy tangles here."

I took a comb out of my kit and handed it to her.

Alicia methodically worked the little plastic comb, section by section, through her long, dark strands.

"Thanks for the loan of a shirt. You pack kind of light."

"I didn't know I was packing for two. And I didn't plan on staying long. I just came down here to get you."

"To get me."

"I don't have the details sorted through yet, but I figure we can swim across into Texas along some deserted stretch and—"

"Are you insane?" Alicia turned to me. "What if we're caught? Didn't you hear what Woodstead said? I have to be a freaking saint, or they throw me right back into that god-awful prison again. How anxious do you think I am to be beaten and raped?"

"Keeping you out of prison is exactly why I'm going to get you across the border. I don't know how much time Woodstead's influence has bought you, but we'd best assume not a lot. We'll just slip across the Rio Grande into Texas. People do it every day."

"And people get caught every day. And if the police catch me making a run for it, it'll be as good as a confession. You think the Prosecuting Attorney will listen to a damn thing Woodstead has to say after that?"

"But what evidence could they possibly have against you in the first place?" I tried to make sense of it. "What motive?"

"Well, I do stand to gain from Dr. Salazar's death. There's this contract with the State Historical Society that says if Dr. Salazar can't fulfill his duties, like if he's too sick or whatever, the Assistant Director assumes his position."

"They think you murdered someone just to bag a promotion at work?"

"It's no little promotion. See, Dr. Salazar is an Art professor – was an Art professor. Anyway, he teaches at the University here in Chihuahua, but last summer he's up in Chicago as a visiting professor, and I have him for one of my last classes for my master's degree. But when he wasn't lecturing, mostly he's hustling to fund this project down here to restore the murals at the Palacio de Gobierno. I volunteered to help with the fund raising, and when I got my MFA, he offered me the Assistant Director's position. But it was entirely Dr. Salazar's project. And to be fair, he did all the heavy lifting with the financing. So while my salary is okay, Dr. Salazar inked in a bonanza for himself, plus some dandy perks, like an expense account and a chauffeured car. He did all right."

"And now *you'll* be doing all right."

"With the Director's salary and prestige, I could live like the Duchess of Chihuahua. For the next eight months or so, anyway."

"Okay, a windfall of money counts as motive. I'll give 'em that."

"You louse." Alicia threw the comb at me. "I didn't kill him. Actually, I kind of liked the old geezer."

I thought for a moment. "But they'd have to have something more than motive."

"You mean like where I was at the time of the murder?"

"Oh yeah, that's right. You said you were right there."

"About twenty feet away from him. Not much of an alibi, huh?"

26

I sat on the bed and wished I had a beer to help me think. "You said Salazar was shot. You didn't have a gun in your purse, or anything, did you?"

"No. But the police said I used some old gun that was there at the Museum. One of Pancho Villa's old pistols, I guess. Of course, I told them they were crazy. But they looked really closely at my hands, and one guy even brought them up to his nose and sniffed them. They ignored anything I said and just talked to each other in Spanish. It was frustrating as hell."

"And you and Salazar were locked in a museum?"

"It used to be Villa's old house, his hacienda. It's a museum now, and it's pretty huge inside. It's the Museum of the Revolution in the guidebooks, but nobody calls it that. The windows are barred, and the big double doors in back are padlocked. And at the time that Dr. Salazar was shot, the iron gate at the front entrance was locked."

This was bad, all right. "So, it was just you and Dr. Salazar."

"And the murderer."

"Yes, of course. And the murderer," I said. "But how do you get locked in a museum?"

"Okay, here's the layout." Alicia came over and sat next to me on the bed. "Every couple of weeks, we'd take the Restoration group out for some photographs. Pictures of various members of the group examining murals and tapestries and statues. That sort of thing. We'd send the pictures up to Dr. Salazar's colleagues at the Chicago Art Institute to be included in a newsletter. You know, with a little blurb to remind the patrons of the Arts that we're down here carrying out the important work they'd paid for and to hint around at the other historical wonders that need restoration and that we'd be only too happy to tear into. We'd already photographed the living bejesus out of the Palacio de Gobierno. So now, we're fishing around for the next project. We took the group over to the Cathedral, a couple of times, and then finally, to Pancho Villa's Museum. I don't know how many pictures actually get into the newsletter, but Dr. Salazar said that you have to keep sending them, or the money people tend to forget about you, and you have to start all over from scratch to fund a new project."

"So, Salazar is always trolling the fat wallets to fund the next one."

"That's how the game is played."

Mostly to give me a moment to take it all in, I took the time to retrieve the comb from where it had landed on the bed, but once I had it, I just held it.

"All that explains why you were at Villa's Museum," I said, "but not why you were locked in."

"Okay, so we're all at the museum – Dr. Salazar, his wife, the project's three other workers, and me. It's Monday, so the place is closed. But two soldiers are there on guard duty, and Dr. Salazar had arranged for them to open the place up for us—"

"Wait a minute. Soldiers?"

"Villa's Museum is owned and operated by the Mexican army. How's that for irony?" Alicia stood and began to pace in front of me while she talked. "So the soldiers let us in that afternoon. And Eduardo, our handyman, takes a bunch of photographs of us, singly and in little groups, out in the courtyards and inside the

28

various rooms around the hacienda. After a couple of hours, it's getting late in the afternoon, and the two soldiers have us all herded together and are trying to move us toward the exit, because their shift is almost over. But suddenly, Dr. Salazar gets the bright idea of having his picture taken, while he's sitting in Pancho Villa's car. You know, the one Villa was ambushed and killed in."

"The car is inside the hacienda?" I asked.

"It's parked in one of the courtyards. After all, Villa's wife would have inherited the car, after her husband was assassinated, and she lived in the hacienda until she died. And now the old car is the museum's main attraction."

"And that's why Dr. Salazar wants his picture taken in Villa's car. For the newsletter."

"Yes, but the soldiers say that Dr. Salazar only paid for two hours, and anyway, they're about to hand off the museum to the evening watch. Teresa, our student artist, translated this for me, and frankly, I was happy we were wrapping it up. Then out of the blue, Lydia, that's Dr. Salazar's wife, announces she's buying everyone drinks at a nearby restaurant, including the soldiers. And in the meantime, Dr. Salazar can get a few last-minute photos of himself taken. Lydia appoints me to stay and operate the camera. Which was okay with me. Lydia and I don't get along too well. And Lydia says the soldiers can just lock the place up for half an hour and take a break."

"And the soldiers were okay with deserting their post?"

"No. Well, I guess, technically, one of them did. But the other soldier said he'd wait out under the portico and have a smoke. But still he had to lock the front gate, because that was procedure. Again, Teresa translated for me. And we were supposed to give him a yell when we were done with the photographs, and he'd let us out."

"How long does it take for a couple of snapshots?" I asked. "Couldn't everybody have just waited?"

"I don't know what led up to this. I must have been busy on the other side of the courtyard when all of this was cooked up. But Lydia likes to take charge of things, and Dr. Salazar seems to always defer to her."

"Okay, they all leave, and the soldier locks you and Salazar inside, while he goes out for a smoke."

"Right. So it takes me a while to get the camera set up on the tripod, because I have to get back far enough and there are all these tree limbs to contend with. And meanwhile, Dr. Salazar has to go use the public men's room, and it takes old men forever to freaking pee. And when he finally gets done, I have to help get his slow ass sitting in the old car – he's not much of a climber, anymore. So, at long last, I go back to the camera, and I have my face up to the viewfinder, framing up the shot, and then suddenly there's this enormous sonic boom. I about went deaf. But I knew it was a gunshot, because I see Dr. Salazar draped over the steering wheel like a rag doll. And I ran over to him and—"

"Weren't you afraid of getting shot, too?"

"I don't know. I just ran to him, okay?" Alicia's eyes gave me a moment of defiance. "Anyway, there's a hole you could stick your finger into in his forehead and a big chunk gone from the back of his head. And I'm panicked, and then I remember about the soldier, and I run out of that courtyard and on through the little

30

courtyard going for the entrance gate. I run into the soldier just outside the Admission Office. He's all wide-eyed, and he grabs me by the arm and asks me something in Spanish."

"Did the soldier have a gun?"

"I don't remember. Anyway, I tell the soldier Dr. Salazar's been shot, but I don't know if he understands me. But we run together back to the old car. The soldier takes a quick look at Dr. Salazar's head and – oh yeah, he had a pistol, because now he's panning the courtyard with it, you know, looking for something to shoot. Then he rattles off something in Spanish again, motions for me to stay put, and runs off back to the front of the building."

"He must have gone to phone for help in the Admission Office."

"I guess, but anyway he never came back. So I'm standing around, trying not to look at Dr. Salazar, trying to hold it together and not be sick. Then I don't know how long it was before policemen and ambulance crews and soldiers all start spilling into the courtyard. There's this chaos and lots of commands yelled in Spanish. And then some big hard-ass in a starched shirt is firing questions at me, but in English. I explained the best I could, and I thought I was okay, because the police gave me a ride back to the Vista Suites. But then, like I told you, I was arrested the next day at the Palacio de Gobierno. So now, I'm public enemy number one."

Alicia sat next to me on the bed again, as I ran through what she'd said in my head.

"And the account you just gave me, is that what you told the police?"

31

"Maybe not word for word. I was just answering the questions, thinking I was helping."

"I can't see that you hurt yourself any with it," I said. "But still, being right at the scene of the crime and having a motive written right in a signed contract. Damn." I thought for a moment. "Did you say they found a gun?"

"The museum has lots of guns on display. Apparently, I used one of them."

"Trust me, if they could prove that, you wouldn't be sitting here." I stood, walked to the dresser, and laid the comb on top, before turning to Alicia. "I was serious about helping you get across the border. But if you're determined to stay here, what you need is a lawyer. Woodstead gave you a list. The best I can do for you now would be to send you what money I can raise when I get back to Chicago."

"No, Francis. I need you here." Alicia stood and her hands went to her hips in the same motion. "I'm going in to work this morning and assume the Directorship. And you're going to find out who killed Dr. Salazar, so I'll be cleared."

"*I'm* going to find the killer? Are you crazy? Where do you come up these ideas? I just fix broken machines. Your lawyer can hire a private detective, if that's what you want. I wouldn't know where to start."

"But you believe me. You know I didn't do it. Anybody I could hire down here would just take my money and wave goodbye, as I'm dragged off to the gallows. And you speak Spanish, so you can talk to people here. They won't be scared of you, like they are, the police. Is that too much to ask? And just let *me* take care of raising the money. Hopefully, my cell phone is still on my desk hooked up to the charger."

I leaned my back against the wall, looked upward at nothing in particular, and let out a sigh. "I'd be better at sneaking you past the Border Patrol."

"No, what you're better at is figuring things out. How else could you fix your precious machines? So now, it's my situation that needs figuring out." Alicia's hands dropped from her hips, and silently on bare feet, she came over to lean against me, her head on my shoulder, her fingers toying with a button on my shirt. "I'm precious too, aren't I?"

"What makes you think so?"

"You're here, aren't you?"

She let me think about that for a few moments, before pushing off, letting our eyes meet for only a second, and stepping over to the dresser. With her back to me, she resumed combing her hair in the mirror, patiently waiting for me to acquiesce, confident that I wouldn't walk away again.

Chapter 3

Taking her slim watch from the top of the dresser, Alicia glanced at its face, before sliding it onto her wrist. "I'd better get a move on."

She stepped over to the bed and began to rummage through the clothes in my suitcase. "My blouse and skirt are destroyed. That monster's blood is all over them. And I don't have any makeup. My first day as Director, and I get to turn up looking like a scarecrow."

She looked fine, of course – well, maybe a little powder to cover up the bruise.

Alicia selected my pair of khaki shorts, took them into the bathroom, and closed the door.

I sat on the bed and gave some thought to the murder weapon the police decided Alicia had used – supposedly, some old handgun from a museum display. I could only assume that either the police had found a recently fired gun with no fingerprints on it, or some gun from a display case was missing entirely. Either way, there'd be no proof that Alicia had handled the murder weapon.

Not that Alicia was unfamiliar with guns. When I was an Electronics Technician in the Navy, assigned to a Destroyer home-ported in San Diego, Alicia and I would routinely join a group of friends for tailgate picnics out in the desert, where we target practiced with an assortment of handguns and rifles for amusement. I had an old Smith and Wesson, model 52, pistol, a hand-me-down from my grandfather, and Alicia became quite proficient with it. Almost without fail, she could punch a hole in an empty beer can at twenty yards and send it skittering off over the desert scrubland. And if the can happened to pop up in the air high enough to give her time, she'd fire once more and usually, to the awe of the rest of us, hit it again in mid-flight.

Naturally, we asked her how she did it. But she just told us that she simply pointed the gun at the can and pulled the trigger, and that she didn't want to analyze it or think about it, for fear she wouldn't be able to do it anymore.

My thoughts were broken, when the door opened and Alicia stepped out of the bathroom, ready to assume the directorship of the Restoration Project. Her body feminized my shirt nicely. The khaki shorts, however, were a loose fit.

"I need your belt."

I got up from the bed, ready to oblige. But Alicia's hands beat mine to the buckle, which she quickly unfastened. She whipped the leather from around my waist, the tail end exiting the final loop with a snap.

Once she'd cinched the belt around her own waist, Alicia returned to the open suitcase to appropriate my sandals. "I need these too. Heels with shorts would send the wrong message."

***

The sky was clear and the morning air smelled fresh for our walk to the Palacio de Gobierno. Alicia said it'd be quite a hike, but she needed to do a little shopping on the way. We had to wait, while a clerk unlocked and pushed back the metal, security gate from the front of a shoe store, opening for the day. I paid for Alicia's new athletic shoes, which she wore out of the store. I grumbled, to no avail, about having to carry my returned sandals in a plastic bag. At a drug store, Alicia burned through some more of my pesos, buying such essentials as makeup, a hairbrush, and nail polish.

During a quick breakfast at a small café, Alicia carefully applied her new makeup, using the mirror on the inside lid of a small plastic case. Her practiced hand skillfully blended in the highlights and shadows, accentuating her facial features and all but erasing the bruise mark made by the lustful jailer.

As we left the café, the sun peeked over the city skyline, casting a harsh light on the thickening morning traffic and warming the sidewalks, where street vendors were staking out turf and setting up shop for the day. Several tall, important-looking buildings and monuments were festooned with colorful, sparkling strands of decorations, some spanning five and six stories.

"What's with the bling on the buildings?" I asked.

"It has to do with the Independence Day celebration," Alicia said. "Something wonderful happened in 1810. It's like our Fourth of July."

"Viva la México."

"Exactly."

We crossed through a park where green-roofed kiosks, dedicated mostly to the business of shoe shining, nestled among smooth-barked trees. Off to our right, a traffic policeman on a Segway rolled along the sidewalk checking parking meters. And as we neared the street on the opposite side of the park, the morning sun reflected off a statue of Miguel Hidalgo mounted on a pedestal with one hand held aloft and the other holding some, apparently important, document. Arrayed below the folk-hero priest were statues of four other assassinated, historical luminaries.

"That's where we're going." Alicia pointed across the street. "The Palacio de Gobierno."

The large, ornate building took up a whole city block. Greco-Roman trimmings and false balconies framed each tall window.

Alicia and I jaywalked at mid-block, heading straight for a pair of suitably large, wooden doors. Once inside, we passed through a short entryway that opened into a bright central patio open to the sky. Three tiers of walkways with arched supports like Roman aqueducts rimmed the expanse of tiled patio. Dominating the center, an eagle-topped spire loomed above four statues, each facing out with its own compass point of view. Just beyond the tall arched columns on the ground floor, I could see the series of murals that Alicia had described to me, painted high up on the back wall of the lofty colonnade. Indians fighting invading Spaniards, Mexican peasants overthrowing land barons, priests directing the construction of a cathedral – on and on they continued around the patio, all larger than life, overwhelming in concept, and vibrant in color.

Alicia made straight for a small knot of people gathered in front of a mural commemorating Miguel Hidalgo's execution, wherein eight rifle barrels were perpetually leveled at his chest at point blank range.

The four people turned to Alicia's approach.

"Sorry I'm late," Alicia said. "Teresa, we'll be proceeding with the color match on the assassination panel. Carlos, we have some sort of mold along the bottom. See what works on it. And Eduardo, I'll need the camera on the tripod with the wide lens."

Alicia then turned to a smartly dressed woman, whose classic Hispanic beauty was hardened by the dramatic contrasts of her makeup and severity of her black hair, tightly pulled back and secured in a bun at the nap of her neck. I put her age at mid-forties and her look at fashion-magazine perfect.

"Lydia, how absolutely brave of you to come into town today. Dr. Salazar was such an inspiration to the project," Alicia spoke soothingly, and then to me,

"Francis, this is Lydia Salazar. Dr. Salazar's wife."

"Miss Elton, I am...perplexed that you are here," Lydia Salazar spoke in chilled English, ignoring my presence. "I am just now dismissing the workers. Surely the project can no longer be completed. My husband is dead. It is ended."

"Oh Lydia, you poor dear," Alicia continued to placate. "It must be so terrible for you."

Dr. Salazar's widow fixed Alicia with a look of haughty disdain. Then, as though she could no longer hold back, her words burst out in rapid fire, "Why are you not in jail?"

Alicia stiffened, but fired right back, "The police made a mistake."

The two women locked hostile stares. Then without a further word, Lydia Salazar turned and stormed away, clicking pointedly across the patio tiles on stiletto heels.

"Eduardo, take the Land Rover. See that she gets back to her ranch all right," Alicia instructed the good-looking young man whose black hair was thick, oiled, and combed straight back. "But return here immediately. I have another assignment for you."

While Eduardo scurried after the retreating figure of the late professor's widow, Alicia turned to the two remaining workers – one, a finely-shaped, young woman in her early twenties who exemplified the striking beauty of Mexican youth, and the other, a well-fed, middle-aged man with a pair of glasses hanging from a cord around his neck.

"When you are grieving, sometimes the words come out wrong," Alicia set aside the flare-up with the widow, before moving on to the introductions. "This is Mr. Francis Elton," she started, but quickly added, "No relation." Then further amended, "I mean now."

The young woman and the older man shifted their looks of curiosity from Alicia to me, and then back, as Alicia attempted again to clarify. "We were married once…when we were young."

Feeling that our history had come out uncomfortably early, I forced a smile and, with a slight nod, managed a dry "Hello."

"Francis has come to help me discover the truth about Dr. Salazar's murder," Alicia soldiered on. "The police, of course, acted rashly when they took me into custody. And although they allowed me to leave, it seems they still require some convincing." Alicia took a breath, before continuing in a softened tone. "I know this is a trying time for all of us. But we must persevere and complete the restoration work, so that Dr. Salazar's last project will be a success and … and a tribute to his tireless efforts to conserve this … these historic works of art."

The two workers gave Alicia several seconds of light applause. I belatedly joined in for the last couple of claps.

"Teresa is an art student at the University here in Chihuahua," Alicia restarted the introductions, "and Carlos is a conservator on loan to us from the Art Museum in Mexico City." Alicia put a hand on my back, ushering me into handshake range. "As for Francis, apart from occasionally helping me out, he primarily travels the Earth as a field service engineer."

I shook Carlos's outstretched hand, as he struggled with a greeting in English. When I responded in Spanish, his face lit up, and he grabbed my shoulder and gave it a hardy squeeze. I then turned to Teresa and held her hand. She spoke English with a light and pretty accent, "Welcome to Mexico. Carlos and I are very happy that you come to help Miss Alicia."

"I'm sure it's only a misunderstanding," I said.

In response, Teresa simply smiled with brilliantly white, straight teeth.

"Well, you have your assignments." Alicia was back in charge. "I have some phone calls to make. And then I'll be with you."

Teresa and Carlos moved off to the assassination mural.

Alicia turned to me. "Hang loose, Francis. When Eduardo gets back, I'll have him drive you over to Pancho Villa's Museum, so you can see for yourself where it happened."

"Eduardo's also the chauffeur, then?"

"He's our jack-of-all-trades," Alicia said. "See that scaffolding?"

Teresa, in tight blue jeans and a paint-speckled, man's dress shirt with rolled up sleeves, was silently rising up in front of the large mural, while standing on a platform that ascended within the confines of four, vertical pipes. It looked like she was having a smooth ride.

I was still watching, as the platform came to a stop about twelve feet off the ground and Teresa set about her work.

"It's easy to look beautiful when you're twenty," Alicia said, breaking my spell.

But lovely as the sight of Teresa was, I was drawn to the platform lift's mechanism. As I approached it, I could see the four upright pipes were attached to each other in a weldment, similar to the frame of a fourposter bed, but on wheels, so it could be pushed from one mural to the next. I had to get close to see that each corner of the platform was welded to a large nut that rose with the rotations of a threaded rod within each slotted pipe. The threaded rods had sprockets fitted near the bottom and turned in unison by means of a continuous chain that was driven by an electric motor. A cord ran from a panel box, mounted on the base, up to a push-button control unit, which now hung by the last few feet of cord that Teresa had left draped over the safety railing.

I'd seen a similar mechanism before in a couple of auto factories on ergonomically correct workstations, designed to adjust the table height over a twelve-inch range to accommodate tall, or short, workers. So here was that same idea, but scaled up and applied to scaffolding.

"It was the first thing Eduardo made." Alicia had come up behind me.

"The pretty-boy made this?"

"Perfect hair on a man doesn't mean anything down here," Alicia said. "Dr. Salazar needed a powered platform that we could work off of. One that could move around easily and raise us up to work on these big panels. A regular scaffold wouldn't do, since Dr. Salazar's climbing days were long over, and a hydraulic scissors lift still requires scrambling up a four-foot ladder to get to the platform. So Dr. Salazar called some professor friend at the Technological College and asked what could be custom built. The friend put Dr. Salazar on to a former student. Shortly after that, Eduardo shows up, Dr. Salazar describes what he needs, Eduardo makes a quick sketch, they shake hands, and two weeks later we had this."

We both stepped back far enough to view the entire platform again.

"So then, Salazar hired Eduardo full time?" I asked.

"Pretty soon thereafter," Alicia said. "Frankly, he does a lot more work out at Dr. Salazar's ranch than he does here. I know Eduardo built some sort of powered carousel to exercise Lydia's horses. Anyway, he's on the Project's payroll as the chauffeur – of all things – but unless we need him here for something specific, I mostly only see him when he drops off Dr. Salazar in the morning and picks him up at the end of the day. But on the plus side, he takes his photography assignments seriously, and he can fix whatever breaks. And he's the best one of us at the computer. When we bought the new digital camera, he installed the software, and taught me how to upload pictures and e-mail them to Chicago for the newsletter."

"And he's the chauffeur."

"There's a line in the Project's budget for a driver," Alicia said, "but not for a handyman. And anyway, Eduardo enjoys cruising in the Rover, as much as Dr. Salazar enjoyed living large." Alicia consulted her watch. "Now, you'll have to amuse yourself for a while. I didn't get my purse back, so I need to put a freeze on my credit cards, before I buy some policeman's wife a new wardrobe."

Left to myself, I wandered along beneath the arcade that surrounded the spacious interior patio area. I kept between the pictured walls and the arched supports, staying out of the late morning sun that beamed down on the open patio and was already heating up the floor tiles. It was a walk through Mexican history, as I viewed the series of heroic, and sometimes horrific, murals. Looking up across the patio to the second-floor level, I could see, above its railing, even more murals, as though the Mexican people's appetite for wall art were insatiable.

Eduardo was back at the Palacio de Gobierno in just over a half an hour. This didn't seem like enough time to have taken Lydia Salazar as far as a ranch outside the city. Maybe Salazar's stern widow had further business in the city that day. Perhaps making funeral arrangements. In any case, soon after the skilled, young man's return, Alicia brought the two of us together.

"Eduardo, this is Francis. He'll be helping me deal with the local police, so I can devote my time and energy to moving our project along. I want you to drive

43

Francis over to Pancho Villa's Museum." Alicia turned to me. "Go look at it, Francis. You'll understand it all better, after you've seen it yourself."

Chapter 4

Setting a quick pace, Eduardo led me past a broad staircase. Looking up the stairs to the first landing, I caught a fleeting glimpse of stained glass. But we pressed on without pause, eventually turning down a hallway on the opposite side of the building through which Alicia and I had entered. Leaving the main patio area, we passed through a little indoor garden. And now, as I turned and looked up high above us on the interior wall that was the back of the staircase, I caught a full view of the two, impressively large, stained glass windows, each depicting a robed female figure – one bearing the scales and sword of Justice and the other, the book and sword of the Written Law. I commented on the beauty of the stained-glass artwork, but Eduardo didn't respond, his mind apparently focused on something other than twin characterizations of the Rule of Law.

Outside the Palacio de Gobierno, an equally massive building across the street was undergoing a total renovation. Its interior was so stripped down that you could see all the way through its shell to the street on the other side. A temporary sign indicated it had once been the Federal Building and was about to become a new museum.

"Times must be good to afford a big project like that," I said in Spanish, again attempting to engage Eduardo in conversation.

"For Chihuahua, it does not matter," Eduardo replied this time. "There is always money for grand public buildings and statues. Our Mayor thinks of little else."

But Eduardo wasn't looking at the Federal Building, or at me, when he said this. When I followed his gaze, I spotted a forest green Land Rover, parked within an arc of orange cones that blocked off a traffic lane. Also within the coned-off area was a large crane, whose engine and counterweight swung around, passing over the Rover's hood with barely a foot of clearance, as the crane's cables lifted equipment up to the roof of the former Federal Building. Figuring that the precariously parked Land Rover was the one belonging to the Restoration Project, I could now understand Eduardo's distracted behavior, particularly if the crane had been idle when he first parked there. But the swing of the crane wasn't Eduardo's only worry. Just outside the coned-off area, a uniformed officer of the traffic police had just stepped out of his patrol car and was already writing on his pad.

It appeared that Eduardo had gambled and lost. But as we neared the illegally parked Rover and the ticket-writing policeman, Eduardo merely asked me, "Can you give me a hundred pesos for parking?"

I didn't quite understand what was going on, but the request was for little enough money. I extracted a hundred-peso note from my wallet and gave it to Eduardo, who left me standing, as he engaged the policeman. The policeman and Eduardo shook hands and spoke for a minute, before the policeman openly took the money. Then, apparently heeding the call of duty, the policeman turned his attention to the nearest traffic lane and with hand gestures managed to free a trapped line of cars.

I joined Eduardo and spoke in English, since the policeman was still within hearing distance. "Did you arrange this with the traffic policeman, when you parked here?"

"No. It is only the price of a minor parking ticket," Eduardo answered in passable English. "Do you understand?"

"Yes, I understand all right. The *mordida*."

"It is the same in America?"

"No," I said. "In America, offering a bribe would just insult the policeman and erase any leniency that he might have shown you. It's better to just take the ticket and mail in a check for the fine."

Eduardo merely shrugged at this, perhaps wondering how Americans, with their quaint customs, made it through their working day.

As I walked around to the passenger side, Eduardo remotely unlocked the Rover's doors with a button press on a key fob and said he had a quick phone call to make. I slid into the front seat, and Eduardo remained outside the Rover with his cell phone to his ear. Muffled by window glass, the only part of Eduardo's conversation I caught was "*Museo de Pancho Villa*", and that was only because he'd had to raise his voice over the roar of the next lift of the crane. As the crane's counterweight filled my view through the windshield, I guessed that Eduardo was probably telling his girlfriend he'd be late, because he had to take some gringo sightseeing.

Eduardo finished his call, but instead of getting behind the wheel of the Land Rover, he remained outside, leaning against the side of the Rover. I was beginning to get annoyed at being inconvenienced, when I heard his phone's electronic ring tones, followed by a few muffled words from Eduardo. Soon after that, the driver's door opened, and Eduardo finally got in and started the Rover. As he edged forward into a turn between two orange cones, I waited, expecting an apology, or at least an explanation, for the delay, but none was given.

The pliable traffic policeman now held up a line of cars, allowing the Rover to pull out, and we drove away from the city's center on Avenue 20 de Noviembre.

We cruised along at a gentlemanly pace for several minutes, before Eduardo turned off the wide avenue and headed down a side street. After a few blocks, Eduardo abruptly pulled the Rover to the curb, said he'd only be a minute, and disappeared into a convenience store.

I wondered whether Eduardo was unsociable by nature, or merely preoccupied that particular day.

Fifteen minutes later, just as I was about to follow him in and find out what was taking so damn long, Eduardo reappeared with two plastic bottles of Aquafina. Again, he offered no explanation, but simply handed me an unasked-for, plastic bottle of cold water and drove back to where we'd turned off Avenue 20 de Noviembre and continued on.

About three quarters of an hour into our leisurely-paced trip, Eduardo turned the corner onto Calle 10a, and we descended a long hill through an older residential district. In our descent, we passed between two long rows of plain, single-story houses that shared adjoining walls and were set back from the street only by the width of a narrow sidewalk – as though it were one long adobe-walled motel. At the end of this two-block-long line of residences was a much larger building with a tall portico that extended right out over the sidewalk, its doubled columns anchored at the edge of a stretch of yellow painted curb. The portico was centered on the large two-story building that continued on as a single-storied wall for, perhaps, seventy-five feet and ended a corner turret at the cross street. The turret featured the type of tall, narrow slits that are typically associated with defensive guns. Eduardo parked at the curb, just beyond the yellow paint.

"This is the hacienda of Villa," Eduardo said in Spanish. "It is now his museum."

Eduardo and I climbed the front steps under the portico of Villa's Museum, only to find the entrance blocked by a black ornamental iron gate, on which hung a red-lettered sign stating: 'Museum Closed,' in both Spanish and English. I was about to express my disappointment when the gate swung open and a uniformed policeman stepped out. But instead of turning us away, as I'd expected, the policeman stood to one side. Wordlessly, Eduardo walked on through the open gate. My feeling of uncertainty, as I followed Eduardo in, turned into a moment of apprehension, as I heard the gate clang shut behind us.

I caught up with Eduardo, who had stopped just outside an open door to our left. "Why were we let in?"

"I telephoned ahead and secured permission," Eduardo said, as though it were all in a day's work for a chauffeur-slash-handyman.

Above the open door, a large sign read: 'Admission.' Inside were two soldiers. One stood behind a counter, reading a newspaper that was laid out between display racks, crowded with souvenirs and postcards for sale. The other soldier, sitting in a chair to one side of the counter, nodded at Eduardo, before taking a leisurely swig of water from a clear plastic bottle.

"I will wait in here," Eduardo said, "while you look around."

With no regrets that the unsociable Eduardo wouldn't be accompanying me, I walked alone into a little courtyard with a small square of trimmed grass and shrubs, a modest central fountain, and a dwarf fruit tree. I strolled past windows and open doorways through which I could see furnishings from the turn of the last century. A sign said these rooms were the living quarters of Villa's wife, Luz, until her death from old age. My pace quickened when I spotted up ahead, through a passage leading to the next courtyard, a vintage, black touring car parked under the shelter of a colonnaded walkway. This would be Villa's car, and according to Alicia's story, also ground zero for the scene of the crime.

As I neared the old car, the first thing that caught my eye was the emblem on the chrome-plated radiator cowling, proudly proclaiming: 'Dodge Bros. Detroit'. The bullet holes from Villa's assassination still punctured the radiator and continued in a random pattern along the driver's side of the car. The doors and cab body reached only half the distance between the running boards and the canvas top, leaving the upper half wide open to incoming projectiles. I leaned over the sturdy chain strung between the columns and peered inside. If Dr. Salazar had spilled any blood on the weathered and torn interior, it had been thoroughly cleaned up.

A green, vinyl awning, tightly stretched on a metal frame, extended the shade out from the covered walkway, further sheltering the old car. The awning looked new and had obviously come way too late to save the sun-split leather seats and deteriorated canvas top.

I remembered Alicia telling me that she'd set up the camera on a tripod, as far back from the driver's side of the touring car as she could get, without leaves and branches getting in the picture. Looking directly away from the driver's side door, I saw the heavily vegetated area that included several trees that topped out at about the second story roofline. I paced the "twenty feet" that Alicia had estimated as the distance from the old Dodge to her camera's location. My paces showed that it actually might have been several feet beyond twenty, but it was still within easy handgun range. And a professor's head is a lot bigger target than a beer can. So, at first glance, it wasn't looking too good for Alicia's proclaimed innocence. But on the other hand, in this larger open-air courtyard, there were plenty of trees, tall ornamental grasses, and columns for some other potential shooter to hide behind – not to mention, several shadowed doorways. So, Alicia's hidden assassin explanation wasn't out of the question, either.

I decided to do a little exploring, to see how easily someone could move about the old hacienda unseen.

Walking beyond the tailgate of the vintage car, I saw, painted on an adjacent wall of the lower colonnade, heroic murals depicting Pancho Villa and his men in action. It now made more sense that Dr. Salazar would bring his group here, given his never-ending pursuit of future restoration contracts.

Immediately on rounding a corner, to my left was a passageway that led back to an opening in the wall that allowed viewing of Villa's old Dodge on the passenger side. Passing that by, I saw ahead of me a carriage and wagon from a bygone-era, and I soon entered what proved to be yet another walled-in yard. This one featured an old cannon, mounted on wooden-spoke wheels. The open, interior side of the turret was in the far corner. To my right, large double-doors were padlocked together, and near the corner to my left, was an emergency exit door, clearly marked and fitted with a modern panic bar. To my reckoning, the emergency door would open onto Calle 10a, about halfway along between the portico and the corner turret. If an assassin's timing were right, the emergency exit could have been how he made his escape unnoticed. I filed that away in my head with the feeling that Alicia's story may have gotten a little boost.

Returning to the large courtyard that contained Villa's touring car, I climbed a stairway leading to the upper colonnaded walkway that gave access to the second-floor rooms, filled with displays of artifacts and photographs from Villa's time. As I turned the inside corner of the walkway and continued on, I could see, between the treetops, the green awning sheltering Villa's car on the lower level across the courtyard. From this higher angle, the awning blocked my view of the upper half of the old, black Dodge. Obviously, the shot that killed Salazar couldn't have come from this level, or there'd be a hole in the awning's fabric. I was beginning to think detective work wasn't so hard after all.

I moved along to the next inside corner of the upper walkway, but looking through an open doorway, something caught my eye. Instead of turning, I went straight and entered a long room that may once have been two rooms, since off to my right there was a step down about midway in its length. What had caught my eye was the beginning of a series of long glass cases, full of elderly handguns and rifles, extending down the center of the room. Unlike the elegantly machined works-of-art under the glass display counters in US sporting goods stores, these guns bore witness to rough, outdoor use, and lots of it. These were tools, not showpieces, and all could stand a damn good cleaning - certainly before *I'd* attempt to fire one. And even if someone got past the padlocks on these glass-topped cases, chances were that the firing pins had been removed anyway. It was hard to imagine the police would think someone had used one of these old relics to shoot Dr. Salazar.

The long room fed to the left into another room, where a saddle and spurs on a sawhorse were on display. From this room I stepped out onto a second story walkway, overlooking the smaller courtyard I'd first entered, when I began my self-guided tour. Moving past more rooms - one containing a period wooden desk and chair, some worn-out books, and an old typewriter -

I descended a flight of stairs and found myself outside the Admission Office again. Inside the office, Eduardo now sat on a chair, talking to the soldier with the water bottle. At the counter, the other soldier continued with his newspaper.

I turned to a sound behind me and was confronted with a large, stern-faced man wearing a neatly pressed, white shirt. The butt of a black, holstered semiautomatic peeked from behind his right side. The plainclothes policeman simply pointed toward the small courtyard. It appeared that permission to enter Villa's Museum would come with a price after all.

I reentered the small courtyard, as silently ordered, and encountered another plainclothes policeman, who blocked the passageway leading to the elderly black Dodge. He pointed toward a door just off to his left.

Thus herded, I entered a spacious bedroom – its decor typical of Villa's era. But my eyes immediately went to the grip of a large handgun, holstered in worn leather and hanging on one of the posts at the head of the bed. From across the room, I could tell only that it was a carved grip in the hue of old piano keys and dotted with two points of red. No plate glass shielded this gun from curious fingers, just a velvet rope within the bedroom to separate the tourists from the furnishings on exhibit.

I caught a whiff of a freshly lit cigarette. In the reflection of a mirrored armoire, a slender man in a black suit exhaled gray smoke. I turned to face him.

He was tall for a Mexican and had a pair of dark, mean eyes. He stood with his back leaning against a wall, his mean eyes fixed on me. He took another pull on his cigarette and blew out another small cloud, smoking in a public museum with impunity.

"What is it that you wish to see here?" His English was without accent, like that of a network newscaster, back in the States. "Why have you come to Villa's Museum today?"

I wasn't happy that I'd attracted such high-level attention so soon.

"I'm a tourist," I said.

"A tourist. No, I do not think so." He took in more smoke. Through an exhaled haze, he said, "You are the man that Miss Alicia Elton has sent for."

"Maybe you'd better tell me who you are."

"Certainly. I'm Commandant Arroyo of the State Ministerial Police." He didn't bother to show a badge.

"Perhaps, you'd be kind enough to tell me *your* name."

"It's Francis Elton. I thought you knew who I am."

"You are related to Miss Alicia Elton?"

"Her ex-husband."

"Then it is Mrs. Elton," Commandant Arroyo corrected himself.

"I think she prefers Miss."

The Commandant paused to cycle more smoke through his lungs. "It's interesting that she has summoned her former husband, at this particular time." He tapped his cigarette, letting ash fall to the floor. "Are you a lawyer, Mr. Elton? Or, perhaps, an agent of the American government?"

"A field service engineer. I troubleshoot and repair automated machinery."

He looked at me hard for a moment. "That, I think, we must verify."

Now that I'd managed to trap myself in a police interrogation, I figured I might as well try to pick up on what pieces of evidence the police had against Alicia. Maybe, I could refute them, one by one, and keep Alicia from getting rearrested. Anyway, it sounded easier than rooting out an unknown assassin.

"Look," I said. "I'm just the guy Alicia turns to when she needs a hand with something. She asked me to come over here to Villa's museum to look around, maybe find some indication of where the real killer was standing when he shot Dr. Salazar."

Through smoke, Commandant Arroyo said, "We have tested a column on the second-floor walkway and found considerable gunshot residue. The shots came from there."

"Wait. That can't be right. I was just up there. The green awning would block the shooter's view."

"The awning had been damaged and removed at an earlier date. The workmen replaced the material just yesterday. There was only the framework of aluminum tubing on the day of the murder."

"In that case, it couldn't have been Alicia who fired the gun." I thought I had him. "She was down in the courtyard behind the camera when Salazar was shot."

"Is it impossible that Mrs. Elton went up to the second story walkway to do the shooting?"

"Move farther away to take the shot? Why would she do that?"

"In order to bolster her self-portrayal as an innocent bystander. For Alicia Elton's story to hold together, the fatal bullet had to originate from somewhere other than the area near the camera on the tripod. A downward trajectory of the bullet passing through Dr. Salazar's skull satisfied this need." Commandant Arroyo pinched the glowing ember off the end of his cigarette, let it fall to the wood floor, and stepped on it. "The deception may well have worked, had her motive not been so transparent."

I successfully stopped myself from then asking where Alicia was supposed to have laid her hands on a working gun. Unfortunately, I couldn't stop my eyes from glancing at the holstered revolver, slung by its belt on the bedpost.

Arroyo smiled. He then unhooked the end of the velvet rope from the stanchion nearest him and walked over to the holstered gun at the head of the bed. "When left alone with Dr. Salazar, after the others in their party had embarked on their pilgrimage to the Café Iguana, Alicia Elton came into this room to get the murder weapon. This gun." Arroyo placed his hand on the grip.

I couldn't let that go unchallenged. "Are you telling me that all the old guns on display around here actually work? They're just old, rusty museum pieces, aren't they? Do you think Alicia carries penetrating oil and ammunition around in her purse?"

I was feeling better now, but it was short lived.

"This is not the gun that is supposed to be here," Arroyo calmly said. "It's not the stylized Colt carried by Pancho Villa in his later years. True, this is a single action Colt from the days of General Villa, and the special grips look like those in the photographs of

Villa's actual Colt. But the serial numbers do not match the museum's records."

Arroyo gave the exposed grip a couple of taps, before continuing, "Also, we removed the grips and quickly found that they are not, in fact, made of carved ivory, as they would've been in Villa's day, but of molded plastic. Artistically disguised, painted by a skilled hand, but modern plastic, nonetheless."

The implication, concerning the artistic application of paint, was not lost on me.

Arroyo pulled the revolver out of the holster and held it barrel up. "This gun was brought to Mexico from the United States, where guns and ammunition are abundant and easily purchased. It was disguised for the purpose of substituting a functioning firearm for the non-functioning museum piece. Mrs. Elton is perfectly capable of completing these tasks. However, what Mrs. Elton could *not* do, after she shot and killed Dr. Salazar, was to clean the barrel and chambers, before returning the gun to this holster. There wasn't time. And the soldier who came running at the sound of the shots told us that he could not say whether the woman who was left alone with Dr. Salazar had just run *past* this room or had just run *from* it, when he stopped her in the foyer."

Arroyo changed the gun to his other hand to reverse it, and offered it to me butt first. I hesitated, thinking about putting my fingerprints on a murder weapon.

"The gun is unloaded now," Arroyo said, "Feel free to examine it, while I examine your passport."

Since my fingerprints would be on top of the Commandant's, I drew my passport from my pants pocket and exchanged it for the gun.

Arroyo thumbed through my passport with its multitude of stampings, before taking a notebook and pen from his jacket, and writing down the information printed on the identification page.

The revolver had some serious heft to it. The head and neck of a long-horned steer with ruby red eyes were raised in bold relief on the right-side grip and filled my palm comfortably as I held it, offering a lot of purchase. I knew from experience that big caliber guns with smooth grips tend to require a he-man's grasp to keep the gun from rotating when fired.

I laid the gun in my left hand and focused on the beautifully painted faux grain of carved ivory. The long lines were randomly spaced and somewhat faded, as though by exposure to the sun, and the delicate angled cross-hatchings were fainter and without pattern. The false gold medallion, embedded above the raised steer head, could fool the eye, too.

The ruby colored, probably glass, eyes of the steer stared back at me. Okay, I silently told the steer, you're an excellent reproduction. Now, let's see if you could have shot anybody.

Shifting the weight of the revolver back into my right hand, I opened the loading gate, thumbed the hammer back two clicks to the half-cocked position, and rotated the cylinder. There were no unfired cartridges or spent casings in the chambers. I brought the gun up to my nose. The pungent smell of burnt gunpowder was still strong.

I closed the loading gate and eased the hammer back down with my thumb, as my index finger slightly pulled the trigger. Then, I thumbed the hammer fully back, hearing four clicks along the way, and saw the firing pin in place on the hammer. I aimed the gun at the floor just in front of me, pulled the trigger, and watched the hammer smack onto an empty chamber.

"You are familiar with guns, Mr. Elton?" Arroyo asked without looking up from his writing.

"I own a couple."

"And Mrs. Elton. She, too, is familiar with your guns?"

I hesitated. "No, I bought them after we were divorced."

"Ah, after you were divorced," Arroyo said. "Yes, of course."

Arroyo stowed away his notebook in a jacket pocket and walked back to where he had been standing when I first entered the room. He picked up a briefcase from the floor, brought it over, and laid it on the bed. He also laid my passport on the bed, but out of my reach. Arroyo opened the briefcase and extracted a large photograph of a Colt revolver with a steer-head grip.

"This is a blown-up version of the photograph of Pancho Villa's Colt from the museum's catalog." Arroyo handed it to me. "Notice that the gun in your hand and the gun in the photograph are visually identical."

Admittedly, the photograph seemed to be of the gun I was holding. The point, of course, was that it wasn't.

I returned the photograph to Commandant Arroyo. He put it in his briefcase, closed the lid, and then, to my relief, handed my passport back to me. As I was pocketing the passport with one hand, I held out the duplicate Colt to him with the other.

"Just one moment," Arroyo said, not taking the gun. "Perhaps a little demonstration is in order. We'll go to the spot from where the shots were fired."

Carrying the old gun, I followed Arroyo, as he led me out of the room, past Villa's old touring car, and up the flight of stairs to the second story colonnade level. We rounded the first interior corner we came to and stopped at the second column beyond it. It was almost the exact spot where I'd looked between the treetops and spotted the green awning that shaded Villa's old Dodge near the far corner of the large courtyard.

"Notice the dark marks here on this column." Arroyo pointed to two elongated smudges on the inner arch. "They have tested positive as being gunshot residue."

"I'll have to take your word for it."

"The test result speaks for itself," Arroyo said. "And since you are familiar with revolvers, perhaps you'd care to prove something to yourself. Brace your gun hand against the edge of the column and align the attitude of the barrel to the long residue mark that is angled downward."

Not wanting to take his word for something else, I raised the gun up to a firing position, rested the back of my wrist on the column's edge, and held the gun barrel along the long mark.

"Notice," Arroyo said, "that you are now sighting down to the old car and that the gases that would emanate from the cylinder's loose fit would produce the shorter mark."

I glanced at the smudges again. There was no refuting Arroyo's point. So, I tried a little nitpicking.

"When I sight down there, all I see is stretched green vinyl," I said. "Am I supposed to guess that no parts of the framing crossed in front of Salazar's head?"

"I have a photograph of one of my men sitting in the driver's seat on the day of the murder, taken from this vantage point. The crosspiece of the frame passed by him at his neck level."

I again held the gun out to Arroyo. He took it this time.

"A head shot," I said, "using an old handgun, at what, seventy or eighty feet? Even steadying your hand against the column, it'd be one hell of a shot."

"But not out of the question for someone who has had the opportunity to practice with shooting the murder weapon."

"Nor is it out of the question that someone else was up here that day," I said. "Someone who could have taken the gun from the bedroom sometime earlier, waited for his chance, maybe even thought that Dr. Salazar was alone, since he might not have seen Alicia setting up the camera under the trees. He shoots Salazar, and after Alicia runs to the front gate to call for help, he returns the gun to the holster and runs off for that yard with the cannon. By then the soldier has come inside, and the killer slips out through the emergency exit."

Commandant Arroyo shoved the gun under his belt, freeing up his hands to extract another cigarette from his pack. He took his time lighting up.

"There was no one else," Arroyo said, when the smoke cleared. "Among the photographs taken that day of members of the Restoration group all around the museum, there are several showing the gun still in its holster in the bedroom. Also, we have verified that at the time of the murder, except for Alicia Elton and Dr. Salazar, everyone who had been admitted to the museum had left the building. The front gate was locked, and a soldier was posted just outside. No one else came in."

"But an assassin could have been let in earlier through the emergency door."

"The emergency exit has an alarm mechanism that is triggered when the panic bar is pushed," Arroyo said. "And as to the big rear doors near the old cannon, the padlock is in place and unmolested, and the dust is undisturbed."

He was having it all his own way. I took a swipe at him. "So, if you've got the case against Alicia all sewn up, what's the big idea of having your Sergeant strip-search her, *after* she'd already showered and changed her clothes?"

"He is *not* my Sergeant!" Arroyo flared. "He is of the Municipal Police, and he is a moron. His brutish behavior provided that shameless chameleon Woodstead with an outrage, which he used to extort the release of an accused murderess."

While Arroyo struggled to regain his composure, a tense stillness descended on the former hacienda, as though even the birds were holding their breath. Knowing that the gun wasn't loaded was my only solace during the long minute it took for the rage to gradually subside from Arroyo's face. I had an idea that the failings of others with whom he had to share the planet were a constant source of aggravation for Commandant Arroyo.

With his flash of anger ended, Arroyo commanded, "Come," and immediately strode briskly back toward the stairway, forcing me to hurry to keep up.

"Do you know how difficult it is to legally purchase a firearm in Mexico?" Arroyo asked, as we descended the stairway. "It's not like Texas. You cannot buy a pistol at a gas station in this country."

"I imagine there's a lot of paperwork, but—"

"The paperwork is unimaginable. A wait of a year or more is normal. And you must travel to Mexico City in order to buy your firearm from the DCAM. Even to buy from a private owner, both buyer and seller must present themselves to the Government in Mexico City. This makes old handguns rather precious, does it not?"

"I guess so."

"You guess correctly. And this is a forty-five-caliber revolver." Arroyo held the gun up for me to see over his shoulder, as he walked ahead of me. "It is absolutely forbidden to possess a forty-five-caliber handgun or even a single forty-five-caliber cartridge in Mexico. Did you know that?"

"No, I didn't."

Arroyo said nothing further, as he led me back past the ancient Dodge touring car and into the bedroom with the now empty holster at the head of the bed.

"I'm certain you'll agree," Arroyo turned to face me, "that it would be rather easy for a US citizen to cross the Rio Grande into Texas on a day trip and buy an elderly revolver, plastic steer head grips, and ammunition."

"But that US citizen would *not* find it so easy to bring the revolver and ammo back across the Rio Grande into Mexico."

"There are those who make a living from cross-border smuggling. They don't advertise, but they can be found."

"If you think Alicia would ever set foot in some lowlife bar, for any reason, you're sadly mistaken," I said. "She wouldn't even consider it."

"Then let us consider the artistic skill needed to transform new, white plastic into aged ivory for the grips." Arroyo again tapped the plastic with a fingertip. "And that the murderer had to be in a position to know well in advance that Dr. Salazar's group would visit Pancho Villa's Museum on a day it was closed to the public." Arroyo's mean eyes fixed on mine. "And consider how easily Alicia Elton could tour the museum a day or two ahead of the group's visit, replace Villa's Colt with a fully functioning and loaded duplicate Colt in this holster, and walk away with the museum piece in her purse."

While I stood there unable to form a counterpoint, Commandant Arroyo calmly opened his briefcase on the bed and laid the substitute Colt next to it. From the briefcase, he withdrew another aged revolver. This one was plain, the grips made of smooth stock wood. He stepped over to the head of the bed and slid the plain gun into the holster.

"A gun from one of the glass cases on the second floor," Arroyo explained. "We cannot disappoint the tourists."

Arroyo came back and placed the duplicate of Villa's ornate Colt into his briefcase.

"Exhibit One must remain in my custody." Arroyo smiled at me briefly. It was not a nice smile.

65

"Anyone would have access to the duplicate Colt," I finally found an argument. "This room is unguarded."

"Yes, it's unfortunate that the security camera that you see as a black globe in the entryway arch takes video only of the area just outside the Admission Office. It's the only functioning camera within the building. The outdoor security cameras mounted along the roof edges above the courtyards haven't worked in many years. A problem with the system, I'm informed. The repair parts are no longer available."

I hadn't noticed any security cameras at all. They're so common now that, unless you're a thief – or, I suppose, a police detective investigating a crime – seeing them doesn't even register anymore.

I stepped out of the bedroom and into the first courtyard. I saw the black globe hanging over the arch in the entryway between the foyer and the first courtyard. It looked like the one of those cameras at a bank on the wall behind the tellers – the type that mostly keep watch over the handling of the money.

I looked up at the roof edges above the first courtyard. I didn't see any security cameras, functioning or not, but there was an empty bracket that might have once held one. I turned and walked through the arched hallway that led into the larger courtyard, stood next to the old car, and scanned the roof edges. I spotted one, above and perhaps twenty feet to the right of the column with the gunshot residue, pretty much opposite Villa's Dodge. The security camera was an old one, all right, given its large size and the utilitarian, three-sided, sheet metal cover. I could easily accept that replacement parts for such a relic would be only a dim memory, even to the most seasoned clerk at an electronics supply house.

"It would have been an interesting piece of video, I agree." Arroyo joined me in gazing up at the security camera. "However, it would merely have shown us what we already know. Professor Salazar was shot while sitting in the old car."

"It would also have shown Alicia rushing to his aid within seconds of his being shot."

"If you wish to fantasize..." Arroyo didn't bother to add the shrug.

"I take it," I said, bringing my gaze back down to earth, "that there was no picture in the digital camera Alicia was using that shows the Professor sitting in the old Dodge."

"There was not," Arroyo said. "Perhaps, Mrs. Elton was busy with other matters."

"Gloves." The thought popped into my head. "If Alicia had no gunshot residue on her hand, either she wore gloves, or she didn't shoot the gun. And you didn't find any gloves, did you."

"What is it that you know about gloves, Mr. Elton?"
"Alicia said one of your detectives sniffed her hands. And when he didn't smell the odor of burnt gunpowder, I would assume your men would start searching for discarded gloves. And if they'd found any gloves, I'm pretty sure you would've mentioned it by now."

"It's true that her hand showed no visual stippling and didn't smell of burnt powder. That was in the report," Arroyo said. "However, thin latex gloves are readily available and easily concealed. They are also easily disposed of, along with the empty cartridge casings, with the flush of a toilet."

This hadn't gone well. My repeated attempts to refute the evidence against Alicia, point by point, had gotten me exactly nowhere. I was now more than willing to chalk up the morning as a loss. Plus, I'd had more than enough face time with Commandant Arroyo.

I was still working up an exit strategy, when Arroyo said abruptly, "You may leave now."

I was relieved, but mystified.

"All right then," I said. "Well, we'll probably meet again."

"I was telling you that you may leave Mexico now." There were those mean eyes again.

"I don't understand."

"I have taken a good deal of my time to explain in detail and to show you conclusively that Alicia Elton murdered Dr. Salazar. It is pointless for you to further cast about on her behalf. Also, it's burden enough on my available manpower to keep a watchful eye on our capriciously released suspect. And I'd prefer that her flight-risk potential not be amplified by the on-going presence of such a devoted ex-husband."

Arroyo looked past me and made a head movement. The two plainclothes officers reappeared, but they didn't close in. Yet.

"I told Alicia that I'd stay and help."

"The only assistance Alicia Elton requires is that of a defense attorney," Arroyo said. "Both Mrs. Elton's version of what occurred that afternoon and the Prosecuting Attorney's case against her will be presented to the Court. After due consideration, a decision will be reached and Mrs. Elton's fate determined. There is nothing you can do that will change any of this."

If it were anyone but Alicia, I'd have grabbed my suitcase and headed straight for the airport. "As I said before, we'll probably meet again."

Commandant Arroyo's mean eyes never wavered. "If you remain in Chihuahua, you may be sure of it."

Chapter 5

One of Arroyo's men followed about ten feet behind me. I stopped outside the open door of the Admission Office and rapped twice on the wood frame.

In Spanish, I said, "I am finished here."

Eduardo caught up with me, as the uniformed policeman opened the iron gate and stepped out ahead of us.

Out under the portico, the policeman whistled and waved at a tour bus that was parked at the yellow curb and kitted out in the guise of an old-fashioned trolley car – except for the modern advertisement for Victoria beer, running along its length.

The bus driver announced to his passengers in English and Spanish that they could now disembark and enter the Museum of the Revolution. Eduardo and I stood to one side, as tourists of many nationalities – my own countrymen attired as though for a backyard barbeque – filed out of the bus, trooped up the portico steps, and entered Villa's former hacienda.

On our way to the Land Rover, I instructed Eduardo to drive me straight back to the Palacio de Gobierno. "No delays this time," I added.

The harshness in my tone drew a quizzical look from Eduardo, but I wanted it understood that I was wise to the part he played in my involuntary encounter with Commandant Arroyo.

On reflection though, it shouldn't have been surprising that I'd attracted the attention of such a high-level police official. After all, it wouldn't have been a mere Sergeant arguing with Consular Agent Woodstead in the Prosecuting Attorney's office.

In any case, my focus now was to get back to the Palacio de Gobierno, as quickly as possible. Letting a busload of tourists tramp through the crime scene was a sure sign that Arroyo was no longer looking for "further evidence" at Villa's Museum. And that pretty much left him with only one place to squeeze out additional proof of Alicia's guilt. Alicia herself.

Once we were belted into our seats, Eduardo swung the Rover around the block, returning to Ave. 20 de Noviembre. He then drove at a good clip, heading directly back to the city center.

"What did the State Police want with you?" Eduardo found his voice again.

"Just a few questions." I figured he could ask his amigos at Headquarters, if he was so damned curious.

***

When Eduardo and I arrived at the Palacio de Gobierno, Carlos and Teresa rushed toward us in agitation and excitement. Teresa's flurried, high-pitched Spanish was incomprehensible to me. I turned to Carlos and his slower, more methodical speech for an explanation of what had happened.

"Miss Alicia has been arrested again," Carlos said. "Two policemen came in and went straight to her. They took the artist's brush from her hand, and they led her away, one on each arm."

"She kicked at the policemen's ankles," Teresa had calmed down enough to add. "Miss Alicia shouted, 'Tell Francis.' Then they were gone."

Eduardo's look of concern wasn't too convincing. But I was done with Eduardo.

I asked Carlos, "Did the policemen wear uniforms? Did they have a piece of paper that they showed to Alicia?"

"No uniforms, but with badges and guns on their belts," Carlos said. "They showed no documents. They said only, 'You will come with us.'"

"Which way is the jail from here?" I was done with the Rover, too.

Carlos pointed, and I immediately headed for the door.

Hurrying, almost at a run, down the sidewalk in the direction Carlos had indicated, I kept a lookout for a taxi. I slalomed through lunchtime shoppers and street vendors, and perilously dodged through traffic when crossing against the light. My fear was that Arroyo had decided to coerce a confession from Alicia to satisfy the Prosecuting Attorney's requirement. If I could get there before they started, I could demand that Alicia's lawyer be present. True, Alicia didn't actually have a lawyer yet, nor did I have Woodstead's list of Consulate-approved attorneys at hand, but stopping the backroom tactics was the first priority. I'd fill in the blanks later.

Finally, I spotted an empty taxi coming up behind me. I stepped into the street and hailed it with waving arms. And once again, I found myself directing a taxi driver to take me to the City Jail. This time, I arrived in a fighting spirit.

***

Amid the crush of people waiting in the jail's visitor area, I saw no discernible pathway through to the long counter at the far end of the large room. Regardless, I plunged into the crowd, moving forward as rapidly as I could, not bothering to excuse myself.

Ahead of me at the counter, two peasant women, dressed in colorful blouses, full skirts, and shawls, were making a passionate appeal. The porcine officer standing behind the counter had three chevrons on his sleeve, two blackened eyes, and a strip of thick tape spanning his swollen purple nose.

The Sergeant sent the traditionally garbed women away with a dismissive wave of his thick hand. I was up next.

"Sergeant," I addressed him in Spanish. "Two State Police officers took Alicia Elton away from the Palacio de Gobierno this morning. Is she here? I must see her."

The Sergeant didn't even bother with the pretense of checking. "No, there is no one here by that name. Come back tomorrow."

I reached across the counter and dragged a lined, yellow notepad and a pencil over to me. Before the corpulent Sergeant could respond to the breach of protocol, I wrote "Alicia Elton" on the pad, slid it back to him, and tapped my index finger on Alicia's name. "She is here. Commandant Arroyo ordered two of his officers to bring her here."

"Commandant Arroyo told you this?"

"Yes."

The Sergeant touched the white tape that held his nose in place, winced, and began shuffling through the papers stacked on the counter. He then picked up his telephone and poked at the numbers. I overheard him asking in a low voice about Alicia and mentioning

Arroyo's name. Presently, he grunted and returned the phone to its cradle.

"You must wait."

"For what reason was she brought here?"

"You must wait."

I received my own dismissive wave of the Sergeant's hand. Immediately, the next hopeful supplicant pushed his way in front of me, and I was reabsorbed into the shifting press of people crowding the aisles between rows of fully occupied, plastic chairs.

After ten uncomfortable minutes spent pressed within the throng, a door off to one side of the visitor's area swung open, and a young man, who looked like he'd had the crap beat out of him, emerged with a jailer still firmly gripping his arm. An extended family rose up from a row of plastic chairs with a whoop of joy. The jailer quickly disappeared behind the closing door, as the family rushed to the young man. As though the music had suddenly stopped, I moved quickly to become one of the lucky ones to plant myself on a vacated chair.

The newly released, battered young man, engulfed in the family's collective bosom, was swept out through the double doors, and gradually, the flurry of excitement subsided. As the large, overpopulated room settled down once again to wait, I took out my cell phone, noted the time, and put it away. I stared at the floor for what I was sure was at least an hour, but when I again checked the time, only fifteen minutes had passed.

After another ten minutes, I left my seat and approached the long counter. The portly, broken-nosed

Sergeant was gone and in his place was a bored-looking policeman with two chevrons sewn to his shirtsleeve.

"Corporal, can you tell me the status of Alicia Elton?" I asked in Spanish. "Is she being questioned? Has she been allowed access to an attorney?"

The Corporal slowly lifted his head to look at me from beneath half-closed eyelids. "There are many people. It all takes time."

I tried the magic name again. "Commandant Arroyo informed me that she is here and that I was to notify him when I arrived."

"Her name again?"

I reached to the yellow notepad and slid it over in front of him. The Corporal looked down at the pad, picked up his phone, and asked about Alicia.

A few seconds later, the Corporal hung up, took a moment for a yawn, and said, "A test for the residue of spent gunpowder on the hands is being performed. It all takes time."

What had I done? *I* was the one who brought up Alicia's hands and gunshot residue to Arroyo. Therefore, it was *my* bungling around, not knowing what I was doing, that got Alicia dragged back to jail again. A swell ex-husband *I* turned out to be.

A door behind the Corporal swung open, and the portly Sergeant appeared with a mug of steaming coffee. The handle of the mug could only accommodate two of his fleshy fingers.

"Commandant Arroyo has been informed that you are here." The mug landed hard on the counter, resulting in a significant loss of dark brown liquid. "If Commandant Arroyo wishes to speak to you, he will speak to you. What *you* wish for is of no consequence to *him*."

"I am not going away."

"*That* is of no consequence to *me*."

The Sergeant picked up his mug, turned, and waddled back through the door to resume his break. As the Corporal lethargically brought out a roll of paper towels from under the counter, I relinquished my place at the counter to the petitioner behind me.

Having lost my seat, I walked over to a vacancy along a wall and leaned my back against it. I stayed there, intermittently glancing at the time on my cell phone, for the next half hour. Then from out of the crowd, a thin, young man, whose unkempt hair and sparse goatee were both an anemic yellow, slithered over and asked, in sotto voce English, "I wonder if, by chance, a businessman, such as yourself, might have some extra storage space in your hotel room? Not much, really, just enough to accommodate a few suitcases. Let's say, five?"

"Five."

"Yes." He kept his sun-reddened face uncomfortably close to mine. "It seems I find myself in the awkward position of having more cash than secure square footage. My partner is currently being questioned, owing to a miscalculation on his part, so I feel it prudent to reposition the luggage for, say, twenty-four hours – just until I can arrange for alternate means of transportation for the journey north. You've no particular objection to payment in pesos, do you?"

I could understand his singling out a compatriot, especially one whose presence at a foreign jail might well indicate a certain familiarity with calculated risk. And truth be told, given my financial straits, I can't say I wasn't tempted.

"I'll pass," I said. "I have problems of my own."

Out of the corner of my eye, the damaged-nosed Sergeant reappeared at the counter. I turned my full attention to him, and his blackened eyes glared back.

The Sergeant then spoke a few words at the Corporal's ear.

Shortly thereafter, two uniformed policemen parted the crowd, as they approached me. The young man who had more suitcases than were good for him vanished.

"Sergeant Gameros orders the Gringo to be more comfortable to wait outside," one of the officers took a fair stab at English.

Rather than being manhandled, I exited the main doors under my own power.

***

But I didn't more comfortably wait outside. I climbed into a taxi that had just emptied its passengers onto the curb in front of the jail.

"Where do you wish to go, sir?" The driver asked in Spanish, as the taxi pulled away.

"To the United States Consulate. Do you know where that is?"

"Yes, sir. In the City of Juarez. It is a long way, four hours. I must call my dispatcher." The driver reached for his radio microphone.

"Wait a minute," I said. "Is there no United States Consulate here in the City of Chihuahua?"

"No, sir."

We moved along with the traffic, apparently on our way north to Juarez. I had a queasy feeling in my stomach. I needed to talk to Consular Agent Woodstead, and I had no idea how to contact him. The very least the slick bastard could've done was to give me his card.

"Can you ask your dispatcher to find the telephone number for the US Consulate in Juarez?"

The taxi driver radioed his dispatcher, who, after a short delay, relayed the Consulate number to him. I dialed the number into my cell phone, as it came through the speaker. After five minutes on the phone with the Consulate in Juarez, I had the address of a building in Chihuahua that housed what was termed "the informal Chihuahua office of Consular Agent Richard Woodstead." I withdrew a dollar from my wallet, borrowed a pen from the driver, and jotted the address in the empty space next to Washington's picture. With the Consulate still on the line, I asked for Woodstead's phone number, thinking maybe I could get things started before I got there. I was informed that Woodstead was scheduled to be in Mexico City that day and was given the phone number for his secretary. I added it to the front of the dollar.

I rerouted the taxi driver to the address I'd been given. I tried to reach Woodstead's secretary, but the "battery low" message popped up on the screen. After a couple of futile tries, I shoved the useless device into my pocket.

The address turned out to be on the north side of the city, so it wasn't long before the taxi pulled to the curb in front of three stories of cut-stone façade in a block of newer office buildings. As a former Navy electronics technician, I couldn't help but notice the array of antennas sprouting from the roof.

The dark blue Lincoln Town Car was parked at the curb in front of us. Maybe, I'd caught a break, for once. I paid the driver, tipping generously for his help, and he sped off.

As I climbed the steps, the door at the top swung open, and Woodstead's stout driver stepped out. He looked down at me briefly and then scanned the street, holding the door open with the heft of a fat leather satchel that he carried in his off hand. Richard Woodstead next emerged from the building, crisply suited and carrying a slim briefcase. As the door swung closed behind them, Woodstead started down the steps with his driver on his near flank. The driver kept an eye on me. The weight of the satchel on his arm seemed to make the unnatural bulge under his suit jacket more pronounced.

As they were about to pass me by, I spoke up,

"Consular Agent Woodstead, a moment of your time."

Woodstead and his driver stopped on the steps. The driver's free hand slid beneath his jacket toward the bulge.

"Have we been introduced?" Woodstead asked.

"You handed off Alicia Elton to me at the Court House yesterday and dropped us at her motel. I gave you six hundred dollars."

"Ah, yes. Forgive me. You were mostly facing away from me in the front seat." Woodstead's eyes now studied my face. "And your name again?"

"Francis Elton."

"And you're the husband."

"We're not married anymore."

. "Well, perhaps that's for the best. Now, what brings you here? It'll have to be fast. I have a flight to catch."

"The police have Alicia in jail again."

"Whatever are they up to this time?"

"I have an idea it's about something I said to Commandant Arroyo, concerning gunshot residue."

"You've been talking to the Commandant?"

"I bumped into him at Villa's Museum. Immediately afterwards, he ordered that Alicia be brought in for a gunshot residue test."

"A GSR test now? Rather clumsy of our Commandant. Does he think the woman doesn't wash her hands?" Woodstead's tongue made a dismissive click. "In any case, Arroyo is still blocked from holding her, while he pretends to expand his investigation. So, if he can't think up something else with which to charge her, he'll be forced to release her within twenty-four hours. Assuming he plays by the rules."

"I'm worried they'll try to get a confession out of her, the old-fashioned way," I stated my deepest fear.

"Yes, that's quite likely."

"I went straight over to the City Jail," I pressed on, "but I had no luck in getting her out again. Obviously, I don't have your clout. And if you remember, I used up all the money I'd brought with me on her first arrest."

"The money, which you never seem to tire of mentioning, is used to promote goodwill with the local police in general and, more importantly, for the occasional fashionable dinner with ranking officials and their ambitious wives. Thus, in the event that a lovely

80

American lady is arrested for murder, my phone call gets through, and, circumstances permitting, the cell door is persuaded to swing open. Naturally, an unofficial slush fund is maintained for this purpose. I'm sure you can imagine why it's unofficial. Now, I believe we have discussed your money quite enough. Perhaps, we can dispense with the topic."

This was going badly, and I would've loved to sock that smug snobbish puss of his. Instead, I restated my appeal, "I hoped that you might, once again, use your influence on Alicia's behalf."

"This is becoming tedious." Woodstead sighed. "But I suppose Arroyo thinks he's cleverly found a loophole in the Prosecuting Attorney's instructions." He brought his wrist up for a glance at his watch. "I'll see what I can do by phone on the way to the airport."

Woodstead left me standing, as he turned away and, accompanied by his driver, proceeded on down the steps. At the curb, the driver opened the back door of the large sedan, but Woodstead paused for a moment, his back to me. Then over his shoulder, he said, "Ride with me to the airport, while I make the call."

I would've preferred to be riding back to the jail and to Alicia's rescue, but I dutifully hustled down the steps and over to the far side of the Town Car. Woodstead's driver climbed in behind the wheel, and I slid into the back seat next to the Consular Agent.

Woodstead already had his cell phone to his ear, as we sped away from the curb. He spoke in his crisp Spanish, rapidly running through Alicia's situation, ending with Commandant Arroyo's delayed, and therefore bogus, need for a GSR test on her hands.

Woodstead then asked the person on the other end if he would take on Mrs. Elton's defense. Apparently getting a yes, Woodstead instructed him to go to the City Jail and secure Alicia's second release. He added that her husband would be there shortly to take her off his hands. I wasn't happy with the prospect of having to correct my marital status once again, but I guessed Woodstead couldn't be bothered to go into side issues.

"Who's the lawyer?" I asked, when he closed his phone.

"Your Spanish is better than I thought." Woodstead reopened his phone. "Just a moment. I have to preempt our favorite Commandant's tendency to overreach." After a flurry of button beeps, Woodstead again held his phone to his ear. He informed the person on the other end that a US citizen named Alicia Elton had been taken to the City Jail for a curiously belated examination of her hands for gunshot residue. He stated that he fully expected that any questioning of Alicia Elton by the police would wait for the arrival of her lawyer and take place in the lawyer's presence. And he further expected that Alicia would be free to leave with her lawyer, whenever the lawyer decided to end the interview. This time I had no idea who he was speaking to.

After ending the call, Woodstead switched to English. "That's the best I can do at the moment. It's quite important that I am in Mexico City this afternoon. As to your question about the lawyer, his name is Enrique Ponce. A distant cousin of my wife, her mother's side, as it happens. One of the newer crop of defense attorneys."

"As long as he can stand up in court and tell the jury Alicia's side of the story—"

"That's not quite how it's done here."

I turned to the Consular Agent. "Surely, there'll be a trial."

"Yes, of course. Just not one with a jury," Woodstead said. "Luckily, however, your former wife got herself accused of murder in one of the few Mexican states that have fully transitioned from the old inquisitorial system to the new adversarial one. So, yes, her lawyer can stand up in court and tell her side of the story, but it will be the judge who decides her guilt or innocence. Apparently, the elder judiciary felt that blatant appeals aimed at the heartstrings of the laity was a reform too far. Still, there's no death penalty. At least, they're civilized."

As we rode on in silence, I mentally digested this information. I could only hope that judges and prosecution attorneys here weren't too cozy.

Woodstead broke the silence, by stating, "There is something you don't know about the murder weapon."

"That Villa's revolver with the carved ivory grips wasn't the gun that was used, but that an old Colt, with plastic grips painted to look like old ivory, was?"

"And how did you come by that knowledge?"

"Commandant Arroyo showed me the disguised old Colt when I was looking around Villa's Museum this morning. I don't know when plastic was first used for handgun grips, but I'm pretty sure it was after Villa's time."

"I wasn't privileged to inspect the murder weapon, myself," Woodstead said. "I understand that, aside from the decorations, it's as old as Villa's fancy Colt. Did it look to be in working order?"

"I handled it. The mechanism operates freely, and the firing pin is in place."

"Ah. Something we weren't sure of." Woodstead withdrew a small, leather notebook and pen from his jacket pocket and jotted something down. "It's true that Villa's actual gun from the bedroom display was not the murder weapon. This is largely because Villa's gun has been in Chicago, since well before Dr. Salazar's murder."

"Chicago? What's it doing in Chicago?"

"Since your wife didn't tell you—"

"Ex-wife didn't tell me."

"Yes, of course." Woodstead again brushed aside the legalities. "Well, I suppose it's possible that she wasn't a party to all of it, although it's not hard to imagine that she was somewhere in the mix. Someone had to fabricate the counterfeit grips, after all. And she's rather adept with paint, isn't she?"

"Paint doesn't explain how Villa's Colt got all the way to Chicago."

"I was getting to that," Woodstead said. "Dr. Salazar had been stealing rare artifacts from various storage rooms for several years. Through some unknown broker, the plunder was then off-loaded into the private collections of the heavily-moneyed class. However, with the recent economic downturn, the purloined items started resurfacing in various consignment shops and estate auctions throughout the US and Europe. Assorted Departments of Antiquities could not avoid seeing the red flags waving in their faces, and the hue and cry went out. Find the perpetrator and bring him to justice. As though museums weren't bloated with a lot of old, dusty refuse for which they have no exhibit space, anyway."

"Wait. Go back. Salazar was stealing from museums?"

"Easy pickings, apparently," Woodstead said. "It took some serious digging into who, in the past few years, had been given access to the back rooms of the involved museums. Lists were compared, and Dr. Salazar's name had an uncanny knack for popping up, typically as someone's guest. Given his stint as a visiting lecturer up in Chicago, the sneaky boys arranged to take a surreptitious peek inside any package arriving at the Art Institute with Salazar's name on it. I, personally, would have expected this exercise to bear more futility than fruit. And yet, one sunny day, a package does arrive at the Art Institute, addressed to Dr. Salazar and postmarked from Houston. Inside the package, FBI agents found an old handgun, flaunting ivory grips, one of them sculpted into the head of a long-horned steer, with sparkling rubies for its eyes."

"Pancho Villa's Colt," I said.

"Precisely. It was a major score for the Bureau, even if it wasn't the Aztec fertility figurine, or what-have-you, that they were hoping for. A mini-cam was duly set up in Salazar's office to capture a glimpse of the hapless minion they assumed would come to fetch it. They don't think Dr. Salazar himself had his fingers directly in the black market. More likely, he's just the thief. The one they really want is the unscrupulous broker. Of course, they wouldn't mind also collaring the receiver of the stolen goods, alias some rich old fool with a huge yen for possessing the actual Colt carried by Pancho Villa – in a country packed to the rafters with firearms, mind you."

"You're saying some gun collector actually put in an order with the crooked broker for a specific museum exhibit?"

"Either that, or the broker, being a well-connected sort of scoundrel, anticipated his wealthy client's desires," Woodstead said. "In any case, ultimately, no one came to retrieve Villa's Colt from Dr. Salazar's office at the Art Institute – undoubtedly because of the stupendous dust-up the Bureau caused, while investigating the old Professor's previous filching. That, of course, has bunched the silk unmentionables of our Lords and Masters. And now, with Dr. Salazar's murder, they have no one to arrest at all and are left holding an aged handgun with tasteless decorations that the Mexicans are screaming to have returned."

"Maybe, the broker hired an assassin to shut Salazar up."

"That's the current viewpoint of our esteemed Federal Bureau of Investigation." Woodstead gave a derisive sniff. "But the choice of murder weapon doesn't quite fit, does it?"

"A headshot at that distance calls for a small caliber rifle, not a big honking horse pistol that sounds like a bomb going off. And anyway, why wouldn't the killer bring his own gun?"

"And now you have the Mexican authorities' viewpoint," Woodstead said. "Thus, their focus remains on the beautiful, but allegedly deadly, Alicia Elton. They feel certain that she was in league with Dr. Salazar in the theft of Villa's Colt and thus was well aware that a functioning firearm was residing in the holster in the bedroom. The Prosecuting Attorney intends to offer ruthless ambition, as a motive. I understand the coveted Directorship falls to the Assistant Director, should Dr. Salazar become incapacitated. Death, of course, being the ultimate incapacity."

The Town Car came to a stop midway along the loading zone in front of the airport terminal. Woodstead and I remained sitting in the car, while the driver got out and opened the trunk. Several nicely dressed, but humble looking, would-be porters rushed forward. But as a unit, they stopped and backed away, giving Woodstead's driver plenty of space, as he carried the heavy, fine-leather satchel into the airport himself.

"I'm worried," I said, "that the lawyer you arranged for won't have much to offer Alicia by way of a defense."

"Don't underestimate the Bureau's desperate desire that the official solution to their otherwise bungled investigation should be that a rogue antiquities broker paid his cross-border smuggler to silence Dr. Salazar permanently. They've invested too much time on this to come up empty. At minimum, they'll need to arrest the smuggler."

"So, the FBI's theory of the murder is Alicia's defense?"

"For as long as it remains viable," Woodstead said. "Unfortunately, the smuggler-as-hit-man theory is embarrassingly thin on particulars when it comes to the events at the scene of the crime. Naturally, the State Ministerial Police are not cooperating. And the Rio

Grande would flow backward, before Arroyo would allow the FBI to put one of their own Special Agents on the ground here." Woodstead pushed back his jacket sleeve for a glance at his watch. "And so, at last, we get to the point of your ride to the airport with me. Evidently because I'd already stuck my toe in the muck, I received an encrypted request, this morning, to look further into the Salazar murder locally, for our friends at the Bureau – quite unofficially, of course. The Bureau's theory is absolute nonsense, but I would like to tell them that I have a man on it."

It took me a moment. "Me?"

"You came to me today, once again seeking my help to free your former wife from the rigors of South-of-the-Border-style incarceration. And I, once again, accommodated you. I thought perhaps you'd return the favor. Quid pro quo, if you've kept up on your Latin."

"Look," I said, "my blundering around this morning is exactly what got Alicia carted off to jail again. So, I don't think—"

"I merely need a set of open eyes and receptive ears, moving freely among the late Dr. Salazar's associates. That seems little enough to ask, doesn't it?" Woodstead brought his slender brief case onto his lap and reached for the doorknob. "Any tidbit that seems relevant enough to pass on, simply drop by my office for a chat. Or if I'm not there, scrawl it on a piece of paper and hand it to my secretary."

We both exited the vehicle through our separate doors and met again on the sidewalk. Woodstead extended his hand, and as we shook, he said, "I can count on you, can't I?"

"Yes, I suppose so, but—"

"Good man." Woodstead released his grip. "And a note of caution, be very careful not to run afoul of the local police, especially Commandant Arroyo. 'Quite unofficially' is code for 'you are on your own'."

Chapter 6

Inside the airport terminal, Woodstead and I parted company. I watched, as the Consular Agent strolled causally past the lines of passengers who waited patiently for their luggage to be x-rayed, before queuing up again to have their passports and tickets mulled over by pretty, uniformed clerks. Woodstead barely gave any of this activity a glance, as he carried his slender briefcase on past the last of the competing airlines' check-in counters and, with fluid ease, simply disappeared through an unmarked door.

As I scanned the terminal for an ATM, Woodstead's driver, no longer carrying the heavy satchel, walked right past me without so much as a nod and exited the terminal through the sliding glass doors. Through the glass, I watched as he slid behind the wheel of the Town Car and pulled away from the loading zone, undoubtedly moving the luxury vehicle to some secure VIP parking area.

I returned to my quest for an ATM. When I found one, I milked it for three-hundred-dollars-worth of pesos, as a cash advance against what was becoming an increasingly uncertain future.

With my wallet fattened, I strode directly to the lounge and rewarded myself with a cold bottle of Corona, for being so unwitting as to accept Woodstead's assignment – not that I had much choice in the matter. Along with my last swallow of beer, I occurred to me that all those taxi rides had seriously chewed through my previous cash-on-hand. So, pressing my credit card still further toward financial ruin, I presented myself at the Avis counter, rented a Ford Fiesta, and drove myself back to the city.

I had to stop once to ask a traffic policeman for directions, but eventually I found my way back to the City Jail. A block away, I found a tight space at the curb, begrudgingly left between two large SUV's, and into which I managed to successfully insert the diminutive Fiesta.

The former crowd in the jail lobby had mostly dispersed during my absence, and there was neither a hostile Sergeant nor a lethargic Corporal manning the long counter. A quick check of the time on my phone showed it was after two in the afternoon, putting us squarely within the lunch and siesta period. This circumstance made it easy to pick out Alicia and a gray-suited young man seated together in a sparsely occupied area of plastic chairs. As I neared them, the young man was rapidly typing on a laptop computer, balanced on his knees, while Alicia quietly spoke.

I sat down next to Alicia. "Glad to see you're out."

Alicia turned to me. "Where've you been?"

"Soliciting Woodstead's help in getting you set loose again." I looked past Alicia to the young man's quizzical face. "I take it you're the lawyer. I'm Francis Elton."

"My ex-husband that I told you about," Alicia placed me in context.

The young man carefully set his computer on top of a briefcase that lay on the empty chair next to him, and stood. "Enrique Ponce. Attorney for the Defense," he said in accented English. "Welcome to Mexico."

I got to my feet and shook his hand above Alicia's head.

"I appreciate that you came straight over here," I told him.

Enrique Ponce and I retook our seats.

"Thank you very much for getting me arrested again, Francis," Alicia started right in. "Some prick, calling himself a *Comandante*, told me that you demanded a test for gunshot residue on my hands."

"Actually, I—"

"They slathered my hands all over with some noxious chemical. God only knows what it was. It smelled carcinogenic." Alicia's eyebrows lowered. "Is this your idea of helping me?"

"They test for elements from the discharge of the gun," Ponce explained. "It is routine, but it is far too late. I suspect they use it only to bring Mrs. Elton here to induce the confession. But I arrive in time to put a stop to that." The lawyer sat up a little straighter.

"The *Comandante* guy was game for some inducing, alright," Alicia said. "Saying they had all the physical evidence they needed now and how the judge would go easier on me, if I just told the truth. And was he ever pissed at that jailer who let Mr. Ponce in the room."

"Consular Agent Woodstead makes one of his famous telephone calls, I am sure," Ponce said. "Because I find that I am able to bring Mrs. Elton out to these chairs without the usual difficulty."

"Is there someplace we could go for a drink?" I asked. "I'd like to put some generous distance between us and the police."

Ponce stowed the laptop in his briefcase and stood. He offered his hand to Alicia, who used it to smoothly rise to a standing pose.

"I do love a gentleman. Francis, do you see how it's done?"

"There is a nice little restaurant near my office," Ponce said.

***

Enrique Ponce's car was parked in a lot near the jail. I rode with the lawyer and Alicia to where I'd parked the rental car, extricated it from its tight space, and followed them to other side of the city. After parking the cars, we walked between tall, red rubber cones that restricted the street to pedestrian traffic only. The effect was an open-air shopping mall with shops and restaurants at sidewalk level and with offices and apartments on the floors above. Cordoned-off dining areas, containing white plastic tables and chairs, extended out from the several restaurants into what, at other times of the day, I assumed, reverted back to traffic lanes. Enrique Ponce led us to one of these table groupings on the shaded side of the street.

After a waiter took our drink orders, Ponce pointed up toward some anonymous window on a building across the street. "My office is up there on the third floor. When we are finished with our drinks, there are some documents that require Mrs. Elton's signature."

"I'll sign anything that'll keep me from being arrested every day," Alicia said. "It's getting on my nerves."

"You are not yet arrested," Ponce said. "You are summoned for questioning only. If Commandant Arroyo gets an arrest warrant from a judge, you will remain in jail until your case is decided."

"I take it that Alicia filled you in on what happened," I said, "the day Salazar was shot."

"Yes, I have her words." Ponce tapped his briefcase.

"Do you know," I asked, "that the murder weapon is not the actual fancy revolver worn by Pancho Villa, but another old Colt made up to look like it?"

Ponce didn't verbally respond, because at that moment, the waiter arrived with our drinks. Instead, Ponce brought his laptop out of his briefcase, opened it, and clicked away at the keyboard. Not quite in cadence with Ponce's typing, Alicia tapped her fingers on the table, impatient for the waiter to unload his cargo and move on.

"What's all this about a duplicate gun?" Alicia demanded when the waiter was out of earshot. "Who told you that?"

"Separately, both Commandant Arroyo and your pal Woodstead," I said. "And Woodstead also says Villa's actual Colt turned up in Salazar's office at the Art Institute in Chicago."

"Dr. Salazar's office at the Art Institute was a little cubicle with his name handwritten on a piece of paper pinned to the outside," Alicia said. "They're probably using it for a storeroom now. How the hell did Villa's gun get there?"

I leaned in to keep my voice low. "The FBI thinks Dr. Salazar stole Villa's Colt from the Museum and had a professional smuggler take it across the border and up to Houston. From there, it was mailed to the Art Institute in Chicago." I glanced around make sure that I wasn't generating interest from beyond our table. "And to cover his theft, they say Salazar put a substitute Colt with fake ivory grips in the holster in the bedroom exhibit at Villa's Museum."

"Faked how?" Alicia asked.

"A damned clever paint job on cheap plastic grips, probably bought on-line. One of them was made from a mold with a long-horned steer head, so with the paint, it looked like the carved ivory one on Villa's gun."

Enrique Ponce looked up from his computer screen. "This substitute pistol. Was it in working order?"

"Yes, Arroyo let me handle it," I said. "I took a sniff of its barrel, too. And I didn't have to get my nose especially close to know it had been fired recently."

"Then the police must not have found Mrs. Elton's fingerprints on the gun," Ponce said, "or she would not be with us now."

"They're saying she wore gloves."

The lawyer smiled with a nod. "It is what policemen typically say, when they cannot link the suspect to the murder weapon."

"But what I don't get," Alicia said, "is the part where Dr. Salazar steals Villa's gun. Why would he do that?"

"According to Woodstead," I said. "Salazar had a little cottage industry going on, stealing dusty antiquities from museum storerooms and selling them on the black market. The FBI caught on and was watching his office at the Art Institute. That's how they got the first peek when the package with Villa's gun arrived."

"I can't believe this," Alicia said. "You'd think Dr. Salazar made a damn nice living lecturing at the University and leading restoration projects."

"What makes him change?" Ponce wondered.

"Apparently, a chronic need for money," I said. "And lots of it. That wife of his certainly looks expensive."

"That bitch."

Ponce laughed. "She is like Villa's wife. Villa must steal the cows for money to buy guns up in Texas for the Revolution. Meanwhile, Villa's wife buys the expensive furniture and tapestries for the hacienda. It is a funny thing."

When he noticed no one else joined his merriment, Ponce quickly dropped his smile.

"Still, Salazar took an awful risk," I said. "Even with the storeroom thefts, once the museum pieces started turning up in the antiquities market, someone was bound to notice."

"Maybe he thought they were all going directly into private collections," Alicia said. "You know, just from one storage area to another."

"But this time," Ponce said, "he steals an item on display. This is very different from the storeroom thefts. This forces him to produce the substitute pistol, before he steals."

"Woodstead thinks a wealthy gun collector put in a specific order," I said.

"But this is not Dr. Salazar's method," Ponce argued. "Perhaps this time, it is not Dr. Salazar who makes the theft. Perhaps someone knows of his other thefts and knows also of the desire of the wealthy gun collector. And it is this someone who disguises a pistol that can actually fire to look like the museum pistol of Villa and then steals the real thing. Therefore, the dead professor takes the blame for the theft, and the someone gets the money."

Enrique Ponce kept his eyes on me, as he spoke, only flicking them once in Alicia's direction at the end.

"Enrique, sweetheart," Alicia said, "as my lawyer, other than suspending your doubt about my innocence, what is it exactly that you are going to do to earn your four thousand dollars?"

While Alicia's lawyer explained Chihuahua's, newly reformed, criminal trial process to her, I signaled the waiter for another round of drinks. Ponce's explanation was pretty much the same as what Woodstead had told me. However, Alicia's reaction was somewhat more volatile than mine.

"No jury? Seriously? How is that reform? How is getting dragged before some old fogey who arbitrarily decides your fate somehow not still the freaking Inquisition?"

"I can now cross-examine witnesses and challenge the prosecution's evidence," Ponce came to the new justice system's defense. "There are now the plea negotiations and the presumption of innocence. These are major reforms that faced major resistance."

"And yet," Alicia again objected, "no one felt that a trial by jury was worth the trouble."

"I will admit that, without a jury, our trials lack the theater embraced by the American courts."

"When we're talking about a life sentence, I want all the theater you can muster."

"You may console yourself that, in Mexico, the sentences are much shorter than in the United States," Ponce said.

"An innocent inmate might find that less than consoling." Alicia downed the last of her cocktail.

The arrival of the waiter with a new round of drinks necessitated a pause in the debate over the new justice system. As soon as the waiter left, I jumped in.

"Arroyo must be taking some heat from above for not arresting Alicia yet. What's holding him back?"

"The original Lead Investigative Officer rushes to arrest Mrs. Elton," Ponce said. "This allows Consular Agent Woodstead to cleverly argue not for dismissal of the murder charge – which is to ask for too much – but for a temporary release, until a more thorough investigation is completed. Unfortunately, this stimulates Commandant Arroyo to take over the case."

"Why unfortunately?" Alicia asked.

Ponce turned to her. "Who among the investigative officers subordinate to Commandant Arroyo will now discover evidence that contradicts your guilt?"

"Oh."

"Today, the Commandant attempts to sneak an easy goal," Ponce went on, "but again he is blocked by the political skill of Consular Agent Woodstead."

"And again, I adore him," Alicia said.

"But you must not underestimate the skill of the Commandant," Ponce said. "Behind each point that the Prosecuting Attorney presents to the judge, there will be the irrefutable evidence, supplied by Commandant Arroyo. If the Commandant cannot verify a fact, he will not include it in his report. For a defense attorney, it is like attacking the stone with the scissors."

Ponce let that image hang in the air for a moment, before summing up, "Therefore, Mrs. Elton, you must take no comfort that you are not yet arrested. At a time of the Commandant's choosing, you will be." The lawyer's eyes swung to me. "And you also, Mr. Elton. Now that you involve yourself in this matter, the Commandant watches also for *your* first misstep."

***

The little restaurant began to fill with office workers from the street's upper stories, stopping in for afterwork drinks. Meanwhile, the conversation at our table moved on to the FBI's theory of the murder (which, Ponce agreed, was rather short on details) and to the living arrangements that Alicia and I had been obliged to make (which, Ponce remarked, would surely pique the interest of the State Ministerial Police). We then decided to have dinner where we were. But since it was only half past five, Ponce took Alicia across the street and up to his office to sign the paperwork. I stayed behind to keep our table.

I added a shot of Tequila to my next beer order, to help me cope with the thought that, sooner rather than later, I'd have to call my boss and attempt to talk him into letting me extend my stay in Chihuahua. My only bargaining chip was to propose that I make a courtesy call at the Ford Engine Plant on the northern outskirts of the city, where my company had installed a couple of large, production line machines. I knew I'd have to sweeten the deal by assuring him that I could score a hefty, spare-parts order. I'd worry about the consequences of failing to do so, later.

Eventually, the after-work drinkers drifted off and there was lull before the dinner hour. In anticipation of the return of Alicia and her lawyer, I put in an order for our next round.

The waiter arrived at the table with our drinks, just as Alicia and Enrique Ponce were coming back across the street. Instead of his briefcase, Ponce carried a sheaf of papers in his hand. I tossed back the second tequila, chased it with a sip of beer, and wondered why paperwork was coming my way.

"It was too stuffy up there to think." Alicia sat and took up her fresh drink, almost in one motion. After a restorative swallow, she elaborated, "And everything's in Spanish, and I'm not getting what Enrique's trying to translate to me."

"Will you help, Mr. Elton?"

The Spanish legalese was tough going for me too, but together, Ponce and I plowed through it. And I did my best to convey it all in layman's terms to Alicia.

At one point, after seeing the words 'in the matter of the death of John Salazar, PhD,' I wondered out loud,

"Why is his name John and not Juan?"

"Oh, I know that one," Alicia said. "His father was Mexican and his mother was American. He was born in Texas – his parents were in graduate school there – but he grew up in Mexico City, where his parents later taught at a college. He was named for his grandfather, the American one."

"So, John Salazar was a US citizen?" I asked.

"He held dual citizenship," Alicia said. "He showed me his two passports at the border, when we first came down here in the Land Rover."

"I'll bet that was handy," I said.

"He circulated between Mexico and the US, like it was Illinois and Indiana," Alicia said. "He told me he considered all of North America to be his home. He was an amazing guy."

We sat in silence for a moment, following this mini-memorial to the Professor of Fine Arts. Then Ponce brought us back to the legalities of securing his services. He had me write a paragraph in English at the end of the contract, stating that Ponce and I had verbally translated the text to Alicia. Each of us initialed this paragraph at the margin, and Alicia signed her full name at the bottom, as though she understood any of it.

Ponce folded the papers and stuffed them in the outer pocket of his suit jacket. "Tomorrow morning, I will start on my opening statement."

"I'd really appreciate it, if you could get my purse back," Alicia said. "I don't expect there'll be any money left in it, but if my credit card's still there, it'll really come in handy when it comes time to pay you. Getting my luggage back would be a big plus, too."

"I will see what I can do." Ponce didn't sound too enthusiastic about this errand. I gathered that writing up legal arguments was what really made him feel alive.

We finally got around to dinner, and because none of us had eaten since breakfast, we ate with ravenous appetites and without conversation. After dinner, a small group of musicians, who had been playing at a nearby restaurant, came and set up near the outer end of our restaurant's bar. It was pleasant just to sit and listen to the carefree music under the darkening sky, sip after-dinner Kahlua and coffee, and not think about the hole I was digging for myself.

***

Arriving back at the Hotel Miramar, I turned the rental car over to a hotel employee, who drove it away to some mysterious off-site parking lot.

A brief elevator ride later, we entered our room, and Alicia walked immediately into the bathroom. Through the closed door, the shower knobs creaked, the pipes banged, and after a short delay, a spray of water hissed, as Alicia began what had quickly become her post-incarceration ritual.

I was drawn to the window by the sound and flash of distant fireworks. But the pyrotechnics were short-lived – probably just some backyard celebrating. Now, the only lights were electric ones, and the only sound was of water splashing on Alicia's skin. I had a nice inner visual of the soap bar, sliding around the hills and valleys of that skin. I was introduced to those contours during my Navy days, when I was still in Electronics Technician school at Great Lakes. Like many of my fellow sailors on weekend liberty, I'd take the Saturday morning train down to Chicago. But unlike most of them, at one point my reason for making the weekend journey changed from just hanging out in the Loop to actually spending time with a pretty girl.

I'd met Alicia by chance at the Art Institute, one rainy morning, and to my amazement she suggested lunch at the café in the Modern Wing. The lunch went quite well, and the after-lunch part went amazingly well.

From then on, I had a standing weekend date for the rest of my year of tech school. I lived for those weekends, but dating a girl as pretty as Alicia had a dreamlike quality to it. Deep down, I kept expecting it to suddenly end.

It took four years of tumultuous marriage, a crowning heated argument, and a swift, matter-of-fact divorce, but end it finally did. Just not suddenly.

Several, post-Navy years later, after picking up where I left off and completing my engineering degree, I moved to Chicago for a job. And by twist of fate, Alicia and I had a second, chance meeting. This time, it was at a cocktail party given by a couple with whom, at the time, neither of us knew we were mutually acquainted (actually, I knew the one guy, and Alicia knew the other). Soon afterwards, we began dating again, although sporadically and for periods of varying lengths of time. These dating periods were always initiated by a call from Alicia (needing my help with something), and it was always Alicia who brought them abruptly to a halt. I guess she'd learned not to drag it out.

At the soft creak of a door swinging open behind me, I turned from the city lights of Chihuahua. Framed in the bathroom doorway, Alicia stood poised with wet hair and the drape of a bath towel held to her collarbone.

She probably thought she had all the essentials covered. "Francis, would you hand me—"

I'm not sure what made her stop. My guess would be the look on my face.

"Just a minute." Alicia quickly stepped back and swung the bathroom door closed.

Warm, damp, flowery air wafted over me, as I told myself that this was no big deal. I'd seen her body before. Plenty of times. Still…

The door reopened. The bath towel was now wrapped completely around her, providing wholly adequate coverage. Gripping the towel's overlap tightly to her chest, Alicia stepped to the foot of the bed, snatched a t-shirt and boxer shorts from my open suitcase, and quickly retreated back into the bathroom. The door closed, and the lock clicked.

I stood there, replaying the last minute in my head. But it was clear she hadn't meant to entice me. She just needed something to put on. And I knew she'd be on guard when she came out again. Unless I gave her some space.

I spoke through the bathroom door. "I'm going to go find a cigar and a beer."

"You do that, Francis."

***

The hotel's restaurant was still open, but only a few tables were occupied. The bar was empty, except for a bartender and a waiter quietly talking together. The bartender peeled himself away long enough to set me up with a cold beer and inform me that I was out of luck concerning the cigar.

I forced the image of Alicia's body to the back of my mind and concentrated on the more practical matter of her plight. One thing for certain was that I'd have to keep on the good side of Consular Agent Woodstead. And as he'd made clear, that meant I had to keep feeding him information to pass on to the FBI. But so far, the only information I'd come up with, that

104

Woodstead didn't already know, came from Commandant Arroyo. And I sure as hell didn't want to talk to *him* again. And I didn't think there was much chance of my running a supposed smuggler to ground, or for that matter, bolstering any other aspect of the FBI's theory. It all seemed pretty hopeless.

I lingered through a second beer, before deciding that Alicia must be in bed by this time. I paid up and returned to our room.

The room was dark, when I entered. I showered and brushed my teeth, before climbing into bed. Alicia was on her side with her back to me. I didn't exactly spoon her, but I was aware she was wearing the t-shirt and boxers. Not a particularly receptive signal.

"You don't smell like a cigar." Alicia's voice held no hint of sleepiness.

"I struck out on that quest." Like a camel seeking to put its nose under the tent, my hand came to rest on Alicia's hip where I judged the hem of the t-shirt would be.

Without physically responding, Alicia said, "You remember when my father died, and you helped me clean out his garage, so my mother could sell the house? You remember, after we finally had it all done, that, for the first time since our divorce, we buried the hatchet?"

"That's one way of putting it."

"And you remember, after the fire in my apartment building, how you let me stay at your place while you were gone? And how we waited until I finally got all resettled back into my apartment, before we had the thank-you sex?"

"Okay, I see where this is going." I rolled onto my back.

"It's just that when we do the award ceremony, while we're still in the middle of the task-at-hand, the goal kind of gets lost. I don't have to cite instances, do I?"

"A couple of times things got a little messed up, sure, but—"

"We'll get around to it when all this is over. I promise."

I lay there, staring into the darkness. I don't know for how long.

Chapter 7

The next morning, I tipped a hotel employee for retrieving my rental car from its undisclosed location and drove Alicia to work. We arrived in the city center early enough for me to find a parking spot along a stretch of curb without meters, a couple of blocks from the Palacio de Gobierno. Another plus was that it wasn't far away from the small café where we'd breakfasted the day before. Along our walk to the small café, I stopped and bought an issue of the previous day's El Diario from a vendor who operated his business from a large, wooden crate that crowded the sidewalk.

Once we were seated at a table, I browsed through the front section of the newspaper, while we sipped coffee and waited for our food.

"Ah, here we are." I folded the paper open at the third page and translated for Alicia. "Professor Shot At Villa Museum."

"Does it say anything we don't know? Does it mention me?"

"Just a second." I scanned down through the article.

"Oh, here. It says the police are questioning the Professor's assistant. Probably, that's you."

"Assistant *Director*. Can't they get anything right?"

"Okay, let me go back to the start. It says John Salazar, PhD, was shot and killed, while sitting in Pancho Villa's Dodge...um, the car that Villa was driving, when he was assassinated in 1923...Revolutionary hero. Yeah, we know...Although normally closed on Mondays, the museum was opened

107

specially for the Restoration Group for photographing…And here's where they say the police are holding you for questioning. Wait, it continues on page five." I unfolded the paper, flipped to page five, and refolded it. "Oh, here's your name. Professor Salazar and his assistant, North American artist Alicia Elton, MFA, were alone in the Museum at the time of the murder. But here, is this right? It says there were two shots fired. One of the bullets hit the Professor in the head, killing him instantly."

"That's not right. There was only one shot. Did the neighbors say that? Maybe there was an echo."

"A police source said that."

"Well, he's wrong. I know what gunfire sounds like."

"I think, for now, it might be better for you to downplay your previous experience with firearms."

"Just put the stupid newspaper away. You're just upsetting me."

The waiter arrived with our breakfasts. As he set the plates on the table, I brought up another matter.

"I have to call my boss this morning. I'm going to try to talk him into letting me have a few extra days down here by making a courtesy call at the Ford Engine Plant. You know, look over the machine, talk about problems, make sure they have spare parts. That sort of thing."

"What are you doing? You're supposed to be helping *me*."

"I'm trying to hang onto my job."

"And I'm trying to stay out of prison."

"It'll only take a couple of hours."

"God." Alicia gave me her exasperated sigh. "If you feel you must."

"Even if my boss agrees to it, he'll still punish me. Does that make you feel better?"

Alicia was quiet for a moment. She then said, "Francis, I want you to know I really do appreciate your doing this for me." She reached over and placed her hand on mine.

"You didn't seem particularly appreciative last night."

Alicia withdrew her hand. "We had that discussion."

***

Leaving the rental car in the free parking spot, Alicia and I walked the few blocks to the Palacio de Gobierno. As soon as we arrived, Alicia went directly to Carlos, who was on a tall stepladder, dabbing with a cloth at the lower reaches of some other idealized historic event, which, I supposed, was the next mural slated for restoration.

I detoured to take a second look at the platform lift, which was still positioned in front of the Hidalgo panel. The lift again struck me as a nice piece of work, even though this time it wasn't adorned with the youthful beauty of Teresa. In fact, Teresa was nowhere in sight. For that matter, Eduardo didn't appear to be lurking around, either.

As I walked over to rejoin Alicia, I heard her attempting to communicate with Carlos in English, separating her words and over-enunciating them, as though that helped. At issue was the original color of a skirt worn by an on-looker in the foreground of the mural.

With his reading glasses perched almost at the tip of his nose and a solvent-soaked cloth held in suspended animation, Carlos looked down at Alicia from his height on the ladder, listening with a lowered brow. Occasionally, he'd brighten, nod his head, and struggle with a few English words in response. But the communication wasn't going well.

I waited for a lull, before I asked, "Just the two of you then today?"

"Looks like," Alicia said, while her eyes remained on the area where Carlos had been dabbing. "I don't know what's become of Teresa. Eduardo, I never know about." And then she commanded, "Carlos, let me up there."

I told Carlos in Spanish that Miss Alicia desired to take his place on the ladder.

Carlos climbed down, and I helped him reposition a work light, while Alicia climbed up.

I waited for her to make a few dabs of her own with the cloth, before I asked, "Can I use your computer to email my boss? It's hard to get through to him. It's better if he just calls me."

"My password is 'Picasso', upper case 'P' with two esses." Alicia's dabs with the cloth moved successively outward along the on-looker's skirt. "There!" Alicia startled both Carlos and me. She leveled an accusing finger at a fold in the paint-rendered skirt. "There's the edge of some old crappy repair. See where some insensitive hack patched it with something straight from a pre-school pack of Crayolas?"

"*¿Qué?*" Carlos looked in askance up to Alicia, down and over to me, and then back up.

110

"Damn, I wish Teresa would show up," Alicia said. "We might as well be using smoke signals."

"You want me to stay and translate?" I asked. "I mean, I don't know the Spanish for crayons, off the top of my head, but..."

"No. We actually get more done, because we can't stand around and talk. Go send your e-mail." Alicia then tapped on the old repair and relayed her critique down to Carlos, "Amateur."

"*Si, chapucero*," Carlos agreed that the repair was shoddy.

Since they'd somehow come to an accord by themselves, I left them and walked across to the Project's makeshift office and supply room. Once seated in Alicia's chair, I opened her laptop, typed in 'Picasso', and went online. I kept the message down to a request for a call back and my cell phone number.

When I returned from sending the e-mail, Alicia had placed a box of paint tubes, brushes, and a tablet of paper palettes onto the platform of the automated lift and was stepping aboard.

Before she lifted off, I told her, "I'm going to walk back to the rental car, while I wait for my boss's call."

"As long as you're just wandering around, how about wandering over to the Cathedral. Maybe, Teresa's there. She's kind of religious, and she's stopped off, on her way to work, to pray, before. It might be some Saint's Day, or something." Alicia pushed a button on the motor control pendant and began her ascent. "And if you see her, tell her to get her tight little butt over here. We're behind schedule. I need her."

***

111

I spotted the twin steeples of the Cathedral over the treetops of a small park, the perimeter of which was guarded by numerous five-foot high, fiberglass sculptures of sitting Chihuahua dogs, individually painted in festive colors and patterns – one in calico, another with star constellations, others with leopard spots, tiger stripes, quilted patchwork, or other fanciful motifs. In the center of a large patio just in front of the Cathedral, a statue of some Spaniard, wearing a large flop-brimmed hat, gallantly held a hand aloft, as though inviting the pigeons to use it as a rest area.

The Old World façade of the Cathedral had a baroque center section, replete with columns, tall arched openings, and saintly figures. Flanking this were two bell towers, which rose above the center section's crowning angel, reaching toward the heavens.

The massive entry doors were open and inviting. I mounted the broad steps, put my cell phone on vibrate, and went in for a quick look.

There was a large wall of intricately carved wood that screened the nave from the bright sunlight and diverted the entering faithful to either of the two side aisles. I went to the right and soon had a clear view, beyond the rows of mostly empty pews, of an ornate altar at the far end of the nave. No Mass was in progress, but three nuns sat side-by-side in the front pew. In the rows behind the nuns, individual worshipers, bowed in silent personal prayers, were scattered beneath the immense emptiness created by the vast ceiling, arched high above them.

A young woman, seated just off the aisle about halfway back from the nuns, turned her head toward the hollow bang of a kneeler, swung to the upright position by a departing believer. Although the young woman wore a multi-colored scarf over her hair, I thought she looked like Teresa. I couldn't be sure. Beautiful as Teresa was, I'd only seen her twice, and the young woman's head soon turned back to an attitude of prayer.

Not wishing to intrude, I backtracked out through the main entrance.

She could have been just another pretty Mexican girl in a city chocked full of them. But Alicia had asked me to keep an eye out for Teresa, so when I spotted an open side door, far down the street running along the side of Cathedral, I dutifully walked down to it.

After climbing the two steps up to the side door, I poked my head in. In front of me was the broad space between the nuns in the first pew and the wide steps leading up to the altar. Scanning the pews, I spotted the colorful scarf. And with a frontal view, I was now fairly certain the young woman's beautiful face, cheeks damp with tears, belonged to Teresa.

I pulled my head back and exited the side door without delivering Alicia's message. A woman in tears is a woman with problems. And I already had one of those.

***

Not long after I'd remembered to change my phone from vibrate back to ring tone, the electronic notes sang out.

"Francis, what's going on? You were only supposed to be gone for two days." My boss came through loud and clear.

113

"Do you remember Alicia, my ex-wife? She was at my thirty-fifth birthday party. The one at Sally's house. We were toying with getting back together around that time."

"Oh yeah. Alicia. Way too good for you. What about her?"

"Well, she's been working on a project here in Chihuahua, and she's run into a little trouble with the local authorities. She sent for me, because I speak Spanish. I'm working with the U.S. Consulate and her lawyer. And Alicia's not locked up or anything. But this professor who was her boss on the Restoration Project was killed, and there's been a lot of misunderstanding about what exactly happened. But it's not like it takes up every waking minute of my day. So, I thought I could zip over to the Ford factory and conduct a little company business, while we're getting things straightened out down here."

"This is your *ex*-wife, Francis. The 'ex' part means you no longer have to deal with every moronic situation she gets herself into. I have a couple of exes myself. I know whereof I speak."

"It'll probably take a few more days to straighten it out," I soldiered on. "See, Alicia doesn't speak any Spanish and—"

"Okay, okay. I got it the first time. I guess I could give that young, project engineer, down there at the Ford plant, a call. What's his name? I've got his card somewhere here in my...Oh, here it is. Diego Ortega. That's a great name. You could get laid a lot with a name like that. Maybe not so much in Mexico, but you know that bar in Cleveland, down in the Flats?"

"Yeah, I know the one," I played along.

"Women there are crazy about Latinos. Name like that, you'd get laid a lot."

I wondered if my boss was still drunk from the night before. "So anyway, you'll give Ortega a call? I could get over there this morning yet."

"I'll call him. But if Ortega doesn't have time for you, this will count as vacation days. Plus which, you know the unwritten rule about screwing up is carved in stone. And going AWOL is screwing up, big time."

"Yes, I know."

"And you know that Thanksgiving is coming soon."

"I know."

"But there's no Thanksgiving Day in Canada."

I knew there actually was, but I said, "I know."

"And I need to leave a babysitter for the new machine startup at GM in Saint Catharines, so I can bring the guys home for the long weekend. And you're my man, because you screwed up."

"I got it."

"But before that, I've got a treat for you. You know where Porto Alegre is?"

"No."

"It's in Brazil," my boss said. "You'll have a fine time speaking your Spanish there."

"They speak Portuguese in Brazil."

"They do? Well, that's stupid. Anyway, it's a Massey-Ferguson plant. You know, tractors. They crashed three tools in a row. I'm sending them some new tooling this week. They'll have it by next Wednesday, but you'll be flying out this coming Monday, because it takes forever and a wake-up to get there. Figure out what they're doing wrong, set them straight, and you should be back home in plenty of time for...let's see..." I could picture my boss puzzling over his calendar, his hung-over brain, pounding. "Well, nothing at the end of September...Hey look, Columbus Day for us *and* Thanksgiving Day in Canada. Well, I'll be damned. But that's in October. You'll be done with Brazil long before then. Sound good?"

"Peachy," I said. "So, you'll call Ortega?"

"Soon as we hang up. I'll have Sally call you back when it's a go. And sell Ortega some goddamn spare parts, will you? I'm tired of the Nazis in Accounting looking at me like my department's some kind of gigantic lodestone."

***

My rented Ford Fiesta was in sight, by the time I received the call from Sally, my boss's secretary. She told me Diego Ortega not only had time for me that morning, but also had asked how soon I could be there. So, it was pretty clear I was walking into a problem. I just hoped the problem was only a broken machine.

When I arrived at the Ford Engine Plant, Ortega was waiting for me in the reception area. He shook my hand, rushed me through the ritual paperwork, and walked me at a faster-than-comfortable pace out to the machine.

On the way through the factory, Ortega related how the machine had been hobbling through the last few days, producing marginally acceptable parts with a high rate of rejects and many stops and starts. Scrapping out engine blocks at a thousand bucks a pop explained why Ortega was bringing me along at a brisk trot. And before we even reached the steps leading up to the catwalk that

116

ran the length of the massive machine, I could hear the honing stones slamming into contact with the cylinder bores and making eagle screeches with each thrashing, vertical stroke. Computer-controlled, high precision machines typically operate *below* the decibel level of a rock concert. I mounted the catwalk with a certain amount of regret weighing on me.

Several workers were gathered at the control console, idly talking, but ready, I supposed, to jump into action and get the machine running, should it suddenly stop once again. I shook hands all around, a custom seemingly observed in the factories of all the industrialized countries, except the United States. And then all eyes were on me.

The first thing that struck me was that the second honing station took way longer to complete its cycle than the other three stations. I knew it was actually timing out, rather than ending the cycle when the bore came to size. This should have lit a fault light, and the machine should have stopped. But neither of those things happened. I turned to the computer screen on the console. The Fault Page was displayed, but was blank. I brought up the page that displayed the finished sizes of each station. The tool in the second station hadn't done much honing, beyond what you'd get if it just slapped around inside the bore without expanding. So, of course, the major squawking came from the third station, as those stones attempted to hone off all the material not removed by the previous station, plus the material it normally was supposed to hone away. Removing double the material, in the same amount of time, meant doubling the feed rate, which makes lots of noise and lots of scrap product.

I changed screens, brought up the program's ladder diagram, and paged down to the line that should have triggered the fault output on the second station. I was looking for an "inhibit" that, I felt confident, had been placed in the logic by someone who just wanted to keep the damn thing running. Since I knew what I was looking for, it was pretty easy to find. I then worked backward through the logic and found I was missing the input from a proximity switch that should have made contact each time the piston reached the top of its stroke, which in turn would have signaled the honing stones to incrementally expand.

I had the machine operator stop the machine, but leave the power on. I monkey-climbed up to the top of the vertically mounted, hydraulic cylinder on the second station and verified that the little green LED - indicating power to the switch - was lit. When I climbed down, I deleted the "inhibit" from the line of programming, had the operator power down and lockout the machine, and pointed out to Ortega the switch I wanted replaced. Ortega assigned two of his electricians to the task, and the rest of us broke for lunch.

***

Lunch in the factory's cafeteria was free for Ford employees and, apparently, also for visitors from afar. I took my place in line and received generous portions of food, doled out by cheerful ladies in white smocks and hairnets.

118

As we dug into our food, Ortega asked in Spanish, "Do you think the proximity switch is our only problem?"

Since Ortega didn't also mention my correction to the altered program, I had an idea I was looking at the guy who'd inserted the inhibit. However, since Ortega was also the guy in charge of ordering the machine's spare parts, I let it slide.

"After the switch is replaced," I told him, "the second station will start doing some work for a change. Then we have a lot of adjustments to make on all the stations. We will have a busy afternoon."

"We once had a technician here who knew electronics and machinery as well as you," Ortega said, "but he left us about six months ago."

"Eduardo," piped up one of the repairmen sitting at the table with us. "He was very good."

My ears pricked up at the sound of the name.

"Eduardo? I know the artists working on the Restoration Project at the Palacio de Gobierno. There's a young man named Eduardo, who is their handyman. Could he be the same Eduardo?"

"Maybe," the repairman said. "He was crazy to quit his job at Ford."

There were general grunts of agreement with this all around.

"I think it is the same Eduardo," Ortega said. "Sometime after he left us, he came to me to buy an old workstation unit with an adjustable table height. We were discarding it. He said that it was for a platform he was to build at the Palacio de Gobierno. I was happy for him to find work. Ford charged him only the scrap metal value of the unit. I helped him with the paperwork."

"He was crazy to quit," the repairman said again.

"He was a very skilled technician," Ortega said. "We would not need your help today, if he was still with us."

"Why did he leave?"

"Arrogance," Ortega passed judgment. "He knew more than anyone else. And he would tell you so. And he said that any other factory would quickly make him an engineer. It was a song that he sang very many times."

The others at the table nodded and laughed.

"Six months ago," Ortega went on, "Eduardo finally approached the Chief Engineer. He demanded to be promoted to engineer status on the spot, or he would quit. Without hesitation, the Chief Engineer dismissed him."

"So, Eduardo's gamble did not work," I said.

"It is crazy to demand of the Chief Engineer," Ortega said.

"Crazy," the repairman echoed.

Just as the crowd of workers in the cafeteria had thinned out, another wave came in. The two electricians who were assigned to replace the switch were with this new group. Ortega left our table and went over to them. When he came back, Ortega said, "The new switch is installed."

"You seem happy with your crew," I commented.

"They are skilled men. And skilled men are difficult to find."

"Do they all go up to work at the border factories?"

"No. The pay is very low at the *maquiladoras*."

"But the auto factories, Ford and GM, they pay well, don't they?"

"Yes, perhaps as much as thirty percent of an American worker's pay. But at the *maquiladoras*, skilled workmen are paid only about ten percent of American wages," Ortega mapped out the economics. "And the women who work at the sewing machines are paid almost nothing. Our great friends from America, Europe, Japan, they would make slaves of us all."

***

It was nearing three in the afternoon. I'd had Ortega's crew dial back all hydraulic and pneumatic pressures to their factory settings, before we started tweaking. There followed a couple of hours of cat-whisker tuning, before the abused stones in stations two and three settled back in and the massive honing machine began sending hundred percent "in spec" engine blocks on down the line.

After a wrap-up meeting with Ortega, during which I scored a fair-to-middling parts order, the young engineer delivered me back to the lobby. We shook hands, and I stepped out into the afternoon sun, just as the day shift was leaving for home.

The exit from the parking lot was temporarily blocked. A long line of gaily-painted buses was backed up out onto the road, each bus waiting to take its load of workers back to their neighborhoods. While waiting for the bus traffic to disperse, I leaned against the rental car and selected the number of Windy City Machinery from the directory in my phone. When I put in the extension number at the prompt, Sally answered.

"This is Francis. Is the Big Cheese in?"

"I haven't seen him since he left for lunch. You all done at Ford?"

"Yeah, tell him I straightened out a machine problem, and I snagged him a parts order."

"I'll write him a note," she said, and then, "Francis, suddenly you're down for the whole Thanksgiving weekend at Saint Catharines. What the hell did you do?"

"I needed a few extra days here in Chihuahua. Personal business."

"Personal business. In Mexico. You."

I imagined her finely shaped eyebrow arching.

"It's a long story. I'll tell you about it when I get back."

"Yes, well, buy a girl a drink when you do."

"Sure thing," I said, while secretly hoping that whatever current problem she was apparently having with her husband would over with by then.

"And you're flying down to Porto Alegre this coming Monday on United at six fifteen in the morning. The woman at the travel agency says it's way down on Brazil's southern coast, almost to Uruguay, so it's like eighteen hours of travel time. You might want to take a book."

"I'll try to be back by—"

"Do *not* miss that flight, Francis. You know he only has two punishments. And you're already down for the one where you keep your job."

Chapter 8

On my way back downtown, I stopped at a large supermarket to buy a six-pack of beer. I also bought three plain dress shirts. I'd only packed for a two-day trip, and with Alicia sharing my shirts I had my doubts the hotel laundry service could keep up.

When I arrived at the Palacio de Gobierno, the only person from the Restoration Project I saw was Carlos. And he was packing up for the day.

After the handshake, I asked Carlos, in Spanish, "Is Alicia still here?"

"She is in her office." He pointed across the interior patio.

As I turned to go there, Carlos put a hand on my arm.

"You must tell Miss Alicia that it is correct for her to attend the funeral tomorrow." Carlos straightened his spine, rising to his full five-foot-three. "I will be there by her side. I know that she would not murder Professor Salazar or anyone else. I will not allow it to be said of her."

"Thank you, Carlos. That makes two of us." I clasped him on the shoulder, as he maintained the noble look on his face. I added, "But the Professor's wife...It might be uncomfortable for both Lydia and Alicia to—"

"It is only vanity."

"Well, I am not sure that is exactly what—"

"You are not Mexican. I do not fault you for this. But you must see as a Mexican sees to understand the conflict between Lady Salazar and Miss Alicia. They are

123

both beautiful women. But they are no longer young – not young like Teresa. They cannot compete with youth. But they can compete with each other. Do you not see that they remember very well the children's story, 'Who is the fairest of them all,' in the judgment of the mirror that speaks? The vain Queen is threatened by the beauty of her rival. It is the nature of women."

"I bow to Mexican wisdom."

Carlos nodded curtly in acknowledgement, and returned to gathering up the chemicals, paints, and brushes he used to preserve the aging works of art.

Entering the Project's office, I stopped short, unsure how to proceed. Alicia sat in her chair, swiveled a quarter turn from her desk and facing toward the door. At her feet, Teresa knelt with her head and arms collapsed onto Alicia's lap. Her printed scarf was clutched in both hands, and her back and shoulders quivered with each successive sob.

Alicia had been stroking Teresa's long, black hair, but on seeing me enter, she raised her hand and made a brush away gesture with her fingers. I quickly retreated, and quietly closed the door after me. I turned and saw Carlos approaching the Project's office, carrying a cardboard box, full of art supplies.

"Alicia and Teresa are going to need more time alone," I told him.

"Yes. I saw that Teresa was unhappy." Carlos set the box on the floor near the office door. "I hope that it is only an affair of the heart that troubles her."

With Carlos standing unoccupied in front of me, Woodstead's words – the ones about my being his eyes and ears within Salazar's inner circle – played back in my head.

"Carlos, let me buy you a beer on your way home."

Carlos grinned. "You are most generous. There is a cantina near the house where I have rented a room."

"How about that restaurant near Pancho Villa's Museum?"

"The Café Iguana?" It took only a moment for merriment to leave Carlos's face. "What is it that you want?"

"Alicia's lawyer asked me to talk to you and Teresa and Eduardo," I lied smoothly. "Maybe, you can recall something from the day Salazar was killed – something that would help Alicia with her defense. I thought that if you were back at the Café Iguana, you might remember that day more clearly."

Carlos studied my face. Although he still appeared wary, he asked, "Do you have a car?"

***

Carlos helped me navigate our route toward the Café Iguana. I was getting better at finding my way around Chihuahua, but I was far from feeling confident.

We parked on Calle 10a, just past the restaurant on the corner. Out on the sidewalk, I took a moment to look down the hill toward Villa's Museum. I could see the railing enclosing the roof of the portico and, above it, an edge-on view of the arched ornament centered on the decorative eave atop the museum's second story. I made a mental note to get back inside the museum for another look at things – this time without a police commandant directing my attention.

Inside the Café Iguana, the savory aroma of slow-roasting beef hung at nose level. But no one was eating yet. The Iguana's patrons at this hour, like Carlos and me, were having a drink on the way home. The hard, reflective surfaces of tile and stucco amplified the din of surrounding chatter. Carlos and I sat across a table from each other and brought our heads in close to talk.

"That afternoon," I began, "on the day Salazar was shot. As I understand it, you and the rest of the group left Dr. Salazar and Alicia at the museum and all came here."

"One soldier stayed behind," Carlos said. "I saw him lock the iron gate across the entrance, before he lit his cigarette, out under the portico. Lady Salazar brought Eduardo, Teresa, the other soldier, and me here for refreshments. We waited for Miss Alicia to complete her photographs of Professor Salazar sitting in the old car."

A waitress appeared, took our order, and left.

"Did any of the group leave this café during your time here?"

"We all remained here, until we heard the sirens and saw the police cars and the ambulance go by."

"Did you hear the sound of the gun firing?"

"Yes, we heard it, but at that time, we did not know what it was."

"How many shots?" I asked.

"One shot."

The waitress placed two cold bottles of Dos Equis before us and moved on.

"When you heard the shot, was the cantina full of noise, as it is now?"

"Yes," Carlos said, "but the sound of the shot was much louder than the talking. Naturally, it caused all the talking to stop for a moment, but then it was quickly dismissed and the noise level rose again."

"How much time passed between the gun shot and the sirens?"

"Who can say? Ten minutes? Fifteen? Then with the sirens, of course, everyone knew the sound must have been the report of a gun. The young soldier jumped up and ran out of the restaurant. I think that he must hurry back to the museum." Carlos drained his beer bottle.

I caught the waitress's eye and held up three fingers. The waitress, middle-aged plump with a still pretty face, soon brought the required number of beers to the table. Without having to ask, the waitress placed the extra beer in front of Carlos.

"Thank you, my lovely one," Carlos said.

The waitress and Carlos exchanged smiles, as she moved on to her other customers.

"What did all of you talk about, sitting at the table that day?" I resumed my probe.

"Oh, no one main subject," Carlos said. "There were many small conversations at our table. Heads together to be heard. There were many voices around us. Is this important?"

"Perhaps, not. But I wonder...was there was any feeling of tension? Was it a friendly gathering?"

"Teresa did not seem very happy to be seated next to Lady Salazar. She leaned in close to me, and we talked mostly of art and the Project. The soldier from the Museum was across the table. He looked as though he wanted to talk to Teresa. I could see that he was

127

building his courage, but looking and drinking was all he did. A young waitress – not this one, another – she flirted with Eduardo. The handsome Eduardo, you know. Lady Salazar watched him with strict eyes and lips. Of course, Eduardo made the effort to be attentive to Lady Salazar, but it is natural that the young waitress distracted him."

I excused myself from the table and left Carlos to catch up on his drinking, while I went to the men's room. A sign saying '*baños*' hung over the entry to a hallway. As I walked the hallway keeping an eye out for a more gender-specific sign, I cast a glance, through an open door, into what looked like the manager's office. Farther down and across the hall, I finally spotted the word '*hombres*' gouged out in script on a wood placard affixed to a door. I went in.

My mission completed, I threaded my way back through the tables and chairs. I saw Carlos coming from the opposite direction. We didn't speak, as we passed each other. There was no need.

At our table, the plump waitress was slowly clearing away the empty bottles – stalling, I supposed, until I returned. I took my seat and ordered three more beers.

As she wiped the wet circles of condensation from the table, the waitress commented, "Your friend is a happy man."

"He is an artist," I said. "He likes to…" As I arranged the Spanish words in my head to complete my response, something triggered a return to that long-ago Saturday morning when I was a young Seaman, down from the Electronics School, trying to keep my civilian clothes dry by wandering around the Chicago Art

Institute, until the rain outside stopped. In an alcove, a young woman with long dark hair and shapely legs stood, with her back to me, before an Old Master's painting of a Parisian street scene. She was sketching the painting in pencil on a pad of drawing paper. I strolled up and stood a little apart from her, pretending to admire the painting. Out of the corner of my eye, I saw that she'd paused her sketching and was looking at me.

"You're a sailor, aren't you." It was more accusation, than question.

"Yes. How did you…" I turned and got my first good look at her face. Wow, considerably out of my league.

Her defiant green eyes bore into mine. "What are you doing here?"

"I like to look at beautiful things."

The green eyes softened, and the pink lips smiled.

And for once in my life, I had blurted out the right answer. Sure, I'd categorized her as a 'thing', but for God's sake, I told myself, shut up, don't try to fix it, you're ahead, just let it—

"¿Señor? ¿Está bien?"

The waitress's Spanish tugged me back. "No. I mean, yes. I am fine," I struggled to answer in Spanish, through the fog of remembrance. "My mind just wandered for a moment. Yes, my friend is an artist, and it makes him happy—" I almost finished with 'to look at beautiful things.' But that now seemed like sacrilege. I backed up, "It makes him happy to drink beer and talk to attractive women."

The waitress did a good job of holding her delight in reserve, but it still shined through, as she turned and carried the empty beer bottles back to the kitchen. I hoped I'd successfully covered for drifting off.

A few minutes later, Carlos returned from the men's room and seated himself, just as the waitress, coincidentally, arrived with fresh beer.

"I ordered another round," I told him. "I hope you have time."

Eying the waitress, as she distributed the beer bottles on the table, Carlos said, "I can only thank you for making this enchanting goddess reappear."

The waitress remonstrated Carlos with a light, play slap on his cheek, followed by a lingering drag of her fingertips across his thinning hair. She sashayed away from our table.

"The younger ones slap harder," Carlos voiced his experience, followed by a smile. He then drew his pair of cold ones closer. "If you have more questions concerning the day of murder, they cannot continue past these two. I have an appointment."

"Fair enough." I took a chilling swallow and launched back in. "On that afternoon, did anyone from your group leave the table to make a phone call or use the bathroom?"

"Yes, naturally for the bathroom," Carlos said. "And for the e-mail."

My head came up. "The e-mail?"

"Lady Salazar excused herself from the table. I noticed that her drink was only halfway gone. I wondered about her capacity. For a woman still in her middle years, I mean. And then Eduardo left for the men's room, shortly afterward. And soon, I also felt compelled, but I was drinking a little faster than the others, you understand, and beer has that effect on me."

"So, the three of you left the table."

"Yes. Teresa and the soldier remained. Perhaps, I thought, the young soldier will now find his voice." Carlos finished the remaining third of his bottle in one drain. "And then I saw a peculiar thing."

Carlos set his empty down, wiped his lips with the back of his hand, and clasped his next full one. I leaned in, hoping a "peculiar thing" might become a "relevant tidbit."

"As I am in the hallway, on my way to the bathroom, I hear voices. I look into what is the manager's office, and I see Lady Salazar sitting at the desk in front of a computer. And Eduardo is there. He is pointing, instructing. Is this not strange?"

"It is, go on."

"That is all I saw. My errand was urgent, and I continued on to the bathroom. And while I was there, conducting business, Eduardo came in and used the other fixture. Then, another peculiar thing. Eduardo said to me, 'Lydia wanted to check her e-mail. I had to help her.' But I did not ask him why that he and Lady Salazar are in the manager's office. It is not for me to ask this. Although, it is natural for me to wonder."

Carlos took an extended swallow from his next beer.

"So," I prompted, "when you and Eduardo left the bathroom, was Lydia still on the computer, when you passed by?"

"Yes, she was still with her e-mail."

"Did you tell the police about this?"

"I answered to the investigative officer only what he asks," Carlos said. "He asked only 'who of the group were at the restaurant' and 'how long had we been there, before the sound of the gun fire.' I responded only to these two things. When a policeman inquires, it is unwise to know too much."

"So, it was sometime after you and Eduardo returned to the table that you heard the gunshot."

"It was soon after Eduardo and I returned. But we did not realize that it was a gunshot. It was only a loud noise."

"But by then, everyone was back at the table?"

"Yes, we were all there."

"Even Lydia?"

"No." Carlos raised his index finger in the air, as if he were halting the proceedings for a point of order. "No, Lady Salazar was not back to the table yet."

"When did she get back?"

"A little later, I think. She arrived with the waitress and another round of drinks that she had ordered." Carlos smiled. "She is a lovely woman."

"So, Lydia returned to the table after the sound of the shot, but before the police and ambulance went by?"

"Oh, yes. Because when the police went by, it was Lady Salazar who said that we must hurry back to the Museum. That something is wrong."

***

At the end of his last beer, Carlos announced that he was overdue for afternoon drinks with his landlady. I paid the tab, while Carlos paid a final visit to the men's room, and together we left the Café Iguana.

132

At Carlos's direction, I drove to a house in a westside suburb, where for the duration of the Restoration Project, he had leased an apartment. Carlos said his landlady's late husband had built the apartment, as an addition to the back of the house, for just such casual rentals. I wondered if the addition was now also used for the casual afternoon drinks.

When I stopped and let Carlos out at the curb, half a dozen children swarmed out of the house and surrounded him. He led them off to the back yard, prattling away with them like a favorite old uncle.

I returned to the Palacio de Gobierno to give Alicia a lift back to the hotel, but found the Restoration Project's storeroom locked. I looked at the time on my cell phone screen and discovered that it was after seven. I'd spent more time at the Café Iguana with Carlos than I'd realized. I called Alicia.

Alicia answered her phone with, "What."

"Ah, sorry I missed you. I didn't realize—"

"Where *were* you? I had to take a taxi back to the hotel. It ate up about half the pesos you gave me."

"I was talking to Carlos at the Café Iguana." I immediately regretted mentioning a café. "Then I gave him a ride home."

"How considerate of you."

"Well, I came back to get you, but—"

"Just forget it. At least, my luggage found its way back to me, so that lawyer is finally being of some use."

"I don't suppose your purse—"

"No, that would be too much to hope for."

"Probably, Commandant Arroyo's holding onto it to restrict your—"

"I may not be here when you get back. I have to look into something for Teresa."

The image of Alicia with Teresa's head on her lap flashed before my mind's eye.

"Wait, I'll go with you," I said. "I can be at the hotel in ten minutes."

"No, this doesn't concern you. I have to do this alone."

"It's already getting dark out. It wouldn't be safe for you to be walking around alone."

"It's okay. I'm pretty sure the police are following me. There was a car right on the taxi's bumper all the way back to the hotel. The driver kept complaining about it. I picked out 'imbecile' and 'police' from his rant."

"You don't know that it was a policeman. And even if it was, you don't know if he would come to your aid, if you were being mugged. I'm on my way. You wait there. Just wait ten minutes—"

"Don't tell me what to do."

There was a click and then nothing.

I'd heard that phrase, "don't tell me what to do," often enough when we were married. I heard it with increasing frequency toward the end.

***

I entered the hotel room, expecting it to be unoccupied. I set the bag, containing my new shirts and the six-pack of beer, on the table next to the TV. It was then that I caught the sweet, balsamic scent of sandalwood. I turned to see Alicia standing at the mirrored dresser, calmly brushing her hair. She was dressed in tight blue jeans, black high heels, and a fitted western-style shirt. As she turned from the mirror, a simple silver cross on a light chain glinted from the v-shaped reveal of several upper buttons left unfastened. Her dark hair spilled down over her shoulders, her eyes were outlined in black, and her lips were the color of a fire engine.

"I see we're wearing our hunting outfit," I said. "What's the quarry?"

"I waited, because I need a translator. You don't need to ask a lot of questions."

"What's going on with Teresa? Why's she crying in church and sobbing on your lap?"

"See, those would be like questions."

"Well, here's another. Where are you – No, wait, I think I can read the signs. From the way you're dressed, I can tell that you're going to a bar and that you're going to talk to a man. Since you changed your mind about my not going with you, I assume that it won't be a nice hotel bar. You say it's about Teresa, but I'm thinking it's also about Salazar's murder. So, why not tell me about it? I came all the way to Mexico to help you. I can't help you, if you hold back on me."

"Okay, it was a mistake to include you. I'll just do it alone."

"You can't go to that bar alone. Do you know how hot you look?"

"Yes."

"It's just asking for trouble. Don't be stupid."

"I'll do whatever the hell I want. And what's stupid is me trying not to hurt you."

Alicia took three purposeful strides toward the door. I stepped into her path and caught her arm.

"Then hurt me and be done with it. Then I'll go with you. Tell me what Teresa said."

***

Alicia sat on the desk chair, her heels off, her feet propped on the bed, the chair tilted back. I stood at the window, looking at nothing, waiting to take the hit. We each held an opened can of room-temperature, Mexican beer.

"According to Teresa," Alicia started, "for the last couple of months, once or twice a week, after the rest of us had left for the day, Dr. Salazar stayed behind in the Project's office and worked on a painting, a full figure nude. Teresa was his model. I know this is the part that hurts right up front, because it brings back memories of those terrible arguments that blew up our marriage. I wanted to avoid telling you, but nothing after this makes sense, unless you know this part first."

I looked out over the darkening rooftops of Chihuahua and took the punch to the heart. Back when my ship was home-ported in San Diego, Alicia and I had been married for several years. Despite my being a Petty Officer Second Class, we were perpetually broke.

But Alicia was relentless in her pursuit of a career in Fine Art. Eventually, she found out that posing nude as a live model for an advanced art class would make her an employee of the University, which meant she was eligible for free tuition for her own art classes. When I returned from a three-month cruise and discovered what she'd been doing, I went insane with jealousy. Of course, I demanded that she stop, and of course, Alicia stood her ground. In the short term, this led directly to

136

my discovery that divorce doesn't solve jealousy. Much later, I discovered that time doesn't either.

Beyond the rooftops, a distant upward streak of light burst into the green, white, and red colors of the Mexican flag. The crack of the explosion took a couple of seconds to reach the third floor of the Hotel Miramar.

"I didn't want to throw it in your face again," Alicia said.

I turned away from the window, abandoned my untasted beer on top of the dresser, and went over and sat on the end of the bed, close to Alicia's feet, but not facing her. "Just go on."

Alicia took a breath. "So about a week before Dr. Salazar was killed, Teresa was posing, and Dr. Salazar was painting away – I assume he painted as slowly as possible. I mean, two months for a simple nude? It's not like he's painting it on the ceiling of the Sistine Chapel – Anyway, it seems this time Teresa forgot to call her boyfriend, Antonio, to tell him not to pick her up after work that day. So Antonio comes into the Project's office and finds his girlfriend naked, and Dr. Salazar eyeballing her, more or less professionally, over his easel. Antonio socks Dr. Salazar a good one, knocking the old man and the easel and everything to the floor. Antonio vows that he'll kill Dr. Salazar, if he ever gets his girlfriend naked again. Antonio then starts breaking up the place and flinging things around like an angry gorilla. Teresa gets her clothes back on, and she and Antonio leave."

Alicia took a swallow of warm beer, made a face of disgust, reached the can over to the desk, and set it there. "So Teresa spends the rest of the night with

Antonio, trying to calm him down, since his blood is still at a boil. But she finally gets him rocking in the cradle, you know, and so she figures he's all reassured. She comes in to work the next morning and apologizes to Dr. Salazar for Antonio's behavior. And Dr. Salazar says it's okay, that he hasn't been in a fight over a girl in a really long time, and so he's wearing his bruises with pride, et cetera."

"All better then," I said.

"True enough, in that Teresa still has her job. But Dr. Salazar says the painting is all messed up. However, he can fix it, if she'll pose for him just one more time. He says he's got an apartment that no one else knows about, so Antonio couldn't possibly stumble in on the two of them again."

"She fell for that?"

"No. Teresa is beautiful, but she isn't dumb. Well, not that dumb. After all, she's an artist too, and it's beginning to dawn on even her that two months is a hell of a long time, I don't care what you're painting. Couple that with an invitation to a secret apartment, and finally, the alarm bells begin to clang away in her pretty little head. So she politely declines. But then, as she's walking away from Dr. Salazar, she sees Carlos loitering nearby, and she wonders if he's overheard all of this."

"Do Carlos and Antonio know each other?"

"I get that impression," Alicia said. "So now, it's several days later, the day of the shooting, and we're all at Pancho Villa's Museum doing the photo op. Teresa borrows my cell phone and calls Antonio at the bar where he goes after work and waits till it's time to come pick her up. But this day, she calls and tells him not to come to get her at the Palacio de Gobierno, because she's at Pancho Villa's Museum with Dr. Salazar and the gang, taking photographs."

"At least, she's getting better at keeping Antonio informed."

"But in this case, she thinks it worked against her. Well actually, more against Dr. Salazar. Because she thinks that Carlos might have gotten talkative, as he does with a few beers in him, and told Antonio what he'd overheard. And she thinks that, after she called Antonio from the museum that day – given what she said, plus it being from an unfamiliar phone number – that Antonio got it in his head that Dr. Salazar was getting his darling Teresa naked again – this time for photographs. And that Antonio tore out of the bar, drove heart pounding to Villa's Museum in a jealous rage, climbed over the wall, grabbed one of the Museum's guns, and shot Dr. Salazar dead."

"Does Antonio keep a collection of ammunition in his glove compartment?" I asked.

"I don't think logic is Teresa's strong suit."

"I take it Teresa didn't go to the police with any of this."

"Teresa couldn't tell the police, because she loves Antonio madly. And she couldn't tell the priest, for fear he'd damn her to Hell for getting naked for money and having it off with Antonio before marriage. She said the first time the police came and got me, she thought I'd just be questioned and released. And when I showed up at work the next day, she thought everything was going to be okay. But then, when I was dragged off to jail the second time, kicking and screaming – well, you know, I was upset – she was sure I was going to rot in prison for a murder that Antonio committed."

"Didn't she bother to ask Antonio if he killed Salazar?"

"She says Antonio told her that he never left the bar, until she called him again, after the shooting, to come and pick her up at the Café Iguana. But Teresa wasn't especially convinced. I get the idea she's caught Antonio lying to her before. So, when she finds me today back at the Palacio de Gobierno, she breaks down, and this whole Shakespearean tragedy she's built up in her little brain comes tumbling out, and she's crying and begging for forgiveness, and it takes me forever to calm her freaking down."

I stared at the floor and ran it all through my head again, before I finally tumbled. "So, we're going over to Antonio's after-work bar to prove his alibi, so Teresa can stop beating herself up."

"That took almost a whole minute, Francis. Maybe you should eat more fish." Alicia brought her feet down from the bed and slid them into the black high heels. "The bar is called the Gato Negro. Let me check my face, and we'll go."

Chapter 9

Turning off the same boulevard I had driven earlier in the day on my excursion to the Ford Factory, Alicia and I left the security of bright streetlights and plunged down a dark side street in a barrio on the north side of the city. A desk clerk at the Miramar had penciled an X, for us, on a city map to indicate the approximate location of the Gato Negro. The clerk had to call a friend for the information, after his Google search had turned up nothing. According to the clerk, his friend also mentioned that there were at least a hundred nicer places within the city limits to get a drink.

I took a left at the second cross street, and even though the sign was small and illuminated only by my headlights, by driving slowly and eyeing every sign on the street, we found the Gato Negro Cantina.

The cantina stood within a tight row of shops and warehouses on our left. Parking was restricted to the business side of the street only. It was evident that this was in order to maintain two-way traffic on the narrow street and have curbside parking at all, because the right-hand side of the street featured a ten-foot-high block wall running its length, separated from the traffic lane only by crumbling curbing and a thin line of weeds. I drove past the Gato Negro, giving the area a further scan. The tight turning ratio of my "economy" rental came in handy for performing a U-turn at the next intersection. I drove back toward the cantina, pulled into the long stretch of open space along the sidewalk, and nosed up to the last car of a four-car line running back from the cantina's front door.

Despite the parked cars, the entire street, including the cantina, looked closed for the night. Using what ebbing residual light was left in the evening sky, Alicia and I made our way along the deserted sidewalk to the heavily scarred door beneath the Gato Negro's minimalist sign and entered.

The interior lighting was almost as dim as the twilight outside. The air reeked of stale cigarette smoke and neglected beer taps. To the left, a utilitarian bar ran along under the elbows of seven patrons, all men. Two empty pool tables – their worn, green felt illuminated by low-hanging light fixtures with flyspecked bulbs – dominated the center of the room. Tables and chairs from the aluminum-and-vinyl era were scattered about on a checkerboard of tired, black and white, linoleum squares. The tables were empty, except for one at the back, where a lone man sat with some papers spread before him under a bright table lamp. The eyes of the men at the bar, the bartender, and the man at the far table had all looked toward the door, when Alicia and I entered. They remained on us, as we ventured in deeper.

"I don't think I'll be using the ladies' room here," Alicia privately remarked. "Assuming they have one."

We took a table near one of the pool tables. The men at the bar continued to observe us, talking low among themselves.

"You want anything?" I asked Alicia.

"Just get me a beer," she said. "A cold one, this time. In a bottle, with the cap still in place."

I stood and walked to the bar. No eyes tracked me. They stayed on Alicia.

I ordered, "*dos Victorias*." When the gaunt, sad-eyed bartender set two bottles in front of me, I snatched them away, before he could open them, and laid out some peso notes. When the bartender returned with my change, I spoke in Spanish again, "The lady wants to talk to you. Will you come to our table?"

The bartender looked passed me toward Alicia.

"With much pleasure."

I returned to our table and removed the caps with the bottle opener blade of my Swiss Army knife. The bartender came around the far end of the bar and joined us.

"What do you wish, my beautiful one?" he asked in Spanish.

"Francis, tell him I only speak English."

"The lady does not speak Spanish," I translated for her. "She desires information concerning a regular customer of this establishment."

"Who are you?" the bartender asked.

"I am Francis, she is Alicia, and this is a countryman of yours." I showed him the portrait of some long-dead statesman on a two-hundred-peso note I'd drawn from my pocket.

The man who'd been sitting with his paperwork now approached us. His pencil mustache was neatly trimmed, but he was too pot-bellied to successfully carry off the black, shiny dress shirt and canary-yellow slacks. He announced in Spanish, "I am Ignacio Baez. I own this cantina. What do you wish of my bartender?"

143

I realized I'd been too open with my bribe. "The lady has challenged your bartender to a game of pool." It was the best I could come up with on the fly. "I hope that he can accept."

"I can see that he will receive two-hundred pesos, if he wins," Baez said. "And I know that he does not have two-hundred pesos of his own, if he loses. What does he bet?"

"If he loses, he tells the lady about a young man who comes in here almost every day, after work. His name is Antonio."

I watched for a glimmer of name recognition in the cantina owner's eyes. Baez gave away nothing.

The bartender was also watching Baez, waiting to be told what to do.

"Yes, Felipe, you may play the game. I would never hear the end of your weeping, if I did not allow you to play with this splendid woman and win your two-hundred pesos."

The bartender eagerly stepped to the nearest pool table and began to rack the balls in a diamond shape.

"Francis, what's going on? You're supposed to be translating for me."

"You're going to shoot pool with the bartender. He gets the equivalent of fifteen dollars, if he wins. If he loses, he tells us about Antonio. Looks like they play nine-ball down here."

"He'll be shooting with such a big woody, it'll probably get in *my* way."

Alicia took a swallow of her beer, stood up from the table, and walked over to the line of cue sticks on a nearby wall. Every set of eyes in the bar followed her movements.

Alicia sighted down the taper of the stick she'd selected and then rolled it on the green felt of the other pool table. Satisfied that the stick was reasonably straight, Alicia methodically and theatrically chalked the end of her cue stick, while striking a flattering pose, for the benefit of her fans at the bar.

The bartender took a stick from the rack, chalked it aggressively, and waited.

"Do they lag for break down here, or what?" Alicia asked me.

"I don't know the words for it to ask." I turned to the bartender and said in Spanish, "You have the honor to start the game, sir."

The bartender came to mock attention. "The Sovereign Nation of Mexico insists that the honor rightly belongs to America the Beautiful."

That brought on a good deal of laughter and cries of "Viva!" from the men at the bar. Baez and I laughed along with them.

"What was that all about?" Alicia asked.

"Your break. Mexico insists."

Alicia bent low, sighted on the white cue ball, and then sent it slamming with a sharp crack into the yellow "one" ball at the head of the diamond-shaped mass of object balls. The "one" ball stayed fixed, and the cue ball backed up seemingly in slow motion, while the other eight, colored balls scattered, as though fired from a shotgun. The balls careened off rails and collided with each other, but none sank into any pockets. The bartender was left with a clear line at the "one" ball, and absolutely no chance of sinking it.

The bartender gamely tried to make his shot, apparently without considering what opportunities his futile attempt would leave for Alicia. When the playing field resettled, Alicia was left in excellent position to sink, at least, the first two balls in the numerical sequence.

"Gracias, my innocent," Alicia murmured, as she lined up her shot.

Alicia made the "one" and "two" balls easily. Her setup for the "three" ball was doable, but not necessarily a cinch.

"I see that your lady knows this game," Baez said. "Does Felipe have a chance at winning your two-hundred pesos?"

"No," I said.

Alicia was not a magician at the pool table. She was not any better than the average barroom player at bank shots and combination shots. But with the clean shots, cue ball hits object ball at just the right spot to drive it directly into the pocket, she was unlikely to miss, even on a rough barroom table. 'Just relax,' she would tell me. 'Don't think about it, just do it.' Her natural eye-hand coordination served her well, no matter what tool she was using. Be it cue stick, artist's brush, or handgun.

"What is it that you wish to know about this customer of mine, this Antonio?" Baez asked me.

"Do you know him?"

"Not by name. We have many men who come here in the afternoon on their way home from work. More than a few come from the Ford factory. I like them. They have money."

"I was at the Ford factory earlier today. I helped the repairmen fix a broken machine."

"Do you repair broken machines? Then I have one for you. I had a man working on it, but he does not come back with the new part. My customers from the Ford factory recommended him to me. He is the Great Technician, they tell me. Easily he will repair my Coke machine, they tell me. And yet, my Coke machine remains broken." Baez pointed beyond the far end of the bar to a red vending machine from the Art Deco period. "I bought it for the children, when they come here on Saturday mornings with their fathers, while their mothers do the shopping. It was a beautiful arrangement. The men give the children their change. The children buy the soft drinks from the Coke machine and play on the pool tables. My bartender can concentrate on selling the beer and the liquor. That is where I make my money. It was a grand idea. I would open my cantina on Saturday mornings with joy in my heart. But now on Saturday mornings, I must help Felipe behind the bar to sell the soft drinks to the children, because my Coke machine is broken."

"So, the technician never came back?"

"At first, he does not appear at all. Weeks go by. Again and again, I say to the workers from Ford, 'Where is the Great Technician? Bring to me the Great Technician.' They say that he is busy with his new situation. They say that he no longer works at Ford. 'Find him,' I plead. 'Ask him again.' And then just last week, my heart sings. The Great Technician finally appears in my cantina. And just as they say, he opens my Coke machine and immediately extracts the broken part. He tells me that he will find a replacement part. He tells me that he will soon be back. But to my sorrow, the Great Technician never returns. And my Coke machine remains broken."

"Perhaps the replacement part was difficult to find," I said. "It is a very old machine."

"That I cannot say." Baez grasped my arm. "But *you* can fix machinery. Come. Come and look at my Coke machine."

I glanced over at the pool table. There were only the "eight" and "nine" balls left, and Alicia was shooting. The game would soon be over.

Baez drew me toward the red machine. From his pleated, yellow trousers, he produced a ring of keys and used one to open the front of the dispensing machine. It swung on its hinges to reveal slanting shelves that fed the bottles of soda pop by gravity.

"There." Baez pointed. "There is from where the part is missing. The technician took it with him to match it to a picture that he would find on the Internet."

Two wires hung uselessly. Missing was the part that electro-magnetically pushed its metal core forward to release a mechanical stop, allowing a bottle to drop into the customer access area in response to the right combination of coins.

"Do you know what part is missing?" Baez asked.

"Yes. A solenoid for the bottle release action."

"Excellent. Here, let me give you the model and serial number. It is what the Great Technician said he needed to find the replacement part."

148

Baez stooped down and withdrew a pen and somebody's business card from his shirt pocket. He began to copy down two strings of numbers from a metal label riveted to the machine.

Before he finished, I heard Alicia call out from across the room. "Francis! A little help here!"

One of the men, a big one who had been standing at the bar, was now at the pool table. I could see the green of a two-hundred-peso note in his hand. The bartender was trying, unsuccessfully, to deal with him.

I quickly returned to the pool table and placed myself between Alicia and the big man. I spoke to him in Spanish, "The lady has finished playing the game for the night."

"I have the two hundred pesos to bet." The loud and belligerent blast of hot, beer breath washed over my face.

"Put your money away," I said. "I will buy you a beer. Let us return to the bar. I will buy beer for you and all your friends."

The giant hand formed a fist, engulfing and crushing the green currency. Then, a pudgy hand landed gently on the heavy shoulder above the balled fist.

"My friend wishes to buy you a beer," Baez appeared from behind the big man. His hand stayed on the heavy shoulder, as Baez looked up toward the big man's face. "Do not insult my friend."

The big man looked down at Baez.

"I know," Baez quietly told him, casting a brief glance toward Alicia. "I have eyes also."

The hand on the big man's shoulder slid down to become a hand at his back, as Baez steered his large patron back to the bar.

I caught up with Baez, added a one-hundred-peso note to the two-hundred for the original bribe, and handed the money to Baez. "Is this sufficient?"

"It will buy beer for all these men and also tequila for Felipe and myself." Baez snatched the money from my hand.

"I still need to talk to Felipe."

"I will attend to the bar. Talk quickly." Baez slid the business card with the Coke machine's numbers into my shirt pocket and tapped it. "Do not forget. I need my Coke machine. I cannot afford to hire a Yankee, but you and your lady will drink all night for free."

"I will see what I can do."

I returned to Alicia and the bartender at the pool table.

"This'll only take a couple of minutes," I told Alicia. "And then we'll get out of here."

I switched back to Spanish, "Felipe, do you know a young man named Antonio, who comes here in the afternoon to wait, until it is time to pick up his girlfriend from work?"

"I know Antonio."

"Do you remember that he was here two days ago, on Monday?"

The bartender thought for a moment. "I can only say yes, because he is here every afternoon during the work week."

"On Monday, Antonio received a cell phone call, while he was at this bar."

"His cell phone has an amusing song when it rings."

"And you heard the amusing song on Monday?"

"I remember. The vendor was here to restock the bar. He commented on the amusing song. The vendor comes on Mondays."

"After that phone call, did Antonio stay here at the bar, or did he leave soon after the call?"

"Antonio leaves."

"You are sure that he left right after the phone call?"

"He drinks the last of his beer and leaves."

I sensed Felipe's growing impatience with my questions. But I needed to be sure.

"Then it was just one phone call?" I pressed him. "Or was there a phone call, some time passes, and then another phone call?"

"I remember the song of his cell phone only one time."

"Felipe," Baez, called from the bar. "It is time to return to work."

"I must go." The bartender seemed relieved to return to his duties.

I said my thanks to Felipe's back, the ritual handshake on departing having been omitted in his haste.

"What did he say?" Alicia asked.

"That Antonio left right after receiving only one phone call from Teresa."

"Are you saying it's actually possible that Antonio killed Dr. Salazar?"

"He has a stronger motive than you, and he lied about where he was at the time of the murder," I said.

"And that's exactly how I'll put it to Commandant Arroyo tomorrow morning."

***

We were on our way out of the Gato Negro, my hand on the doorknob, when Baez waylaid Alicia.

"Lovely Lady, I desire to say 'goodnight' to you," Baez surprised me by speaking in heavily accented English. "It is not with frequency that we are honored with the company of a lady here."

"I guessed that," Alicia said.

"I desire you to know that always my pool table is here for you."

While the parting words continued, I opened the door to the street and poked my head out. There was no source of illumination, other than the light spilling out from the Gato Negro. Knowing that it was just a matter of pupil dilation didn't make the void less black.

Baez finally wrapped up his farewell, and Alicia followed me, as I stepped out onto the sidewalk. When the door to the Gato Negro closed behind us, I had new respect for the expression 'dark as a wolf's mouth.'

As we moved along the line of only-vaguely-perceived parked cars, my eyes gradually became conditioned enough for me to discern a figure in motion up ahead. From somewhere behind us, there came a brief wash of light, and in those few seconds, the moving figure ahead became a shabbily dressed man, lingering on the sidewalk near my rental car. Then the light went out with the sound of a door closing. I put my arm in front of Alicia, and together we stopped. Now that the tapping of Alicia's high heels had ceased, I

152

heard the sound of heavy footsteps, approaching us from behind.

"A few pesos for a poor man?" The dark figure in front of us asked in such mumbled Spanish that, had I not anticipated his request, I would not have caught it.

I took the car key out of my pocket and pressed it into Alicia's hand. "When we get to the car, unlock your door, get in, and lock it again. Then start the engine and unlock the driver's side."

Together we moved aggressively forward. The beggar gave ground. Apparently, Alicia had kept her wits and quickly found the key slot in the dark with her fingertips, because I soon heard the rasp of the key sliding in. I also noticed that the sounds of footsteps coming up behind us had stopped. I turned and positioned myself such that my back was not turned to either man. In the brief time the dome light switched on, I could clearly see the second man, dressed in work clothes, now standing just off the curbside front fender of the rented Fiesta. It wasn't the big man who wanted to shoot pool with Alicia, but this guy was big enough. As for the beggar, he'd straightened his stance, no longer looking humble. The car door closed, and we were again plunged into darkness.

As the engine coughed to life, I asked, "How many pesos will buy my new friends a drink?"

I grabbed some coins from my pocket and gave them a toss. As the coins tinkled on the concrete, I turned and threw myself onto the hood of the rental car and scrambled inelegantly over to the driver's side. I pulled the door open, slid behind the wheel, shifted into reverse, and smacked into a car behind us. I cranked the wheel, dropped the stick into drive, hit the gas, and we shot away from the curb like a launched torpedo.

A right turn at the first intersection would've taken us back to our hotel, but I was still in flight-mode, and my foot wasn't leaving the gas pedal. But another block later, I'd calmed enough to know it was time to leave the barrio and get the hell back onto the main thoroughfare, heading downtown. As I slowed to take the next corner, a set of headlights came up quickly behind us.

I really didn't think the two muggers had a car handy, but after I'd completed the turn, the headlights in the mirror stayed right with us. I was forced to stop two blocks later, where the side street met the brightly lit boulevard, streaming with heavy evening traffic. I could now easily see in the mirror that the car trailing us contained a single, broad-shouldered man. As I waited anxiously for an opening in the traffic, another check in the mirror showed a cloud began to envelope the car behind us. There was a loud hissing sound and a sickening odor, like sugar and rubber being burned together.

I finally got my chance, and I floored it, making a sweeping left onto the boulevard with that satisfying squeal you get from punishing rental-car tires. The car behind us never emerged from the cloud of green steam. And the little Fiesta rolled with the evening flow back into the city.

"Quick thinking back there." Alicia allowed me a rare compliment.

"Nice reaction time on your part." I wanted to add how happy I was that, for once, she had done exactly what I'd told her to do. But I had the good sense to leave it unspoken.

***

I pulled into the loading zone in front of the Hotel Miramar, longing for a cold beer and a light supper – to be immediately followed by a soft pillow. A hotel employee bounded out and opened Alicia's door for her. I managed on my own, and as I rounded the back of the rental car, I ran an eye over the damage, resulting from my bumper-car departure from the Gato Negro. The taillights were intact, although the battle scars on the paint job were clearly noticeable. I'd have to allow time for the extra paperwork, when I returned the rental car to the airport.

The hotel employee drove the rented Fiesta off to some far-flung lot. On entering the Miramar's lobby, we were greeted by loud, pounding Latin rhythms emanating from the hotel's restaurant and bar.

"That sounds like fun," Alicia said, already drawn toward the music.

I stayed with her, as we passed by the front desk, busy with a knot of men in suits and ties, all trying to check in at once. We also bypassed the elevator doors, standing open and inviting, before arriving at a hostess station. While the hostess continued to puzzle over her computer screen without noticing us, I looked in and saw that the hotel's normally sedate restaurant had somehow morphed into a crowded, raucous nightclub. At the far corner, a flamboyant disc jockey worked at a soundboard flanked by two giant stacks of woofers, midrange speakers, and tweeters. The mingling at the bar was three deep, and the tables were full – a few

155

patrons dining, but most just drinking. The women wore cocktail dresses or chic office outfits. The men, for the most part, were in jacket and tie, although there was the occasional open collared, gaily colored, dress shirt.

"We're a little under-dressed for clubbing," I had to speak louder than normal to point this out.

"Oh, everyone knows Americans dress like farm workers," Alicia spoke directly into my ear. "We're fine."

"*Buenas noches*." The eyes of the pert, young hostess had finally left her computer screen and found us standing before her.

Alicia stepped up to the hostess. "Do you have a table? We'd like something to eat."

I quickly moved forward and translated this into Spanish, over Alicia's shoulder. I added that we were guests of the hotel, hoping our residency would count for some extra consideration.

Apparently, it did. Holding the stiff, glossy menus before her as a wedge, the young hostess led us deep into the throng. The entire gamut of perfumes, from flowery to woodsy, competed for air superiority, as we made our incursion. The hostess established a narrow beachhead at the bar and parked us, until a table became available. I reached past Alicia and rested my hand on the bar edge, with a five-hundred-peso note sticking out from between my fingers. The bartender responded, and I ordered a margarita for Alicia and a beer for myself.

When the drinks, eventually, landed in front of us, I grabbed up the beer and took in a hearty swallow. Immediately, I felt my blood pressure lower and smooth out, as the wonderfully cold, lightly hopped beer flowed over my tongue, soothed my throat, and settled my stomach.

Alicia tasted her opaque green drink. "Oh wow, this is good." She brushed salt crystals from her lips, while looking over my shoulder. "Isn't that my lawyer over there?"

I looked to where Alicia was pointing. Enrique Ponce sat at a table with two other men. All three were in business suits, drinking and laughing.

"Let's go say 'hi'," Alicia said. "I want to thank him for getting my luggage back."

"Well, he's with friends. Maybe we shouldn't…"

But Alicia and her margarita were off, heading toward the party of three.

I tipped the bartender well for being prompt with my change, jammed the remaining peso notes in my front pocket, and set off through the crowd in pursuit of Alicia.

When I arrived, all three men were still standing, and Ponce was completing the introductions. Alicia briefly caught and released the fingers of each extended hand in turn, while holding her delighted-to-meet-you smile on high beam. When my presence was noticed, Ponce performed the introductions again, this time in Spanish, and I worked through the ensuing, manly handclasps.

Ponce then invited Alicia to sit down with them. I helped Alicia with her chair, and the three men regained their seats. There was no fifth chair, so I stood behind Alicia and hoped this wouldn't take long.

"Enrique, thank you so much for getting my clothes back," Alicia spoke to her attorney at normal volume, during a lull in the music.

"It was my great pleasure. I see that they still fit you exceedingly well – despite your lengthy prison stay."

Alicia gave him a playful push, in reply.

Ponce then explained to his two friends, in Spanish, that he had successfully retrieved his client's luggage from the evidence storeroom at the City Jail.

I leaned forward and translated into Alicia's ear.

"But all my underwear is missing," Alicia objected to her lawyer's statement. "I have no bras and panties."

Ponce quickly relayed this information to his two friends, and when one of them accused Ponce of stealing the lady's pretty undergarments, all three broke into laughter. I wondered how long they'd been drinking, but I laughed along too. It was infectious.

"What are they laughing about?" Alicia asked over her shoulder.

"Ponce's friends are accusing him of stealing your underwear."

"In that case, please inform my attorney that, if he's wearing my undies right now, I don't want them back."

I translated this for Ponce's friends, and there were more hoots, along with much arm punching.

The hostess tapped me on the shoulder and told me our table was ready. Alicia and I said our goodbyes, and we moved away through the stares of the other patrons, leaving the three friends to their inebriation and camaraderie.

We were seated at a table near the small dance floor, which, despite the insistent disco-like beat the DJ was cranking out, at the moment, was unoccupied – although there was quite a bit of swaying to the music among the young women within the crowd up near the bar.

"How did Ponce happen to be here?" I moved my head close to Alicia's to ask. "Did he say?"

"Turns out, one of the characters at Enrique's table is the hotel's accountant. When Enrique dropped off my luggage, the two of them decided to call the third friend and have dinner here."

"They'd better get to eating something soon."

"Us, too. I think whoever's in charge of watering down the booze must've taken the night off."

I caught the eye of a waitress tending to a nearby table. After she came over, took our order, and departed, a young man wearing a red vest arrived from the bar with a chilled pitcher of margaritas and a pair of stemmed glasses. I looked over to Ponce's table, and the lawyer gave me a wave of his hand. I waved back.

"Compliments of the Attorney for the Defense," I informed Alicia, as I rationed out two cocktails into the salt-rimmed glasses.

Alicia stood and blew Ponce a kiss. When she sat back down, she said, "I should be buying *him* a drink. If he hadn't managed to get my luggage back, I wouldn't have anything to wear to the funeral tomorrow."

"What time's that happening?"

"Well, I don't know when or where, because I was tied up with Teresa and her tears, and then I didn't get a chance to ask Carlos. I was going to, when he brought his supplies back to the office at the end of the day. Turns out he left the supplies outside the door and went off with his drinking buddy, never to be seen again."

I could've argued that I was indirectly working on her behalf, during beer time with Carlos, but I didn't want to argue. So, I took another sip of a drink that was way too sweet tasting, despite looking remarkably like swamp water.

"I almost asked Teresa about the funeral," Alicia said, "but she was such a mess I was afraid she'd freak out, if I brought it up." Alicia stood again, this time to extract her cell phone from a front pocket of her tight jeans. "Maybe, I could give Carlos a call." She pushed buttons with her thumb. "Actually, given my foreign language skills, it might be better if *you* talk to him."

"He was going to have a few drinks with his landlady, when I dropped him off," I intervened on Carlos's behalf. "And I'm not sure what goes on after the children go to bed."

Alicia sighed and slid her phone away, before regaining her seat. "I'll call him first thing in the morning, then. But I'll still need your help with the translation."

Our food arrived, and the dinner conversation – what I could hear of it – turned to talk of color matches and brush stroke techniques. Mostly, I ate and pretended to listen. I neglected my margarita and ordered beer at the first opportunity, relinquishing the rest of the pitcher to Alicia.

As the busboys cleared the plates from the tables of the last few diners, the DJ ramped the music down from its frenzied beat and volume. The lighting dimmed, until the LEDs of the electronics shone as bright points of blue. Couples, at last, began to appear on the small patch of dance floor.

Alicia poured the last of the cocktail mix from the pitcher into her glass and downed it. She placed the empty glass on the table and pushed it away from her.

"Dance with me," she said.

"Well, you know, me and dancing…"

"Nobody's asking you to jitterbug."

Resigned to my fate, I stood and helped Alicia rise up onto her high heels. She grabbed a handful of the back of my shirt for stability, as we maneuvered single file between a pair of intervening tables and onto the dance floor.

The dance floor was small enough to be crowded by five couples. We were the sixth. Nevertheless, we claimed a small patch of real estate, just as the DJ put on an Eagles ballad from the seventies. The selection may or may not have been a nod to Alicia's western shirt and jeans, standing out among the more sophisticated displays of women's wear, but her face still wore the appreciative smile she'd bestowed on the DJ, as she spun around to face me, and we slid into the slow-dance embrace.

Alicia's hair was a soft cushion, as she laid her head against mine. "I remember this song from when I was a little girl. Ellen and I would dance in the living room with our teddy bears. We were Cinderellas at the ball, and the teddy bears were our Prince Charmings." Alicia's head slid down to my shoulder, and I adjusted my hand on her back to accommodate the new position. I noticed that something was missing.

I turned my face into Alicia's hair. "You're not wearing a bra."

She lifted her head slightly. "I know." She laid her head back down.

"A little daring, don't you think?"

Alicia picked up her head again. "I told you the police stole my underwear. After I took a shower, my only bra was too sweaty to get back into."

"But you went to that lowlife bar without—"

"It's not body armor, Francis. And that's why I wore this cowgirl shirt. It has two breast pockets." Alicia brought her lips close to my ear and whispered, "So my nipples wouldn't show." While she was in the neighborhood, she teased my earlobe with her teeth. "I have no secrets from my teddy bear. Tonight, I went totally commando."

In full response to this news, as soon as the Eagles let their Western love song trail off into the sunset, I steered Alicia back to our table. A leather-bound folder, with a corner of the check peeking out, had been discretely placed on the table. I hastily calculated the tip in my head, overpaid from the wad of pesos notes from my front pocket, and closed them within the leather folder, not allowing Alicia a chance to sit down – even though she looked like she was fading fast.

I caught Alicia, as she stumbled. "Time to call it a night."

"Okay," she said languidly. "Or we could just sleep here."

***

Once we were inside our hotel room, Alicia gave me a perfunctory goodnight kiss and climbed onto the foot of the bed. She proceeded forward on hands and knees, until her head hovered over the pillows, and then dropped over on her side and rolled onto her back. I quickly locked the door, kicked off my shoes, and was on the bed next to her, lying on my left side, leaving my dominant hand free.

I worked on the seemingly innumerable buttons of her Western shirt, gradually revealing the warm, rolling topography beneath. The closure button on her blue jeans was somewhat more challenging. And then instead of a zipper, I was faced with more buttons. But before I could stoically persevere, Alicia's fingers were in my hair, pulling my face back up toward hers. I had only a brief scan of the previous points of interest, when a sudden heavy pounding on the door caused my head to jerk free of Alicia's grasp.

A raised voice demanded in Spanish, "Open up, Mister Elton! We are the police!"

The sound of a key turning in the lock sent the blood rushing back up to my brain. I quickly slapped a pillow over Alicia's body, which she immediately embraced, curling up with it.

As I sprang from the bed and onto my feet, three men, wearing neatly pressed, casual wear, confronted me in the small hotel room. The desk clerk, holding his passkey in a trembling hand, peered from behind the policemen and mumbled his apologies. The room seemed to shrink even further in size – along with my ardor.

The policemen wore badges and guns on their belts.

One of them announced in Spanish, "I am Corporal Valdez of the Chihuahua State Ministerial Police. Commandant Arroyo has instructed me to bring you to his office at the Delegation, at once."

"Look, Corporal," I responded in Spanish, "this is not a good time. At present I am occupied with—"

"I can clearly see what I have interrupted. Put on your shoes. You will come with us."

"Wait a minute. If it is a matter of money." I brought my wallet out. "If you could just give me an hour, a half hour even. You could post a guard outside the room and—"

"No amount of money that you can offer would entice me to explain the delay of an hour to Commandant Arroyo."

One of the other officers kicked my shoes toward me. I put my wallet away, sat on the bed, and put my shoes on. The moment they were tied, the shoe kicker grabbed me roughly by the upper arm and pulled me up on my feet.

As Corporal Valdez led us out of the room, I looked back at Alicia, peacefully sleeping off the pitcher of margaritas. She held the pillow tightly. Her red lips moved. They seemed to form the words, "teddy bear."

Once we were all out in the hall, the desk clerk gingerly closed the door and locked it.

The Corporal ordered the officer who didn't have hold of me, "Remain here. No one enters or leaves this room without the permission of Commandant Arroyo."

The desk clerk touched the arm of the officer who was to remain. "I will get you a chair." He hurried off.

I was brought along, still in the policeman's grip and trailing behind Corporal Valdez, as he strode toward the elevator. I was already dreading the perp walk through the lobby.

Chapter 10

An involuntary ride in the back of a police car has a way of dramatizing the images of the passing cityscape, especially when illuminated by streetlights. The parked cars, storefronts, and fire hydrants appear too sharply delineated; a windblown sheet of newspaper seems to carry unsettling significance. And for the first time, I noticed that the divided highway with the shallow, cement-lined Rio Chuviscar as its median, had a name. The unmarked police car took the ramp onto the Teo Borunda Expressway and picked up speed.

When we eventually exited the Teo Borunda, as far as I was concerned, we could have been anywhere within the city. But, when the police car swung into a driveway that led past a grim two-story building, cast in no-nonsense concrete and bathed in the harsh glare of security lights, I had no doubt that we'd arrived at Commandant Arroyo's base of operations – and what, I supposed, Cpl. Valdez had meant by "the Delegation".

Again trailing behind Cpl. Valdez, I was walked across the back parking lot and up a set of exterior spiral stairs. At the top, Valdez keyed in a code and opened a plain steel door. We then proceeded along a hallway flanked on either side by more steel doors, although these featured narrow windows, providing a peek at warrens of cubicles lit by the glow of screen savers. The only open door was the last one on the right, and Cpl. Valdez led the way on through it. As Valdez stepped to one side, I was brought to a halt in the center of the room.

Commandant Arroyo sat behind a large, mahogany desk – the focal piece of a spacious, yet stunningly Spartan, corner office. The impression was of an environmental void, too hostile to support any form of existence, but law enforcement. The smell of spent cigarettes alone would have choked a cactus.

A wooden chair with scarred armrests was brought over, and I was plunked down onto the seat.

Arroyo began in English, "Mr. Elton, I'm sure you're aware that it was in response to your activities this evening that you were brought to my office."

"I can't think of any activity that would warrant being roused out of bed in the middle of the night." Angry as I was, I left unsaid the activity I was engaged in, at the moment of the rousing. "What is it that couldn't wait until morning, when, incidentally, I fully intended to come to your office to speak with you anyway?"

"Yes, I understand that, for a gringo, the hour is considered late." Arroyo leaned forward, moving his forearms off padded leather armrests and onto his desk. "I doubt that it would surprise you to learn that, subsequent to her conditional release, we have been keeping a close eye on Alicia Elton. Nor should it surprise you that I was to be immediately informed, should either Mrs. Elton, or you, violate the law, or intentionally elude one of my investigative officers. Tonight, you did both."

"What the hell are you talking about?"

I slid forward in my chair, about to stand up. A heavy hand clamped down on my shoulder and pulled me back into my seat.

Arroyo calmly ordered, in Spanish, "Have Sergeant de Leon step in here for a moment."

A minute later, a man of about my age, wearing workman's clothes that didn't for a second make him look like a workman, entered the room and stood before Commandant Arroyo.

"Sergeant," Arroyo stayed with Spanish, "tell Mr. Elton what you reported to me when you telephoned earlier this evening. Pass over his suspicious behavior inside the Gato Negro, and—"

"Wait," I said, in English. "What suspicious behavior?"

"We are establishing the facts of your *criminal* behavior, at the moment," Arroyo rebuffed in English. He kept his hard eyes fixed on me, as he returned to Spanish. "Sergeant, go to the part where Mr. and Mrs. Elton leave the cantina."

"In English, Commandant?"

"In Spanish," Arroyo said. "Mr. Elton seems to understand it well enough."

"Yes, Commandant," the Sergeant responded in Spanish. "When the Yankees left the Gato Negro, I followed them in the darkness to their car. I had parked my car right behind their rental car, so that I would be able to drive straight out and catch up to them."

Oh, crap! My mind raced ahead. Hit and run on a police car. This was not good.

"A dome light comes on," de Leon continued. "Alicia Elton quickly enters the car and closes the door. It is dark again, and the car engine starts. I hear Mr. Elton say something to a beggar and then the sound of coins spilling to the sidewalk, as Mr. Elton hastily pays

167

the beggar. The shadow of Mr. Elton crosses over the hood of his car. The dome light briefly comes on again, and he is behind the wheel. He smashes back into my car and then rapidly drives away."

"It was an accident."

"That," Arroyo said, "has yet to be determined. Continue, Sergeant."

"Yes, Commandant. I run to my car to give chase. The beggar attempts to interfere, as I believe he was paid to do, but I put him to the sidewalk. Once in my car, I pursue the fleeing suspects. But the damage that the Yankees have inflicted on my car is too great. It has lost too much fluid. My car overheats and stalls. I call Corporal Valdez and send him to the Hotel Miramar, in case the fugitives return there. Then I call you, Commandant, because with the deliberate destruction of property, a law has been violated, and also Mr. and Mrs. Elton have intentionally eluded me."

"Thank you, Sergeant," Arroyo said. And then to me, he asked in English, "Did you understand all that was said, Mister Elton?"

"I didn't misinterpret the Sergeant's words," I said in English, "but the Sergeant misinterpreted my actions."

"Then let me pick up your evening's busy saga where Sergeant de Leon left off." Arroyo still spoke in English. "Before leaving my ranch, I alerted the Traffic and Security Police with a description of your car. I also notified the Federal Inspection Station out on the highway to Juarez, concerning your fugitive status. On my way in to my office, Corporal Valdez called to report that the desk clerk at the Miramar had not seen

you or Mrs. Elton return to the hotel, and that when
Corporal Valdez went to your room to verify this, he
noted that your suitcases and clothes were still there."
Arroyo leaned back in his chair. "However, Corporal
Valdez was astute enough to also note that there were
surprisingly few men's clothes, even though he found a
receipt indicating that you had recently purchased more.
And although there was a reasonable amount of
women's clothing, there were only two pieces of ladies'
undergarments to be found." Arroyo smiled. "We, of
course, understand that the ladies tend to be quite fond
of their undergarments. They find it difficult to leave
them behind."

"In this case," I said in English, "I believe it was a
fondness for ladies' undergarments harbored by one of
your officers that accounts for their absence. After
Alicia's lawyer returned her luggage – luggage that *your*
men had confiscated – she discovered that all her bras
and panties were missing."

"Ah, yes. The lawyer." Arroyo was unfazed. "I was
just getting to him." He switched back to Spanish.
"Corporal Valdez was on the sidewalk, outside the
Hotel Miramar, giving instructions to two investigative
officers, who were to remain on watch at the hotel. He
noticed that some guests from the hotel's weekly
cocktail party were being loaded into a taxi. While
Corporal Valdez was making sure that there were no
Yankees among those being loaded, he was informed
that one of them was an attorney named Enrique Ponce.
At that point, the night desk clerk came out to inform
Corporal Valdez that he had just seen Mr. and Mrs.
Elton leave the cocktail party and enter the elevator."

Arroyo leaned forward to drive it home. "Thus, it is clear that this evening you and your ex-wife launched an attempt to flee the country, first by disabling Sergeant de Leon's car and eluding him, and next by laying low and hiding within the crowd at the hotel's cocktail party, waiting for the search to grow cold. While there, you arranged for a consultation with Mrs. Elton's attorney. However, in the end, you were obviously dissuaded from your folly by the cooler head of Mr. Ponce, because we next find that you have aborted your plan and returned to your hotel room. This is what your own actions have told us. And now you have the audacity to sit there and assert that you and your ex-wife have committed absolutely nothing of an illegal nature at all, this evening."

"You've got this all wrong," I said.

"Did you damage Sergeant de Leon's car this evening and speed away?"

"Well, yes, but—"

"Then I did not get it *all* wrong," Arroyo said. "Therefore, let us now focus on your alleged accident, involving Sergeant de Leon's car."

"I can explain that," I said. "When we left the Gato Negro, it was seriously dark out on the street. So, I was on my guard. And as Alicia and I approached our car, ahead of us in the darkness a man asked for money. And at the same time, I heard footsteps behind me. I assumed the beggar had a confederate, and we were trapped. As soon as Alicia was safely locked in the car, I tossed some coins at what I believed were *two* beggars. You know, just to satisfy them for the moment. That's when I scrambled across the hood to the driver's side, got in, and sped away from danger. I'm sorry I banged into the Sergeant's car, but I didn't know, at the time, that it was the police that we were fleeing from."

My words were greeted with silence. But for good or ill, my version of the story had been told. Still, I began to wonder if I would soon be enlisting the legal services of Enrique Ponce, for myself.

I sensed that no one else in the room would speak without being specifically asked to do so by the Commandant. For his part, Arroyo remained leaning back in his chair with the stern expression that I was coming to identify as his thinking face.

When Arroyo finally did speak, it was in English. "Mister Elton, you said that you had planned to come here tomorrow to talk to me. You may tell me, now, what you intended to say."

"I was hoping we'd eventually get around to it," I said. "This afternoon, Teresa – she's an artist who worked for Dr. Salazar on the Restoration Project – she told Alicia that she believed her boyfriend, Antonio, killed Dr. Salazar out of jealous rage."

Arroyo took this in for a moment. "What would cause this boyfriend to be so angry that he would kill Dr. Salazar?"

I recounted Teresa's tale about posing nude for Dr. Salazar, while he depicted her in oil on canvas, and Antonio coming in on them and knocking Salazar down, threatening to kill him, if he ever got his girlfriend naked again.

"An understandable response," Arroyo commented.

I went on about Teresa's first call to Antonio at the Gato Negro, telling him she was with Dr. Salazar at the

Museum, which Teresa believed gave Antonio the wrong idea, and then about the second call she made to him, after the murder, when Antonio told Teresa he was still at the Gato Negro. And about Teresa fearing that, instead, Antonio, consumed by anger that Salazar was ogling his sweetheart again, had gone straight over to Villa's Museum, after the first phone call, and shot Dr. Salazar.

Commandant Arroyo again leaned forward in his chair to ask, "And this young woman, Teresa, told you this?"

"She told Alicia. And Teresa's going through all kinds of anguish, because she's certain Alicia will be sent to prison for a murder she didn't commit." I felt good that I'd found an opportunity to say the last part.

"And this is why you and Mrs. Elton went to the Gato Negro earlier tonight?"

"Yes," I said. "To find out if Antonio told the truth as to his whereabouts when he received the second phone call. But the bartender at the Gato Negro told us Antonio received only one phone call that afternoon and left right afterward. That means Antonio not only threatened to kill Dr. Salazar, but also lied about where he was at the time of the murder. So that's why I intended to come and talk to you tomorrow morning."

Commandant Arroyo leaned back in his chair and lit a cigarette. As though this were a signal, the other policemen in the room also lit up.

As a gray haze was forming in a thermal layer just below the ceiling, Arroyo, having completed a series of contemplative puffs, laid his cigarette aside, and made a business of pulling a clean sheet of paper and a pen from a desk drawer. "The girlfriend, Teresa, what is her family name?"

"I don't know."

With his pen still poised above the blank paper, Arroyo looked at me. "And this Antonio, do you know *his* family name?"

"No."

Arroyo placed the pen onto the blank paper with affected care. "Ordinarily, I would now assign Sergeant de Leon to the task of questioning Antonio, Teresa, and the nameless bartender."

"His name is Felipe," I said.

"However, you have disabled Sergeant de Leon's car."

"I do have collision insurance. It says so on my rental papers."

"Insurance does not fix a broken car. A mechanic does. The insurance company will require estimates for the repair. Then the work must be performed, but only when the mechanic has the time in his schedule. It will be many days. And yet, I need Sergeant de Leon in his car tomorrow morning, out doing his job. How will you make this happen, Mr. Elton?"

Before I could respond, Arroyo filled in the blank himself.

"The answer is with money," he said. "A premium paid up front will ensure that the repair of Sergeant de Leon's car is the mechanic's first priority tomorrow morning. You may work out the details for reimbursement with your insurance company at your leisure."

I'd taken the precaution to sign up for extra insurance when I'd rented the car at the airport. A fat lot of good that was going to do me now.

But I had an alternative. "I will repair the Sergeant's car, myself."

"*You* will repair the car?"

"Yes."

"You are now an auto mechanic, Mr. Elton?"

"I told you that I repair machinery. An automobile is a machine. Make the Sergeant's car available to me tomorrow morning. I will make it mechanically sound again." I fervently hoped it was just a damaged radiator. "The dents and scratches can be dealt with later by the insurance company."

Commandant Arroyo thought for a moment and then asked in Spanish, "Did you understand all of this, Sergeant de Leon? Is this acceptable to you?"

"If my car is rapidly returned to service, then yes, Commandant," the Sergeant's voice came from just behind me.

"It appears then that we shall soon discover Mr. Elton's prowess with a wrench," Arroyo said.

"I will be back here first thing in the morning," I said over my shoulder in Spanish to Sergeant de Leon, "to start on the repair."

"No," Arroyo said. "You will remain as our guest tonight."

I swung my head back around. "You've no cause to do that," I unconsciously switched back to English. "I've done nothing wrong."

"I have not yet decided that," Arroyo said, in English. "Let me have your passport once again."

174

"Why? Nothing's changed, since the last time you saw it."

I received a sharp poke to the back of my shoulder, and looked up to see Sgt. de Leon glowering down at me. I handed over my passport. Arroyo drew back his center desk drawer, dropped the passport in, and closed the drawer.

"Hey!"

"I will keep your passport here in my desk along with that of Alicia Elton, until your stay here in Chihuahua is completed." Then, in Spanish, Arroyo ordered, "Corporal Valdez, take Mr. Elton to the City Jail. There will be no paperwork. Instruct the Desk Sergeant to keep him seated in the lobby, until Sergeant de Leon arrives for him in the morning."

A firm hand grasped my upper arm and lifted me out of the chair.

"Wait a minute. Jail?" I had to turn my head to protest, as I was removed from the Commandant's presence. "You can't do that. You have to follow the law too, you know."

I was still sputtering about my rights as a US citizen at Corporal Valdez's back, as his fellow officer manhandled me along the hallway, out the steel door, and into a circling descent down the Delegation's spiral staircase.

***

Except that it was now deserted, the lobby of the City Jail was an old familiar sight. My police escort roughly deposited me front row center, facing the long imposing counter.

"You will remain in this chair, until Sergeant de Leon arrives in the morning," Corporal Valdez outlined my sleeping arrangements in Spanish.

I still had a little fight left. "Am I under arrest?" I asked in Spanish.

"You are not," Valdez said.

"Then I may choose to leave."

"That you remain here as instructed, or that you again attempt to flee, who can say which would please the Commandant more?"

Cpl. Valdez left me with that little riddle to ponder, while he and his partner went up to the counter and spoke quietly to the nightshift Desk Sergeant. Shortly thereafter, the two investigative officers left.

The multiple rows of empty plastic chairs, repeatedly burnished by the backsides of the countless people-who-must-wait, gleamed under reduced, afterhours lighting. The debris from the day had been swept from the floor, and there was a faint odor of lemon-scented ammonia. The nightshift Desk Sergeant busied himself at the counter with some paperwork, ignoring me. At one point, he disappeared into the office behind him for a good ten minutes, before reappearing with a fresh cup of coffee.

I thought it was pretty sporting of Arroyo to give me a ten-minute head start, but I figured that heaping more suspicion onto Antonio was a better bet. And to advance toward that goal, I had to get Sergeant de Leon's car running again. So, I'd have to let my detention play out and wait for morning.

This wasn't the first time I'd been forced to pass the night lying across a row of plastic chairs. Years of traveling the industrialized world provided me with repeated opportunities to sleep in an airport boarding area, because of a cancelled flight. And the chairs at the Chihuahua City Jail were similarly bracketed together with no intervening armrests.

I took off my shirt, rolled it up, and laid it two seats away. I then slid down onto my shoulder, reaching with my free hand to adjust my rolled-up shirt into the least unpleasant position under my head. After bringing my feet up, I lay, knees bent, on my side across four, hard plastic seats. I closed my eyes and tried to console myself that, at least, I'd had the sense to shy away from a business deal that would have inevitably led to Cpl. Valdez discovering five suitcases full of God-knows-what, when he searched my hotel room.

I did manage to log some sleep time, but it wasn't uninterrupted slumber. Several times, during the night, various detainees were brought in by traffic and security policemen, had their paperwork processed by the Desk Sergeant, and were taken away through the door at the far end of the room. A few minutes later, the arresting officer would re-emerge through the door and return to the nightly fray. Each time this routine concluded, it took ever more rock-and-roll oldies replaying in my head to lull my brain back to unconsciousness.

***

The hand pushing on my shoulder belonged to Sergeant de Leon. Daylight beamed in through the tall, narrow windows. I sat up, achingly stiff from my night on the plastic chairs.

This morning, a freshly pressed dress shirt covered de Leon's burly torso. He had fifty pounds on me, but didn't carry the big belly of a man of his weight. I doubted he'd have to wrestle much with a perpetrator, before slamming him to the ground and cuffing him.

"I assume you slept well," De Leon spoke in Spanish, as he pressed a plastic-lidded paper cup of coffee into my hand.

I couldn't trust my voice just yet. I gingerly pried up the lid. The aroma was enticing, but it was the first, bitter sip of drive-thru coffee that fully woke me up. "Just give me a minute," my barely-moistened throat let me say, as I leaned back in the plastic chair. "Let me work up some blood pressure."

I took a full medicinal swallow of the fast-food version of morning brew. Thankfully, its signature scalding temperature had greatly diminished during de Leon's ride on whatever alternate means of transportation he'd had to arrange for that morning.

"It is time." De Leon's patience was apparently quick to find its limit. "You will attend to my car."

Despite its awful taste, I downed the rest of the coffee, put on my shirt, and stood. "Lead the way."

I buttoned and tucked my shirt, as I walked with Sergeant de Leon to a parking lot adjacent to the jail. The lot was enclosed with a high chain-link fence, topped with concertina wire, whose razor-edged coils of steel glistened in the morning sun. A gate guard, busily checking ID's and granting admission to the cars arriving for the day shift, waved us in through the pedestrian gate, after a cursory glance at the badge Sgt. de Leon held up.

De Leon led me along a row of parked vehicles to a car that had been left abandoned in front a corrugated-metal, utility shed. The driver's side of the car's front bumper was shoved in, jammed beneath the fender. Scrape marks from the impact, along with smeared paint in the color of a certain Ford Fiesta, marred its surface.

"This is my car. See what you have done to it," de Leon said.

The damage didn't look all that bad. The car wasn't new, maybe ten years old, but still, I figured, its bumper would be mounted on a pair of shock absorbers that would accommodate a minor hit. And I didn't think I'd smacked into it all that hard during my hasty getaway.

I dropped down on my hands and knees and looked up under the front end. The shock absorber's rod was shoved in. Hopefully, it was just stuck, not bent. I gave it a test pull, but it didn't budge.

I got back on my feet. "The bumper was designed to come right back out. It needs only a little extra persuasion."

Sgt. de Leon nodded, but looked doubtful. I hoped he wasn't fussy. I didn't want to buy him a new bumper just because of a few scratches.

De Leon opened the driver's door and popped the hood. "And the radiator?"

I undid the catch, raised the hood, and peered in. Plastic cowling and fan blades blocked my view of the radiator's cooling fins on the interior side, but the fan was positioned too far back to have made contact without a lot more front-end damage. I crouched down to view the exterior side through the grill, but again saw no damage. However, there was a shimmering greenish puddle on the concrete beneath the engine, and green beads of liquid still clung to the underside of the hood.

"I cannot tell where the damage is," I said. "Can you call a tow truck? We will have him bring water for the radiator, and then we can run the engine and find the rupture. We can also use one of his chains to pull the bumper back out."

When de Leon brought out his cell phone, it occurred to me to call Alicia and explain my disappearance. I slid my hand into my pocket and quickly discovered I had no phone. Maybe I left it back in the hotel, or it fell out of my pocket at the jail. I didn't know. But I decided Alicia was probably still sleeping off her margaritas anyway and went back to examining the cooling system of the car I'd smacked into.

When I moved around to the side, I saw a green stain where coolant had been leaking down the outside of the fan cowling. On looking closer, I noticed frayed strands of wire mesh poking out on the underside of the upper radiator hose. I reached in and felt the tear with my fingertips. I knew that this was not the result of my car hitting his bumper. The hose, deteriorating with age, had to have been dripping for quite some time. Its weak spot along the seam had finally burst, undoubtedly, from the overwhelming steam pressure generated by a combination of low coolant level and high engine exertion – such as when de Leon had floored the accelerator to catch my quickly departing rental car.

"The tow truck will be here soon." De Leon put his phone away.

"I think this tear in the hose is your only problem."

De Leon looked into the engine compartment, but merely shrugged. "You are the mechanic."

I wondered how long de Leon had known he'd been losing cooling system fluid. A few weeks? A month? How often had he just added more water, rather than spend the money and time to take it in for a repair?

Eventually, the tow truck lumbered through the open gate, the driver exchanging waves with the guard. I signaled the tow truck to park in front of de Leon's car. After the driver descended from the cab and the handshaking was completed, I turned to my task. I hooked a chain to an iron loop on the back of the truck, dragged the chain by the other hook over to de Leon's car, and attached it to a metal bracket behind the bumper on the stuck-in side. I then grabbed the two, plastic gallon jugs of water that the driver had brought and emptied them into the radiator. I had de Leon start the car, put it into reverse, and just let it drift back on its own in idle. When the chain jumped up tight, the bumper popped out and the drifting car halted.

The tow truck driver smiled and gave me a nod of approval. He even took care of the chain himself. I had de Leon shut off the engine, before the played-out radiator hose became too hot to handle. I borrowed a screwdriver and pliers from the tow truck driver and, with a little fight, successfully removed the torn hose.

De Leon told me that the Police Department would pay for the tow truck, but I would have to provide a generous tip for the driver. I negotiated a ride to the auto parts store to be included in the deal, so I didn't feel too heavily ripped off. De Leon later told me that the career of a tow truck driver is much more lucrative than that of a policeman.

**

181

In a taxi that I paid for, De Leon and I returned from the auto parts store to the fenced parking lot next to the City Jail. It didn't escape me that, had I not been forced to spend the night laying across pieces of plastic shaped for sitting, I would've had at my disposal the car that I'd gone to the expense of renting – not to mention that I was beginning to lose count of the number of times I'd arrived at the City Jail in a taxi.

Using a screwdriver and pair of pliers I'd bought along with the replacement parts, I set to work on de Leon's car. Within twenty minutes, the new hose was installed with new clamps and the system was topped off with fresh coolant.

"How do you know how to do this?" asked Sergeant de Leon, who, I noticed, had displayed a rather hands-off approach in assisting me.

"In America, mechanics are expensive. So, if you are young and have no money, you learn to fix the simple problems for yourself."

"In Mexico also, mechanics are expensive. So, with no money, if it is broken, it stays broken."

"I bow to your capacity to do without," I said.

"Each of us has his own idea of what is essential."

With his vehicle back in working order, Sgt. de Leon gave me a ride back to the Hotel Miramar. As we rode, de Leon said, "I will use the time your repairs have saved me to talk to Antonio Peron."

"How did you discover Antonio's last name so quickly?"

"Some of our investigative officers brought the members of the Restoration Project back to the Café Iguana, where they were questioned along with the other customers and staff. Antonio was there to pick up his Teresa when it came time for her to be questioned. He was not a witness, but his name was taken down, because we had spoken to him."

"When the investigative officer spoke to Antonio, did Antonio say that he was still at the Gato Negro when the shooting occurred?"

"I read over the notes last night. Concerning Antonio Peron, only his name, his place of employment, and that he came to the Café Iguana to pick up his girlfriend, after the shooting, were recorded. I will now go the sporting goods store, where he works, and talk to him."

I perked up at this. "The sporting goods store," I said. "Does it sell ammunition?"

"Aside from the government store in Mexico City, only a few select stores and gun clubs can sell ammunition in Mexico. But not even the Government can sell forty-five-caliber ammunition."

Despite knowing I should probably just let it go, I persisted, "But surely, on the Black Market—"

"If you were an investigative officer, Mr. Elton, you would understand that the murderer needed to know beforehand that the revolver in Villa's bedroom was functional and that Dr. Salazar would be present at Villa's Museum on that afternoon," de Leon said. "These are the considerations that a skilled professional would use to develop his list of potential suspects. Not who, in all of Mexico, had access to the illegal ammunition."

Sgt. de Leon swung his car into the loading zone in front of the Hotel Miramar.

After getting out, I leaned down and spoke through the open window. "Only one boyfriend, in all of Mexico, had both threatened to kill Salazar and lied about where he was at the time the killing took place. Does that rate a consideration for your suspect list?"

"I will find out where Antonio was and why he lied to the girl," de Leon said. "Thank you for repairing my car."

"It was my very great pleasure to be of assistance." I said this in English, because it wouldn't have sounded sarcastic in Spanish.

***

There was an empty chair outside our hotel room door. Inside there was a light scent of sandalwood. But this time, only the scent. I looked longingly at the soft, inviting bed. But instead of flopping down, grateful of the pillow, I showered, brushed my teeth, and put on some laundered clothes.

A knock on the door made me flinch at first, but opening the door revealed only a housekeeper and her cart of linens.

I stepped back and in Spanish said, "Please come in. I was just about to leave."

The housekeeper gave me a smile, as she came in, leaving her cart in the hall. Holding the stack of fresh towels against her light blue uniform, her eyes swept the room, stopping momentarily on the still-made, but rumpled, bed, before she continued on toward the bathroom. At the doorway to the bathroom, the housekeeper paused, turned toward me, and said in Spanish, "Please enjoy your stay in Chihuahua."

It was a nice way of saying "goodbye", especially in a voice that had a pleasing mellowness some women acquire in late middle age.

"Permit me to ask," I took advantage of the moment. "Is it the custom in this hotel for me to leave a tip each day or is a combined total at the end of my stay preferred?"

This time, her eyes did the smiling, as she said, "Either way is fine. We are always happy when guests from America stay here. Or perhaps from Canada?"

I stepped over to the desk and took an envelope and pen from the arrangement of hotel stationary next to the TV. After a glance at her name tag, I wrote "Violeta" on the envelope.

"I will put the total in here on the day we leave. The envelope will remind me."

The housekeeper took the fresh towels on into the bathroom, and I stood for a moment before leaving, trying to think of what I was forgetting. The housekeeper re-emerged with the used towels. On the way out to her cart, she detoured to pluck a bath towel, hanging from the back of the desk chair.

Making a fuss about adding the towel to the bunch and keeping her eyes on her work, she said, "There is a grand gossip among the housekeepers that there was a policeman guarding your room all last night."

I supposed that if she could find out anything more, she would score a substantial triumph among the other housekeepers.

I chose my words carefully, not the least because the door to the hallway was still open. "The police requested that I go with them to give a statement concerning a traffic accident involving a patrol car. They left a man here in case a statement from Mrs. Elton was also needed. In the end, it all turned out to be nothing."

The housekeeper brought her load of towels out to the hallway, dumped them into a bag on her cart, reentered, and went straight into the bathroom again, effectively cutting off further discussion. Apparently, my answer fell short of the threshold for scandal.

Having won my way clear of my hotel room, I was riding down in the elevator when I finally remembered what I'd forgotten – or rather, forgotten again. My cell phone was still on the charger, next to the TV. But I wasn't about to go back for it and risk rekindling the housekeeper's inquisitiveness. At least, I'd had the wit to slip the screwdriver and pliers into my back pocket, before I left, being mindful not to leave non-tourist related items lying around to further stoke the fires of speculation.

Down at the front desk, I requested that my rental car be brought from the off-site lot and was informed that Alicia had already taken it. I took a deep breath, let it out slowly, and had the desk clerk call for a taxi.

***

When I entered the central patio at the Palacio de Gobierno, I spotted Alicia raised high up to the upper areas of a mural on the platform lift. She appeared rather overdressed for restoration work, wearing a trim black skirt and jacket with the black high heels she'd worn the night before. Far below her, a large herd of gray-haired tourists was moving along the continuum of wall art. Those of the group strolling nearest the murals found themselves stymied by the obstruction of the platform lift and eddied in confusion at its base. Unconcerned with the plight of their obstructed fellows, the rest of the meandering oldies flowed past the lift, drawn onward by the sound of the tour guide's ever-retreating monotone.

I waded in through the tourists, and in only as loud a voice as I thought was necessary to reach her, I called, "Alicia."

Fiery eyes blazed down from on high. "Francis," Alicia's voice was hushed, but stern. "Get me down." She picked up the push button pendant by its cord and shook it at me. "This stupid thing is broken again."

I scanned down the length of the cord to locate the control box. I reached to my back pocket for the screwdriver, and immediately realized that I'd unwittingly left the screwdriver and pliers on the seat of the taxi. The lack of a good night's sleep was kicking my memory's butt.

I dug out my Swiss Army knife. The flat-ended blade with the bottle opener notch on the side wasn't as comfortable to use as a regular screwdriver, but, at least, I had a version of the requisite tool at hand. I pivoted the appropriate blade out, knelt down, and set to work.

The temporarily stymied members of the elderly tourist group had, by this time, mostly rejoined the herd at its tail end, but a few remained to watch me remove the screws, as though I were one of the attractions on view.

Once I had the cover off, I was confronted, as I expected, with two motor control relays, one for up and one for down. Of course, they were not labeled as such. So, since it was a blind choice, I simply picked one and used the knife's flat blade to give its core a momentary test push into the coil. When the relay contacts came together, the platform lift jerked upward.

"Francis!" This came as a loud bark from above.

The lingering onlookers, frightened by the sudden lift movement and Alicia's shout, scurried away.

I manually closed the contacts on the other relay. This time the platform descended, the four threaded rods rotating slowly, bringing Alicia back down to earth.

Alicia opened the little gate on the platform railing and negotiated the two steps to the floor with as much dignity as her heels and skirt would allow.

Then she lit into me. "What were you trying to freaking do, squash me on the ceiling?"

"Please. No thanks are necessary."

Alicia's simple white blouse beneath her jacket held an ornate silver broach, pinned in place over the top button. I recognized the broach; it had belonged to her grandmother. Alicia's makeup was reserved, her hair tied back, and her eyes moist.

"Oh, Dr. Salazar's funeral is today." I, at last, put it together. "And you're missing it, stuck up there on the platform. That's why you were crying. Alicia, I'm sorry. I got tied up with the police. But maybe, if I drive you over there right now, you can catch the last part of—"

"That's not why I was crying. And I wasn't *crying*, damn you." The moist eyes dared me to contradict her. "I was going to go to the funeral, but I got up late with a hangover. And *you* had disappeared. I called your cell phone and heard it vibrating two feet away from me, next to the TV. So, I don't want to hear any whining that I stole your car."

"Maybe there's still time—"

"And maybe I know where the damn funeral is being held." Alicia looked away for a moment, regained control, and then recounted, "Before I left, I tried calling both Carlos and Teresa, but apparently, they'd already turned their phones off for the service. On a guess, I drove over to the Cathedral, but nothing was going on there. Then I came over here, hoping Carlos might still be waiting for me. But he wasn't. So I'm standing around, not knowing what to do, and I look up and see a chip had fallen out on this mural, showing a little triangle of white. So I put a little burnt umber on a brush, and I take the lift up. And the buttons worked fine. I cover up the white patch for the time being, and push the 'down' button, and nothing. I push it again and again. But I'm stuck up there. So I'm going out of my mind, I can't get down, and all these geriatrics are milling around under me, and they're useless, and as usual, *you're* not around, and I'm going to prison for murder, and I didn't kill anybody, and every time I work my ass off for something I really want, everything freaking blows up in my face."

Tears welled up in Alicia's eyes again. I started to embrace her. But she forcefully shoved me away.

"Don't you try to hug me. Where were you this morning?"

"Some State Police officers came and carted me away last night, about five minutes after we got back to the room. You were asleep."

"What did the police want?"

"The car I backed into when we left the Gato Negro, it was a policeman's car. A plainclothes officer, who was following us. The police held me all night."

"Who had my blouse open? You or the police?"

"Uh, that was me."

Alicia turned and swiftly crossed the patio, each step an angry report off the hard tile floor. The door to the Project's office slammed closed behind her.

The nice thing about getting a cat down from a tree is that it only scratches you.

***

The elderly tourists, shepherded by their tour guide, began their exodus from the Palacio de Gobierno, heading for their waiting bus and, I supposed, the promise of a box lunch.

I turned my attention to Eduardo's automated lift. The pendent with its 'up' and 'down' buttons lay on the floor of the platform, where Alicia had thrown it. I could see that its cord had been pulled out from the pendant's compression fitting by about an inch, exposing four, colored wires, extending beyond where the sheathing ended. I unplugged the power cord from the wall and set about removing the screws from the pendant's cover. With the cover off, I wasn't surprised to discover a wire had been jerked free from its terminal screw.

In the aftermath of Alicia's spike in temperament, it was relaxing just to mindlessly perform the simple repair. I almost regretted how little time it took.

With power restored, I had the pendant in my hand and was about to give it a test when, close behind me, a voice demanded, "What are you doing?"

In my head, I leaped in the air, but in reality, I just took a quick step away. Turning back, I saw Alicia standing with her hands on her hips. And as my heart rate settled back down, I summoned up a normal voice. "I fixed your damned pendant. And don't sneak up on a guy like that."

"I forgot I was wearing stealth heels. What broke on the pendant?"

"The cord must have caught on something. Pulled a wire off its connection."

Alicia relaxed her stance. "It's gotten caught on things, a few times before. Eduardo always takes care of it, but he hasn't shown up much lately. Sorry I was such a bitch."

An apology from Alicia was so rare it took me a moment to respond.

"I can understand your being mad at me for going for the score last night," I said. "When you were vulnerable."

Alicia crossed her arms under her chest and looked down at the tiles, as she spoke. "Well, when we were dancing, I was feeling all...I mean, we did have an awful lot to drink, and I guess...Well, I remember kind of mauling you. So..." Alicia lifted her chin, and her grandmother's broach flashed, as it caught the light. "So I wasn't acting like a lady. And so, I accept that it was half my fault. But apparently, the police barged in and saved my honor anyway." Her green eyes looked straight into mine. "So, no harm done."

I sensed that we'd just made up. But I was wary. I knew that anything I might say now could be used against me later. I played for safety.

191

I pushed the 'up' button on the pendant. The platform obediently rose up. I tested the 'down' button, and the platform dutifully lowered back down.

"There you go," I said. "Back in business."

"Yes, so much easier to discuss machinery."

"I thought we were done."

Alicia took the pendant away from me. "Eduardo was supposed to have converted this to a remote control." She tossed the pendant onto the platform floor. "He found what he needed on the Internet from a company that sells remotes for model trains. I put it on the Project's credit card. I don't know if it ever came or not."

"If it did, looks like he didn't get around to installing it."

"He spends more time now at the Salazar Ranch than ever. I practically never see him around here. I'm not sure what to do about him."

"He's a little too chummy with the police for my taste," I said.

"Well, if they've recruited him to spy on me, they're not getting much for their money."

"My stomach's growling. Feel like some lunch?"

"It's not even close to two yet."

"It's past noon, and I'm way past hungry. We can eat with the tourists."

"Okay, but no booze. I'm still in recovery. Give me a minute to lock up.

***

At the restaurant, we had the dining room all to ourselves. The waitress brought us our club soda and iced tea. She told us it would be a while for the food.

192

"I thought we were going to a restaurant that catered to tourists," I complained.

"Look how I'm dressed," Alicia said. "I can't sit with people off a tour bus. Anyway, I like this place. The food isn't greasy."

I took a sip of iced tea and wished I'd ordered beer. "Some good came from my being abducted by the police in the middle of the night. This morning Sergeant de Leon went off to ask Antonio where he really was, at the time Dr. Salazar was shot."

"How'd you pull that off?"

"I'm not sure," I said. "Especially since De Leon didn't really seem to consider Antonio a viable suspect."

"As long as they're busy doing something other than hauling me off to jail, I'm good with it."

The waitress poked her head out from behind the door to the kitchen, perhaps to reassure herself that it was still just the two of us sitting there, and withdrew again.

"You look like you need a nap," Alicia said. "And while you do, I'm going to change my clothes and go out shopping for underwear. I've been feeling a little too free and easy lately."

"What are you using for money? I thought you didn't get your purse back."

"I do get a paycheck, you know. And since I handle the accounting for the Project, the woman at the bank knows me, and she cashes my check without asking for I.D. And we talk for a while, if they're not busy. I think mostly so she can practice her English."

"You handle the accounting? What did Salazar do all day?"

"Originally, Dr. Salazar handled all that, as part of overseeing the project. But there was an audit by the State Historical Society, a couple of months ago, and it turns out Dr. Salazar had some explaining to do. He claimed that the double entry system had somehow gotten away from him." Alicia raised an eyebrow for a moment. "But I guess the Historical Society didn't want to halt the Project halfway through. So they swallowed hard, but they made Dr. Salazar relinquish control of the money. So that's how I became the responsible adult."

"Stealing museum exhibits, smuggling, and now embezzlement. Where does it end?"

"Evidently, with a bullet to the forehead."

***

I'd switched from iced tea to beer when our food, at long last, found its way out of the restaurant's kitchen. After lunch, the combined effects of alcohol, food buzz, and sleep deprivation signaled in my brain that it was siesta time. Back in our room at the Miramar, I flopped down on the bed and was asleep, before Alicia left for her shopping.

Hours later, Alicia woke me by bursting noisily into our hotel room with a riot of colorful shopping bags, which she dumped in a clutter next to me on the bed. I sat up and was rewarded with the first hammer of a headache.

I held my forehead. "You left some stuff for other people to buy, didn't you?"

"I've been out having girl fun. It's like slamming a shot of estrogen."

"No problem with the language?"

194

"Oh, the clerks and I stumble through it. They know that at some point I'll need to know 'how much.' They either write it on a piece of paper or tap the numbers on a pocket calculator. Then I pay. It's simple."

I stood, and my headache began to pound in earnest.

"Is there any aspirin?"

"Now you turn your back, while I put my new undergarments away." Alicia was full of herself. "No, wait. Look at this." Alicia pulled some shimmering red material out of a bag and held it to her body. "It's a silk chemise. Isn't it pretty? One of the shop girls said 'naughty, naughty' in English, when she showed me this. All the other shop girls laughed and shoved each other." Alicia looked directly at me. "This is for the night you tell me the police have arrested Dr. Salazar's murderer, and I can stay on as Director and finish restoring the murals."

I pushed through my headache, searching for something reassuring to say to this. Finally, I offered, "Maybe that State Police Sergeant's talk with Antonio will lead to something."

It was every bit as lame as telling her to hope for the best. But what else was there?

Alicia turned away and stepped over to the dresser. She pulled open the top drawer, carefully folded the red silk chemise within it, and slid the drawer firmly closed. Then she picked up a brush from the top of the dresser and started in with long strokes, not looking at me, but with her jaw set.

Nothing I could say now would fix it. So, I bailed.

195

"I'm going out to find some aspirin," I said. "Let you have some space. To deal with your new stuff, I mean."

***

Out on the sidewalk in front of the Hotel Miramar, the afternoon sun cast long, crisp shadows. As I embarked on a walk to a nearby pharmacy, I noticed two men standing on either side of a car parked a little way up the street. They leaned with forearms on opposite roof edges, smoking cigarettes and talking across the top of the car. I recognized both of them.

Sergeant de Leon stepped back from the passenger side of the car, as I approached. The other man – the officer who'd gripped my arm and led me away from the threshold of passion the previous night – slid into the driver's seat and drove off.

De Leon waited on the sidewalk, standing directly in my path, as I approached him.

"Sergeant."

"Mister Elton."

"Do we shake hands? I'm unfamiliar with the art of surveillance," I said in English.

"In this circumstance, no," de Leon responded in his heavily accented English.

I switched to Spanish. "Did you get a chance to look into Antonio's alibi?"

"It will sadden you to know," de Leon replied in Spanish, "that Antonio can prove that he was nowhere near Villa's Museum, at the time that the murder took place."

"But Antonio was not at the Gato Negro, as he told Teresa. I talked with the bartender—"

"Antonio visited a former girlfriend who works at Los Artesanos, a handicraft store. Naturally, Antonio could not tell this to his present girlfriend, Teresa. However, the former girlfriend and two other clerks at the store all confirm that Antonio was there and had received a call on his cell phone. After he finished the call, Antonio told them that Teresa's employer had been killed. Then he left to go for Teresa and take her home."

"I suppose that means that Alicia is back to being your number one suspect."

"She never stopped being our number one suspect. But I am sure that Commandant Arroyo appreciates your suggestion that we test the alibi of Antonio Peron. The Prosecuting Attorney required that we pursue a more thorough investigation into Dr. Salazar's murder, before concluding that your wife did it. To be frank, we could think of nothing further to pursue. That is, until you provided us with an alternate suspect – one just plausible enough to justify further investigation, and then to be easily eliminated."

Having just scored a goal for the opposing team, a headache was now the least of my worries. I needed to just stop, smoke a soothing cigar, and take stock of the situation.

"Sergeant, can you point me to the nearest store where I can buy a good cigar?"

"There is a tobacco shop on a street further down the hill." De Leon pointed in the opposite direction of my intended route to the pharmacy.

"Is it easy to find?"

A car pulled to the curb near us. The man behind the wheel was the officer who had been assigned to sit outside our hotel room the night before.

"Ah, very good," de Leon said. "The afternoon watch. This frees me to walk with you. It is not far."

As De Leon and I set off on our downhill walk, I asked, "Is your car still running well?"

"It is with pleasure that I drive without fear that the engine will boil over."

"Since last night, you mean. Since our accident."

"Yes," de Leon said. "Yes, of course, since the accident."

After two blocks, we rounded a corner, and I spotted the tobacco shop sign, half a block up ahead.

"I'm looking to buy a Cuban cigar," I said. "I paid a lot of money for one when I was in Spain. It burned well, but I expected the flavor to be great, not merely okay. But it would not be fair to judge all Cubans by a single cigar. I intended to give them a second chance, while I am here."

"And you will again pay a premium for the myth," de Leon said. "You desire the Cuban, only because it is prohibited in your country. We will find you a fine Mexican cigar."

We entered the shop. After a brief perusal through the glass window of a large humidor, I bought six Mexican panatelas for the price of one Cuban robusto. I laid out the equivalent of about twenty dollars for the cigars. The matches were complimentary.

Emerging from the tobacco shop, I trimmed the ends off two cigars with the scissors of my Swiss Army knife and handed one to de Leon. We lit up.

To my unexpected satisfaction, the wrapper leaf was just slightly oily to the touch, and the warm smoke smelled and tasted deliciously sweet and spicy.

"I commend you on your advice." I blew out a white cloud.

"Yes, this is most excellent." De Leon gazed at the even burn for a moment. "Ordinarily, I would not accept such a small bribe."

For the first time, I saw the State Police Sergeant smile, even if only briefly.

"Then I must be careful not to ask for a large favor in return," I said.

There was a second brief smile, before de Leon said, "There is sadness in my little joke. For the traffic and security police the pay is very low. So, taking the little cut to ignore a minor offense became, over time, an accepted tradition."

We turned the corner and started the uphill climb.

"For the State and Federal Police, it is different," de Leon went on. "We investigate major crime and are paid as professionals." De Leon took another draw on his cigar and blew out the smoke. "Of course, for some, it is never enough."

"You couldn't pay me enough to be a policeman," I said. "Not even if I were made a Commandant."

"For Commandant Arroyo, money is not a consideration. He is a wealthy man. His family owns several large cattle ranches in Texas. He attended university there. And he personally owns a gentleman's ranch here, outside the city. With such wealth, he is incorruptible, even for the drug lords. And this only adds to his power. Commandant Arroyo is either much respected or much feared. He has no preference."

"I think I saw that last night," I said. "He must have many enemies."

"Naturally so. But he is vigilant. And he has allies."

"Allies like you?" I asked through a puff of smoke.

"I am one of a few. I must be vigilant also."

We continued uphill in silence for a few more puffs.

With Antonio officially cleared of any suspicion, and thus having made matters even worse for Alicia, I grasped at my only other straw. "The Federal Bureau of Investigation believes that Salazar's murder was arranged by a corrupt antiquities dealer up in Chicago, who—"

"The murder of Dr. Salazar took place here in Chihuahua. It is a matter for the Chihuahua State Ministerial Police."

"Then Arroyo is not willing to listen to the FBI either?"

"Your FBI presented us with their hired-gunman theory, but they have not presented us with one fact that we can verify. Even the little story that you brought to us – the girlfriend, Teresa, and her suspicions of the boyfriend, Antonio – was superior in that respect." De Leon held the last of his cigar by its band, as he took a final puff. When the smoke cleared, he said, "Therefore, all verifiable facts still point directly to Alicia Elton, as the murderess."

We were back at the front doors of the Hotel Miramar, back to our starting point. Our shared cigars were becoming too hot to hold.

"Tell me," I said. "How much time do I have to prove you wrong?"

"Who can say? If the FBI can deliver some verifiable evidence to support their theory, the time will lengthen. If we gather more incriminating evidence against your wife, the time will be cut short. But I can tell you this. The influence of Consular Agent Woodstead in this matter is steadily being consumed. And before it burns his fingers, he will have to let it go."

Sergeant de Leon let his cigar remnant fall to the sidewalk, to be crushed under the State Ministerial Policeman's shoe.

Chapter 11

As I entered our hotel room, I caught a glimpse of red silk, just before Alicia closed the top dresser drawer, picked up her hairbrush, and returned to tending her long tresses.

As I closed the door, Alicia turned from her reflection in the dresser's mirror and looked me over, tilting her head theatrically from side to side.

"Drugstore out of aspirin?"

"I bumped into Sergeant de Leon." I propped myself against the desk to give my legs a rest from their uphill exertions. "He found out that Antonio has a solid alibi for the time of the murder."

"So it was the bartender who lied?"

"No, Antonio lied to Teresa, all right. But he was actually at a handicrafts store, chatting up an old girlfriend, not gunning down an old art professor. Two other clerks back that up."

"Great, I'm still in the soup, and I can't even reassure Teresa about her boyfriend, without ratting him out."

Alicia took her hairbrush with her, as she stepped away from the dresser. She sat on the edge of the bed, just holding the brush and staring ahead.

When I dropped down next to her, Alicia said, "You smell like my apartment building after the fire."

"I smoked a lovely Mexican cigar."

"How nice. Now go stand over there," she pointed with her brush, "so I can breathe."

I went to the window, lifted the lower pane, and remained there in exile.

"Now that Antonio is out of the picture," I said, "maintaining Woodstead's support is more crucial than ever. And to do that I have to supply him with some sort of report to pass on to the FBI."

"Like what?"

"They seem keen on finding out who smuggled Dr. Salazar's stolen antiquities out of Mexico. Maybe it'd help if you can think of any strangers you saw Salazar talking to."

Alicia gazed at her hairbrush for a few moments, before looking up. "There was that guy who gave me the creeps that sometimes came into the lounge at the Vista Suites."

"Home of the 'pompous little popinjay'?"

"Well, it's a pretty nice place really. Very upscale. And they have this Social Club Building with a classy lounge, and there's a swimming pool just outside, overlooking the city."

"But it's open to anybody?"

"They serve free breakfast in the morning, just for guests staying at the motel. But in the late afternoon and evening, it becomes a lounge where you can entertain friends or business acquaintances that aren't necessarily staying there. Like on Fridays, Dr. Salazar and I began going to the lounge for 'happy hour' to discuss the progress of the Project. Pretty quickly, it became like our Friday after-work routine."

"What about the creepy guy?"

"Oh, him. Well, most times we'd get to the Vista Suites around five thirty, and I'd dash over to my room to freshen up a little and change out of my work clothes. When I got over to the Social Club, sometimes Dr. Salazar would be at the bar talking to this hunched-over guy who always needed a shave and whose wardrobe consisted entirely of faded-wallpaper shirts and khakis. But as soon as I showed up, Dr. Salazar would give the guy a pat on the shoulder and come and lead me over to a table."

"So, the creepy guy always got there ahead of you."

"Not always. Sometimes, the creepy guy would come in after we got there and just go up to the bar. And the next time Dr. Salazar found he had to visit the men's room, on his way back, he'd stop and talk for a little while with the creepy guy, before coming back to the table."

"Was the creepy guy American or Mexican?"

"Definitely not Mexican. My guess is American. But I never heard his voice."

"Ever ask Salazar who he was?"

"He just said he was a guy he knew. Nothing more," Alicia said. "But what creeped me out were those whiskey eyes, looking at me like he wanted something. Something nasty. I got a little shiver right now, just talking about it."

I thought for a moment. "So where was Eduardo? Didn't he drive you and Salazar over there in the Rover? Especially, to go drinking."

"No, for the Friday 'happy hour' jaunt, Dr. Salazar always drove the Rover himself. It pissed off Eduardo to no end. He's pretty possessive about the Rover. Dr. Salazar would knock off about three on Fridays and take the Rover to run his errands, then he'd swing by the

Palacio and pick me up around five, and off we'd go to the Vista Suites. It saved me a taxi fare one day a week, and he paid for the drinks. Who could holler?"

"And the creepy guy always turned up every Friday?"

"Oh, no. Just sporadically. I couldn't stand it otherwise." Alicia started to brush her hair, but then stopped in mid-stroke. "You don't suppose the sporadic meetings coincided with Salazar's pocketing something from some museum earlier in the week?"

"Damn, I hate it when you do that."

"Get ahead of you? It's not that hard."

"Okay, let's just run with it for a minute," I said. "Salazar establishes a Friday-after-work-drinks routine with you at the Vista Suites. In fact, it becomes so normal that, if you miss a Friday, people ask where you were, the next time they see you."

"We missed one Friday, because of the meeting with the Historical Society after the audit that I told you about. And the only other Friday we missed was when Dr. Salazar was out of town. But I showed up anyway. Until all this happened, I really didn't have much else to do at night, except go to the lounge and talk to the other regulars."

"And Salazar talked to other people too when he went there, didn't he? Not just the creepy guy?"

"True enough. The creepy guy was just one of the people Dr. Salazar would stop and talk with." Alicia perked up. "Oh, so you're thinking this is what makes the Vista Suites such an excellent place to meet up with a smuggler. Dr. Salazar talks with lots of people, so nobody thinks anything about it when he talks to the creepy guy, too."

"Yeah, I was getting there," I said, a little annoyed at being bested again. But now I was thinking about the exchange. Hard cash and stolen antiquities changing hands couldn't happen in the open. "Did the creepy guy always leave before you and Salazar did?"

"Always before I left, anyway," Alicia said, "because after Dr. Salazar headed home, I'd stay on at the Social Club and talk with a woman there I'm friends with. But now you mention it, the creepy guy always left a little while after he'd talked to Dr. Salazar. Like another shot of whiskey and off he'd go."

"Okay, good. So, let's figure that when Salazar stole a museum piece, he merely had to green light the smuggler. It could be any pre-arranged signal that was meaningless on the face of it. The time and place were always the same. And he'd use his established habit of slipping out early on Fridays to run errands as cover for when he needed to retrieve the stolen booty from some hidey-hole and stow it in the Rover. Then just like normal, he'd pick you up at five and drive you to the Vista Suites. And to the regulars at the lounge, it looked like you were bringing Salazar to the lounge as your guest, not Salazar intentionally going there to hook up with a smuggler."

"And after their little business meeting," Alicia jumped in, "the smuggler would leave the money in the Rover and transfer the stolen object to his own car. That's why he had to leave first."

"I was about to say that."

"And before you ask, yes, Dr. Salazar always locked the Rover when we got to the Social Club," Alicia raced on. "So that means the creepy guy has a valet key to the Rover. And if the FBI finds the key in his pocket, then they have their smuggler." She'd ended with a bright smile on her face, but quickly dropped it. "Sorry. I did it again."

"No, that's all right. You knew Salazar always locked the Rover. I didn't."

But I really hadn't thought of the key business at all. And admittedly, it did sting a little.

"So maybe we figured some things out," Alicia said, "but you think it's enough for Woodstead? I mean it's just us talking. And when you get right down to it, so what if Dr. Salazar occasionally spoke to some lowlife on Fridays?"

It was my turn for a flash of insight – at last. Because the thing was, I didn't have to prove any of this. My deal with Woodstead was just to gather some tidbits to pass on to the FBI. And now I knew where to get them. But I needed Alicia to go with me. And that would take a bit of finesse.

"You know," I began, "*today* is Friday."

"You can't be serious. The Vista Suites? Those bastards threw me out. You want me to go back there?"

"Just to the Social Club part. I need something verifiable to give to Woodstead. You said so yourself."

"But they humiliated me."

"Did they? I thought you put them right in their place and walked out with considerable dignity. That was my take."

Alicia considered for a moment. "Well yes, I suppose I did."

"And you can go back to the Social Club and talk to your friends any damn time you want."

"You're damn right I can." Alicia stood up from the bed. "Just give me a minute to touch up."

It took more than a minute. While I brushed my teeth and put on a fresh shirt to dampen the odor of cigar smoke, Alicia changed back into the skirted business suit that she'd intended to wear to the funeral. The blouse she chose was not the snow white one she'd had on earlier, but a cream-colored silk one, left unbuttoned far enough to reveal a turquoise and gold, Aztec-style pendant laying on a field of smooth, pale skin.

At the desk, Alicia loaded an assortment of makeup containers, a few tissues, a comb, and her cell phone into a small handbag that matched her black high heels. I supposed the handbag was another of her shopping spree acquisitions.

I pulled on my sport jacket, so I'd look more like part of the set, and hustled to keep up with Alicia on our way to the elevator.

***

The Motel Vista Suites, perched high up the north slope of the river valley, was coming up fast on our right. Alicia said that it'd be easy to sidestep the management in the main building and proceed directly to the Social Club. As soon as my tires rolled onto the paving bricks that circled the central fountain, Alicia pointed to an opening between the main building and a high wall. The opening, from my prospective, looked like the edge of the earth, but I drove forward on blind

208

faith, and abruptly the little Fiesta plunged down a steep, single lane of stone pavers leading to a lower parking area. I kept my foot mashed on the brake pedal, and the ABS system kicked back furiously all the way down and was still spanking the bottom of my foot, as I wheeled, nose first, into a parking space, bumping to a stop when the tires encountered the curb. I had to sit for a minute, before getting out of the car and joining Alicia on the sidewalk, where she waited with that superior smile of someone who'd been on the thrill ride before.

Inside the Social Club's lounge, a cathedral ceiling studded with skylights loomed above an expanse of white floor tiles, where polished wood tables and chairs shared floor space with plush, white leather couches. Through a wall of glass sliding panels on the far side was a view of the swimming pool, beyond which was endless blue sky, presumably with the central city somewhere below. The lounge was heavily peopled, the chatter level high.

A middle-aged woman, tending toward the heavy cruiser class and bristling a shock of red-dyed hair topside, hailed us with a waving hand. Holding a pink cocktail relatively steady in the grip of her other hand, she came steaming toward us, heedless of the shoals. People grabbed for their drinks, as she jostled chair backs and table edges in her determined passage.

"Girlfriend, where you been?" The alarming woman bear-hugged Alicia, sloshing a good bit of pink cargo over the side. "Lord, but I missed my Honey Pot."

"Oh, Marybeth, I missed you too," Alicia said, when she was set free. "Sorry I've neglected you. It's a long story."

"Well then, you'll just have to tell Marybeth every little thing." The woman moved her focus to me. "And who's this? Darling girl, you traded the old one in on a new model."

"Well, he's used, but he's only had one owner."

"Anyone I might know?"

"Francis is my ex," Alicia said. "I told you it's a long story."

"Honey Pot, you are just *full* of astonishments. Let's get you a drink."

Marybeth took a moment to scan me, head to toe and back, with a critical eye, before we threaded our way, single file, through the tables and chairs toward a long bar, lined with high swivel chairs. We reassembled at one end of the bar, and as I assisted the ladies up on their perches, Marybeth reopened the topic. "So this one is Francis, and he's from before."

"He comes in later, after things had already gotten crazy." Alicia turned her back to me and leaned in toward Marybeth.

I ordered some drinks, while the two women kept their heads close together and their voices low. When the bartender moved off to fill our drink order, I surveyed the lounge's generally upscale clientele, looking for Dr. Salazar's smuggler, a.k.a. the creepy guy. I spotted what had to be him about half the length of the bar away from us. The bleached-out shirt was in keeping with his mop of unruly hair, chin stubble, and moist, reddened eyes. The bartender paused in preparing our drink order to refill the creepy guy's shot glass with amber liquid – apparently, without needing to inquire. The awful eyes that Alicia had described swung in my direction, and I turned away. Sensing that his eyes remained on me, I stared at the row of liquor bottles on the back wall of the bar and wondered what to do next. I really hadn't thought this through. Step one was 'find the guy'. Step two probably involved something more than sitting half a bar length away and avoiding eye contact.

I heard Alicia say to Marybeth, "Excuse me a minute. I have to go to the ladies' room."

I stole a glance at the creepy guy. He downed his fresh shot and stared ahead at nothing. I caught Alicia's arm, as she slid off her stool. "Is that the guy Dr. Salazar always talked to? The faded shirt half way down the bar?"

Alicia looked. "Yes, that's him. Now turn me loose."

Alicia made her way through the tables of afternoon drinkers toward the entrance, where the restrooms were located. The whiskey eyes now followed her journey.

I turned to Marybeth and found myself face to face with her.

"Okay, Francis from the past, what's your story?"

"My story?"

"Why you're here. Alicia and I been close as two peas, ever since we met. She never once mentioned *you*."

"Didn't she tell you? She called me to come help her, because the local police think she shot Dr. Salazar. Mistakenly think."

"And you just come right down here. Her ex."

"I'll help her out of a jam, if I can, if she asks."

"*My* ex wouldn't tend to me if I was snake bit."

"I guess some exes are willing to help out and some aren't." I meant it to sound philosophical, rather than noble.

"Uh huh. I'd say that's mighty accommodating of you. And now I'm wondering what it is that this Yankee boy wants. I bet pretty Miss Alicia knows. I bet she's got it dangling right out in front of Mr. Francis the Ex. Just out of his reach."

Marybeth watched my face, while I sorted through several responses and rejected each in turn.

I finally opted to move the conversation the hell off me. "Can I ask what brought *you* down here? You sound like you're from Texas."

"I sure am." Impossibly, Marybeth perked up even further at the mention of her State. "And if you care to know, I come down here, because my factory shuttered itself closed and sent all the jobs down here to Mexico."

I slid over onto the seat Alicia had left empty to ask with less volume, "You're working for Mexican wages?"

"Oh, shoot no. God Almighty, I'd starve to death. But it's sort of comical. See, us girls up in Fort Worth are making up the wiring harnesses for the jet planes. Well, the stockholders, they're making money, but it ain't never enough for them boys. You know that. So they button up our factory and run us off and move the harness making down to Chihuahua, so as the Mexican girls can do it just about for free. Well, it's a right nice plan, but they forgot one thing. Ain't nobody, Mexican or otherwise, ever been born with the know-how to make up a jet plane's wiring harness. And with your jet planes, some things are awful important. Oh, they send the supervisors down here, but them boys, they don't know nothing about the part where you use your hands – which I guess was right shocking news to the stockholders. So, my old company comes and asks, won't some of us Texas girls go down and show them Mexican girls how it's done? And here's the comical part. They're paying us more money to show the Mexican girls how to wire up the harnesses, than they used to pay us to wire them up our own selves. And on top of that, we're staying for free in this deluxe motel, and the stockholders are buying all our food and liquor. It's downright comical, ain't it?"

"What's comical?" Alicia rejoined us.

"The law of unintended consequences," I said.

"Not when you're living it." Alicia climbed onto the high swivel seat that I'd left vacant. She then observed, "Francis, Marybeth's glass is empty."

"Generally," I said, "I'd let the stockholders refill it, but this one's on me."

Marybeth slugged my shoulder. "Shoot, he's funny. Honey Pot, you brought us a funny one."

"He's a scream all right."

Waving her hand, Marybeth caught the bartender's attention. "Nicky, the funny one wants to set us up again."

"Francis," Alicia leaned against my arm, "that creepy guy's staring at me. Why don't you go punch him in the nose. Or at least, go talk to him. That's what we came here for, isn't it?"

"Who we talking about, darling?" Marybeth asked.

"That creepy guy in the faded shirt down the bar," Alicia said.

"Oh, him. Nicky says his name is Butch, but I can't believe somebody's mama would actually name her baby 'Butch'." Marybeth leaned across me toward Alicia, supporting herself with one hand on the bar surface, the other gripping my shoulder. "One time he's in here," she kept her voice low, "and Nicky comes to me and says that a gentleman named Señor Butch wants to buy me a drink. Well, I look down the bar at him. And I'm gonna own up, I been down here a long time without once being asked to the dance. But he don't look right to me at all. So I tell Nicky, 'Take this drink back and keep that liquor-sotted mis-creation away from *me*'."

Her account concluded, Marybeth shifted her weight back onto her seat, much to my relief.

"Well, Francis, what are you going to tell Woodstead?" Alicia asked. "That his name is Butch, and he has an eye for the ladies? Seems a bit thin, doesn't it? Now go strike up a conversation, while Marybeth and I catch up."

Reluctantly – because I had no idea what to say to him – I carried my drink down the bar toward the faded-patterned shirt. But in my mind, I was already building a case against him. Assuming he smuggled the substitute Colt revolver into Mexico for Salazar, there's no reason he couldn't have brought along some forty-five-caliber cartridges, too. And by the looks of him, I didn't think murder-for-hire would present him with any sort of moral quandary.

I set my drink on the open space left by other bar patrons, who chose to allow the creepy guy a wide berth. But I remained standing – to better facilitate a hasty retreat.

"Hi, you're Butch, right?"

His head turned slowly. "Who're you?"

"Oh, I'm with—"

"I *know* who you're *with*," his slurred baritone scolded, "what I *asked* was who you *are*."

It took me a few seconds to recover from his breath. Still a little dazed, I blurted, "I'm Francis Elton." I damned myself for not substituting a phony name, but pressed on. "I'm part of the group working on restoring the murals at the Palacio de Gobierno."

Butch tossed back another double shot of liquor.

"Where's Salazar?"

This didn't sound like a question Dr. Salazar's killer would be asking. But maybe he was being clever. Except that clever and whiskey-besotted never come in the same package. And this guy's *sweat* smelled like Jack Daniel's.

"Unfortunately, Dr. Salazar is down with a severe headache. I'm taking his place."

"I don't like it."

The bartender poured a refill from a freshly opened bottle, and Butch sampled it, as though deciding if it were to his liking.

Butch set his shot glass down. "You bring the Rover?"

"Uh, no. I drove my own car."

Inflamed eyes glared at me. "You tell Salazar I don't deal with flunkies. You tell him this is business. And I don't like to deadhead back. And if he can't deliver, then we're done."

Butch slammed the rest of his whiskey and pulled a crumpled wad of peso notes from his pocket. He separated out three, light brown, hundreds and dropped them on the bar. Then, pushing off from the bar top, he slowly spun on his stool, found the white tiled floor with a cautious toe of one of his grayish sneakers, and ambled off unsteadily toward the door.

As soon as Butch was through the door, I was quickly up and across to it. I held the door open just enough to see him get into a maroon Chevy Malibu with an Avis rental car sticker on a corner of the windshield. As the Malibu backed around for the steep climb up to street level, I jotted down the license plate number on a bar napkin.

When I returned to Alicia, she was alone at the bar.

"Get anything?" she asked.

"A Texas plate number. And without a doubt, Butch is the smuggler. Where's Marybeth?"

"Powdering her nose." Alicia opened her new handbag and dropped in her cell phone. "We're all going out to dinner tonight. Enrique knows a really great place. Not only high-class, but excellent food, to boot."

"Enrique?"

"I have a lawyer named Enrique Ponce. I think you've met him."

"It's just I'm a little surprised that—"

"I think Enrique would be perfect for Marybeth. She's been down here such a long time, without having been dated."

"She's got a good ten years on him," I said, "and by 'having been dated' do you mean—"

"I told her five years, and you shut up about it. And yes, that's exactly what I mean."

I saw Marybeth exchanging a few pleasantries, in passing, with some people she apparently knew, as she came tacking back through the tables toward us.

When she docked, Marybeth asked, "Now, Alicia honey, are you going to supper in those clothes? 'Cause I don't want us looking like ying and yang, when we go out."

"Yes, I'm fine with this outfit, but you be yourself tonight. We're going to have fun."

"Well, you come help me pick out something nice, something lawyers like." Excitement was fairly dancing in Marybeth's eyes.

Alicia touched my arm. "Francis, you have to go report in to Woodstead. I'm going to go with Marybeth back to her room, while we get ready. We're going to scoop up Enrique at his office at seven, so you be back here no later than six thirty."

"Why so early?"

"Because we're going to the Symphony first."

My heart sank. "Chihuahua has a string band?"

"A Philharmonic Orchestra, for your information. Enrique was going to take his mother, but she couldn't go. And he didn't want to miss it. They're playing traditional Mexican music tonight, because of the Bicentennial. So he invited us, and I said we'd be honored. And before you start whining, a dose of refinement will do you some good. Life isn't all oily gears and circuit boards."

"I just love music," Marybeth enthused.

I could guess what kind of music Marybeth loved.

***

I walked with the women across the lower parking area to Marybeth's motel room, so I'd know where to find them when I came back. As Marybeth went on into the room, I drew Alicia to one side.

"What made you decide on your lawyer for Marybeth's blind date?"

"He's single and has a decent job, and he's fluent in English. How many men like that do you think I know down here?"

"How did you know he's not married?"

"No ring, for starters. And I've been in his office. There were photographs on the wall of his parents and his graduating class and him sitting on a horse, but no picture of a woman about his age with or without kids. And the part about taking his mom to the symphony simply confirmed what I already knew." She looked at me steadily. "Want to know how I know he's not gay?"

"I'll take your word for it."

***

I still had the dollar on which I'd written the address for Woodstead's Chihuahua office and the map from the excursion to the Gato Negro Cantina. Woodstead's office building turned out to be in the same general area of the city as the Motel Vista Suites, so it was just a ten-minute drive, and I was there. There was no Town Car out front this time. I parked, mounted the front steps, and pulled open an unusually heavy door.

Once inside, I walked down a broad hallway lined on both sides with steel doors, faux grained with paint to look like wood. Between the doors, along the walls, church-pew-type benches were placed beneath out-sized oil paintings that depicted scenic views of nothing in particular. At the far end of the hallway there was an open door, beyond which I could see a desk presided over by a young woman of what I now thought of as routine Mexican beauty.

I crossed the threshold and stood before the secretary's desk.

"Good afternoon," I said in Spanish. "I am Francis Elton. I wish to speak to Consular Agent Woodstead, if he is here."

The secretary had written my name on a pad of paper, before I'd finished speaking.

"May I ask the nature of your business with Consular Agent Woodstead?" she asked in English.

I switched to English. "The Consular Agent asked me to gather some information, concerning the murder of Professor John Salazar. I'm here to deliver that information."

The secretary wrote a note under my name. "I will see if he is in for you."

She picked up a phone, pushed a button, and after a short delay, related my business in Spanish. Apparently, she hadn't spoken directly to Woodstead, because we then waited. Meanwhile, the secretary returned to her computer work, and I perused the room.

Large, framed photographs of President Obama and Secretary of State Clinton hung on either side of an outsized relief of the US State Department seal. On an adjacent wall, there was a grouping of smaller photographs of nicely dressed, important-looking people, whose identities I couldn't guess. A US flag, draped from an upright pole, stood in one corner, it's

Mexican counterpart in another. For an "informal Chihuahua office," it seemed to have a lot of official-looking trappings.

"Consular Agent Woodstead sends his apologies. He is heavily engaged this afternoon."

I turned to face the secretary, who was gently replacing the phone onto its console. I hadn't heard a ring or a buzz.

She added, "Would it be convenient for you to write out your information, and perhaps, wait as long as your time permits, in the event that the Consular Agent has a free moment?"

Before I could respond, the secretary extended a clipboard toward me that held a blank sheet of paper with a pen resting on top. When I took the clipboard, she pointed to a pair of guest chairs and returned to her work.

I sat, laid the clipboard on the armrest, and wrote: 'Dr. Salazar had numerous brief contacts with an American named Butch in the lounge at the Motel Vista Suites. These contacts were infrequent, but always on a Friday around 5:30 p.m. and maybe coinciding with Salazar's thefts. I presented myself to this man as Salazar's agent. From our conversation it was apparent to me that this man is the smuggler. He lost interest in me when I told him I was not driving the Restoration Project's Land Rover. It is likely that Butch carries a spare key to the Rover and transfers the stolen item to his own car in the motel parking lot. He drives a maroon Chevy Malibu. Avis rental. Texas plate - TU 4703.'

I handed the clipboard, pen, and paper back to the secretary.

She pressed an intercom button and spoke in English, "I have a written message for Consular Agent Woodstead."

Immediately, from a side door a taller-than-six-foot, muscular, young man with black skin and a firm jaw appeared in the room. The close-cropped hair, the white tee shirt showing at the open collar of his crisp dress shirt, the razor creased trousers, and the fact that he was the first American black man I'd seen in Chihuahua all week, clearly announced "Marine in sheep's clothing." And those massive hands, even at ease, looked like they could efficiently kill with a quick twist of a neck.

In meeting the Marine's gaze, the secretary's eyes took their time sweeping upward, finishing with a slow, deliberate eyelash swing. As her back arched, her breasts rose up a notch and a whiff of meadow-sweet perfume drifted through the still office air.

The big Marine received the paper without a word and retired from sight behind the side door.

I wondered how often during the day the secretary looked at that intercom button, knowing how easily she could command that fine vision of manhood to appear.

After ten more minutes of waiting, I was at the point where I'd have to leave immediately, if I were to get back to the Vista Suites by six thirty. I stood and told the secretary that I was due at another appointment.

"I will inform Consular Agent Woodstead that you are leaving." She picked up her phone.

I didn't wait for her to finish the call. I retraced my steps along the broad hallway flanked by the many doors. Halfway to the exit, a door just to my right swung open, and Consular Agent Richard Woodstead

221

materialized, like a conjurer's trick. He placed a hand on my arm to stop me, while his other hand pulled the door closed behind him – but not before I caught a glimpse of several, conservatively suited, Hispanic men sitting in plush leather armchairs.

"Mr. Elton, I'm so pleased I was able to catch you. Just a few quick questions, if you can spare the time." Woodstead's hand remained on my arm.

"You read my note?"

"Indeed, I did. The FBI will contact the Avis people. Discovering the smuggler's identity will now be a simple matter."

"Anything for the cause."

"And that a spare key to Salazar's Land Rover could be found in the fellow's pocket and, thereby, identify him as the smuggler. Actually, that was brilliant."

"Actually, Alicia thought of it."

"In that case, let us hope she came up with it by way of astute deduction, rather than prior comprehensive knowledge of the smuggling operation." Consular Agent Woodstead again left no doubt that he believed in Alicia's innocence about as much as Commandant Arroyo did. "Now, there's something in your note that requires clarification. You implied, but did not quite say, that the smuggler was waiting at the Vista Suites, and at the appointed time, today to meet with Dr. Salazar." He squeezed my arm. "Today. Is that true?"

"He was there less than an hour ago, and yes, he asked me where Dr. Salazar was."

Woodstead's hand left my arm. "Rather odd behavior for the FBI's number-one suspect, wouldn't you agree? Keeping a rendezvous with our rogue professor, subsequent to killing him."

"I thought about that, but then this Butch guy couldn't be sure I wasn't FBI myself. Maybe, he thought he was being clever by asking where Dr. Salazar was."

"For a murderer, I should think being clever would entail a quick absconding back across the border and never setting foot in Mexico again," Woodstead said. "Odds are the smuggler is unaware that Salazar is dead."

Woodstead drew back a few inches of jacket sleeve and looked at his watch for a long while, too long to be merely checking the time.

I was getting low on patience, when, at last, Woodstead lowered his watch arm.

"Well," he said, "perhaps we should let the FBI draw its own conclusions. The data from the smuggler's car rental contract should gratify them for a day or two. And with luck they'll nab the smuggler crossing into Texas with the Land Rover's spare key inexplicably in his possession."

"Will gratifying the FBI keep Alicia from being arrested again?"

"I can keep Commandant Arroyo in check only as long as you keep bringing me little infusions, such as you have today, to provide life support for the Bureau's moribund investigation. I believe I have already explained that." Woodstead's tone edged toward a rebuke. "And to that end, I have an additional task for you."

I knew I wasn't going to like my new task.

"I need you to bring the Land Rover over here to this building," Woodstead said.

"You're telling me to steal a car?"

"Not at all. How you get it here is completely up to you," Woodstead said. "We just need to give it a quick look-over."

"That might be tricky. The chauffeur, Eduardo, treats the Rover like it's his own. Even Salazar only got to drive it on Friday afternoons."

"On the contrary," Woodstead said. "According to the FBI, the Land Rover, with Dr. Salazar at the wheel, has been up to Texas and back within the last several weeks. And that, coupled with your information about the transfer of stolen property in the Vista Suites parking lot, has piqued the Bureau's interest in the Rover. They'd like their forensic experts to have a good sniff at it. They'll fly them down from Houston. Your part is merely to bring the Rover to my doorstep." Woodstead placed a hand on my shoulder. "I believe your words were 'anything for the cause'. And we wouldn't want our fair damsel to get her lipstick mussed in some nasty old Mexican dungeon, would we?"

The man could sure turn a screw. "I'll do my best."

"Excellent." Woodstead's hand left my shoulder with a departing tap. He then withdrew a small leather folder from an inner jacket pocket, extracted a business card, and handed it to me. "Call this number, well ahead of your projected delivery of the Rover. I'll need some lead time to get the appropriate people down here." He tucked the leather folder away. "And now, I'm afraid I'm neglecting my guests. And I'd rather not have that particular cohort in there conspire without me."

Chapter 12

My tardy return to the Vista Suites, caused a flurry of activity, as Alicia bustled an obviously excited – on the verge of giggling – Marybeth toward the rental car. Happily, Marybeth's dark, richly flowered blouse and plain skirt was not the square-dance outfit I'd anticipated. Her wild shock of hair, though still an unnatural red, was now swept-back and hair-sprayed into a sassy pompadour. Finely worked, Mexican silver hung from Marybeth's neck, above an ample display of cleavage. And a practiced hand at makeup had smoothed and tinted away the last five years, while bringing out a surprisingly attractive pair of brown eyes.

"Can you believe it, Francis?" Marybeth exclaimed, as I opened the rear door of the little Fiesta for her. "It ain't even dark out, and Alicia's got me up in the Full Betty."

"I'm sure the payoff will be worth it."

Alicia socked me on the arm. "You look lovely, Marybeth," she said. "Now let's not keep Enrique waiting."

On our way to pick up Enrique Ponce, Alicia phoned ahead to apologize for our being late. After closing her phone, Alicia told us, "Enrique's going to wait for us in the restaurant below his law office."

With the car parked, we made the short walk up the blocked-off street to the restaurant. The Attorney for the Defense was wearing a suit and tie, as though ready for court. He sat alone at a table among a scattering of late-afternoon drinkers in the outdoor dining area, which was again cordoned off – this time by a pink ribbon strung between the temporary plastic posts, defining the restaurant's annexed territory beyond the curb.

Enrique Ponce was biting into a wedge of lime, as we approached. An empty shot glass rested on the table before him. When he noticed us, he dropped the lime wedge into the shot glass, touched his fingertips to a paper napkin, and stood.

Alicia introduced Marybeth to her date and suggested that we all call each other by our first names. Enrique then seated the ladies, and I signaled the waitress.

"Was that tequila?" Marybeth pointed to the shot glass. "Let's *all* have a big ol' slug of tequila."

With my latest assignment from Woodstead still on my mind, I was ready for a double.

But Alicia intervened, "I think a lovely white wine would be more appropriate, as a prelude to an evening at the Symphony and the elegant dinner that Enrique has planned for us."

Marybeth and I exchanged looks of shared disappointment, which were amplified when the waitress arrived and informed us that the wine list for this small restaurant consisted entirely of a choice of sweet or dry sherry. Since the dry came chilled, I opted for a bottle of it.

"Marybeth comes from Texas," Alicia prompted. "You have relatives in Texas, don't you, Enrique?"

"Everyone in Mexico has relatives in Texas," Enrique replied.

We all laughed, although primarily as a release from the awkward tension inherent in the initial stages of a blind date. After that, the table talk flowed freely enough. And to our good fortune, the dry sherry was young and inexpensive enough to taste like a mix of equal portions of bottom-shelf vodka and bottled lime juice, rather than the fortified, liquid dirt flavor of the rigorously aged and pricey variety.

While Alicia was telling Marybeth about her shopping trip, Enrique produced a dark blue necktie from his coat pocket and reached it in my direction.

"A tie is not exactly *required* at the restaurant where we will dine after the symphony," Enrique said, "but I would not want you to feel uncomfortable."

"Actually, what makes me feel uncomfortable is wearing a tie," I said. "So given the choice—"

"It's not a choice." Alicia broke off her shopping story to bring me to heel. "We're being ladies and gentlemen tonight, Francis. And like a gentleman, Enrique graciously offered to provide a tie for you when I called him and we set this up." She then confided to Enrique and Marybeth, "I doubt if Francis even owns a tie."

"I still have the one you gave me to wear to your father's funeral." I was fairly sure this was true.

"Perhaps, at the symphony," Enrique was the voice of reason, "a tie would not matter as much. There will be students there. But at the restaurant, you would feel out of place."

I took the necktie with a grace I didn't feel and fed it around under my shirt collar. During my serial attempts to tie the knot and have the ends come out right, I noticed the others at the table watching me with curiosity. To divert their fascination, I asked, "This restaurant we're going to, it's pretty classy then?"

"Originally, I was very lucky to have reserved a table for my mother and me at only a week in advance," Enrique said. "It was only because I attended school with the maitre d' that he gave me a table resulting from a cancellation. When I called this afternoon and asked if it was possible to make the reservation for four, I was again lucky, because the cancellation had *been* for a party of four, and therefore, was easily managed. I can only hope that our good luck will continue and rub off on Alicia's current difficulties."

"For the record," Alicia said, "I don't care *what* I have to rub for luck."

"Now you got your fella putting on a tie for you," Marybeth admonished. "No call for you to sweep the field. Comes to rubbing someone's magic lamp, I got skills too."

We all laughed again, but this time I noticed Enrique's laugh sounded forced, and his eyes anxiously scanned the al fresco dining area, perhaps seeking an opening in the encircling pink ribbon.

***

I put the sherry, Enrique's tequila, and the waitress's tip on my credit card, and the four of us left the little restaurant. We rode in my rental car, so I had to be on constant alert for directions issued from the back seat. To my annoyance, Enrique proved to be one of those people who wait till you're at a point where he himself would begin his turn, before telling me to make a right or a left.

228

Having survived some hasty (and often exciting) cornering, we arrived at the University early enough to secure seats near the center of the theater. We settled in to wait, thumbing disinterestedly through our programs and making minor comments to one another.

At the appointed hour, however, the orchestra came bursting out of the gate with Beethoven played at breakneck speed. This grabbed my attention and held it through the entire piece. However, once the musicians' pent-up energy had been spent, the conductor slowed the pace for a soporific tour through the Romantic Period. At one point, I was wakened from a light doze by a sharp jab in the ribs, special delivery from Alicia. After that, I managed to stay with it, the pain she'd inflicted having some remarkable hang time to it. But later, when I noticed that Alicia's chin had come to rest on her collarbone, I had the satisfaction of bumping her shoulder and watching her head snap back up to attention.

At intermission, while the ladies with their purses went off to freshen up, I moved over a couple of seats to talk with Enrique. What I had in mind was to provide him with an opportunity to earn that shot of tequila I'd bought him.

As I plunked down next to him, Enrique commented, "Such fabulous music. And after the interval, they will play the great traditional music of Mexico."

"I'm looking forward to it," I said. "Say, I wonder if you might do a favor for me."

The young lawyer visibly stiffened. "What favor do you ask?"

229

"Consular Agent Woodstead wants to have some forensic scientists from the FBI examine the Restoration Project's Land Rover. He wants me to bring the Rover to his office building, but that might be troublesome. From what I gather, the Rover is parked out at the Salazar ranch when Eduardo isn't using it."

"And Eduardo is…"

"The Project's chauffeur and handyman. And the trouble is he hasn't shown up at work lately, which puts the Rover out of my immediate reach. But I was thinking. If the Rover is the property of the Restoration Project, then Alicia, through her attorney, could insist that it be brought back to the Palacio de Gobierno. Then, I can simply take it from there over to Woodstead's office. But if the Rover was Dr. Salazar's *personal* property and so now belongs to his widow, Lydia, I doubt I could persuade her to part with it for an afternoon. Not the least because she thinks Alicia should already be in jail for her husband's murder."

"Ownership can be established through the vehicle's registration." Enrique drew a pen and small notebook from his jacket pocket. He seemed relieved that it was just business. "What is the license plate number, please?"

"I don't know."

"Once you provide me with the license plate number, or better yet, the vehicle identification number, it will be a simple matter." Enrique put his pen and notebook away.

Alicia and Marybeth returned, and I sidestepped out to the aisle to let them in. As Marybeth entered the row and excused herself past people's knees, Alicia confronted me in the aisle.

"Francis, what kind of knot is that?"

"Well, I didn't have a mirror and—"

"You're not tying up the Queen Mary." Alicia tore my knot apart.

Alicia made a quick business of re-looping and stuffing the tie. An unexpected, downward jerk tightened the knot, which was then rammed up into my throat. Satisfied with her work, Alicia patted my lapel, turned, and gracefully moved along the row to her seat. I followed, apologizing for scuffing people's shoes.

When we'd regained our seats, Marybeth commented, "Seems your Francis finds it difficult to come to grips with his neckwear."

"How he manages without me is a complete mystery," Alicia said.

The orchestra filed onto the stage for the second half, the lights dimmed, and the audience hushed.

The traditional Mexican music was much more interesting than the Old World classics. A male and a female singer alternated their solos, until together they sang what must have been the National Anthem, because the whole audience came to their feet, and everyone, except us Yankees, sang along.

Then the singers left the stage, and the orchestra launched into an instrumental piece. Right from the outset, it was wild and fast – the strings swirling and soaring up and around in the high ranges, the woodwinds scurrying about the midrange in counterpoint to the strings, and the horns out-shouting them all with furious staccato accents on the up beats, rapid-fired with exacting precision. The percussion section pounded out urgent and incessant rhythmic patterns on the snares, underscored with body-wracking punches and roaring flurries from the kettledrums. I felt as if I were riding with Pancho Villa's cavalry, galloping over the rolling hills dotted with sentinels of Socorro cacti, and then sweeping down through the broad plains and thundering past longhorn cattle grazing by a river. It was exhilarating, happy, fantastic music.

When it was over, I came right up to my feet, beating my hands together and shouting "Bravo!" The Guest Conductor, a diminutive Asian in a tuxedo, raised the orchestra up from their chairs to accept the unanimous standing ovation, then leaped from his podium to give the comely first-chair violinist a tight hug, and then flitted back over the podium to bestow upon the radiant first-chair cellist an equally enthusiastic squeeze. By contrast, the trumpeters, in the afterglow of their rigorous, open-throttle performance, coolly touched respect knuckles.

"You liked that one, Francis?" Alicia stood next to me, still clapping her hands.

"It was worth sitting through all that drudgery in the first half."

"I knew if high culture smacked you hard enough on the nose, you'd finally get it."

The singers came out together for the last number, which brought the audience solemnly to their feet again with the opening notes. Many mouths moved along with the singers' words, which I didn't quite get, and at the end many tears were wiped from the cheeks of the older generation. Enrique told us the song had, for all practical purposes, become the National Hymn. And I saw him turn slightly to sneak an index finger wipe just below each eye, himself.

That wrapped up the concert, and we all filed out of the auditorium.

"I liked the lady singer's voice," Marybeth declared, as we moved through the parking lot. "She sounded like she was going for Opera. Damn, that girl could holler."

***

It was well after dark now, and once again I drove the rental car through the Chihuahua streets, informed by Enrique's backseat navigation. Although I was thoroughly lost, the architectural style of the more prominent buildings suggested that we were now in an older section of the city.

Finally, Enrique said we were close enough to the restaurant to start looking for a place to park. I drove along the unbroken line of parked cars, eyes sharp for an opportunity. When a car pulled out ahead of me, I accelerated toward the vacancy, quickly established a claim, and maneuvered into the open spot along the curb. When we got out and formed up on the sidewalk, we three Yankees were transfixed, gazing across the busy street at a majestic, colonial mansion that was lit-up from the outside to showcase red-tiled conical roofs atop imposing turrets that towered above the tall shrubbery that encompassed the property.

"Oh my," Marybeth said, "It's like a castle."

"Yes, it is a very old house." Enrique was looking at his watch. "We are already deep within the open time of our reservation."

As Enrique hurried us on, we passed right by a first-class-looking restaurant, which I, at first, supposed was our destination, and crossed a busy, multi-lane street at an intersection. On the far side was another stately old mansion, which, pretty obviously, had been converted over to fine dining, given the understated sign out front and the packed, parking area that surrounded the building. Before we climbed the front steps, Alicia stopped me to fasten my collar button and cinch up the knot on my tie, both of which had somehow worked their way loose at the symphony.

Once we were ushered through the front door, the grandeur from a prosperous, long-past era was on display. Immediately before us was the curving upward sweep of a grand staircase, beneath which a musician worked diligently at the keys of a concert grand piano. We were promptly received and led off to a front room that must have once been the formal parlor, but was now filled with smartly dressed patrons seated at tables draped in white.

The combined drone of multiple conversations and the clinking of silverware imparted an air of excitement within the carefully preserved walls and ceiling of the stately parlor. We were shown to a table near the front windows. While I seated the ladies, Enrique engaged in a prolonged handshake and words-in-confidence with the maitre d', before finally breaking free with departing, hearty, *compañero* slaps to sides of each other's upper arms.

Once in his chair, Enrique took up the extensive wine list that his pal, the maitre d', had left on the table, studied it briefly, and conveyed his choice to a hovering waiter. The rest of us pretended to peruse our menus, while surreptitiously admiring our surroundings. Evidently, a protracted journey to the cellar was required, but eventually, the wine did arrive at our table. And after being sampled and approved by Enrique, it was, at last, poured for us. But admittedly, it was worth the wait, because we now sipped wine so refined that its flavor actually changed from hints of one fruit to another, the longer you held it on your tongue – a phenomenon I'd read about, but never truly experienced at the wine tasting parties Alicia occasionally dragged me to. And I could only guess at the magnitude of insult that the dry sherry we'd sipped earlier in the evening must have inflicted on Enrique's cultivated palette.

Enrique and I helped the ladies with the Spanish when we got around to making our choices from the menu. The waiter approved of each of our selections in turn, made a note of them on his pad, and withdrew.

Enrique asked Marybeth how she came to be staying in Mexico, and Marybeth began her long tale of upper-managerial farce.

Beneath Marybeth's saga, I leaned closer and asked Alicia, "Do you know if the Land Rover belongs to the Restoration Project, or to Dr. Salazar, personally?"

"I have no idea," Alicia said. "Why would that matter?"

"Another assignment from Woodstead."

"Just let it go for tonight, will you? Look where we are. Let's just relax and enjoy it."

Marybeth concluded her story with, "Ain't it funny?"

"It is indeed a comedy," Enrique said, "but the happy ending, I think, is that it led to you being here with us tonight."

"Oh my, but you're the smooth one," Marybeth said. "I bet you could talk the pants off a Supreme Court Judge."

Alicia set her wine glass down quickly and coughed into her napkin. Enrique held a smile for a few seconds and then swung his head to me.

"But what of you, Francis?" he asked. "You are divorced from Alicia, yet you come all this way."

"I asked him that very thing," Marybeth said. "He says he's willing to help out his ex when she's in a jam. Can you imagine?"

"He speaks Spanish, and he's helped me out in the past." Alicia came to my defense.

"But to fly such a great distance and at a moment's notice," Enrique pressed the issue. "Are you not the most excellent of former husbands?"

"If I do well, I've been promised a really big kiss," I said, hoping to end the lawyer's line of questioning.

"The last big kiss I gave Francis cost me a very handsome boyfriend," Alicia said.

"Ooh, wait a minute now. This sounds delicious. You got to tell Marybeth all about this one, Honey Pot."

"I don't want to bore Enrique with an old story." Alicia looked directly at him.

Enrique gestured that she continue.

"Okay, so a close friend of mine asked me to be the Mistress of Ceremony for her wedding," Alicia began. "You know, just to keep it organized and take care of the little things that tend to pop up. So the wedding's already happening, and I get a call from the limousine service, saying the driver showed up to work drunk and crashed the limo, before he even got out of the lot."

"Oh no," Marybeth caught on. "There ain't gonna be no limousine for whisking the bride and groom away after the ceremony."

"I know," Alicia said. "What are they supposed to do, walk? Now get this. This Adonis I'd been dating at the time actually suggests that I call a taxi. Isn't that unbelievable? Did William and Kate leave Westminster Abbey in a damned taxi?"

"Oh Lord, what'd you do?"

"So I call Francis and tell him to suit up and bring me the biggest freaking showboat he can lay his hands on."

"And?"

"And damned if doesn't pull up in front of the church in a big, brand new, white Cadillac. Just as the bride and groom are finishing up with their outdoor photos."

Marybeth clapped her hands. "That's amazing, Francis. How on Earth did you make that happen?"

"Well," I said, "the salesman from the Cadillac dealership *did* need a little calming down when I pulled over during the test drive, got out and opened the back door, and the bride and groom piled in."

"I was so happy with Francis," Alicia said, "that I swooped in and planted a whopping huge kiss on his mouth with plenty of breast-to-chest mashing thrown in for good measure."

"Ooh." Marybeth quickly took a big gulp of expensive wine. "Keep going. I knew this was gonna be delicious."

"So Francis jumps back behind the wheel, and they drive off to cheers from the waving crowd. But my Adonis is just steaming mad. He rants that I practically serviced this guy in front of a church and all these people. And I told him I'd have done the same for *him*, if he'd come through with a big, throbbing, white Cadillac, just when I needed it. So my big, handsome boyfriend stormed off, and I never saw him again."

"Oh, my Lord, your stories make me moist in places I should be dry." Marybeth slumped against the back of her seat, but then quickly recovered to lean forward again and ask, "And did you and Francis get together after the reception? You know, to finish what you started?"

Alicia picked up her little handbag, as she rose to her feet. "I think we'd better go powder our noses."

Enrique and I stood, and with mild confusion Marybeth belatedly followed suit. Alicia ushered Marybeth off in the direction of the foyer. They walked in close conference.

Enrique and I regained our seats across the table from each other. We talked for quite a while about the growing acceptance of fine wine, produced in Mexico, but I was impatient to return to my quest.

"About the Land Rover," I inserted, during a lull, "if it turns out that it's the property of the Restoration Project—"

"Tell me," the lawyer interrupted. "How can this be relevant to Alicia's defense?" He quickly held up his hand. "And before you answer, remember that I am not so easily deceived as a Cadillac salesman."

I leaned in and kept my voice beneath the surrounding conversations. "Salazar was using the Rover to transport the stolen antiquities to his smuggler. And the FBI says the Land Rover has been across the border and back recently. So, the Rover is involved, no question. And the FBI thinks a search of the Rover will provide evidence to bolster their murder-for-hire case against Salazar's smuggler. But even if they can't actually pin the murder on him, what evidence the FBI does find that implicates the smuggler will, at least, provide you with an argument for reasonable doubt, as to Alicia's guilt."

"Mexican judges do not doubt themselves," the lawyer said. "Nor, for that matter, does Commandant Arroyo."

"I don't know about judges," I said, "but I think facts will persuade Arroyo."

As Alicia and Marybeth approached our table, Enrique slid in a caveat, "Be careful who you make the fool."

Enrique and I dutifully stood, as the ladies arrived, and we assisted them in getting reseated.

"Have you men managed to entertain each other, while we've been gone?" Alicia asked.

"We've been busy enlightening one another," I said. Then, still standing with my hand on Alicia's chair back, I added, "Now, if you'll excuse me, I'm going to slip away and try to be back before the food arrives."

Alicia grabbed my necktie and drew my ear down to her mouth. "Take a good look into the big room with all the stained-glass when you're out in the foyer," Alicia spoke softly. "But don't let yourself be seen."

Alicia released me, and I made my way through the tables, massaging the back of my neck.

***

On my way back from the men's room, I stood to one side of a wide doorway (through which waiters silently and efficiently came and went) and looked into a large dining room with a high ceiling and two vast, busily-patterned stained-glass windows that swept across two adjoining walls. This large room held a much greater number of diners than the former parlor. In the center of each white-clothed table, a grouping of candles glowed in glass vases of varying heights and in colors that echoed those in the stained glass. But the sight that Alicia obviously wanted me to see was on the far side of the room, directly beneath the expanse of colored art-glass. Lydia Salazar, dressed in prim black, was seated at a table-for-two with Eduardo, the chauffeur and all-around handyman, who wore a dark suit. At the moment, they were busy with their dessert course and ignoring the waiter who was making a show of refilling their wine glasses from a towel-wrapped bottle.

I pulled my head back, went the long way around the grand piano, and returned to our table in the parlor.

Our many loaded plates arrived at the table just when I did. Beneath the resultant fuss and excitement of aromatic and appealing food landing beneath our alerted noses and hungry eyes, Alicia leaned close to me.

"Did you see them?"

"I saw Lydia and Eduardo just finishing up with supper, if that's what—"

240

"My God," she kept her voice low, "do you really come directly from the cemetery, where you've just buried your husband, and have a candlelit, champagne dinner with your chauffeur?"

"Every table had little candles, and people have to eat."

"They're not grabbing a quick beer and sandwich on the way back to the ranch. It takes advanced reservations to get a table in this place. Didn't you hear Enrique? And you saw how they were together. Did that look like employer and employee?"

"I admit it didn't look quite right, but—"

"It looked like they're lovers. And she's got to be well into her forties, and I know he's mid-twenties."

I glanced over at Enrique and Marybeth, as they happily clinked wine glasses, having made some private toast.

Alicia saw where my eyes went. "They're different," she said. "Their ages are closer, and...and the composition is better."

"What're you two whispering about?" Marybeth asked.

"Alicia was just correcting me," I said.

"Why, I think you two boys been behaving like perfect gentlemen all night, springing up out of your chairs, like regular jack-in-a-boxes, every time one of us girls stands up."

"In this case, I was guilty of drawing a parallel, where, as it turns out, none exists," I said.

"Well now, Honey Pot, I never heard of *that* one."

At this point the waiter stopped by and asked us how our food tasted. After we sheepishly admitted that we were busy talking, instead of eating, we immediately dug into the delights of Mexican high cuisine.

***

As he was returning his credit card to his wallet, Enrique suggested after-dinner drinks in the lounge upstairs. The motion passed unanimously, and we headed toward the grand central staircase. As we started up, I saw Alicia looking through the wide doorway into the big room with the stained-glass windows. I looked too, but saw only a busboy draping fresh, white linen over the table-for-two, where Lydia and Eduardo had polished off their champagne dinner.

At the top of the stairs, we entered a different world. I had to withdraw my observation that the old mansion had been left largely undisturbed. Nobody's colonial mansion had a nightclub where the bedrooms were supposed to be.

Colored lights flashed and electronic music pounded in the densely packed lounge filled with the young and fashionably dressed. Alicia was yelling something in my ear, but I couldn't sort her words out from the pandemonium. Through the hot, smoky air, I spotted French doors leading out to a veranda. Using hand signals, I led our group toward a more temperate climate and a less adverse decibel level.

Out on the veranda, where reverberations and body heat were unconfined, the music thumped in more muted tones, and the air was refreshingly cool.

"I don't think we'll find Lydia and Eduardo in there," Alicia said, as she scanned the dance floor through the open French doors. "They're probably home in bed by now."

242

I now belatedly damned myself for missing the opportunity to scurry outside and copy down the license plate number of the Land Rover, probably valet-parked in the restaurant's lot. I tried to console myself that Lydia and Eduardo might well have arrived in some other vehicle, but I knew it was dull-witted of me not to think of this before.

A waiter stepped out on the veranda to gather our drink orders. When he turned to me, I requested Kahlua and coffee. I needed to clear my head, if only for the drive back.

While Marybeth and Enrique were quasi-dancing to some rhythm of their own, Alicia and I stood at the railing. The brightness of street lamps and car headlights emanating from the busy intersection washed out the moon and stars, but the systematic orchestration conducted by the traffic lights provided a comforting substitute for the orderly movements of the universe.

Alicia entwined her arm in mine and leaned against me. It was a rare, pleasant, and unusually sustained moment – until the waiter's Spanish words broke the spell.

"A cognac for the lady, and your Kahlua and coffee, sir."

Alicia and I disengaged, as we turned to accept our drinks.

From across the veranda, I heard Marybeth exclaim, "Ooh, damn, this is good." She poked at a blue colored drink with a pair of narrow, pink straws. "Enrique, honey, how do I tell that boy 'thanks' for this sumptuous liquor?"

"You say '*la cuenta*'," Enrique told her.

Marybeth waved the pink straws at the waiter and called out enthusiastically, "*La cuenta*, my little amigo."

The waiter smiled, gave a curt nod, and headed back to the bar with his empty tray.

Enrique cast a smug smile over at us.

"For the love of God," Alicia said to me. "I can't believe he's playing that joke on her. Doesn't he want to get laid tonight?"

The waiter returned with suspicious promptness and presented Marybeth with a leather folder. Marybeth reached out and took what was being handed to her. When she discovered she'd been handed the bill for our drinks, Marybeth's stunned expression was so artless that, in spite of herself, even Alicia laughed along with Enrique and me. The waiter, who must have seen this fun-with-gringos gag played a hundred times, nevertheless also joined in.

The joke having played out, Enrique took the folder from Marybeth's hand and returned it along with his Visa card to the waiter. The waiter received Enrique's pat on the shoulder and went off to swipe the card.

"You all are terrible." Marybeth wasn't laughing. "I do not believe that I shall ever take supper with the likes of any of you again."

Alicia was quickly at Marybeth's side, her arm around the offended woman's shoulders. "Mexicans just live for this silliness. But it can only be played on the most gracious people, like you, who feel it proper to thank the waiter, when you've had an enjoyable experience."

The waiter came back with the folder, now discretely encasing Enrique's credit card and a receipt for him to sign.

"This should square things for you." Alicia snatched the leather folder from the waiter's hand and sharply smacked Enrique on the forehead with it. "That's for being a damn comedian."

***

As I pulled away from the curb, a sleepy-eyed Alicia was belted in next to me. Enrique's directions for the return trip to his office building again sporadically emanated from the back seat. But this time, in the background, there were curious sounds of activity mixed with Marybeth's giggles, which I took to be Enrique making up for his little prank the easy way.

I was glad we were finally wrapping up the party. It had been a long night. I used Spanish to discretely ask Enrique if Alicia and I would be taking Marybeth back to her motel, after we dropped him off.

Enrique responded in English. "I will see that Marybeth gets back to the Vista Suites safely. But first, we are going up to my office, so I can show her my diploma."

There were more giggles from the back.

Soon, Enrique's directions all but ceased, but by that time, we were close enough to his law office for me to remember the way. And it wasn't long before I pulled to the curb, as close as I could get to the blocked-off street. Enrique spent quite a bit of time and effort getting a tipsy Marybeth out of the backseat. Then after a wave of goodbye, they walked hand-in-hand down the street, along which the white plastic tables and chairs of the several restaurants were being gathered and stowed for the night.

Alicia and I headed back to the Hotel Miramar. As we drove through the dark streets of Chihuahua, I commented, "I'll bet Marybeth has been thinking about Enrique's diploma all evening."

"For her sake..." Alicia paused for a yawn. "I hope he's magna cum laude."

Alicia reclined her seat back a few notches and closed her eyes.

"You know," I said. "I have a diploma around somewhere, too."

"And I had such a lovely evening," Alicia spoke languidly, "this could be the night you put in some postgraduate work."

I picked up speed.

Chapter 13

As a hotel employee drove the rental car off, Alicia and I entered the lobby of the Miramar. Crossing to the elevator, I could see only the top of the night clerk's head, as he worked at a desk behind the counter. I mentally crossed my fingers that he didn't have a message for us, or some other distraction that might break Alicia's romantic mood.

We made it to the elevator without incident and stepped aboard. Just as the doors started to close, a blur of light blue housekeeper's uniform hurried onto the elevator with us. My first thought was that it was pretty darn late for housekeeping service, and then as she turned, I saw her name tag: 'Violeta.' The elevator door closed, encapsulating the three of us.

"Mister Elton, the police came back to your room," Violeta spoke in rapid, breathless Spanish. "Two of them. I was about to go home, but I was sent up to unlock your door."

My internal response was: damn, not now. But resigned to my fate, out loud I asked in Spanish, "Were the police wearing uniforms?"

"They were in regular clothes. The big one showed me his badge. That one looked like a policeman. The other one, the one who carried the briefcase, he did not show his badge to me."

"Were they State Ministerial Police?" I asked.

"They did not inform me," the housekeeper said. "I told them, 'Do not break anything, and do not steal anything.' But they pushed me out of the room and closed the door. They spent a half hour in your room. When they came out, they told me, 'Do not go into the room. Do not tell anyone that we were here.' But after they left, I went into the room. It is my job to keep the rooms clean. But it is okay. The room looks normal."

"Francis, what's going on? I know what *policia* means. Are they in our room?"

I started to answer Alicia in Spanish, but, after a couple of words, I caught myself and started again in English, "They're not in there now, but they were earlier. A policeman and a guy with a briefcase."

"Oh my God, they've stolen my chemise." Alicia had panic in her eyes.

The elevator doors opened on our floor. Alicia started to rush out. I grabbed her by the arm and pulled her back into the elevator, but pressed the side of my foot against the safety bar on the door edge to keep it open. Alicia struggled against my grip.

"Stop fighting me," I said. "Let me think."

Alicia stopped trying to tear away, but I held on to her tensed arm, anyway.

"If they were careful to not mess up the room," I continued speaking to Alicia, "they didn't want us to know they were in there. But why would they care?"

"You mean they didn't ransack the place?"

"The housekeeper said they didn't. So, maybe they added, instead of subtracted."

I felt Alicia begin to relax, and I let go of her.

I spoke in Spanish to Violeta, "I am grateful for the information. But you must not put yourself in danger with the police. Do not tell anyone that you talked to us."

"I know how to not cooperate with the police," she assured me.

I gave Violeta three hundred pesos, and Alicia and I stepped out of the elevator. When I turned to thank Violeta again, the automatic door was already closing and the money was being deposited within the white lace stronghold beneath the light blue cotton fabric.

It was after midnight. Violeta had stuck around all evening, waiting to sell me the information. Too late, it occurred to me that three hundred pesos was probably not nearly enough. I'd have to remember to overstuff her tip envelope.

I spoke softly to Alicia, "Let's go to the stairwell and try to figure this out for a minute."

"Why don't we just go to our room?"

"I have an idea the police bugged it."

"You mean a microphone?"

"Maybe a camera too."

We walked past the door to our room and entered the stairwell at the end of the hall. The uncarpeted stairwell echoed a little, and there was a vaguely pungent odor, but nobody bugs a stairwell.

I stood close to Alicia and kept my voice low, anyway. "The guy who carried the briefcase, I think he was a technician, not a policeman. A hidden microphone could have either a digital recorder incorporated right in it, or a transmitter beaming to a remote recorder, so they could also listen in, live."

"Why would they do that?"

"Arroyo needs to gather more evidence, and you're his only source. His earlier maneuver – the pointless GSR test in order to trick a confession out of you – was thwarted. So now that he's confident we've settled into this hotel, he plants a bug to record us talking about the murder."

"But we can't be sure of that, can we? Maybe they were just searching the room."

"If there's a bug, I'll find it," I said. "I know what I'm looking for."

"And then what? Change rooms?"

"I think it's better to know about the bug and just not give Arroyo anything he could use against you. We'll just be careful what we say."

"I just won't say anything."

"Well, you'll have to talk about something, while I look for the bug."

"What am I supposed to talk about?"

"Something not related to the murder. Maybe, talk about your sister. How you're going to call her tomorrow, or something." Then another thought hit me. "I'd better look for a camera first. I don't think there'll be one. Not much point to it, really. But it'll only take a minute to check."

"A camera would be pretty big, wouldn't it?"

"They've got them down to the size of a pencil now. But there still needs to be a clear line of sight. And if the lens can see *me*, I can see *it*."

***

When we entered, the room looked just the same as we'd left it.

250

I closed the door behind us. "It'll be good to get out of this necktie." As I pulled the knot apart, I visually swept the room, looking for something new or out of place.

"I just want out of these heels. My calves are in knots." Alicia kicked off her shoes, walked directly to the dresser, and pulled open the top drawer. Apparently reassured, she closed the drawer and began to remove her earrings.

I started a closer scan of the walls and furnishings, pretending to be wandering aimlessly, while shrugging off my sport coat and unbuttoning my shirt.

"I think I'll call Ellen tomorrow," Alicia launched into her part. "She went up to Milwaukee with Roger for a couple of days. One of his seminars. They should be back by now."

"How much more could Roger possibly learn about selling insurance?" I kept the patter going.

"Ellen says it's really all about male bonding with the other salesmen. Touching peters, she calls it. Anyway, she gets to do some shopping with the other wives in exotic Milwaukee."

I'd gone over the room twice and had come up empty. I caught Alicia's attention and performed the pantomime of holding a movie camera and cranking. I then shook my head to indicate "no".

For the listening device, I started with the hotel's telephone. After all, a microphone and the low voltage power are already there. Easy stuff.

The telephone on the nightstand was a fairly up-to-date model with the handset on the left, keypad in the middle, and on the right, push buttons, labeled in Spanish for 'front desk', 'message', and 'speaker'.

"I'm calling down for ice," I said for the benefit of any potential eavesdropper.

I picked up and held the whole phone unit, before lifting the handset and pushing the 'front desk' button. The night clerk informed me that the hotel's room service closed at ten p.m. – a fact that I already knew. I hung up and held the handset tight to its cradle, while I inverted it and gently laid it on the bed.

Using the Phillips screwdriver on my Swiss Army knife, I backed out the little screws, held the phone together, as I turned it back upright, and carefully lifted the plastic housing off the base. Interconnecting wiring kept me from completely separating the two halves, but I really didn't need to. I immediately saw what I was looking for. There was a small circuit board, swathed in bubble wrap, with slender, colored wires protruding out and soldered onto the phone's motherboard. The red and green wires had been soldered to the terminals of the microphone used in "speaker" mode, and the black and yellow pair undoubtedly tapped into low voltage power. A blue, fifth wire, emerging from the bubble-wrap and taped on top, was open ended – perhaps an antenna for a radio transmitter, or just a wire for some unused function. In any case, I'd found the bug.

Alicia came near and looked over my shoulder. I motioned for her to follow me into the bathroom.

I closed the bathroom door and flushed the toilet. "The bug is in the phone. At minimum they can record our voices. And very likely, they can also hear everything we say in the bedroom in real time. It's like the 'speaker' function is always on."

"This is beyond crazy. I feel like Mata Hari."

I returned to the bedroom, reassembled the telephone housing, and gently replaced the unit on the nightstand.

"I'm taking a shower and getting into my 'jammies'," Alicia called from the bathroom.

I took off my shoes and stretched out on the bed to wait my turn at the shower. After all, there was still an outside chance Alicia might feel like pursuing the "postgraduate work."

But I soon began to think about the implications of the little circuit board, hiding within the telephone. If Commandant Arroyo felt he needed a recording of Alicia incriminating herself in order to move forward, that definitely bought us some more time – especially if the FBI's smuggler-turned-assassin theory flamed out earlier than we hoped. However, buying more time for Alicia's predicament wasn't exactly helping with my own time constraint, given that my employment status would abruptly change from "full-time" to "seeking", were the Monday morning plane to Brazil to roar up into the sky above O'Hare without me.

The bathroom door opened and Alicia stepped barefooted out from the light, residual fog. She was wearing shapeless pajamas printed in a desert camouflage pattern. Not the most enticing sleepwear, but on the bright side, it's what's beneath the wrapping that matters.

Alicia plucked her hair dryer from the top of the dresser, before turning a critical eye to me lying on the bed. "Decided to sleep in your clothes?"

"No, I was just thinking about—" I remembered the microphone. "About taking a shower myself."

"The bathroom's all yours. I can dry my hair out here."

I stripped down and left Alicia to the noise and heat of the dryer. The shower also had noise and heat, but it was the kind that soothed and massaged. I soon reentered the bedroom, reinvigorated and ready.

Alicia's hair dryer was still coping with her mass of long, dark hair. I moved up behind her, as she stood at the mirror. The hot, herbal scent of her shampoo blew back at me. My hands slipped around to work on the buttons of her camo pajama top.

"Francis, we can't." Alicia kept her voice level beneath the hair dryer's hum. "They'll hear us."

I unfastened the last button and whispered into her ear, "I'll turn on the TV."

"At one in the morning? The other guests will complain, and we'll have the night clerk up here."

"We'll keep it quiet."

"We're never quiet."

Alicia laid the dryer on top of the chest of drawers, leaving it on and vibrating against the wood. As she turned to me, there was a flash of the prize inside, before she re-buttoned her camouflage. She brought her lips to my ear. "How can I let myself go, when it feels like the police are right here in the room with us?"

Alicia turned away, switched off the vibrating hair dryer, and pulled the plug for the night.

***

The next morning, Alicia was already dressed and ready, before I was done shaving.

"I told the Historical Society we'd be finished with the Hidalgo panel this week," she said. "And we're not."

"I'm sure they'll give you a pass," I said, "especially after the week you've had."

"My situation is a little too tenuous for me to be begging for more time. Anyway, half a day's work should do it. Carlos and Teresa will be there. I only need to stay out of jail until lunchtime."

A half hour later, I found a parking space behind the Palacio de Gobierno, near the construction area, and we entered the building, passing through the little interior garden, beneath the stained-glass twin goddesses of Law and Order. We found Carlos and Teresa already at work on the mural. It would have been extremely helpful to me if Eduardo had shown up with the Land Rover, but as usual, he wasn't anywhere around.

Alicia spoke to Carlos and Teresa for a few minutes, before continuing on to the Project's office. I followed her. I needed Alicia to make a phone call for me. A question had been nagging at me, ever since Enrique Ponce wondered out loud why Dr. Salazar changed his method and risked stealing an antiquity that was currently on exhibit. I knew a guy who could ballpark the answer, but we weren't exactly pals.

"Alicia, I need you to call your sister," I said, as soon as we were in the office.

"I thought that was just for the benefit of the hidden microphone." Alicia seated herself at the battered, castoff desk.

255

"I need to ask Roger a quick question. But between Roger and me, it's always been a little strained. So I thought, if you called Ellen for a little confab and then she handed Roger the phone for a few words from me at the end, we could skip a lot of awkwardness and just get to my question and his answer."

"A question about what?"

"Just how much a wealthy gun collector might be willing to pay for Villa's fancy Colt."

"Why would Roger know that?"

"On many boring occasions, I've been on the receiving end of his bragging about writing policies to insure the gun collections for two super-rich brothers. They both collect only rare guns, and according to Roger, they're in a fierce competition with each other, each trying to get the harder-to-find gun. So, with every acquisition they make, Roger adds it to the appropriate policy, and the next time the four of us get together, I get to hear about his latest lump of easy money. Anyway, I figure he'll be up-to-date on what unique and noteworthy guns go for at auction."

"Doesn't Roger golf on Saturday mornings?"

"Sunday mornings," I said. "He brags about his handicap, too. It's all part of his charm."

"All right. I'd like to talk to Ellen, anyway. I haven't had a chance to fill her in, yet." Alicia opened her cell phone. "Make yourself comfortable. It's going to be a while, before we get to your part."

While Alicia recounted all that had recently happened to her, I had plenty of time to formulate and hone my questions for Roger. At last, I heard Alicia tell

Ellen that, by the way, Francis would like to speak to Roger for a minute, if he was around.

Apparently, Roger was around, but not right nearby. I held Alicia's phone to my ear and heard a door opening and closing, and then the rattle of a receiver being picked up.

"So, you're down there in Mexico, too?"

"Just a quick question for you, Roger. You've talked about insuring the rare gun collections of those two brothers, and I was wondering about the value of a particular gun."

"An everyday gun or something unusual?"

"It's unusual, alright. A forty-five-caliber Colt single action with ivory grips. The side that shows in the holster has a bas-relief of a long-horned steer's head carved in it and rubies for its eyes. Pancho Villa was wearing the gun, the day he was assassinated."

"Are you saying that's for *sale*?"

"It's a museum piece now. But I was wondering, you know in theory, if it turned up in the US and was offered for sale to a private collector, what might a dealer ask for it?"

"Offhand, I'd say in the range of the thirty to fifty thousand, but that's with mighty fine proof that it's the genuine article."

"Thirty to fifty. Damn."

"And that's not nearly what General Patton's ivory-handled Colt would bring in, if his family ever let loose of it."

"What's Patton got to do with it?"

"Oh, he chased Villa around the Mexican desert, way back when he was a lieutenant under Pershing. He carried the same model of Colt that Villa did. Lots of people did back then. Old, single-action Colts are common as dirt. It's the guy who wore it that's the big deal. So that's where the armor-plated bona fides come in."

"Well thanks, Roger." I wanted to take my information and run.

"Villa's gun, huh? That'd be a score, all right," Roger mused, before coming out with, "Say, the two of you aren't up to any shenanigans down there, are you?"

"No, nothing like that. Just curious."

"Well, just be careful you don't get Alicia into any trouble."

"I'll do my best. Thanks for the info. We should get together for a beer sometime."

"You know I don't drink."

"Anyway, fun talking with you." I closed Alicia's phone and gave it back to her.

"Well?" she asked.

"Market price for Villa's Colt would be thirty to fifty thousand. So says Roger."

"Then, only about ten times what stealing a dusty piece of crap from a museum storage room would get you."

"Looks like Salazar decided that, if he's going to risk his neck, he might as well make it worth his while."

"You think that's what got him killed?"

"What's important is that the FBI thinks so," I said. "Right now, they're supposing the smuggler was the hired gun. So, if they catch Señor Butch crossing back into Texas and he can't prove he wasn't in Mexico last Monday, he's in for a very rough ride."

"And if he can?"

"He'll still have to name drop the next co-conspirator up the food chain, if he wants to make happy hour. That'll probably be the shady broker, and that's who the FBI's been pining for from the beginning."

"Will any of this take the spotlight off me?"

"For that to happen, the FBI has to place a third person – someone other than you and Salazar – at the scene of the crime."

"And they have a guy working on that?"

"Unfortunately," I said, "you're looking at him."

***

I spent the next half hour helping Alicia search through cardboard boxes. We were looking for a 'before' photo of the Hidalgo mural to show the Historical Society, as a comparison to the completed restoration work.

My third box was a pile of papers, receipts, and photographs. Actually, the papers and receipts helped, because their dates indicated that the photographs mixed within the layers were from the early stages of the Project. I took the box over to an impromptu workbench on sawhorses, pushed brushes and mixing palettes to one side, and dumped the box's contents onto the plywood.

With the pile now chronologically inverted, I scanned the photos, one by one, as I picked them off the top of the jumble, and surprised myself by finding a photo of the pre-restoration Hidalgo panel, fairly quickly.

"I found one."

Alicia hurried over to look. "This'll do nicely. Good job." She hugged me briefly, before returning her attention to the photograph. "This was taken with our old camera. That must be why it's with Dr. Salazar's stuff."

"What's with the stash of old bills and receipts?"

"Oh, that's Dr. Salazar's idea of bookkeeping. This was before it was all turned over to me."

Maybe I'd struck gold. I began skimming through the papers, ignoring anything that didn't look like it might be an auto registration in English or Spanish. But I did pause at a bill from the Federal Commission for Electricity. The billing address was for John Salazar at 702 Angel Trias, Apt. 4, Chihuahua, CHIH. That didn't sound like the address of somebody's ranch. But I would've bet money that this was the secret apartment, where Dr. Salazar wanted to have Teresa pose for him just one more time. I folded the electric bill and stowed it in my back pocket. Maybe I'd go have a look later.

As I continued to search the pile for the registration, a small business card slid onto the floor. I picked it up, and the name of the business caught my eye: South Houston Guns and Ammo. The small print read "New, Used, and Collectibles. Indoor Range."

"Alicia, did Salazar go up to Houston much?"

"He went a while ago to renew the paperwork for having the Land Rover down here."

"So, it's a Texas plate on the Rover?"

"Illinois. He drove it down when we first started the project. I guess he was supposed to drive it back, when we were done. But we're not even close to being done yet, so he had to take the Rover up to the Mexican

Consulate in Houston to renew whatever permit he needed to keep the Rover here in Mexico a while longer. He took care of that stuff. Probably, he kept the paperwork in the glove compartment, like most people."

"I'd sure like to see that paperwork," I said. "If the Rover is the property of the Restoration Project, then as the new Director, you could demand its immediate return. That way, you'd have a vehicle to drive, and I could easily run it over to Woodstead's office building."

"What for?"

"For some FBI forensic types to comb through it."

"Looking for what?"

"I'm not really sure," I said. "Maybe a hidden compartment, or for all I know, pottery shards from some Aztec burial tomb. It's all part of Woodstead's care and feeding of the FBI."

"Well, the Rover's not here," Alicia said. "As usual."

"Maybe there's something here in these papers."

I searched through the rest of the pile, but in the end had no luck. All the while, though, my eye kept going back to that business card. I wondered if the old gun that had been transformed into a duplicate of Villa's fancy revolver started out as a "common as dirt" single-action Colt, purchased from a bargain bin at South Houston Guns and Ammo.

"I really should be helping with the mural." Alicia stood up from her desk, holding the photograph in her hand. "Find anything else?"

"Nothing about the Rover. But I need to come up with some piece of paper to tell me who owns the damned thing." I began returning handfuls of paperwork

261

and photos back to the box. "I may have to just drive out to Salazar's ranch and, if the Rover's there, jot down the plate number. Or, if it's unlocked, maybe even take a peek in the glove compartment. Do you know how to get there?"

"I was never invited. None of us were – except, of course, Eduardo." Alicia paused with her hand on the doorknob. "Francis, you know the Rover won't be parked out by the road. There'll be nothing but trouble, if you go out there."

***

I left the Palacio de Gobierno, climbed into the rented Fiesta, and headed across town. In spite of Alicia's warning, I had every intention of taking a drive out to the Salazar ranch. True, I had no idea where the ranch was located, but I knew someone who would certainly have the address somewhere in his stack of papers. And though he might not normally be found in his office on a Saturday, chances were pretty good he didn't make it home the night before.

On the third floor of the building directly across from the little restaurant with the extremely abbreviated wine list, the name 'Enrique Ponce' and the occupation 'Abogado' were lettered in black on the frosted glass of his law office door.

After I knocked, a full minute passed, during which time I heard the sounds of movement inside. I hoped I wouldn't be confronted with the sight of Marybeth, as she looks when she first gets out of bed in the morning.

Eventually, Enrique opened the door. He wasn't the dapper young man he'd been, the previous evening. He was in the same pin stripe suit, but with an open collar, and his hair stood out in unkempt black shocks.

Thankfully, there was no Marybeth.

"Oh, it is only you," Enrique said in English.

"I brought back your tie." About ten minutes before, it had been a wad of blue cloth, riding around on the dashboard of the Fiesta with a low priority assigned to its return. I handed the tie over. "Thanks for the loan."

The lawyer took the tie. His other hand was still on the interior doorknob. I sensed he was weighing the pros and cons of closing the door in my face.

I quickly said, "Also, I don't know if you remember, but last night you said you'd help me establish the ownership of the Land Rover."

"It is Saturday. Who do suggest that I call?"

Enrique Ponce turned from the door and walked to his desk, the heel of his hand pressed to his forehead. I quietly closed the door behind me and followed him across the room. There was a leather couch, a matching chair, and a plain coffee table grouped as a casual consultation area. The cushions on the couch were mashed down. They didn't look like they would un-mash anytime soon.

The air in the law office was stale and warm, with lingering mixed odors of sex and Marybeth's perfume just at the threshold of perception. As I sat on one of the reservedly cushioned, guest chairs in front of his desk, Enrique walked around and dropped down onto a swivel chair containing a small pillow for his back.

"I did find out a little more about the place of registration," I said. "It will not be a Chihuahua license plate. Probably Illinois."

"I have noticed that, with you, everything is somewhat more difficult." Enrique picked his watch off his desk, checked the time, and strapped it on his wrist. "The registration is a public record that I can obtain by submitting the proper forms. You need only to provide me with the license plate number, and I can begin. I will ask the Department of Motors Vehicles in Chicago if I can use e-mail to speed up the process. Beyond that I can promise you nothing."

"I was hoping to have the plate number for you this morning, but Eduardo didn't show up for work. So, I was thinking that if I knew the location of the Salazar ranch, I could simply drive out there and copy down the plate number. I figure you must have Dr. Salazar's address somewhere in your court papers."

"It is a very bad idea for you to go out there. There are ranch hands that work for Lydia Salazar. A stranger caught sneaking around on her property would be beaten senseless – or worse."

"I'll be in and out, before anyone knows it."

"It is best that we wait until Monday, during business hours. Then, as Alicia's attorney, I will call Lydia Salazar and simply ask for the license plate number."

"You'll tip my hand."

"You are concerned that your scheme with the FBI will be damaged, because an attorney merely asks for some numbers and letters that are openly displayed on the rear of a vehicle," Enrique said. "I am concerned that my defense of Alicia Elton against a charge of murder will be damaged, because your act of trespass at the Salazar Ranch will almost certainly be viewed as willful harassment of the murdered man's widow."

"I promise I won't involve Lydia in any of this."

"Promise instead that you will let me handle this in the proper way."

I could see I was getting nowhere. "Okay, I'll let you take care of it."

"On Monday." Enrique now held his head in both hands, elbows on the desk pad. "Is that all that you want from me?"

"Maybe you'd better get some more sleep."

"I cannot. In fact, it is good that you wake me. I am expecting a client this morning. It is for a divorce."

"I've been through one of those. For the sake of your hangover, I hope this one is uncontested."

Enrique brought his head up. "If it was uncontested, a city clerk would handle the paperwork."

"So, you have to fight it out in court."

"It is much more structured than that," the lawyer said. "In a contested divorce, the plaintiff must prove a valid cause to end the marriage. There is a long list of what is accepted by the court, although the elements of each are quite specific."

"Did your client make the list?"

"Through bad timing, yes. An unjustifiable absence from his wife for more than six months gave her grounds to sue my client for a divorce. Had his girlfriend thrown him out only a week earlier, we would easily win on the technicality. However, as it is, my task consists solely of retaining as much of my client's wealth for him, as I can."

Enrique picked up the blue tie I'd returned to him, slid it around under his collar, and began to knot it expertly without a mirror. When he finished, the tie looked great, but everything above the knot still looked haggard.

"I image Marybeth was quite a handful," I said.

"It is good that I am young."

Chapter 14

I walked the block from Enrique's law office to the rental car and slid behind the wheel, but I didn't start the engine. Instead, I withdrew the two cigars I'd stashed in the glove compartment. I banked one in my shirt pocket for later and held onto the other, intending to smoke it while engaged in a little strategizing. I started patting my pockets, searching for the complimentary book of matches, but became lost in thought before finding them.

Monday, of course, would be too late. Monday morning, I had a six-fifteen plane to catch, out of Chicago O'Hare, if I wanted to keep my job. And because Brazil's southern coast is so damned far away, even changing my itinerary to fly to Porto Alegre right from Chihuahua would still have me leaving Sunday afternoon – not to mention forcing me to pay a hefty premium for the last-minute change – because I'd first have to fly in the wrong direction to get to one of the airline's hub cities in order to catch a trans-continental flight.

So, like it or not, I'd be leaving Sunday for Chicago. Which, in turn, meant I had to deliver the Land Rover to Woodstead sometime before then. And it didn't help that Saturday was almost half gone. And even though Woodstead said he wasn't fussy about how I gained possession of the Rover, given the hazard of ranch-hand rough justice for mere trespass, vehicle rustling out at the Salazar ranch could be crossed off the list, too.

267

Therefore, I was left with the prospect of somehow enticing Eduardo to bring the Rover to the Palacio de Gobierno. Which would require a lure.

Luckily, I didn't have to think too hard to come up with one. That automated platform lift was Eduardo's baby. He'd created it with his own hands, and the chances were zero that he'd allow anyone to touch its inner-workings, but him. I would've bet a whole wheelbarrow of pesos on that.

I started the engine, slid the forgotten cigar into my shirt pocket next to its twin, and eased out into traffic, heading back to the Palacio de Gobierno. For my scheme to work, a certain amount of performance art would be called for, but that was familiar territory to Alicia. As I drove the city streets, I let it play out in my mind, considered the variables, and thought it all the way through a couple of times. There was one aspect I didn't like at all, but it couldn't be helped.

***

I again parked near the construction area across the street from the Palacio de Gobierno. I had to walk around three massive tour buses – their big diesels idling, filling the street with noxious fumes – to get to the entrance. Inside, the public areas were filled with Japanese tourists. They were everywhere – strolling under the colonnades and contemplating the murals, snapping group photos in front of the Four Races sculpture in the patio's center, trooping up the stairways to view the artwork on the upper stories. The young adults, in blue jeans and backpacks, obsessively tapped at sleek, cutting-edge, digital devices, and the seniors, in sensible traveling clothes, lugged their old-school

268

Nikons, strapped around necks or slung over shoulders. The sheer volume of incomprehensible prattle, echoing off the patio's hard surfaces, would have drowned out the entire Chihuahua Philharmonic at full throttle.

There was a yellow caution tape strung on pylons around Eduardo's automated lift, and within the confines of the tape, I found Alicia in close discussion with Carlos. Feeling the pressure of time, I interrupted them.

"Alicia, I need to talk with you for a minute," I had to speak loudly.

Alicia gave a last instruction to Carlos, and he moved off. Alicia and I went into a huddle.

"What is it?" she asked. "We're really busy, and all these tourists being here isn't helping."

"I saw all the buses. Is this normal?"

"Teresa says it's because of the Independence Day celebration tonight. Now what do you want?"

"I still need to get the Rover over to Woodstead's office building."

"And the Rover is still not here."

"I figured that," I said. "But I have a plan."

"Which obviously involves me."

"I need you to call Eduardo and tell him that the platform lift is broken, and that he has to come in and fix it."

"Won't he notice that it *isn't* broken?"

"It will be by the time he gets here," I said. "Then after he fixes it, you tell him that you have an appointment with Woodstead at his office, and you want him to drive you there in the Rover. If he balks, you insist that it's the Project's vehicle and remind him he's still on the payroll, as the chauffeur."

"So you finally found out the Rover actually belongs to the Project?"

"No, but Eduardo won't know that. At least, I think he won't."

"Who's going to explain what Woodstead's doing with the Rover?"

"That falls on Woodstead. It's enough that we get the damn thing over there at all. In fact, in front of Eduardo, it'd look better if *you* demanded to know just what the hell's going on."

"Am I doing this alone?" Alicia put her finger directly on the part of the plan that I didn't like.

"I can't be around," I said. "Eduardo might wonder why *I* couldn't drive you over to Woodstead's office in my rental car. But if Woodstead holds the Rover for more than, say, an hour, give me a call, and I'll come and extract you out of there."

Alicia sighed. "This had better work, Francis."

I lifted the caution tape for Alicia to pass under, and we went into the Project's office. Compared to the cacophony out in the central patio, the makeshift office was an isolation booth. I sat at Alicia's desk and used the landline phone to call the number Woodstead had given me. It surprised me that it was Woodstead himself who answered.

"This is Francis Elton. Glad I caught you at your desk. You said you wanted the Land Rover brought over to your office building. Well, it'll take a little resourcefulness, but if all goes well, the Rover should be there sometime this afternoon."

"I am, of course, pleased that you're bringing the Rover over here in such a timely fashion," Woodstead's tone sounded more matter-of-fact, than pleased. "But I do need some time to get the forensic people down from Houston." Woodstead then began to think out loud, "Let's allow them five hours travel time, flying commercial and flashing their IDs through security. But they've already missed this morning's direct flight, haven't they. So, there's another hour for a stop." There was silence on the line. I let Woodstead work it through in his head. "Well, it will have to be a private plane then. Ferociously expensive, of course. Let's say two and a half hours, if they don't dally. Make sure you give me at least that much time. And I certainly hope that you can deliver, Mr. Elton."

"Alicia will give you a call when she knows a little better about what time the Land Rover will be at your building. I can't be there."

"The Rover is all that I require."

After I hung up, I told Alicia what the problem with the lift would be. She took her place behind the desk, withdrew from the middle drawer a piece of paper with a list of phone numbers on it, and dialed. I noticed a sentence written in Spanish at the top of the page. It was upside down to me, but I saw that it was a crib note for getting Dr. Salazar to the phone.

Alicia read off the Spanish sentence phonically, substituting Eduardo's name in the sentence for Dr. Salazar's. "This is Alicia from the Restoration Project. I would like to speak to Eduardo, please."

Except that she used Standard English vowel sounds, giving her an accent, her reading of the Spanish was surprisingly understandable. I raised my eyebrows to silently express astonishment. Alicia stuck her tongue out at me.

Abruptly, Alicia's attention went back to the phone, and she said in English, "Oh, hello, Lydia. This is Alicia. I was expecting to talk to Eduardo. I'm afraid the platform lift is broken again...Yes, the thing that raises us up and down. It's plugged in, but when we press the up button, it won't go up. I was hoping Eduardo could come into town and get it running again. He's the only one who knows how to fix it."

During Lydia's response, Alicia made a rotating-Ferris-wheel hand motion, as though telepathically urging Lydia to get to the point.

"Oh, he's there with you?" Alicia's hand motion stopped. "How lucky. Can he come right away? We're pretty desperate for the platform today. We're up against a deadline..."

Alicia put her palm over the mouthpiece. "They're talking it over." Alicia listened for another half minute. "Oh, that would be super. We'll be waiting for him. Thanks so much, Lydia. You're a dear." Alicia hung up the phone. "Well, that certainly was the last person on Earth I wanted to talk to."

"But he's coming?"

"Yes, Francis. He's coming. A pack of man-eating dogs couldn't keep him away from his precious contraption. Not even that alpha bitch."

I had Alicia call Carlos and Teresa into the office for a little impromptu meeting, while I walked out to the platform lift. I opened the screwdriver blade of my pocketknife and went to work.

When I was done, a wire was detached from the up-button and the cord was jerked a little way out of the pendant. I poked my head into the Restoration Project's office and told Alicia that I was taking off. She gave me a disinterested wave of goodbye and continued her discussion with Carlos and Teresa.

But I didn't leave the Palacio de Gobierno. I went up to the second floor and positioned myself in the shadow of a column. I couldn't leave without knowing if my plan had worked. I now blessed the commotion and distraction generated by my new allies from Japan.

Within a few minutes, the door to the Restoration Project's office opened, and Alicia, Teresa, and Carlos returned to the Hidalgo mural. Carlos lifted the yellow tape for the ladies to pass under, and Alicia quickly discovered, to her feigned dismay, that the lift platform would not go up. As Carlos and Teresa set up the tall stepladder, Alicia passed back under the yellow tape and returned to the office, pretending to go to make the urgent phone call to Eduardo that she'd already made.

There was nothing left for me to do, but wait.

**

A little more than an hour after Alicia had called him, Eduardo's head of black hair passed beneath me. From above, I saw him cross the patio, satchel in hand, and approach the platform lift. Eduardo shook hands with Carlos and gave Teresa a brief hug. He quickly recognized that the problem would be a wire pulled off its terminal within the pendant. He unplugged the power cord from the wall socket and set to work.

To his credit, Eduardo had the lift back up and running in slightly less time than it took me to sabotage it. But the bad part was that, if everything now continued as I planned, the Rover would arrive at Woodstead's office building an hour too soon. I could have kicked myself for not having the wit to insert a time delay into my program.

Fortunately, Eduardo didn't stop after completing his simple repair. Instead, he took his satchel off the platform, set it on the floor, and dropped down on one knee next to it. Eduardo removed the screws holding the cover on the gray plastic, electrical panel mounted at the base of the platform lift, and then wrestled a wide, but shallow, cardboard box from his satchel. I couldn't make out the words on the box cover, but the colorful picture on it showed an approaching locomotive. This, obviously, was the much-anticipated, model-train remote control that Eduardo had ordered with the Project's credit card, but had never bothered to install. I watched from my aerie, while Eduardo, working with a battery-powered hand drill, mounted the receiver module on the panel board and then wired it into the lift's relay circuitry.

Almost an hour later, as tour guides began to round up and herd the Japanese tourists toward the rear exit, Eduardo stood and called to Carlos, asking him to plug the power cord back into the wall outlet. Eduardo then took a handheld remote out of the box, backed up a few steps, and tested his work. In response to the press of buttons, the platform obediently moved up and down. Carlos and Teresa applauded, and because Eduardo's back was to me, I couldn't see if he was smiling when he made his comic bow.

Eduardo coiled up the pendant's long cord and secured it with a plastic tie-wrap to the side of the control panel. This would be his emergency backup. If the remote control failed, while the lift was extended, someone on the ground could easily bring the platform down again with the push of a button.

As Eduardo finished replacing the cover on the control panel, Alicia came into view from the direction of the Project's office. She approached Eduardo holding herself very erect. Eduardo stood and faced her.

This was the moment.

They were too far away for me to actually hear whether Alicia's words were in the form of a command or a request, but Eduardo's defiant stance indicated that it was the former. And Eduardo's verbal response was loud and clear: "Impossible!"

But Alicia stood her ground, her forefinger jabbing the air in front of Eduardo's chest, as she loudly launched into a scathing reminder of his duties as the Project's chauffeur.

During an ensuing volley of short, angry word bursts between Alicia and Eduardo, Carlos stood and watched from afar. Teresa advanced a few steps closer, but then stopped and listened with her hand at her mouth.

In the end, Alicia's obstinacy, the very trait that had, in the past, caused me so much grief, eventually won the day and, for once, had worked in my favor. Eduardo threw his hands in the air, and I heard him exclaim, "*Vámonos.*"

That was the word I was waiting for: "Let's go."

As Eduardo grabbed his satchel, Alicia turned and briskly led the way toward the heavy doors on the side of the building across from the park, never once looking back to check that Eduardo was still trailing behind her, sulking.

I left my observation post, rapidly descended the staircase, and, avoiding the platform lift, slipped quickly around within the shelter of the lower colonnade and into the short hallway leading in from the park side entrance. I had to be certain that Eduardo and Alicia drove off together. As I stood just inside the threshold, helpfully holding open one of the heavy, wooden doors for some entering visitors, I saw the Rover pass by – Eduardo at the wheel, Alicia in the front passenger seat.

I started to commit the retreating license plate number to memory, but stopped with the tardy realization that what was once so critical was now of no importance.

My part of the plan had worked, although, admittedly, with a little help from Eduardo's fastidious need to perfect his creation. In any case, the forensic experts from Houston would soon be in possession of the object of their desire. And now, it was up to Consular Agent Woodstead to keep Eduardo diverted long enough for the clandestine search of the Rover to be completed. And if Eduardo did tumble onto what was happening, I hoped Alicia would remember to pretend equal amounts of surprise and indignation.

***

I reentered the Palacio de Gobierno and crossed over to the platform lift. Carlos had picked up the cardboard box that Eduardo had left lying on the lift's deck and was carrying it in the direction of the Project's office, when I caught up with him.

"Can I see that box for a minute?" I asked in Spanish.

Carlos stopped and handed the box to me. "I believed that you had left."

"Alicia phoned and told me to not hurry back. That she would have Eduardo drive her to her meeting, since he was already here to repair the platform lift," I gave him my prepared line. "But Alicia also told me that Eduardo had changed something to make the lift better. So, because my work involves automated machinery, I was drawn back by curiosity." I tapped the picture on the box. "I see that he used model train parts."

"It is a remote unit for operating the accessories on the landscape for a model train layout," Carlos said, "for items such as track switches, whistles, and lights. When Eduardo was contemplating which type of remote to buy for the lift, I told him about the model train that I have set up in the garage at my house in Mexico City. For its landscape, I use a remote that raises and lowers a bridge. That is what gave me the idea."

I scanned the specifications, written on the box. "It says that this receiver module can control four separate outputs. But the platform lift only needed two."

"It is the smallest unit that this manufacturer makes."

Still reading the specs, I said, "And a range of three hundred meters. Really? How big is your garage?"

"The receiver module must be hidden out of sight. The signal needs much power, so that it is not blocked by the landscape material," Carlos said. "For the platform lift, of course, the long range is not needed. Again, it is merely what comes with the unit."

As I gave the box back to Carlos, he pulled the handheld remote from his shirt pocket and offered it to me. "Only the red and green buttons are active," he said. "Try it. See how clever Eduardo is."

I took the remote and pushed the green button, which had "up" hand-printed in fine point marker above it. After sending the platform upward a few feet, I lowered it with the red "down" button.

"Very nice," I said. "And with no wires to catch on anything." I handed the remote back to Carlos. "And I am sure that Alicia will appreciate the words written in English."

"Teresa wrote the English words for her," Carlos said. "We are so grateful to Miss Alicia for saving the Project by taking on the duties of Project Director. Where would we be now, if not for Miss Alicia?"

***

I left Carlos and Teresa to put the finishing touches on Hidalgo's assassination. Outside the Palacio de Gobierno, the busloads of Japanese tourists had rolled on to the next attraction, and the air looked and smelled clear – clear enough for me to spot two cars illegally parked in the construction zone, facing out. Leaning back against one car – his own – was Sergeant de Leon. He was talking to a man sitting behind the wheel of the other car. Apparently, having noticed me making my way toward my rental car, Sgt. de Leon broke off his conversation and crossed the street at an angle, set on a course that would intercept me. He'd used this same sidewalk-blocking technique to accost me only the day before, making it feel more like modus operandi than déjà vu.

"Good afternoon, Sergeant," I said, in Spanish, as de Leon mounted the sidewalk and obstructed my path.

De Leon glanced at his watch. "There is still some morning yet. But I am sending my officer to an early lunch. He is not happy. His stomach has a strict timetable."

"A problem with the schedule?"

"He is no longer needed here. Alicia Elton has departed in the Land Rover, and Corporal Valdez is following her. We now follow only to know where she is when the time comes to arrest her."

The plainclothes police officer drove past us, unhappily going to lunch.

"I was given to understand," I said, "that further proof of Alicia's guilt was required for an arrest."

"Then you have misunderstood. The requirement was for further investigation into the murder. Eliminating Antonio Peron, as a possible suspect, fulfilled that requirement. Commandant Arroyo has forwarded my report to the Prosecuting Attorney's office. We wait only for his assent."

I hadn't misunderstood. According to Woodstead himself, he had persuaded the Prosecuting Attorney that the State Ministerial Police had insufficient evidence for Alicia's arrest. This was just Arroyo again turning up the heat. And De Leon didn't cross the street merely for exercise. He was delivering a message. But what was Arroyo hoping for? Was it to goad Alicia and me to actually attempt the desperate escape across the border he'd earlier accused us of? Or, less ambitiously, was this merely to prompt an incriminating discussion about the murder in the presence of the hidden microphone in our hotel room?

Regardless of Arroyo's intent, what his latest ploy really pressured me into doing was to finally stop working for the FBI and to start actively working for Alicia's lawyer. The defense argument that Enrique Ponce would present to the judge would, without question, have to chip away at what the State Ministerial Police were so damned sure about. And since the whole case against Alicia was anchored on the evidence the police had found at Villa's Museum, then that was where I should go to find the proof that they were wrong. However, discovering contrary evidence all by myself wasn't going to cut it.

"I am on my way to Villa's Museum, Sergeant." I hoped my Spanish sounded casual. "Should I assume that you will be following me there?"

"You may assume that we are now indifferent to your wanderings. It is only Alicia Elton's movements that immediately concern us, and Corporal Valdez can easily coordinate that. And for me, this afternoon I am to interview a security guard, who has been in Intensive Care, ever since being wounded during the robbery of a pharmaceutical manufacturer's warehouse."

Damn it, the one time I *wanted* to be followed. But out loud, I said, "I do not envy you. Hospital waiting rooms can be boring."

"I am not the Lead Investigative Officer in this case, so I am content to let his sedation wear off, before departing for the interview. Besides, we have already detained a gringo carrying a suitcase full of specialty medications, used for the treatment of rare and difficult diseases. An extremely lucrative, black market trade. Now that we have one of the conspirators, we soon will know everything."

Having recently spoken to a nefarious, fellow countryman who also had a suitcase problem, I decided that this was one of those situations where, in Carlos's words, it is unwise to know too much. Besides, I had a better use for Sergeant de Leon's idle time.

I began with a small enticement. "When I visited the museum before, I saw only what Commandant Arroyo pointed out to me. I thought there might be something he missed."

"I would not want to be the investigative officer who proclaims that Commandant Arroyo has missed something."

"Still, you might find a second look at Villa's Museum to be worthwhile, if only to keep the crime scene fresh in your mind. From what I understand, the FBI is rapidly building a case against their own suspect, and they are closer than you think."

"Why should I concern myself with the antics of the FBI?"

It was time to reveal my one – admittedly scant – credential. "I thought that you might wish to review the scene of the crime with me, since it is through *my* eyes that the FBI observes the physical evidence at Villa's Museum."

"You could easily be prevented from entering Villa's Museum."

"Yes. From what I am told, that would be the typical hired-ranch-hand's reaction."

The expression on de Leon's face must have been the one he used to scare the *pantalones* off recalcitrant suspects. "I see what you are attempting to do. You hope to find some contradictory evidence that will lead us to doubt the conclusions of our investigation. And you need me there to witness your discovery." Sergeant de Leon took a step forward, crowding me. "It is only because I know, for a fact, that you have not returned to Villa's Museum, since your encounter there with Commandant Arroyo, that I even listen to you." His breath was hot. "Yes, I will follow you there. However, be equally prepared that together we may discover additional evidence *against* your wife. And in that case, it will be *your* unprovoked blunder that triggers the immediate arrest of Alicia Elton."

Chapter 15

On my way to Villa's Museum, the car right behind me was not always de Leon's, but the State Police Sergeant was always somewhere in my mirror. I turned off Avenue 20 de Noviembre onto Calle 10a, the corner where the Café Iguana stood at the top of the hill. De Leon was now right on my tail, as we descended the slope. There were no tour buses outside Villa's Museum. In fact, the whole curbside was empty, probably as a consequence of it being lunchtime for the foreign tourists. De Leon pulled in behind me, as I parked just shy of the yellow paint that designated the reserved bus spaces.

Together, but without speaking, De Leon and I made the short walk to the portico and entered the front gate of the former hacienda. A soldier, looking out from the Admission Office, waved us through. There would be no fee for the State Police Sergeant and his companion. No badge had been shown. The soldier, apparently, knew de Leon by sight.

I stopped, as the thought hit me. "Just a minute, Sergeant. Was that soldier here the day of the murder?" De Leon looked into the Admission Office again.

"He was one of them."

"Then I want to ask him if a man came into the museum, a short time before or after the Restoration group arrived that day, saying that he was part of the group."

"Will you be able to describe this man?"

"Ah, no."

283

"That was also the FBI's difficulty," de Leon said. "We have the statements of both soldiers. They concur that only members of the Restoration group were allowed in that day."

"But that is exactly what I am saying. A man posing as a member—"

"Allow me to point out to you that even soldiers can count. And both soldiers stated there were three men and three women in the group. No more, no less. And we know exactly who those six people are. The State Ministerial Police deals in fact, not fantasy."

De Leon led on through the first courtyard. In passing, I looked briefly into Villa's bedroom and saw the holstered revolver, reassigned from the upstairs display, hanging from the headboard. The plainness of its worn wooden grip made it look much more authentic than the ornate ivory grips on Villa's showy Colt. Ten steps further on, we entered the next courtyard and came to a halt in front of the radiator of the bullet-riddled Dodge – the death car for both General Pancho Villa and Professor John Salazar.

There was activity on both sides of the old car. On the driver's side, a pair of young workmen, up on ladders, were fitting the green vinyl fabric onto the metal frame that reached out into the courtyard and extended the shelter for the old Dodge beyond the covered walkway. I was puzzled with this work-in-progress, since the green fabric had been in place when Commandant Arroyo and I toured the crime scene, a few days earlier.

On the passenger's side of Villa's Dodge, a wide opening in the building's wall, under the covered walkway, revealed eight more feet of tiled floor and the far wall of a passageway coming in from the right. On the tiles, a wizened old man squatted, preparing a mixture of brownish mud on a small square of plywood.

Despite the work in progress, the old car was still completely surrounded with chains attached to the walkway columns and to the sides of the opening in the wall – as they were on my last visit when I leaned over a section of it on the driver's side to peer inside, looking for blood stains. In order for visitors to view the vehicle from the passenger side, a short hike around the end of the building and up the passageway was required. But rather than make that hike, I swung one leg after the other to get over the chain strung in front of the old Dodge and again to get over the section of chain that kept tourists' fingerprints off the exhibit on the passenger side. I went down on one knee next to the old man who was mixing the adobe paste.

"A little repair-work?" I asked in Spanish.

Hostile eyes peered at me from under a sweat-stained and frayed straw hat. "Damned bullet holes." He jerked his head at the wall behind him where two rough chunks of adobe were missing. "Damned police made a mess, getting the bullets out." He shot an apprehensive glance toward de Leon and quickly returned to his mixing.

I stood and went over for a closer look at the large divots that had been gouged deeper and wider by the efforts to retrieve the bullets. One ragged gouge had been made about halfway up the wall, while the other was only a quarter of the way up and to the left. Two holes meant two bullets, but that didn't jibe with what both Alicia and Carlos had told me.

I turned my head to ask, "So both bullets passed right through Dr. Salazar, Sergeant?"

"The first one missed." De Leon, still standing just outside the chain in front of the radiator, pointed with his index finger. "You can see there, near the old man, where it hit the floor tiling and was deflected up and into the wall, where we found it. The second bullet passed through Dr. Salazar's head. It then hit that back section of chain and was deflected downward and to the right. You see that it struck the tile closer to the car and was redirected up to impact the wall higher and to the right of the first bullet. There were traces of blood and tissue on this second bullet, so we know that it was one that killed Dr. Salazar."

"The two people that I asked told me they heard only one shot."

"Some people heard one shot, some heard two shots, and a few heard three," de Leon said. "People hear many things. But two, forty-five-caliber bullets were recovered from the wall, and no others were found, not even in the victim."

I looked at the gouges again. I presumed the efforts to extract the bullets without damaging them further was mostly to preserve the biological traces of the late Dr. Salazar. The lead bullets would have suffered heavy distortion from ricocheting off the ceramic tile, even before smacking into the cement-like adobe. And the one that punched through a human skull and glanced off a metal chain, before striking the tile, would have been truly messed up.

I turned back to de Leon. "I see you took care with preserving the evidence, but surely the bullets would have been badly mashed up already."

"True, no useful striation marks remained intact on the bullets for a comparison test," de Leon said. "But their weight was right for forty-five-caliber, and that is precisely the caliber of cartridges that are used in the single action Colt that we found in the bedroom."

I walked back to the old car and crouched down to inspect the damaged link in the chain. It was a beefy chain for its job – the links looked to be about an inch and a half long and fashioned from quarter-inch steel rod. I sat down on the tiled floor, leaned and propped myself by one elbow on the tile, and sighted up past the damaged link and through where I approximated Dr. Salazar's head would be, as he sat in the driver's seat, posing for his photograph. The first thing I saw was the old, dysfunctional security camera, mounted just above the edge of the roof across the courtyard and sightlessly looking down at me from over the treetops. The camera was a good six feet above and about twenty feet over to the right from the spot on the column where Commandant Arroyo had shown me the gunshot residue. But when I re-sighted past the damaged link to the grey marks on the column, a straight line would pass just a few inches above the middle of the top of the car's bench seat. That would surely place Dr. Salazar's head well out of position for his photographic pose behind the steering wheel.

My gaze swung back to the old security camera, which was sheltered on its top and sides by a sheet metal cover, meant to shield the delicate mechanism from the elements. Whomp. The green vinyl material flopped down into place, cutting off my view.

"Hey," I yelled, then switched back to Spanish, "Stop that. Leave that off for a minute." And then to de Leon, "Sergeant, come and look at this."

The two young men installing the awning put up a clamor about having a job to do. The old man then also began ranting that he was told that the police were finished, that these boys had to get their work done, and that his mixture was setting up. While these protests went on, rather than step over the chains, as I had, De Leon took the long way around, past the rear of the car, around the intervening wall, and up from the far end of the passageway to where I sat waiting.

By this time, the young workers had returned to refitting the awning material, while grousing to each other about the gringo. The old man was still yammering too, although now mostly to himself.

"Silence!" de Leon barked. "Stop working. I will talk to this man." De Leon lowered his eyes to me. They were not happy eyes. "What is it you wish me to see, Mister Elton?"

"Sit where I am sitting," I said, getting to my feet, "and sight along where the bullet hit the chain."

It was slow going for Sergeant de Leon to lower his bulk down onto the tiles. He reclined on one elbow, as I had, and looked at the damaged link.

I dropped down on one knee and pointed. "Look up through where Salazar's head would have been, as he sat behind the steering wheel for his photograph."

"Pull that covering back," de Leon ordered.

The two young men quickly complied.

"Look along the line of fire," I said. "What do you see?"

"Naturally, I see the old, useless security camera. It is the only thing of interest in my field of view. But not far to the left is the second-floor column with the gunshot residue."

"Then swing your line of sight to that column." When I saw de Leon's head slightly turn, I asked, "Is that where Salazar's forehead should be? Just barely above the top of the seatback in the middle of the car?"

"We cannot be sure how the victim's head was positioned at the time of the second shot. After the first shot missed, it would be natural for Dr. Salazar to defensively pull his head down and look up toward the sound." De Leon awkwardly got back up on his feet.

As I rose, from being on one knee, I said, "But Salazar ended up, lying dead on the steering wheel."

"That is how the soldier found Dr. Salazar when your wife led him back to this car. But she could easily have moved the body onto the steering wheel, after he was dead."

"Why would she do that?"

"To misdirect the police."

"Let me get this straight," I said. "Alicia shoots at Salazar from the second-floor column and misses. He ducks down for cover, but peeks up at her from behind the seatback. She shoots again and this time hits him in the forehead. Then she runs along that colonnade, down the stairs, across this courtyard and into the next one, enters the bedroom, puts the gun in the holster, comes back into this courtyard and goes over to the public restroom to flush the cartridge casings and surgical gloves down a toilet. She then comes back out to the old Dodge, pulls the dead man off the seat and lays him on the steering wheel, and finally runs back into the little courtyard again, where she meets the soldier running toward her. During this time, the soldier runs what? Fifty feet? I could beat his time on crutches."

"The soldier stated that he had trouble unlocking the gate," de Leon said. "And that he then went to the weapons locker to get a pistol and load it. Only after that did he see the woman running toward him in the little courtyard."

This contrivance smacked of a soldier covering up for his reluctance to run toward the sound of gunfire. But either way, it's a delay that would make their timeline work. And after all, Alicia wouldn't really know how long she might have spent standing there in shock. And if need be, I was sure Commandant Arroyo would have no qualms about extracting a moment of honesty from a hesitant soldier. All things considered, better to let the soldier's story sound contrived.

I switched to another point. "Commandant Arroyo said that there was no vinyl material on the awning frame that day. Why was that?"

"Old man," de Leon spoke sharply, "why was there no material on this framework on the day of the shooting?"

"The lady threw down the book. It tore the material," the old man said. "These boys removed the material to send it for repairs."

"A *book* tore the material?" I asked. "Where did the book come from?"

290

The old man replied, "The soldiers told me that, two weeks ago, a beautiful lady and an elderly gentleman come with a letter of permission to take photographs on a Monday. They wish to make sure that the soldiers will allow them to enter on a day that the museum is closed. Later on, the elderly gentleman and the beautiful lady argue up there." The old man pointed up through the awning's open framework to a section of colonnade that spanned the passageway between the two courtyards. "From the Admission Office, the soldiers hear the lady yelling. They hear the words, 'old fool' and 'book' and 'brass'. One of the soldiers responds to the disturbance. He sees the beautiful lady take the book away from the elderly gentleman, and she throws the book down. The book is from the office of Villa's secretary, up in front above the entrance. The book is very old and heavy. It has guarding on the corners that are made of metal. The book corner cuts right through the vinyl material that is stretched tightly. Then the beautiful lady says to have the awning repaired. She writes a check. The soldier said it is a check that would replace four awnings. The elderly gentleman gathers the old book, but it too is very damaged. The book is sent to be repaired, also."

"I saw the green vinyl in place two days ago," I said.

"Why do these men work on it again?"

"It was not installed correctly." The old man shot a brief, disapproving look at the young workmen. "These boys must take the material off and put it on correctly. The Captain in charge of the Museum has demanded it."

I saw that de Leon's interest had already moved elsewhere. His eyes were once again staring up toward the old, security camera. I kept quiet and let him think.

"Gentlemen, my mixture is drying."

"Then throw it out!" de Leon snapped. But he followed his outburst by roughly pulling a partial pack of cigarettes from his shirt pocket and tossing it to the old man. "Here, take the boys out for a smoke."

As the three workmen walked off, de Leon returned his attention to the old camera on the far roof. "Are you suggesting that there were two assassins? One shoots from the second floor, bracing his gun hand against the column, but misses, and the other shoots from the roof, steadying his gun on top of the old security camera, and does not miss?"

"I do contend that the fatal shot came from the location of the broken security camera. But I am not yet willing to concede that there was more than one shot fired that day."

"And thus, you would dispute the facts."

"I believe that more than one conclusion can be drawn from them."

"Believe what you wish. We waste our time talking of this."

Wonderful. Instead of injecting doubt, I'd only succeeded in pissing off Sergeant de Leon. And I sensed he was done with our little expedition. So, as de Leon started to turn from me, I pulled the two cigars from my shirt pocket and held one out to him. He stopped and took the cigar from my hand.

De Leon rotated the cigar until the label on the band was in view. He then smiled at the cigar and said, mostly in English, "Ah, *Méxicano*. You are converted."

I removed the cellophane and, using the scissors of my Swiss Army knife, snipped off the tip of my cigar.

Sgt. de Leon tore the cellophane from his cigar with his teeth and bit off the end. With his cigar clenched in his teeth, de Leon lit a match and held it to the end of my cigar, before lighting up his own. Together we retraced de Leon's steps down the passageway, taking the long way around the vintage Dodge, silently drawing in the richness of our first few puffs.

Hoping the moment was right, I said in Spanish, "If a gunshot residue test on that old security camera were performed, no matter what the result, you will have established another fact."

De Leon blew a cloud of smoke. "That would require a forensic technician. I am not prepared to call for one, until I have sufficient reason to do so."

That sounded like a maybe, so I let it simmer on low for the time being. However, I figured I'd bought a cigar's length of ear time with the State Police Sergeant, and I was curious about another item that didn't fit.

"One of the Restoration Group's artists, Carlos, told me that on the day of the shooting, when they were having drinks at the Café Iguana, Lydia Salazar spent some time in the manager's office checking her e-mails."

"I read Lydia Salazar's statement," de Leon said. "She said that she was alone in the manager's office at the time of the shooting and that she heard nothing. I recall no mention of e-mails."

"I intend to go to the Café Iguana, after I leave here, and ask the manager about that."

"Why does this interest you?"

"What restaurant manager allows his patrons to freely use his computer? It is out of the ordinary," I said.

"I doubt that it is relevant. But you are free to indulge your curiosity."

This was nice, except that I wasn't at all sure the Iguana's manager would indulge *me*. On the other hand, I was damn sure that no café manager would blow off an investigative officer from the State Ministerial Police.

As casual as I could make it sound, I said, "So Lydia stated that she heard nothing, during the time that she was alone in the manager's office." I paused for a draw and release of smoke, before adding, "It makes you wonder. How does a person recall exactly where she was at the moment that she heard nothing?"

De Leon wearily asked, "What are you now suggesting?"

"If the manager's office is soundproof, I am not suggesting anything."

De Leon puffed on his cigar, and I noticed he took a departing look up at the defunct security camera, just before we left the larger courtyard.

Okay, I told myself, you can shut up now. You've got de Leon thinking. And thinking is the gateway to doubt.

Still, we were almost up to the iron bars of the front gate, before de Leon announced, "We will talk to the manager."

***

Instead of continuing right on up the hill to the Café Iguana, Sgt. de Leon stopped just outside Villa's Museum, beneath the portico where the old man and the two young workers were still smoking up his cigarettes. De Leon took down their names in his notebook and then sent the workmen home for the day. The old man looked as if he were about to protest, but then turned and glumly walked away. The younger men followed. De Leon stood and watched, until the trio sardined themselves into the cab of a small pickup truck and drove off.

Abruptly, de Leon turned and re-entered Villa's Museum. I wasn't sure what he was up to, but I stayed with him all the way back to the Admission Office.

There were now two soldiers behind the counter. De Leon displayed his badge this time and ordered, "No one is allowed up on the roof without my permission. Also, the wall behind the old Dodge and the damaged tiles are to remain as they are now, and the green awning above Villa's car is not to be reinstalled. Your Captain will be informed of the justification for my orders."

The soldiers looked at one another, but then said, almost in unison, "Yes, sir."

De Leon focused on one of the soldiers. "You were at the Café Iguana with the members of the Restoration Project on the day of the shooting."

"Technically, I was off duty," the soldier immediately went on defense. "Our relief was late, as usual, but the other—"

"How many gunshots did you hear that day?" de Leon demanded.

The soldier hesitated, before saying, "I heard only one of the shots." The soldier watched de Leon's face, and then quickly offered, "Perhaps, a second one came later, during the excitement of the ambulance."

Without a further word, de Leon left the Museum. I hurried to catch up, and side-by-side we walked uphill the two blocks to the Café Iguana – although with de Leon's bulk crowding the narrow sidewalk, I repeatedly had to step off the curb. Finally, I just walked in the gutter, a strategy that almost got me run over by a tour bus rumbling down the hill toward the Museum.

"Your insinuations do not persuade me," de Leon broke his silence, while remaining oblivious to my pedestrian discomfort. "And yet, I pursue them. I will tell you why. On the day after the murder, I went to the firing range. I set up a target the size of a man's head at the distance we measured from the second-floor column to the old Dodge. Eighty-two feet. This is many feet beyond which my fellow officers and I must qualify with our handguns, shooting at a silhouette of a man's torso. With my wrist steadied against a post, I fired a full magazine at the smaller target from my service pistol."

"How did you do?"

"I found that it was not impossible," de Leon said. "But I admit that I would not have qualified that day, if the smaller target and that distance were my challenge. And I must ask myself. Does this woman, a mere painter, fire her antique revolver with more accuracy than Sergeant de Leon of the State Ministerial Police? This, Mister Elton, is from where my doubt arises."

I refrained from enlightening the State Police Sergeant concerning Alicia's skill with a handgun. Better to take his doubt, however ill-founded, and run with it.

***

Inside the Café Iguana, de Leon and I passed right on through the empty dining room – it was too late for lunching tourists and still too early for the locals. We continued along the hallway to the manager's office.

Behind an open laptop computer, a man with thinning hair, wire-rim spectacles, and a '70s-width necktie worked at his desk. Several file cabinets stood against one wall, a bullfight poster hung on another, and a couple of plain chairs faced the manager's desk. Through the window to the manager's right, I could clearly see the flat rooftops of Villa's Museum, less than two blocks away and one story higher than the roofs of the intervening houses that lined the descending slope of Calle 10a.

"I am Sergeant de Leon of the State Police. This man is Francis Elton. He is assisting me. I just have a few questions, concerning the shooting last Monday at Villa's Museum."

"It was most tragic," the manager said. "Please, sit down. I was so surprised to learn that it was John Salazar."

"Did you know Dr. Salazar?" de Leon asked, as he and I sat.

"Slightly. I knew that he was a Professor of Fine Arts at the University, but not much more. I know his wife, Lydia, much better, of course. She was married to my brother Edgar before his death. Also a most tragic death."

"My condolences," de Leon said. "On that Monday, did you allow Lydia Salazar to use your computer?"

"She has my permission to use this computer to check her e-mail, whenever she comes into the city and stops here for lunch. In fact, her chauffeur installed some software recently to make it easier for her. Apparently, he is quite clever with computers."

"Was Lydia Salazar checking her e-mail, at the time her husband was shot?" De Leon had his notebook and pen out now, using his thigh as a writing table.

"I cannot really say. I know that she was here at the Café that afternoon, because she spoke with me. I can only assume that she checked her e-mail, as usual. But on Mondays, I am busy with the inventories in the kitchen and at the bar."

"That is fine. What you have already told me is sufficient," de Leon said. "The others in the group will know if she was seated with them at the time that they heard the shots."

I caught the hissing sound of the final 's' in "*disparos*", as de Leon spoke of shots, plural.

"For now," de Leon added, "I am satisfied about the computer." He turned to me. "Mister Elton, if you have something else to ask this gentleman, you may ask it."

"Thank you, Sergeant." I wasn't expecting this, but I jumped right in. "I do have a question. How many gunshots did you hear that day, sir?"

"How many? Only one. I was with my bartender. He heard it too. I remember that he said that it sounded like the firing of a gun."

I glanced toward de Leon and saw with satisfaction that he was writing in his notebook.

"Allow me to add my condolences for your brother's death," I said.

"Thank you. Many years have passed now, of course. But his was a good life suddenly cut short."

"How did it happen?" I asked.

"Edgar and Lydia were riding their horses in the desert beyond their ranch. A gust of wind caught up a plastic bag. Edgar's horse shied and reared up. He fell from his horse and hit his head on a rock. It killed him instantly."

"So then, Lydia inherited the ranch where she now lives?" I asked.

"Yes, our Uncle, when he died, left his ranch to my brother – Edgar had helped him with his horses toward the end. Then when Edgar was killed, Lydia, of course, inherited the ranch. Such a beautiful, young woman she was, when they were first married. Such refined features. You would not know that she came from one of the poor villages outside of the city."

"Thank you. That is all we require." Sergeant de Leon had, apparently, finished with his notes.

De Leon stood and shook hands with the manager, who seemed confused, perhaps wondering that the interview had ended so suddenly. As I shook the manager's hand, my own wondering concerned what it might take for the State Police Sergeant to finally knock the final "s" off "*disparos*."

***

Out on the sidewalk in front of the Café Iguana, de Leon opened his cell phone.

"I will call for the forensic technician." De Leon punched at the keys. "I cannot have uncertainty. We will soon discover if a gun was fired in proximity to the broken security camera on the roof."

While de Leon called in and set up the GSR test with a technician, with a rush of insight it became clear

299

to me that Alicia wasn't just caught up in Salazar's murder by being at the wrong place at the wrong time. She was set up. And it wasn't by some unscrupulous, antiquities broker up in Chicago. This murder, like all murders, was local.

Just as Sgt. de Leon closed the lid on his cell phone, both our cell phones sang their individual ring-tones. I stepped away from de Leon to answer mine.

Alicia's voice spoke hurriedly in my ear, "Francis, for God's sake, get over here. Your colossally stupid, freaking boneheaded scheme just blew all the hell up, and I'm trapped in the rubble. Arroyo's here arguing and posturing with Woodstead, Lydia's screaming for blood, more police are showing up, and there's this gigantic, black guy who looks like he's just spoiling to bash some heads. I can't understand any of it. It's all Spanish, Spanish, Spanish. But *your* name comes up a *lot*, and it's all about that damned Land Rover."

"Wait, wait. Why is Arroyo there? Why is Lydia there?"

"We had to pick up Lydia on the way. Eduardo brought her into town for some shopping, while he repaired his precious platform lift. That's why he didn't want to drive me over here, but he didn't actually *say* so at the time. And like a dope, I insisted, because *you* told me to. *Now* look at the mess I'm in."

"This is crazy. How did Arroyo get involved?"

"Lydia called him. I guess they're pals. Now get your ass over here, Francis."

I put away my phone. De Leon still had his phone propped to his ear with his shoulder, while he wrote in his notebook.

After de Leon finished his call, he ordered in stern, accented English, "You will come with me to the office of Consular Agent Woodstead."

"Alicia told me what's going on over there," I said. "I was just about to drive over and—"

"No. You will come with me. By order of the Commandant."

***

Sergeant de Leon cruised along with the early-afternoon traffic, his cell phone again at his ear, his spiral notebook balanced on his knee. On the phone de Leon was assigning someone the task of looking up a vehicle's registration. When he read off some numbers and letters, I recognized the license plate number that I'd started to memorize, as Alicia and Eduardo had sped off together in the Land Rover.

While we were stopped at a red light, de Leon jotted something more in his notebook. I stole a look at it, but couldn't read his handwriting. De Leon then put his cell phone and notebook away and sat staring straight ahead, until a honking horn urged him forward with the greening of the traffic light.

As he belatedly accelerated through the intersection, de Leon spoke in Spanish. "Some of the observations that you have brought to my attention today have provoked my interest. But such things have a way of turning out to be nothing. I would not approach Commandant Arroyo with any of it without proof. Your false allegation against Antonio Peron exhausted the Commandant's patience with you. He will hear no more of your conjectures."

I was already aware that I'd lost credibility with Arroyo. However, at the moment, I wasn't talking to the Commandant. So, I pressed on with my agenda. "Assuming that only one shot was fired, when your forensic technician finds gunshot residue on the camera's metal covering, then that shows—"

"It is not a matter of *when* the forensic technician finds the residue, but *if*," de Leon said. "We must wait for the test result, before further exploring your idea. In the meantime, perhaps you can explain why your wife would throw a book down on the awning, causing its removal and, as a consequence – let me point out – opening both lines of fire down to the front seat of Villa's Dodge, the one from the second story column and the one from the rooftop."

"Alicia was not the beautiful lady that the soldier saw throw the book. That was Lydia Salazar. But the elderly gentleman, in the old man's recounting, was certainly Dr. John Salazar. I think Lydia caught Dr. Salazar stealing some rare old book – probably a first edition that he could sell for a good amount of money. In a fit of anger and disgust, Lydia grabbed the book from her husband's hand and threw it over the railing."

"What makes you think that Dr. Salazar was stealing the book?"

"The soldier reported that he heard a woman's voice yell 'old fool', 'book', and 'brass'. But I think that the soldier reported hearing the word 'brass', because later someone – maybe Dr. Salazar, himself – had mentioned that a brass corner protector on the old book tore the awning. But I doubt that the woman's voice actually yelled 'brass'. It is more likely that she yelled 'thief'.

The words are close in Spanish, but cannot be confused in English, even when heard yelled from a distance. And I am sure you are aware that Alicia does not speak Spanish. Not to mention that, if Alicia had yelled in her boss's face, calling him an old fool, I doubt that she would still have been a member of the Restoration Group last Monday."

We were again stopped for a red light, when de Leon said, "Accepting that it was Lydia Salazar who took the book away from her husband, if Dr. Salazar had not attempted to steal the book in the first place, then Lydia Salazar would have nothing to angrily throw down on the awning. Therefore, it could not have been her intent to cause the awning to be removed. In fact, it would be more reasonable to argue that Alicia Elton simply took advantage of the chance opening of another line of fire, allowing her to shoot Dr. Salazar from a less incriminating vantage point, than the one behind her camera on its tripod. Something, you may remember, that we had already deduced."

The light turned green, and de Leon drove ahead.

I couldn't let this stand as fact. "You just found out about book throwing today. Obviously, Lydia neglected to inform the investigative officer who took her statement that *she* was responsible for damaging the awning cover and having it sent for repair. Just like she neglected to hear the firing of a high caliber gun, while sitting in an office next to a window overlooking Villa's Museum, less than two blocks away."

"I was not present when Commandant Arroyo took Lydia Salazar's statement. She would speak only to the Commandant. They share the same social circle. Her ranch and his ranch are near to each other." De Leon put on his turn signal and stopped, waiting for traffic to clear before making a left turn. "But regardless of what Lydia Salazar told Commandant Arroyo, the presence of the green awning in its proper place that day would have only altered your wife's line of fire, not Dr. Salazar's fate."

***

Two police patrol cars, red and blue lights spinning gaily, were double-parked in the traffic lane outboard of two full-size sedans parked at the curb in front of Woodstead's office building. The ultra-plain, unmarked sedans looked every bit as official as the patrol cars.

Positioned in pairs in front of and behind the patrol cars, four uniformed police officers – one, a young woman with dyed-blonde hair, tied in a ponytail – were busily redirecting traffic around the lane they'd blocked.

De Leon held his badge out his lowered window and proceeded slowly, but relentlessly, straight into the traffic snarl. In response, the two traffic policemen on the far side halted the oncoming cars, while the pair on our end, with whistles and hand gestures, hastily cleared a path, allowing de Leon to continue forward until coming to a halt behind the double-parked patrol cars.

Under the hostile stares from ill-treated drivers, de Leon and I got out and mounted the steps to Woodstead's office building. Inside, at the far end of the hallway lined with sleepy oil paintings, a small crowd had gathered in front of the closed door of the lovely secretary's office.

As de Leon and I neared the crowd, I spotted Alicia. She stood within arm's reach of Corporal Valdez and, like everyone else, was focused on a heated argument being waged between Consular Agent Woodstead and Commandant Arroyo. Standing next to Arroyo, Lydia Salazar intermittently injected verbal venom into the argument. Behind Lydia, Eduardo stood, looking at the floor and, undoubtedly, wishing he were somewhere else. Woodstead's stoic driver, his suit coat unbuttoned, was at the Consular Agent's side. Two of Arroyo's officers, in shirt sleeves and with guns holstered on their belts, valiantly maintained a strategic position between the Commandant and the black Marine. The Marine – who had a clear view over the heads of everyone else in the hallway, including Woodstead and me – was, this time, wearing what looked like a size-50, sports jacket. There was no telltale bulge, but I knew he wasn't wearing the jacket because of a chill in the hallway.

During our approach, I picked up on the argument, which at this stage seemed to turn on the fine point of whether the building in which we all were standing was technically a branch of the Consulate in Juarez, or merely rented office space. Lydia's mean-spirited contributions had to do with inheritance and ownership of the Land Rover.

Arroyo noticed us and waved Sgt. de Leon over to him.

I stepped in close to Alicia and asked in a low voice, "What the hell?"

"Evidently, I've stolen a car." Alicia's eyes stayed on the confrontation in front of us.

"I thought Woodstead just needed the Rover for an hour. Just for some FBI lab coats to poke around in it, like the border guards do."

Alicia pressed her shoulder against mine, tilted her head toward me, and spoke beneath the argument, "When we got here, that big black guy was out front. He directed Eduardo to drive around to the parking garage underneath the building, but I noticed in my mirror that he followed us on foot all the way down the ramp with his phone to his ear. And then in the garage, the black guy opened my door and said that Consular Agent Woodstead had some papers he wanted to go over with me, and that my two friends could wait more comfortably up in his conference room, where there were refreshments."

"Well played by Woodstead," I commented.

"I thought so too. And so, we all trooped up to this floor. But before we were reassembled, I could see that Lydia had become suspicious – just by the set of her lips and how she was eyeing things. Suddenly, she snapped a few words at Eduardo, and he disappeared. And I thought, oh God, she's sent him back down to the parking garage. And before I could even think, Eduardo reappears and is all frenzied and gasping out bursts of Spanish. And Lydia got right on her cell phone, and I heard her demanding '*Comandante* Arroyo' and what sounded like 'immediately', except for the ending. Anyway, I thought, freaking great, Francis's elaborate plan to keep me out of jail is going to get me arrested again. And it actually ran through my mind to make a run for it. But this plainclothes cop shows up so fast it's like he'd been hanging around right outside the front door."

I looked past Alicia to see Cpl. Valdez break into a smile, but quickly suppress it, by exploring the inside of his cheek with his tongue.

This was my first hint that Cpl. Valdez understood English. I made a mental note to be careful about what I said around Arroyo's men.

"...and furthermore," Woodstead's voice rose a few decibels in precise Spanish, "that young man drove the Land Rover into the garage of this building of his own free will. Naturally, we take security precautions and run a routine check of all unknown vehicles entering the garage area. It is standard procedure."

"You are in possession of Lydia Salazar's Land Rover without her permission," Arroyo fired back. "It is the very definition of vehicle theft."

"This woman kills my husband, and you protect her," Lydia raged in Woodstead's face. "Now she steals my car, and you protect her once again."

Arroyo briefly consulted with de Leon during Lydia's outburst. Arroyo then played what he must have felt was the ace of trumps. "I have been informed that Temporary Importation papers for the Land Rover were originally filed by Dr. Salazar six months ago and renewed just two weeks ago. Both times Dr. Salazar presented a U.S. registration certificate demonstrating his personal and legal ownership of the vehicle."

"Let us be precise." Woodstead remained unruffled. "It was sixteen days ago that Dr. Salazar reentered the United States with the Land Rover and drove to Houston where he stayed for two nights. And yes, during that time he reapplied for another Temporary Importation of Vehicle permit at the Mexican Consulate.

However, I think you should know that the Restoration Project, a legal entity formed entirely for the purpose of restoring the murals at the Palacio de Gobierno, is on record as the original purchaser of the Land Rover. As a matter of convenience, the Project sold the Rover to Dr. Salazar for one dollar with the stipulation that ownership of the vehicle would revert back to the Restoration Project when Dr. Salazar's association with the Project had ended – which, unfortunately, has come to pass."

It kind of pissed me off that Woodstead knew all of this, but hadn't told me. Of course, I hadn't thought to ask him either.

Woodstead went on, "It was for the purpose of informing Alicia Elton, the new Director of the Project, about this stipulation that I asked her to bring the Land Rover here today, so that its location could be verified and the paperwork for legal transference initiated."

"So far as Mexico is concerned," Arroyo countered, "the Land Rover was registered to Dr. Salazar as the legal owner, and following his death, through our laws of inheritance, his wife, Lydia, now owns the vehicle. The Sovereign State of Mexico does not recognize questionable matters of convenience forged by lawyers in another country."

"In addition to reapplying for the vehicle permit," Consular Agent Woodstead abruptly switched to English, as though to emphasize that he was moving on to a different matter, "while in Houston, Dr. Salazar also did two rather interesting things. The first one involved a visit to an establishment named South Houston Guns and Ammo. According to our Federal Bureau of

Investigation, Dr. Salazar bought a brand new, forty-five-caliber, Colt revolver, fitted with a laser sight, and two boxes of the appropriate ammunition. I'm sure you are aware of his dual citizenship, which facilitated his purchase."

"Given Dr. Salazar's apparent need for ready money," Arroyo responded in English, "it's most likely that this was merely a straw purchase, in order to profit from a quick resale to someone in Texas who is legally barred from purchasing a firearm."

But I had a different take on Woodstead's revelation. Namely, holy cow, the FBI discovered where the real murder weapon came from. Here was a weapon that actually fit the crime. Just turn on the laser sight, hold the red dot steady on the target, and bang, you're a marksman.

"Then perhaps you'll find this more noteworthy," Woodstead soldiered on. "The sales clerk at the gun store told the FBI that he remembered Dr. Salazar from his purchase a month earlier of a rather inexpensive and elderly Colt single action revolver of the type that was popular in the early nineteen-hundreds."

Arroyo asked, "Do you wish to persuade me that Dr. Salazar himself transformed the elderly Colt into a replica of Villa's revolver, unwittingly providing the means for his own murder?"

"It is a comparison of the serial numbers on the sales record to the numbers stamped on your 'State's exhibit one' that will persuade you," Woodstead responded smoothly. "Also, during his latest trip to Houston, Dr. Salazar found time to mail a package to his office at the Chicago Art Institute. The package contained an antique

Colt revolver with a ruby-eyed steer-head carved into one of its ivory grips, which he had at some earlier point liberated from the Villa Museum. The FBI, of course, intercepted the package."

"Naturally, we have already been notified of the FBI's recovery of Villa's Colt," Arroyo said. "And I also remember wondering at the time, if it did not occur to the famous FBI to patiently follow the package to its final delivery point and arrest their mysterious broker for receiving stolen goods."

Woodstead ignored the gibe. "I bring all this up only to inform you of our recent discovery that Dr. Salazar did not, in fact, use his regular smuggler of stolen artifacts to transport the various guns into and out of Mexico. The smuggler is presently in FBI custody in El Paso, Texas, and he was quite forthcoming about the particulars of his cross-border operation, during the course of exculpating himself from Dr. Salazar's murder. Perhaps, you now see that the Land Rover has played a crucial role in Dr. Salazar's gun smuggling activities, and therefore the vehicle needs to undergo a rather thorough scrutiny."

"The Chihuahua State Ministerial Police are perfectly capable of examining a vehicle," Arroyo said. "And our active murder investigation supersedes your combing the ashes of a defunct smuggling operation."

Woodstead withdrew a cell phone from his jacket pocket. "Just let me check that the vehicle has been reassembled and is ready to be released." Woodstead turned away and spoke quietly for half a minute. When he turned back around, pocketing his phone, he stated, "I must insist that the forensic staff be allowed as much time as necessary to examine the Land Rover and process its contents."

Lydia jumped in. "And *I* insist that my vehicle be *returned*. Commandant, this is intolerable."

"The theft of a vehicle has occurred here," Arroyo said. "That cannot be overlooked. Alicia Elton and Francis Elton conspired to steal the Land Rover from its rightful owner. That much is indisputable. And although the theft was performed with your, at least, passive assistance, you, Consular Agent, are, of course, shielded by your diplomatic status. However, Mr. and Mrs. Elton *and* the Land Rover will now come with me."

Bad as this sounded, I didn't immediately protest, trusting that Woodstead would deftly perform some cunning maneuver to save us.

"Commandant," Woodstead wearily spoke in English, "does it truly matter where the Land Rover is parked, before it is, in due course, returned to Mrs. Salazar?"

"*I* will decide what does and what does not matter within my jurisdiction!" Arroyo announced in loud, belligerent English.

Apparently taking Arroyo's outburst as a call to arms, the two plainclothes officers, standing between the Marine and Commandant Arroyo, each lifted a hand to the service pistol, holstered at his waist, and assumed that awkward elbow-stuck-out, cop-on-alert pose, as they spread apart to cover the area. Woodstead's driver slid his right hand beneath the lapel of his jacket, enlarging the bulge under his left armpit. The Marine's massive black hands were clenched, as he stood foursquare and ready for the order to clear the deck of all and sundry policemen. And even though neither Sgt. de Leon nor Cpl. Valdez had moved a hand toward his gun, I was still poised to pull Alicia to the ground, the moment the first weapon was drawn.

Woodstead allowed Arroyo his moment of political machismo, before offering, "Commandant, may I send an e-mail to your office with the phone number of the South Houston Guns and Ammo store? A copy of the sales receipt, containing the serial number of the old revolver that Dr. Salazar purchased, might tidy up a loose end for you. Judges do so love a paper trail. And I am sure the proprietor will be happy to cooperate with the Chihuahua State Ministerial Police. I will make a point of phoning him myself, so he will anticipate your call."

"One of my officers can manage to look up a phone listing."

"Yes, of course," Woodstead said. "No sense making it easy for him."

Much to my relief, Arroyo and Woodstead were back to contesting verbally. Hands gradually relaxed and fell away from pistol grips.

Woodstead continued on his diplomatic tack. "Perhaps my assistance would be more appreciated, if I could arrange with the FBI for the return of a certain stolen Colt worn by Pancho Villa."

"That process, I'm sure, has already been initiated."

"I, too, am sure of it, since I had a hand in the process," Woodstead said. "But it is important to note that the particular department within your government that will receive Villa's gun from the FBI's care has yet to be determined. Naturally, given my position and close involvement in this matter, I could exert a good deal of influence in this determination. And certainly, it could be argued that it should rightly be a high-ranking *police* official who places the recovered, historically important handgun into the grateful hands of the Mexican Army. Perhaps, some type of ceremony would be involved, given this week of national celebration."

"What are you suggesting?" Arroyo asked.

But I suspected that the Commandant was already envisioning his image, front page, top-of-the-fold, ceremoniously returning the stolen cultural icon to a chagrined Army officer of suitable rank.

"I could have Villa's Colt on your desk on Monday afternoon," Woodstead said. "I need only a few more hours in possession of the Land Rover."

Arroyo hardly paused before declaring, "Of course, I would personally take on the responsibility with an item of such historic importance." Then, in Spanish, Arroyo ordered his men, "Take Mr. and Mrs. Elton into custody for the theft of a vehicle. The Land Rover will remain here, pending its return to Mrs. Salazar." Arroyo turned back to Woodstead and asked, "Is this satisfactory for now, Consular Agent?"

Woodstead considered the situation for a bare few of my heartbeats, before sacrificing two pawns. "Yes, Commandant." His Spanish was still crisp. "For now."

"Hey! Wait a minute!" I yelled in English. "Nobody stole a car here." A plainclothes officer, who I hadn't previously noticed, stepped up from behind me and grasped my upper arm. Unnerving as this was, I kept my voice loud. "Alicia simply asked Eduardo to drive her over here, and he did. How is that car theft? They picked

313

up Lydia along the way. Is she guilty of kidnapping too?"

"Conspiracy to commit major theft will be sufficient for the moment," Arroyo said in English. "An agreement has been reached with your Consulate. No further discussion is necessary."

"Woodstead, just give the damned Rover back!" I yelled. For which, I received a rough warning shake that slammed my teeth together, courtesy of the officer gripping my arm.

"I can't believe this," Alicia said. "Richard!"

But Woodstead was again on his cell phone, with his back turned to us.

As the opposing forces began to disperse, Arroyo turned to Lydia and inquired in polite Spanish, "Mrs. Salazar, would you and your chauffeur spare us a moment of your time? We just need your statements in order to press charges. At my office, naturally, where you can be more comfortable."

"Certainly, Commandant," Lydia responded, as though she'd been asked for the next dance. "I would be delighted."

I was about to launch into another protest when the officer holding me jerked my shoulder up, pirouetted me around, and hauled me toward the exit.

Behind me, amid the sounds of scuffling and, no doubt, unladylike kicking, Alicia yelled, "Ow! Take it easy, you freaking ape. Richard, *do* something!"

From a distance, I heard Consular Agent Richard Woodstead offer, "I shall inform Mr. Ponce of your additional legal difficulties."

Chapter 16

As Alicia and I were taken down the steps in front of Woodstead's office building, the hallway emptied out behind us. I was pushed against the curbside front fender of the first unmarked car, and Alicia was positioned at the rear fender. My arms were gathered behind me. I heard the zip of a tie-wrap, as my wrists were snugly bound. Alicia's wrists were similarly strapped together, and the female uniformed officer, summoned from traffic duty, patted her down. I anticipated that my face would be slammed down on the hood. But instead, I was merely bent forward with a firm push. My chest made a relatively soft, although awkward, landing, which allowed me time to turn my head and avoid a nose plant. By U.S. standards, I was receiving the respectful treatment typically reserved for high-class criminals, like upper management embezzlers or insider traders. Following a few cursory pats, I felt my wallet leave my rear pocket.

With my cheek still on the hood, I saw an imposing torso approach. It stopped just shy of the front bumper. I twisted with discomfort onto my left shoulder to see Sergeant de Leon's heavy-browed face glaring down at me.

"You are wise not to resist," de Leon said in English. Then his eyes lifted up from my face, and he ordered in Spanish, "Put the gringos in this car."

Damn it. Just when I had it mostly figured out. Starting with the new Colt revolver, the laser sight, and the forty-five-caliber ammunition, I added a simple firing mechanism and a control unit. Soon, in my head, I had an automated machine, hastily assembled from parts that I knew to be readily at hand, whose dual purpose was to kill Dr. Salazar and leave Alicia as the sole suspect.

Sensing that this was my last opportunity, my words hurriedly tumbled out in English, "Be sure to have your forensic technician check for gunshot residue on the *underside* of the camera cover, too."

De Leon's eyes came back to my face for a long moment, and then lifted again. "Just put the woman in the car for now, Corporal. Leave that front window down, so she can breathe." De Leon's gaze shifted slightly. "And you, stand this man up. I will talk to him." As I was pulled up off the hood to face him, de Leon switched to English. "Why would the forensic technician find residue *under* the camera cover? It makes no sense to hold the gun there, and I doubt that there is space enough to do so. For the sake of accuracy, the shooter would steady his hand by resting it on *top* of the cover."

"The gun was steady, all right. In fact, it was rock solid. But no hand fired it. At least, not directly. That brand new Colt revolver, the one Woodstead said Dr. Salazar bought in Houston a few weeks ago, there's room enough under the cover to strap it to the side of the old, broken, security camera and line it up, using the laser sight, to where a man's head would be, as he sat in the driver's seat. The camera's cover would conceal the gun, and it could easily be fired by remote control."

"Mr. Elton, I grow weary of your fairy tales."

"The revolver was cocked beforehand and had a bottle release solenoid from a Coke machine mounted within the trigger guard. The output module from a model train's accessory controller turned on the laser, and when the red dot appeared on Dr. Salazar's forehead, while he held still for his photograph, a second remote button was pushed, activating the solenoid that pushed the trigger back and fired the gun. The killer could see the rod dot on the target on closed-circuit TV through a miniature surveillance camera that was taped to the barrel of the gun."

"A closed-circuit TV being viewed where?" de Leon asked.

"The laptop on the manager's desk at the Café Iguana. You'd probably need a power booster to extend the range of the café's WiFi, but that's available locally at any electronics store."

"Do *not* tell me that you accuse Lydia Salazar. It is one thing for you to wildly accuse a sporting goods clerk, but I have already expressed to you the level of Lydia Salazar's standing among the aristocratic landowners." De Leon lowered his voice to add, "And, more importantly, that within her circle of friends there is a particular high-level police official."

"She needed Eduardo to set it all up for her," I pressed on heedlessly, "but it was Lydia who pushed the button that remotely fired the gun. She was in the manager's office, and Eduardo was back at the table with the others. There is a direct line of sight to the Museum's rooftop through the office window, so the full range of the model train's remote could be used."

"So, you would also accuse Lydia Salazar of purposely damaging the awning in order that it be removed, even after I explained to you why it was merely by chance?"

"No, I agree that it was by chance. But that chance incident set in motion a plan that featured ironclad alibis for everybody, except Alicia. But they had to do it before the awning was replaced, or they'd lose their line of fire. This forced Eduardo to use whatever he had on hand. Like the remote control that he'd originally ordered for the platform lift at the Palacio de Gobierno. Eduardo finally got around to installing it on the lift today, but there'll be records to show the date he received it. And the owner of the Gato Negro will tell you that Eduardo removed the solenoid from his Coke machine, saying that it was the broken part. But it really wasn't. Eduardo just needed a solenoid in a hurry."

"And from where did Eduardo get a miniature surveillance camera on short notice?"

"For Lydia to know about Dr. Salazar's museum-thefts, she must have been spying on him. I think she had Eduardo hide a miniature surveillance camera in Salazar's secret apartment. I think Eduardo used that same miniature camera for Salazar's murder."

"And now you evoke a secret apartment."

"There's an electric bill in my back pocket."

De Leon stepped around behind me, and I felt a tug on my pocket. De Leon came back around to the front of the vehicle, reading the electric bill.

I plunged forward with, for the most part, supposition. "Dr. Salazar used that apartment to store his stolen artifacts, before handing them off to his smuggler. And the apartment also provided Salazar with a workshop to create a duplicate of Villa's old revolver. And I'm sure he kept the brand-new Colt with the laser there at the apartment, too. Salazar thought nobody knew anything, but Lydia and Eduardo knew everything. And they had access to everything."

De Leon called Corporal Valdez over and handed him the electric bill. "Go to this apartment on Angel Trias Street. Call me when you are inside." De Leon returned to English. "You said that the duplicate of Villa's revolver was not used for the murder."

"Not for the fatal shot, no," I said. "Eduardo used the duplicate of Villa's revolver only to put gunshot residue on the second story column and to place a recently fired gun in the bedroom holster for you to find. Remember Eduardo would not have time to recover the new Colt from under the broken security camera's cover, before the museum was flooded with police, looking for evidence. He'd still be up at the Café Iguana. So, he needed the police to stop looking for both the murder weapon and the location of the shooter."

An angry glare from de Leon prompted me to hastily amend with, "But what Eduardo couldn't avoid was the improbability of making an accurate long shot with that old horse pistol. Which, of course, aroused *your* doubt, leading you to challenge it at the firing range."

The glare subsided, as de Leon thought for a moment. "You are suggesting that the substitute pistol was fired from the second-floor colonnade, one or two days before the murder. But this ignores that soldiers are on security detail at the Museum around the clock. And firing a big handgun makes a big noise."

"So does shooting off fireworks in nighttime celebration. And I've done nighttime guard duty when I was in the military. Rounds are made at hourly-intervals, you don't patrol constantly at a low security building."

A uniformed officer appeared at de Leon's side. "The Commandant wishes to know the nature of the delay."

"Tell him that I am interrogating the car thief," de Leon said. "I will be finished in a minute."

When the officer left, de Leon returned to English. "Why would Dr. Salazar buy a new Colt revolver?"

"I think an earlier attempt had been made on Dr. Salazar's life, and he was scared and felt he needed a gun for protection. It'd take too long to apply for a permit to buy one from the government in Mexico City, and he felt threatened right now. And he'd already smuggled one gun across the border, so he had a proven method to smuggle in another one. He'd probably picked up some tips from his regular smuggler, Butch, for the price of a few whiskeys."

"We know that Dr. Salazar already owned a shotgun. Many prominent ranchers own them for snakes and coyotes. Why would he need another gun?"

"The shotgun is good for out at his ranch, but even in the US, you can't walk around town, carrying a shotgun."

"In buying a handgun for protection," de Leon kept the questions coming, "why would Dr. Salazar buy a new version of the old Colt forty-five that he had purchased to make the duplicate?"

I was working up a headache, trying to quickly come up with answers to things I hadn't thought about. Under this kind of pressure, I doubt even Alicia could think fast enough.

"I wouldn't suppose Dr. Salazar had much knowledge of guns," I started reasonably enough, before sliding into conjecture. "So maybe, when Salazar was in the Houston gun store the second time and was asked by the clerk what kind of gun he wanted to buy, he named the only handgun he was familiar with, a Colt forty-five revolver. Just a guess."

"I think that you make many guesses," de Leon said. "I must not keep the Commandant waiting further. Answer these questions quickly. Where is this new Colt and the ammunition now?"

"I don't know." I actually felt relief, finally saying the words. "I doubt you'll ever find it."

"And why would Lydia Salazar want to kill her husband?"

"I have an idea, but I don't know for sure."

"Vengeance, greed, sex. Pick one."

"It doesn't really fit in any of them."

"So, you have no motive. And you cannot prove that your supposed murder weapon was ever *in* Mexico. And the alibis of the two people that you accuse still stand as being verified." De Leon reached out, grabbed a fistful of my shirt, and jerked my face closer to his. "It is only because you shared your fine cigars with me that I will not inform Commandant Arroyo how you have wasted his time."

Sergeant de Leon shoved me back into the grip of the plainclothes officer who'd brought me out of

Woodstead's office building. The officer led me around the back of the unmarked car. He opened the rear door, backed me up to it, and pressed my head down heavily, shoving me in butt first with my hands still bound behind my back. I made a hard landing next to Alicia and barely had my feet swung inside, before the door slammed shut.

The two patrol cars, outboard of us, drove off, and then Sergeant de Leon's car passed by with de Leon at the wheel and Commandant Arroyo sitting next to him, smoking.

The plainclothes, state police officer, who had stuffed me into the back seat, put the car in drive and followed de Leon.

"*Now*, look what you've done," Alicia lit into me. "I called you for help. Did you think I called you to come over and get arrested with me?"

"Sergeant de Leon *brought* me over to get arrested with you. Arroyo saw a chance to take us both into custody, and he jumped on it."

"So you're saying Arroyo was just *pretending* to be fighting hard to get Lydia her Land Rover back, but really, he was just gauging how badly Woodstead wanted to keep it. And then he maneuvers Woodstead into having to choose between the Rover and us."

"Okay, I guess I didn't pick up on all the wily skills going on," I said. "All I saw was Arroyo jerking Woodstead up by his diplomatic shorts. *That* must have made his icy heart sing."

"My God, how can you be so oblivious? Didn't you see hands moving to freaking guns? I about wet myself." Alicia slumped back in the seat as best she could with her hands bound behind her. "Well, maybe after a few years in prison, I'll look back longingly on dying in a shootout as missing my last chance at freedom."

"We still have hope that the forensic tech that de Leon called for will find gunshot residue under the camera cover. Then maybe de Leon will muster up the stones to tell Arroyo what I figured out about the murder."

"I could hear what you said to de Leon," Alicia said. "And don't get me wrong, I do appreciate the Hail Mary. But you took a big leap from Lydia and her boy toy sharing a candlelit dinner to Lydia and her boy wizard triggering a kill shot with some electronic gizmo. No surprise he didn't believe you."

"I was rushing to get it all in," I said. "Maybe I said some things I shouldn't have."

"Like saying they'll never find the murder weapon?"

"Yeah, might've been better to leave that part out."

"And like de Leon said, you don't actually know that Dr. Salazar brought the new Colt with the laser sight across into Mexico. And that seems key."

"There had to be a second working gun of the same caliber as Villa's Colt," I said. "And if Butch didn't smuggle it in, then Salazar must have." Then I had a thought. "When you were looking through the view finder just before Salazar was shot, any chance you saw a red dot on his head?"

"That view finder has so much extraneous crap on the screen – different colored dots and weird little symbols – who'd notice? I just make sure it's in auto, center the shot, and push the button. I ignore everything else." Alicia turned her face to me. "Is it important?"

"Only if you'd noticed it. Probably too late to bring it up now, anyway."

The hum of the tires and the rush of warm air coming through the open front windows provided white noise. We rode for the next few minutes without speaking.

Then Alicia said, "That broken security camera, it's going to test positive for burnt gunpowder, isn't it?"

I chose my words carefully. "If I'm right about Lydia and Eduardo, yes."

"A *qualified* yes. That's just great. Looks like we should have made that run for the border, after all."

"Our only real opportunity was right after de Leon's car crapped out on him, when we fled from the Gato Negro. You know, to actually do exactly what de Leon thought we were doing. I just didn't realize it then."

Alicia squirmed in her seat. "At least, get this damned tie-wrap off my wrists. I'm losing feeling in my hands."

"How? My hands are tied too."

Alicia cast a look at the State Police officer at the wheel for a moment, before saying, "Well, you know. Maybe, the Swiss Army will come bicycling down the mountain to my rescue." She smacked the side of her knee into mine.

I looked down and saw the bulge of my Swiss Army knife, still in my pants pocket.

"It'll be up to you to fetch it." I hoped "fetch" would be outside the officer's vocabulary, if he understood English.

Alicia turned her back to me, and I slid over so my thigh was positioned under her bound hands.

"Ow," I yelped. Alicia's fingers had grabbed onto the wrong object.

The officer at the wheel snapped at us, in Spanish, "Be quiet back there."

"That was *your* fault, Francis. You know I can't see."

The officer sat up tall and looked in his rearview mirror, trying to get a view of what was going on in the back seat. But then he had to shift his focus back to the road, because, up ahead, brake lights flashed brightly, as de Leon's car abruptly turned left onto a side street. The officer driving us followed, making the hard left. The centrifugal force of the turn drew Alicia's body outward, and I felt the fingertips of her bound hands drift over to the other, admittedly lower, bulge on my thigh. Having found the jackknife, Alicia began working it beneath the material toward the opening of the pocket. Then I felt the weight of the jackknife leave my leg.

"Hold it tight," I instructed. "I'll..." I quickly rejected 'extract' and 'select', as being too close to the words in Spanish. "I'll glom onto the bit I want."

I maneuvered around and found the jackknife, clenched in Alicia's fingers. Through years of familiarity with the multi-tooled jackknife, I managed by touch to get my thumbnail into the correct slot and swing out the minimalist scissors with the bit of spring steel between its tiny handles.

"Part with the gadget," I said.

Alicia relinquished her hold on the Swiss Army knife. As I was reorienting it in my hand, the officer was again craning his neck. I could see his eyes in the mirror.

"We are just saying goodbye to each other," I said in Spanish.

"As well you should." His eyes returned to the road.

Reaching out behind me, with two finger-tips just out ahead of the scissor blade points, I found a span of plastic that didn't touch Alicia's flesh. I carefully moved the open jaws of the scissor blades onto the span and set them to work. It was tough chewing for the little scissors, but in about ten seconds, I'd cut through the thick plastic. I heard Alicia breathe a sigh.

Alicia took the Swiss Army knife from me. I soon felt the little scissors gnawing at my own binding. And then my hands were free. A sudden relief washed over me. As I massaged my wrists, my hands flooded with warmth and my arms ached with newly won freedom.

Alicia closed and returned my jackknife, giving my hand a little squeeze in the process. "You know," she said, "if we'd always worked together like this, we'd still be married."

Now that our hands were unbound, my mind immediately turned to thoughts of escape. I took a look out the back window. The unmarked car dogging us held two plain clothes officers in the front seats. I supposed Lydia and Eduardo were in the back.

So, we were riding in the middle car of the three-vehicle caravan. Any attempt to commandeer our vehicle at a stoplight, or to bail out and make a run for it, would happen in full view of the policemen in the car behind us. So, my only hope was that the car we were riding in would break off, at some point, and take us directly to the City Jail. Then I could overpower—

I felt the car braking to a stop.

Looking through the front window, I was startled to see, neither the austere façade of the State Ministerial Police Delegation, nor even the familiar stark exterior of the City Jail, but instead there loomed in the near distance the Greek-revival portico of Pancho Villa's Museum.

***

The parking spaces along the curb were mostly occupied, so the three unmarked police cars simply pulled into the long yellow-curbed vacancy reserved for tour buses, directly in front of the museum. Arroyo and de Leon disembarked from the car in front of us. The officer who drove Alicia and me got out, as did the two officers from the car behind us, and all three joined Arroyo and de Leon on the sidewalk. Then Lydia and Eduardo were out of the rear car. Lydia's high heels clicked with determination, outpacing Eduardo and rapidly closing in on the conferring State Ministerial Police officers. As she passed us by, Lydia was already demanding, in indignant Spanish, a full explanation for the sudden change of plans.

"Now what?" Alicia asked.

"With any luck," I said, "the area beneath the broken security camera's cover tested positive for gunshot residue, and de Leon laid out to Arroyo what I'd told him about how Dr. Salazar was really shot."

"Francis, please don't be wrong about any of that remote control stuff."

The curbside door flew open. The officer who'd driven us ordered us out.

Alicia swung her legs out and exited the car, and I slid over and climbed out after her. Sgt. de Leon was there to meet us on the sidewalk, but at the moment was looking back toward Arroyo, as the Commandant led Lydia, Eduardo, and the other two state police officers up the steps to the museum entrance.

Arroyo stopped at the top of the steps and commanded in a raised voice, "Give me a few minutes, Sergeant. Then cut the tie-wraps and bring those two in here."

De Leon waved an acknowledgement and turned to Alicia and me. That's when he noticed our unrestrained hands.

De Leon's immediate castigation of the officer who'd driven us for failing to frisk me was punctuated with so many profanities that I could only catch the gist of it. But then just as I was thinking how glad I was to not be the one subjected de Leon's ire, he abruptly turned and caught me up by the arm, pulled me to the edge of the curb, and with a firm hand grasping the back of my neck slammed my face down onto the hood of the car. After a short, rough search, de Leon found my Swiss Army knife and took it from me.

I pushed myself off the hood, rubbed the left side of my head, and congratulated myself for saving my nose, although at some cost to my cheekbone and the corner of my forehead.

Sergeant de Leon swung his attention back to the original subject of his scorn and advanced on him. De Leon opened the main blade of the jackknife, and used the flat of the blade to lift his subordinate's chin, the sharp edge breathtakingly close to the man's windpipe. De Leon shouted, "If he had slit your throat, would you then learn to continue to thoroughly search a man, after you have found his wallet?"

The officer could only stand there, raised on his toes, looking stricken.

"Give me the wallet," de Leon demanded, folding my knife and pocketing it.

The officer dove the upper half of his body through the open side window to the front seat and came out with my wallet in his hand.

De Leon took the wallet from him and, without looking into it, ordered, "Give me the money."

The officer drew a few twenty-peso and fifty-peso notes from his pants pocket.

"Not *your* money. *His* money. All of it."

From a different pocket, the officer reluctantly withdrew a wad containing peso notes whose denominations ranged into the hundreds, along with a modest reserve in US dollars. Looking more aggrieved than contrite, the officer handed the money over to de Leon.

De Leon turned and shoved my wallet and money into my hands, before turning back to his officer. "Remain out here. Let no one else into the museum. And if you continue to *act* like a Traffic Policeman, I can easily arrange for you to wear the *uniform* of a Traffic Policeman."

Still in full anger, Sergeant de Leon grabbed Alicia and me each by an arm and pulled us along with him toward the entrance to Villa's Museum. As we reached the top of the steps under the portico, we were forced to stop and stand aside, due to an outpouring of extremely annoyed tourists, being herded out of the museum by the two soldiers.

As we waited, de Leon spoke in English with a lowered voice. "Mr. Elton, if there is no gunshot residue to be found beneath the cover of the broken camera, it is *I* who will be wearing the uniform of a Traffic Policeman." De Leon's grip on my upper arm was now cutting off blood flow. "And *you* who will wearing a tag on your toe."

"What? You didn't wait for the test result before telling Arroyo?" It was my turn to look stricken. "Oh, man."

"He had already been informed that I ordered the GSR test." Sgt. de Leon released my arm. His shoulders slumped. "When the Commandant demanded my justification for the test, I had only your conjectures to give him."

"Including Lydia's part in it?" I asked.

"About the book throwing, yes," de Leon said. "I told him that, very possibly, she was the beautiful lady. But I thought it best that the Commandant form his own conclusions, concerning whose finger pushed the button that fired the fatal shot. And even then, it may well take her fingerprints on the handheld remote to convince him."

For a sick moment, I remembered that I had also handled the remote. But then, so had Eduardo, Carlos, and Teresa.

"Naturally," de Leon continued, still in English, "I could not tell the Commandant that these ideas

330

originated from you. Believe me, if I had, we would not be at Villa's Museum at this moment." As the last of the tourists cleared the portico and the soldiers retreated into the museum, de Leon added, "But the stakes for all of us could not be higher."

"I was already going off to rot in prison," Alicia said. "By all means, let's give the dice another throw." She turned and followed the soldiers, but paused at the iron gate to look back and ask, "Coming?"

"Proceed, Mr. Elton." Sgt. de Leon pressed a hand on my back. "We can now only proceed."

De Leon and I caught up with Alicia, as we neared the Admission Office. Sergeant de Leon glanced in the direction of the Admission Office as he passed by, before taking the lead with purposeful strides. Alicia and I followed, no longer being escorted as much as being swept along in de Leon's gravitational pull.

In the first courtyard, Lydia and Eduardo waited with the two state police officers just outside the former living quarters of Villa's widow. One of the officers broke away to mumble something to de Leon, in passing, and then fell in behind Alicia and me, as we trekked on through, heading toward the archway that led to the larger courtyard, where the old Dodge was on display. As we filed by, Lydia, standing erect and poised with her hands grasping her purse at waist height, tracked us with piercing bird-of-prey eyes. In contrast, Eduardo, who appeared no longer to be chummy with the police, stood with his shoulders hunched and his eyes furtively casting about.

Beyond the archway, we found Commandant Arroyo, down on the tiles and leaning on an elbow, just outside the chain on the passenger side of the ancient Dodge touring car. I noticed that, in compliance with de Leon's earlier orders, no repair work had been done to the two gouges in the back wall. And because the reinstallation of the green awning also had remained uncompleted, Arroyo had an unobstructed view up past the bullet-damaged link in the chain, through the passenger compartment of the old car, and on toward the far roof where the dysfunctional security camera blindly stared back at him.

As we gathered in front of the radiator of the old Dodge, Arroyo rolled up onto one knee and seemingly effortlessly rose to his feet.

"I see your point, Sergeant." Arroyo brushed imaginary dust off his trousers. "Where is the forensic technician?"

"I saw him sitting in the Admission Office, Commandant."

"Bring him and his gear up to the roof. On your way, have Lydia Salazar and her young handyman brought over here. Also, send to me the soldier who saw the throwing of the book."

"Yes, Commandant," de Leon said, before departing.

One after the other, Arroyo swung his legs over the span of chain before him and then the one in front of the old Dodge to take de Leon's place, just as Lydia and Eduardo came into the larger courtyard, followed by the other state police officer. As they joined us, Lydia started to say something, but Arroyo put a hand up to stop her and turned to the young soldier who was now approaching him.

332

"Private, how do we get onto the roof of the hacienda?"

"There is a ladder on the upper level, sir."

"Take us up there."

There was quite the mob of us now. Arroyo and the soldier led the way, followed in succession by Lydia and Eduardo, one of the state police officers, Alicia and me, and finally the other officer. We ascended the stairs beyond the tail end of the old Dodge, and trooped all the way around three sides of the second story walkway, passing the column with the gunshot residue marks along the way and ending up at the point above the green canopy, where the wizened, old man had said the rare book had been thrown down.

After the soldier unhooked a chain barrier, we all moved into the restricted area and reassembled at the base of a ladder. The ladder, made of welded metal, was permanently bolted in place and extended up to just meet the edge the roof. The end posts of two, short stretches of safety fence, extending away from either side of the top of the ladder, provided handholds for getting off the ladder and onto the roof.

Without hesitation, Commandant Arroyo climbed the ladder energetically, turned, and stood at the roof edge, peering down at us. "Will you join me, Lydia?"

"Commandant, surely you cannot expect me to climb a ladder, dressed as I am." Lydia was smartly dressed in a fitted blouse, tight skirt, and open-toed spike heels.

"Private," Arroyo's eyes were now on the soldier, "which of these two women threw down the old book that tore the awning over Villa's car and wrote a check to pay for the damage?"

"It was this lady, sir." The soldier pointed to Lydia.

"In that case, yes, Lydia. You must climb up here."

Lydia Salazar, a woman undoubtedly more comfortable with issuing commands than receiving them, was outmatched by the authoritative presence of Commandant Arroyo. Swearing Spanish oaths under her breath, she negotiated the rungs awkwardly. The soldier climbed the ladder after her, guiding each high-heeled shoe in its uncertain quest for the next rung. It was quite a while, before Arroyo's outstretched hand could grasp Lydia's arm and aid her arrival onto the flat roof. In the meantime, the rest of us were treated to smooth, brown, shapely legs and pink silk.

Having moved Lydia a safe distance away, Arroyo again appeared at the roof edge and ordered down in Spanish, "The soldier may return to his post. Bring everyone else up here."

As a police officer nudged Eduardo toward the ladder, I translated to Alicia, "We're all going up on the roof."

"Great," Alicia said. "That way, worse comes to worst, I'll have a handy ledge to fling myself off of."

Once Eduardo nimbly scaled the ladder, Alicia, in tight blue jeans and her new athletic shoes took her turn.

Her climb couldn't compete with Lydia's for entertainment value, but the two police officers behind me quietly agreed that Alicia had a pretty butt.

By the time I made it up to the roof, the others had already moved off. Looking back down, I saw Sgt. de Leon arrive at the base of the ladder, accompanied by a smaller man with a carryall bag slung from his shoulder. One of the state police officers was about midway in his climb, puffing with the effort of hauling his own excess baggage up the ladder.

I stepped back from the edge, turned, and started off across the roof. A slight breeze stirred the warm air, as I joined the strung-out line of rooftop travelers, circumnavigating the inner courtyard under the leadership of Commandant Arroyo. The neighborhood looked very different from this vantage. The roofs of the adjacent buildings going up the hill toward the Café Iguana started below my sight line and rose with the upward slope of the street. I spotted the Café Iguana's rear office window at the top of the hill.

The roofing tar, heated by the afternoon sun, was soft beneath its aged crust, and I felt it give slightly with each footfall. Far up ahead, Lydia tiptoed gingerly, while clinging to Arroyo's arm, and so far, had managed to avoid poking a spike heel through the surface shell. Eduardo, relegated to secondary status, trudged along behind them. Just ahead of me, Alicia's hair fluttered with the soft crosswind, as she walked sure-footedly on the crusted tar.

During our journey, I began to ponder why Commandant Arroyo had ordered that we all be brought up to the roof. After all, Arroyo and the forensic technician could easily have taken care of the GSR test by themselves. But then it dawned on me. The vastness of the old hacienda's mesa-like, roof area was deceptive. Because it was interrupted with large, rectangular-shaped canyons (the floors of which were the courtyards below), Arroyo's officers could easily position themselves to block the only route back to the ladder. And any other direction of escape ended at the edge of a twenty-foot drop. Arroyo had maneuvered us into a trap. And whether the GSR test proved positive or negative, here in perhaps the world's largest interrogation room, far from the legal intervention of pesky defense lawyers, is where Arroyo would extract a confession and make an arrest. And I doubted Arroyo had a preference, whether the arrestees were Lydia and Eduardo, or Alicia and Francis. Enrique Ponce was clearly right that one should not underestimate the skills of Commandant Arroyo.

Arroyo finally came to a halt in an area near to the defunct security camera, but about ten feet back from the edge of the roof. He disengaged from Lydia and turned to face the stragglers, as we gradually arrived and grouped up. Sergeant de Leon and the forensic tech, the last to arrive, continued right on to the camera at the roof edge.

De Leon peered over the edge, gazing down toward Villa's old Dodge, while the forensic tech extracted a small tarp from his carryall and spread it open on the roof. The technician then knelt on the tarp, pulled on a pair of latex gloves, and began to methodically bring out his tools and chemicals, arranging them at the base of the mounting bracket that held the abandoned security camera on its perch, some eighteen inches above the roof deck and angled downward toward the courtyard below.

Stepping back from the edge, de Leon instructed, "Take off the cover, Luis, and for now, just test for gunshot residue on the camera."

336

This caused a stir from the direction of Lydia and Eduardo.

"My dear Commandant, I am sure that this is all very interesting to you," Lydia spoke Spanish in a regal tone, "but I must insist that I be driven home now. You may come by my ranch this evening. There we can discuss your ideas about my husband's death quietly, like fellow landowners. But I absolutely must get off this terrible roof immediately."

As the forensic tech removed the screws that secured the cover, Arroyo asked, "How long will it take you to test for the residue, Luis?"

"About ten minutes, Commandant."

"Lydia," Arroyo said, "I must ask for your patience for only a little while longer."

Once the weathered cover was removed, and the camera revealed, the first thing I noticed was the gloss of black electrician's tape wrapped around a section of dull black sheathing encasing a wiring harness that emerged from a hole near the top of the hollow mounting bracket and plugged into the camera, via a multi-pin connector. I suspected that it was from within this bundle of wires that Eduardo had tapped into the 120 volts needed to power his mechanism. Whether the power had simply been left on all this time, or Eduardo had surreptitiously restored it, I couldn't guess. But his use of the tape suggested that, when Eduardo had snuck back up here to remove his deadly apparatus, he'd taken the time to tidy up. And I now began to worry about just how thorough Eduardo might have been with his cleaning rag.

"Alejandro, this is intolerable," Lydia persisted, using what I supposed was Commandant Arroyo's first name. "Surely, a lady of my stature should not be compelled to stand on this unbearable rooftop, while you and your subordinates conduct little experiments."

But Arroyo ignored her and kept his eyes on the forensic tech, who'd just pulled on fresh latex gloves.

From a sealed package, the forensic tech removed a small circular piece of cloth. It looked like what Alicia used to remove her makeup. But when he lay the empty package down, I read the label, printed in English: 'One glass fiber swab' and 'Sandia National Laboratories'.

De Leon leaned over the forensic tech's shoulder and directed, "Get into that gray patch in the crevice just behind the lens."

I looked over at Lydia and Eduardo. Lydia, seemingly oblivious to what incriminating particles the gray patch might contain, was now reasserting her displeasure by glaring, with an irritated set to her lips, at the Commandant's profile. But Eduardo, no doubt acutely aware of the implications, appeared intently focused on the folded edge of the white swab with which the forensic tech probed the crevice.

When the forensic tech moved away from the camera and bent down to process the swab, I stepped in for a closer inspection and was rewarded with the sight of two pairs of quarter-inch diameter, threaded holes that had been drilled and tapped into the side of the camera. In spite of myself, I had to admire Eduardo's workmanship. No duct tape for The Great Technician. He had clamped the gun sturdily to the side of the old camera with a bracket and screws.

I stepped back next to Alicia, so I could watch, as the forensic tech broke a little glass vial of clear liquid within the test kit jar and placed the white swab into the solution. The forensic tech then relaxed and waited, with the rest of us, for what was probably only a minute, but seemed like an hour.

When the forensic tech finally removed the swab, it now displayed an area tinted in pale blue and dotted with dark blue specks. He announced, "We have nitrates, Commandant."

But it was Sergeant de Leon who responded, with an exhaling of held breath, "Excellent, Luis."

I found that I had also held my breath. As I released it, Alicia's hand found mine and gave it the second little squeeze of the day. Evidently, the significance of *"Excelente, Luis"*, coming from Sgt. de Leon at that moment, needed no interpretation.

"Get us additional samples from around the area where you found the residue," Arroyo ordered. "And also, from the inside of the cover. Send them to the electron microscope in Mexico City, so we have something acceptable to submit to the Court."

Sergeant de Leon bent in close over the inoperable camera, snapping photos with his cell phone, while the forensic tech worked through successive swabs, sealing each in its own little bag and labeling it.

Lydia stood erect, her countenance expressing that she was bravely enduring the tedium of it all. But Eduardo looked ill. And although he physically remained in place, Eduardo couldn't control the spasms in his knees, as the little evidence bags began to pile up on the tarp.

Arroyo turned to Lydia and Eduardo, but addressed only the defiant widow in Spanish. "And now, Lydia, you rightly deserve an explanation," he began. "Recently, First Sergeant de Leon approached me with a number of new facts that he had developed, during our extensive investigation into the death of your husband."

At the sound of "First Sergeant", de Leon straightened and struggled to hold back a smile. Still, I wasn't entirely sure that I was witnessing a meritorious field promotion, until I noticed the poisonous looks on the faces of the other two officers.

"These facts," Arroyo continued, "coupled with additional information that I have gathered over the past week, present us with a much clearer picture of the events leading up to the murder of Dr. John Salazar."

"Alejandro, please. I feel that I must sit down for a moment."

"As you may remember," the Commandant again found it convenient to ignore Lydia's entreaty, "earlier today, I proposed that Dr. Salazar purchased in Texas and brought to the City of Chihuahua the very handgun that was used to kill him."

I had a mental eye roll to this. But what's a little revisionism when things are starting to go your way.

Arroyo went on, "The revelation that a modern Colt forty-five with a laser sight and the requisite ammunition was in play, prompted de Leon to express to me his lingering doubt that the fatal bullet was fired by the artfully-created duplicate of Villa's revolver from the location of the second-floor column, where our preliminary examination of the crime scene found residue from a recently fired gun."

Arroyo paused, but Lydia remained stone faced and Eduardo, although still jumpy, now just looked down at the crusted tar.

"De Leon additionally informed me," Arroyo continued, "that, acting on a hunch, earlier today he revisited this museum and reexamined the calculations that were used in establishing the line of fire. This resulted in his discovery of an alternative line of fire that pointed directly to this broken security camera. De Leon immediately called for a gunshot residue test of the camera to confirm his observation, which, ultimately, has led to our little gathering up on this rooftop, this afternoon."

"You have yet to explain to my satisfaction," Lydia said, "why *I* am compelled to be present on this rooftop. If it concerns the damage to the awning, as you led me to believe, I have a perfectly innocent explanation."

"I am well aware that it was, in fact, Dr. Salazar, himself, who initiated the book-throwing incident," Arroyo casually revealed his deception. "Nevertheless, your presence on this roof – and that of your handyman – was still required, because of the curious fact that everyone who was at the Café Iguana that afternoon reported hearing the sound of only a single gunshot. Except for two people."

"I reported hearing nothing, because it is the truth," Lydia simply rolled with Arroyo's new tack. "I can only assume that my husband's assassination occurred during the time that I spent in the ladies' bathroom."

While Lydia was busy amending her alibi, I held no illusions that Eduardo would ever explain that the real reason he reported hearing two shots was because of his

341

foreknowledge that the police would eventually dig two mashed-up bullets from the adobe wall.

But Arroyo's attention remained solely on Lydia. "This is the first time I've heard of your being in the ladies' bathroom. I was given to understand that you were attending to your e-mails in the manager's office when the fatal shot was fired."

"If I heard nothing, then I suppose that I cannot accurately state *which* room that I was occupying at the time a weapon was fired in a museum that is...how far would you say? A quarter of a mile away?"

"The high caliber weapon was fired from the *roof* of the museum," Arroyo countered, "and was clearly audible at that distance to all other witnesses at the Café Iguana. And being physically two blocks away from the scene of the crime absolves no one." Arroyo briefly pointed toward the defunct security camera, as he explained, "There was barely enough room to attach a handgun beneath that camera's cover. De Leon can demonstrate this, if you find it necessary. Certainly, there was not enough extra room for someone's hand to reach in beneath the cover, grasp the gun, and fire it. And yet, as you saw for yourself, our forensic technician found gunshot residue directly on the camera itself, beneath the cover. That is undeniable. Therefore, the gun must have been fired by remote control."

At the words "remote control," Eduardo flinched, like he'd touched a live wire. Lydia, who'd been holding Eduardo's hand for support, gave it a squeeze hard enough to make him wince.

"One of my investigative officers has been dispatched to the Palacio de Gobierno," Arroyo continued. "There, he will verify the recent installation of an electronic device that, when activated by remote signals, operates an elevation mechanism on a work platform. When we are done here, de Leon and Luis will join the officer at the Palacio de Gobierno to perform gunshot residue tests on this device to confirm that it recently shared space with the murder weapon beneath the camera cover. A test for fingerprints will then identify the perpetrator."

Lydia was now actively restraining Eduardo. His leg movements had noticeably increased, and his eyes kept darting across the broad expanse of rooftop.

Arroyo calmly went on, as though unaware of the reaction that his words were provoking. "Another investigative officer has been sent to the Gato Negro Cantina. And if that officer finds that the Coke machine there has recently had its dispensing mechanism restored to operation, Luis will have another stop to make with his test kit. And finally, a forensic team is already assisting Corporal Valdez with evidence collection at a rather interesting apartment on Angel Trias Street."

In an explosion of energy, Eduardo ripped his hand free from Lydia's grasp and tore off running across the rooftop toward a distant edge with the speed of a gazelle. The hounds in pursuit were the two caught-off-guard, state police officers, who had strategically positioned themselves, as I had anticipated, between any potential escapee and the ladder.

While the rest of us silently watched the chase, Alicia's lips came close to my ear, "I need some translation. Why did Eduardo cut and run?"

I leaned in and whispered through her hair, "Arroyo has been explaining to Lydia how he and de Leon have solved Dr. Salazar's murder. Arroyo's been hammering on a lot of points I'd made to de Leon, but mostly nailing Eduardo, even though he never actually mentioned Eduardo's name. You know, going all psychological on him. Finally, it was too much, and Eduardo confessed with his feet."

As we looked toward the far edge, Eduardo skidded to a stop where the uppermost section of a black vent pipe projected up from its attachment to the outside of the building. During his sprint for freedom, Eduardo had opened enough additional lead on the pursuing police officers to afford him time for a short look back at us, before grasping the pipe and gracefully swinging his body out for the climb down. His handsome head quickly disappeared from view.

"Ah, now we see how he gets in and out of this building unobserved," Arroyo said, more to himself than any one of us.

Commandant Arroyo flipped open his cell phone, punched a single button, and raised the phone to his ear. He spoke without haste. "This is Arroyo. A young man wearing a dark brown shirt, and who has no weapon, will soon appear within the perimeter. He is to be detained. I have two officers in pursuit. Alert the men on all four streets. And leave me something to interrogate this time."

Arroyo snapped his cell phone shut.

"Alejandro, he is just a boy," Lydia began to advocate. "You are so forceful, so virile. You simply scared him. His running away means nothing."

Lydia brought out the tears now, and from her purse, a clenched black handkerchief, bordered with a web of black lace, was brought to her mouth.

Arroyo continued to lay it all out. "Eduardo had also hidden a small wireless surveillance camera under the broken security camera's cover. In the manager's office that day, Eduardo called up the transmitted image from this surveillance camera onto the screen of the laptop. He then rejoined the restoration artists and the soldier at their table. And we know from several statements that this is where Eduardo was sitting when everyone heard the fatal shot. Therefore, someone else had to stay behind in the manager's office to stand at the window and point the remote control in the direction of the broken security camera on the museum's roof, while keeping an eye on the computer screen for the right moment." Arroyo extended his arm and pointed up the hill. "You can easily see the manager's office window from here."

When Lydia didn't turn to look, Arroyo lowered his arm and, keeping his eyes on Lydia's face, went on, "When Dr. Salazar sat in the driver's seat of Villa's old car, someone had to push a button on the remote control, sending the signal to turn on the laser sight. When the red dot of the laser appeared on Dr. Salazar's forehead, someone had to push another button on the remote control that signaled Eduardo's mechanism to fire the gun that killed your husband."

"My dear Alejandro, surely you cannot think—" Lydia choked up and her makeup began to streak with an additional outpouring of tears.

"Lydia, we both know that I will follow through with this new evidence of gunshot residue, wherever it leads me." Arroyo's voice was soothing. "In spite of your present situation, I know that always you demand competence in a man, whatever his endeavor. And allow me to assert that your husband's competence came into question, the moment that you discovered that he had resorted to theft, in order to maintain your accustomed level of gracious living."

"Alejandro, I—"

"Permit me to finish," Arroyo's words were velvet. "I can well understand the apprehension of a refined lady who feels certain that her husband will, one day soon, be arrested for such an embarrassing crime, as common theft. And that as a consequence, he would most certainly lose his position at the University and, perhaps even worse, his position in society. But the cruelest tragedy is that this most refined lady would also lose her high social standing – something for which she had worked with such determination, all of her life. That could not be tolerated. To live in disgrace, to no longer attend the private garden parties with the other landowners, as an equal. Something would have to be done, would it not? Action would have to be taken. And certainly, no policeman arrests a dead man for theft."

"And now, you assign to me a motive also," Lydia added a hint of bitterness to the teardrops.

"Not at all," Arroyo said. "I wish only to express to you that I do understand the circumstances that forced you to act. But at the same time, let me reassure you that my report to the Prosecuting Attorney will contain only the facts for which I have absolute proof."

"Proof? And what of *her*?" Lydia jabbed a crimson-nailed finger directly at Alicia. "Alejandro, are you so blinded by her pale beauty? *She* killed my Professor of Fine Arts. Her husband is an engineer. *He* must have done all those technical things for her."

"Hey, I was in North Carolina, working on a machine," I came to my defense in English. "I wasn't even *in* Mexico, until *after* the murder. I can prove it. And you can verify it with one phone call."

"It actually took two phone calls," Arroyo responded in English, before returning to Spanish to continue with Lydia. "Yes, initially, we suspected Alicia Elton. And several days ago, when you called to inform me that Mrs. Elton had ordered Eduardo to drive an American, who had suddenly appeared at her side, over to Villa's Museum, I was still sufficiently suspicious of her to have you instruct Eduardo to take extra time driving this strange man there, so I would be able to arrive and catch him unaware." Arroyo turned to address me, in English. "You may find this amusing, Mr. Elton. We anticipated that the FBI might attempt to slip in one of their agents, despite our refusal of permission. And when you suddenly appeared, we thought that you were the agent. My plan was to present you with the solid facts behind our allegation against Mrs. Elton and send you packing. I was actually disappointed when we found that you were only what you said you were."

"And I was a fool," Lydia was back to bitter Spanish, "to take you at your word, when you led me to believe that your suspicion of Alicia Elton had proved to be well founded."

"As it turned out," Arroyo responded in Spanish, "not even my expectation that together Mr. and Mrs. Elton would attempt to flee back to the United States was well founded."

"That is not proof of her innocence," Lydia said.

"No, but when you called me today – this time to report that Mrs. Elton had stolen your Land Rover – you reached too far. Because as a consequence, de Leon and I learned of the new Colt forty-five revolver with a laser sight that your husband had purchased and smuggled into Mexico. That was the missing piece that de Leon's new theory needed. It is an irony that Dr. Salazar's purchase of the new Colt sealed his fate and that your repeated demands that I put Alicia Elton in prison sealed yours."

"Are you now suggesting that *I* am the one who is going to prison?" Lydia asked.

"For the moment," Arroyo said, "it is only required that you accompany me to my office. Naturally, you may call your attorney and instruct him to meet us there."

Arroyo turned to Alicia and me and spoke in English. "Your passports will be delivered to your hotel. Mr. Elton, you should have no trouble finding your way back to the United States. Tomorrow at the latest." He underscored this with a short, hard stare, before shifting his mean eyes onto Alicia. "Mrs. Elton, you will be required to stay in the City of Chihuahua, until you are no longer needed as a witness. However, I am sure that you will productively spend this time completing your restoration work at the Palacio de Gobierno."

"Do I get my purse back?"

"De Leon will arrange for its return." Arroyo then spoke in Spanish to de Leon, "I will need written statements from the soldier who saw the book thrown and from the managers of the Café Iguana and the Gato Negro." Arroyo clasped him on the shoulder. "Excellent work, First Sergeant de Leon."

De Leon now allowed his smile to beam.

This mini-award ceremony was interrupted by the ring tone of Arroyo's phone.

After listening briefly, Arroyo closed his phone and reported in English (apparently, for Alicia's benefit), "I have been informed that the young handyman, at first, proved elusive, but he is now in safe keeping."

I doubted he meant that in a good way for Eduardo.

***

Lydia Salazar again clung to Commandant Arroyo's arm and again took care with her high heels on the crusted tar, as she was escorted back toward the ladder.

On the far side of the roof, the two officers who had chased Eduardo no longer pretended that either one of them was going to shinny down the vent pipe after the fleeing suspect and had already started their journey back.

De Leon stayed with the forensic technician, who was now dusting for fingerprints. I felt the chances were low that he'd find any. Eduardo may not have been diligent with the crevices, but he'd certainly have run a damp rag over the surfaces he'd touched.

Alicia and I let the Commandant and the haughty murderess in his custody get some distance ahead of us, before trailing behind them.

"See how she keeps her upper body turned in toward him," Alicia observed, "constantly pushing her breast against his arm?"

When the pair ahead of us reached the opening in the short stretch of railing, Commandant Arroyo encountered the tactical problem in getting Lydia, with her heels and tight skirt, down the steep ladder. Alicia and I stopped and watched it play out.

After a couple of failed attempts to coax Lydia into holding onto the posts and stepping backward into empty space, Arroyo finally climbed onto the ladder first and descended a few rungs. Lydia, apparently feeling more secure, now turned around at the roof edge and, holding onto the posts, swung one fashionably tight-skirted leg back toward Arroyo's waiting hand. With Lydia's ankle in his grasp, Arroyo guided it down onto the top rung. After switching handholds, Arroyo's other hand appeared above the roof edge to guide the other ankle down. And so, with some encouragement from the Commandant, and after a playful slap at Arroyo's unseen hand from Lydia, together they began to descend, rung by rung. And just as the crown of Lydia's sleek, black hair sank below the roofline, we heard a pretend shriek of "Oh, Alejandro!" followed by laughter that echoed off the hard, sunbaked surfaces of Pancho Villa's former hacienda. The Commandant had a robust laugh, for someone you wouldn't think laughed at all.

First Sergeant de Leon and the forensic tech, shouldering his carryall, overtook us. In passing, de Leon reached out a fist, I reached out my own, and we silently touched knuckles, like trumpeters after a virtuoso performance in brass.

We waited for the last two officers, one of them limping slightly, to pass us by and eventually disappear down the ladder. My rental car was still parked at the curb below. So, as far as I was concerned, the State Ministerial Police could continue on without us.

There then came the sound of a commotion from the direction of Calle 10a. Curious, Alicia and I walked over to the edge of the roof that overlooked the sloping street that ran past the museum's front portico.

The sound that had drawn us to the roof edge turned out to be a rolling fusillade of snare and bass drums, announcing that an Independence Day Parade had turned the corner and was moving en mass down Calle 10a. The Parade, consisting almost entirely of children dressed in brightly-colored, frilled and feathered, costumes, had almost advanced as far as Villa's Museum. Fanning out from under the portico, de Leon and the other state police officers hurried to their cars, parked along the yellow curb. Soon, Commandant Arroyo appeared, hustling, as best he could, the high-heeled, tight-skirted Lydia down the steps and toward the opened rear door of the lead car – but it wasn't soon enough. Before Arroyo had Lydia situated in the back seat, the parade, along with the crowd of parents, revelers, and tourists that accompanied them, engulfed all cars parked in front of the museum. The parade then came to a halt, while the children performed a dance to a lively cadence of drums and a discordant squealing of flutes. I wondered if First Sergeant de Leon was enjoying the commencement of his new rank, confined in the lead car with a complaining Lady Salazar and a fuming Commandant Arroyo – who, I imagined, was furiously smoking cigarette after cigarette.

While we watched the dancing from our open, roof-edge gallery, refreshed by the light breeze, I recounted to Alicia all that Arroyo had said, along with Lydia's protests.

"I don't get why Lydia resorted to murder," Alicia said. "I mean I can believe she's vindictive enough. But why not simply divorce Dr. Salazar, if he was stealing things? I can't see her snobby friends ostracizing her, just because an ex-husband got himself arrested."

"It's hard to imagine Salazar would've agreed to an uncontested divorce without a sizable buyout. After all, he'd risked his neck, selling stolen artifacts on the black market, to keep Lydia and her horse ranch in high style. But how would Lydia raise the payoff money? Sell the hard-won trappings of her wealth, or, God forbid, her treasured ranch? Hell, no. So, according to your lawyer, Lydia would have to sue for the divorce in court. In which case, she'd have to prove valid cause. But even though Salazar's thefts, no doubt, would qualify as a valid cause, that was the very revelation she was trying to avoid."

"So killing her husband was the next thing that popped into her head?"

"Well, Lydia's first husband went on a horseback ride in the desert alone with her and came home laying across his saddle. So, there may have been some history for homicide as a fallback solution. But I think Lydia's first inclination would be to find out what else was going on at Dr. Salazar's secret apartment, other than storing stolen museum knick-knacks."

"You mean, like a mistress."

"Catching Dr. Salazar in some adulterous affair would nicely provide the type of grounds for a divorce that wouldn't leave a blemish on her social standing."

"So Lydia knew about the apartment all along."

"No way was that apartment going to remain a secret. Maybe, when Dr. Salazar went out on his errands, one Friday, Eduardo followed in a taxi to see what's so damn important that Dr. Salazar has to take the Rover by himself. Or maybe, Lydia found some paperwork, like I did."

"Then Lydia had Eduardo install a surveillance camera there," Alicia quickly caught on, "hoping for evidence of adultery, but instead, the camera recorded Salazar with smuggled guns and ammo."

"Exactly."

"If that's what happened, why wouldn't Lydia threaten to take her evidence to her pal Arroyo, unless Dr. Salazar agreed to a mutual consent divorce with no payoff?"

"Making a threat of that level," I said, "and staying alive long enough to follow through on it is tricky. Especially if the guy you're threatening has easy access to an unregistered, loaded gun. So, Lydia called on her own secret weapon – the technical savvy of Eduardo. And without a doubt, they'd have gotten away with murder, except that Eduardo was rushed to the point where he didn't have time to completely cover his tracks."

"You mean like, if he'd thought to borrow Lydia's black handkerchief and wrap the murder weapon, there wouldn't have been any gunshot residue found on the broken camera."

"Uh, yeah. That too."

"Sorry, I forgot I wasn't supposed to know anything about guns."

"Okay, kudos," I said. "Although, the fabric maybe needed to be a bit more durable than Lydia's hanky. But I admit wrapping the gun didn't occur to me. Which is just as well. It was hard enough getting de Leon to call for a GSR test at all, without *that* possibility gnawing at me."

"Doesn't it bother you that de Leon got all the credit for everything you figured out?"

"I had no other way to put it in front of Arroyo, except through de Leon."

We watched the dancers for a while longer, before Alicia came out with, "You know, if Lydia continues to hotly deny everything, and if Eduardo can take the threats and the beatings and still stay clammed up, some old judge is just going to be totally mystified by all the disappearing guns and gee-whiz electronics, no matter what Arroyo says."

"Dispensing justice is someone else's lookout," I said. "You've been cleared of Salazar's murder, so I'm a happy boy." I took Alicia in my arms. "Just a happy boy, waiting for a lick of that pretty lollipop he was promised."

Alicia planted a deep kiss on my mouth, and was following through with a full body press, when I felt a tingle of vibration on my thigh. Alice pulled away, and spent some time extracting her phone from the front pocket of her tight blue jeans. "It's Enrique."

"You don't need a lawyer now. He can go to voicemail."

"Oh, I think he already did." Alicia started pressing buttons on her phone. "We should invite Enrique and Marybeth to go to the Celebration downtown with us tonight. There'll be music, and we can dance and wave tiny Mexican flags and shout 'Viva!' And at the finale, there'll be fireworks."

"Speaking of fireworks, does that naughty silk lingerie ever come out of the top drawer?"

"It's on tonight's agenda," Alicia looked up from her phone. "Trust me, I'll make it worth the candle."

www.ingramcontent.com/pod-product-compliance
Lightning Source LLC
Chambersburg PA
CBHW030013180626
46810CB00001B/16